LIES, LETTERS,

and the

RING

NANCY LAMOUREUX

PublishAmerica
Baltimore

ISBN: 1-4241-2108-6
PUBLISHED BY PUBLISHAMERICA, LLLP
www.publishamerica.com
Baltimore

Printed in the United States of America

For Richard, my brother

Other novels by Nancy Lamoureux:

Mystery Series:

By Prescription Only   1997

Never Be A Witness   2000

The Conrad Capers   2004

Acknowledgments

Elizabeth Nolan Slez, Rose Kern, and Charlotte Budlong Lamoureux who retrieved memories of their experiences as students in U.S. nursing schools of the 1930's. Helen Svec Mc Carthy and Jeanette Burns Lawall who did the same for nursing schools of the 1950's. To the District Nursing Officer, faculty and nurses of St. Thomas Hospital in London (1980) who brought Florence Nightingale to life in the actual setting for the author. Finally, to a computer guy, Waiman Cheung, who provided Twenty-first century technology to a Twentieth-century century word processing program. Without him, you would not be reading this book.

BOOK I

SARAH

1913—1951

For in the time we know not of
Did fate begin
Weaving the web of days that wove
Your Doom

Swinburne

Chapter One

Sarah ran across the wooden floor of the family kitchen into her father's arms. The four-year-old clapped her hands over her ears, squeezed her eyes shut and buried her head against his chest. It was not enough for she could still hear her mother's cries of pain and fear.

As Spencer Morgan rocked his daughter back and forth in the chair, she begged him, "Please, make Mother stop hurting." She was afraid for her mother who was making grunting sounds, one hand pressed against her huge belly as she leaned against the stove stirring the dinner stew.

Sarah's father stroked her hair, his muscled arms gentle as they rocked, whispering past his harsh, black mustache. "It's all right. You'll soon have a new brother who will run and play with you." He held her cheeks so she had to look at him and the calm in his deep-set, blue eyes told her it would be true.

She remembered once before when he had been away with the logging crew somewhere in Vermont's Green Mountains and she had heard her mother make these same cries in the night. She got up the next morning and a new sister, Beatrice, lay asleep in the crib.

That was two years ago and Beatrice was bigger now and never seemed to stop running or jumping. Both girls had eyes shaped like their father, a trait shared by every member of the family for generations. Still, the girls did have differences. Beatrice laughed a lot while Sarah was mainly quiet. Beatrice had straight hair while Sarah's was lightly curled. And Beatrice could be mean, pinching and hitting.

The worst of it was, their mother favored Beatrice and Sarah couldn't understand why.

Now she watched as her mother gripped the spoon real hard and clutched her belly, crying again. This time, she stopped stirring for a long time. The evening was hot and sticky. Wet stuff like water ran down her mother's face just like on the sides of the stew pot.

Sarah didn't know how it had been when the twins came because it was before she was born. Louise and Winfield were nearly six now. Tonight they were oblivious to their mother's agony as they lay moving aimlessly in the huge playpen their father had built for them.

They never did grow much and both were smaller than Beatrice. They never learned to sit, crawl, or walk and they spent all day drooling, their bodies twisting and stiffening with seizures. Somebody said they couldn't hear or see because they never said words. When they weren't having seizures or sleeping, they bit at their lips, fingers, toes, or anything that got in the way.

Sometimes they bit Sarah if she wasn't careful. It was her job to wipe away their blood and slobber with rags . At night, their high-pitched screams would wake everyone in the house.

Sarah stiffened as her mother let out a loud, prolonged, agonizing scream, dropping the empty serving platter on the floor. When she let the spoon go, splashes from the stew pot snapped in the flame of the stove.

Her father jumped up, sitting Sarah on the chair.

"Lillian, go get on the bed!" he ordered.

"No. You haven't eaten. The twins haven't eaten..." She groaned, doubling over.

"I'll feed them," he said, dragging her to the downstairs bedroom. She groaned again and lay on the bed covering her face with the pillow, rolling her body from side-to-side.

"I'm going to get Mrs. Mead," he said, picking up Beatrice and rushing out the door. "You take care of your brother and sister," he called to Sarah.

She listened apprehensively to her mother's tossing and turning, got into the playpen and held a bottle for Winfield. He flung his head around until she anchored him against the bars of the playpen.

From the bedroom came a piercing scream. She jumped out of the playpen and ran to her mother, hitching herself up on the high bed. Her mother had thrown off her clothes and lay naked, her huge belly heaving and tightening. A wetness was spreading on the sheets, some of it bloody like Winfield's and Louise's fingers and arms. Even so, she gathered Sarah to her and hugged her.

Suddenly, her mother let go of her, turning away, groaning, bouncing Sarah to the floor.

The front door opened and Spencer Morgan strode in with Mrs. Mead, in her clean, ironed, cotton dress, her hair done up in a neat bun. She had a box of supplies, grabbed extra linens from the closet, went into the bedroom and closed the door, muffling the cries.

Shaken, Sarah followed her father from the house. He had scooped up Winfield and Louise and placed them in Sarah's arms as she sat next to him. She knew it would be a hard ride with the two wriggling the whole way and she tried to hold their chins so they wouldn't turn and bite her. Beatrice lay asleep on the seat. He drove them in the horse and buggy to their cousins' house. The horse slogged slowly down the hill leading from their house, along the road, past the Congregational Church which she recognized by its spire piercing the sky. She saw shadows of the neighboring farms set against these Vermont hills where they lived, halfway between Burlington and St. Albans on the edge of the Lamoille River. They were protected on the other side by the Green Mountains that went the whole length of the State and beyond.

Sarah's great, great grandfather had settled there nearly a century before and, isolated from easy access by outsiders, his generation was left to its own devices. The family had intermarried until today almost everyone in the community was related, either as a cousin, aunt, niece, nephew, or grandparent, until the ancestral lines were no longer clear.

Once in awhile, a French-Canadian would come into the town to woo one of the cousins and they would bundle down, finally marrying. But there were only a few of those families among the seventy-eight people who struggled in this remote, sometimes alien valley.

As soon as her father took them into her Aunt Ethel's and Uncle Rigby's house, they led her cousins, Sam and James away. They never smiled, just said "goodnight", stepped over Winfield and Louise lying on the floor and went to their bedrooms. The Morgans were alone in the living room.

Sarah quickly fell asleep. The next thing she knew, her father was carrying her and placing her in the buggy again.

"You have a new brother," he whispered to her excitedly, as he went back into the house to get Beatrice, Winfield and Louise.

When they reached home, her father carried her into the house. Mrs. Mead tried to stop him, but couldn't because her arms were loaded with soiled bedclothes. Spencer Morgan stood Sarah on the floor next to the crib where her new brother lay. Her mother had her face to the wall.

Her father carefully pulled back the handmade quilt covering the baby. Then, quickly, he threw the cover over the baby and turned on his wife, his voice low and threatening.

"If you had seen a doctor, this wouldn't have happened."

"He's fine." Lillian's voice was faint. *"...all that Mind, God, is or hath made, is good..."*

"You and that damned religion."

Lillian slowly turned over in the bed, glaring at him, her eyes burning. "Its got nothing to do with my religion. It's because you violated me when I was with child. You're never coming to my bed again." There was a tired hatred in her voice. "Never, ever..."

In a fury, he picked up her book, Science and Health, from the bedside table and flung it against the wall, just missing her head. "Don't worry..." He slammed out of the room.

Sarah knew they were mad at each other because of the baby. She took the quilt and pulled it away from the baby's face. "What's his name?" she asked her mother.

"Elbert...from the Bible," she answered wearily.

Sarah leaned over the crib to talk to her new brother. "Hi, Elbert." She was disappointed that he didn't respond, not even to moving his arms and legs. She took his tiny hand and waited for him to wrap his fingers around hers. Instead, he suddenly became frenzied, biting his lips, pulling her finger to his mouth. She yanked free, scared.

She could tell from his dull eyes that he couldn't see and would never know her. He looked and acted just like Winfield and Louise.

Sarah left the bedroom. Her father had put Beatrice to bed, fed the twins, and was putting them back in the big playpen, wrapping the strips of cloth around their arms to keep them from biting themselves in the night. Sarah went to bed by herself and as the hours passed, she could hear her father's restless breathing from the living room where he lay on the couch.

After that night, her parents never spoke again or shared the same bed. When the first snows came, her father, who had signed on with the Northwest Logging Company, left for the winter. Sarah waited for him to return the following spring, but he didn't.

As the seasons passed year after year, summer, fall, winter, spring, over and over, her mother became even more bitter. Their house was one long season of winter. Sarah feared her father would be gone forever, her father who was the only one she trusted and who loved her. Gone. She grieved for him, but he must not have known how much she missed him. If he had, he would surely have come back home.

Once when Sarah was nine, she saw the postmark on a letter from him to her mother. It was sent from Burlington, Vermont. There was lots of money in it which Lillian put in her pocket. After that, her mother got real mean. She treated Beatrice all right, but she hit Sarah if she was the least dissatisfied about anything.

Her meanness never quit. Sarah realized that her father had been right. Her mother was to blame for everything, the twins, Elbert, the hate in their family, the way the townspeople were against them. Her mother and that religion of hers.

Louise was the lucky one. When it happened, Sarah cried, but she was secretly glad for her sister. In her eleventh year, Louise went to heaven. Probably bled to death because they ran out of cotton strips to bind her arms and hands and she bit all of her fingers clear off.

Chapter Two

The morning after Louise died, Sarah and her family realized that the townspeople knew when they saw Uncle Rigby riding up the wet, sloppy road to their house. His horse snorted, protesting the steep pull and cold air. Centered on the back of the flat bed wagon was a coffin Uncle Rigby had made. He said that staying up the night to finish it was the least he could do for the poor child who had suffered so.

Lillian Morgan barely nodded, showing him as much feeling as anyone outside their home would ever see, which was close to none.

He had come alone without his wife or sons and apologized for not staying for the burial.

Lillian must have dug through the snow and hard ground preparing Louise's resting place for the hole was there when Sarah and Beatrice woke up in the morning. There was no breakfast that day. Instead, the two girls bundled up and went outside with their mother. The lid to the coffin was already sealed, but they had to help their mother drop it into the ground. Even though Louise had been tiny, with the coffin, she was heavy and they tugged and pulled before it finally fell into place.

Then the sisters stood quietly next to their mother by the grave outside the sugaring barn which had not been used for years. After the burial, maybe Lillian would melt down the maple sap in the kitchen. But for now sugaring was forgotten while she picked up handfuls of dirt mixed with snow, slowly dropping them on the coffin.

She recited from her Science and Health book: *"If death restores sight, sound, and strength to man, then death is not an enemy but a better friend than Life."*

For once, her mother made sense, at least in relation to Louise. Sarah stared at her sister's coffin and wondered if she would be cold at night and in the winters, but reassured herself that the ground above would keep her warm. And in the summer, there would be a friendly blanket of grass. Maybe in heaven, Louise could smile and see.

Eleven years of seasons had passed and eleven blankets of sod had been laid down since that burial.

Today there was going to be another funeral. Most everyone in Riverfork would be there. It was Mud Tuesday in March, considered by many Vermonters to be the beginning of the new year. Until now, winter had kept them indoors.

Sarah and Beatrice leaned against the pane of the front window of their home, their breath leaving steam on the cold pane. Along the road below, people sludged through the mud and melting snow heading toward the Congregational Church. There they would say their last for Yedda Montgomery, mother of the town's only physician, forty-two year old, Dr. Joseph Montgomery.

He had been born in nearby St. Albans, and been brought to Riverfork as a small child, when his father took over the pastorship of the church. Sadly, Pastor Montgomery died when Joseph was ten. After that, mother and son became inseparable. Even after he returned from his medical studies, the eligible ladies in town somehow understood that he was unavailable for marriage.

Although Dr. Montgomery was well-thought of and was present at most community functions, weddings, christenings, funerals, his life was otherwise secluded.

Sarah had seen him close once at the post-office when she had gone to collect mail for her mother. The doctor was tall, taller than she'd thought when she'd seen him on horseback heading out of town on a visit to someone ailing. His eyes were a sympathetic gray-brown mixture the color of the logs that moved down the Lamoille River to Lake Champlain. She noticed his strong, sensitive hands, a mustache giving width to his narrow lips.

Both Sarah and Beatrice wanted to go to the funeral, but Lillian decided that only Beatrice could go.

"I have to tend this maple sap and you have to take care of the boys," she told Sarah. "Besides, Beatrice has a cleaner dress and her hair is fixed." She surveyed Sarah's blood-stained dress, stains that would never wash out, that she had gotten from Winfield and Elbert who bit and tore at the strips of cotton protecting their scrawny hands and arms.

"It will just take me a minute to change," said Sarah. "The boys will be all right the little time I'll be gone."

"Don't argue!" Lillian snapped, barely slowing as she stirred the maple sap she was boiling down from the bucket brought in from the tree that morning. The steam from the syrup made everything sticky, the walls, the windows, the furniture. It had been easier in the days when she'd used the sugaring barn.

But then, for Lillian, nothing had ever really been easy. Her mother had died in childbirth and her father was killed in a marble quarry accident. She was an orphan when she was six with seven brothers and sisters. The children were farmed out to relatives throughout the New England States, all except for the retarded ones who were put in an institution. Lillian stayed in their hometown of Riverton, but her lucky sister, Elizabeth, was sent to live with a maiden aunt in Boston.

Years later when Elizabeth came back to visit, she brought tales of the larger than imaginable city which had buses, cars, libraries, public buildings of all descriptions, politicians, newspapers, and movie theaters where Elizabeth spent afternoons idolizing Mary Pickford.

Most exciting was the new religion Elizabeth had taken on and that she taught to Lillian, the religion which ruled her for the rest of her life.

When she was eighteen, she became attracted to Spencer Morgan, her cousin, whom she had seen at family reunions, mainly funerals. It was as though she was seeing him for the first time, his dark hair, his husky build. When he came back from logging that winter, they married. Louise and Winfield were born two years later.

With the Vermonters respect for privacy, the neighbors left Lillian alone, although there were dark words spoken in kitchens that it was against God's will to be so independent in choosing a religion. Surely, this was the cause of her misfortunes.

After Spencer left her, she was shunned even more than before until bitterness and isolation had taken her over and she hardly cared.

All she had left were the children and hard work. She did her best but it was never enough. She couldn't afford waste, but now, most of the maple sap would have to go. She didn't have the time or the energy to use it all.

The heat and moisture from the boiling sap became so intense in the house that before the day was out, they would have the doors and windows opened wide.

Sarah followed Beatrice into the bedroom they shared. Beatrice pulled on her bonnet, smoothed her skirt, plumped the sleeves of her blouse, fastened her high-topped, black shoes more tightly and threw a heavy shawl over her shoulders. "Sorry, Sarah," she whispered excitedly. "I'll watch everything and tell you about it as soon as I get home. I promise to hurry."

Sarah bit her lip and went to the front window, watching Beatrice hurrying down the hill to join the crowds moving towards the church, people who were as remote to Sarah as a day when Beatrice wasn't getting her way.

Although she didn't think about it much anymore, there was a time when she knew that if her father were here, things would be different.

When Beatrice had become just another figure in the crowd, Sarah turned back to the living room, which was directly beside the kitchen. She didn't need to be told the order of her chores. With her mother occupied making the syrup that had to be cooked down the day the trees gave up the sap, she'd be doing everything else. There would be the bathing of the two boys laying in the playpen making purposeless movements with hands that had never learned to identify one object from another, their unseeing eyes rolling aimlessly. Sometimes they would screech, their voices high-pitched and crow-like.

Although Winfield was years older than Elbert, neither had grown larger than a five-year-old. If possible, they had become dumber with age. Sometimes she thought Elbert could hear, but she knew Winfield couldn't. He never stirred when Elbert made his whining, screeching cries.

While waiting for their bath water to heat, Sarah combed and twisted her own long hair into a bun and then went to the playpen. As her mother stirred the maple syrup, she reminded her, "Better start the bread."

"Beatrice makes the bread," Sarah answered, absentmindedly. "She can do it when she comes back." As soon as the words were out, she knew she'd made a mistake.

When the stirring of the metal spoon against the sides of the kettle ceased, Sarah turned around where she was kneeling next to the playpen taking off Winfield's soiled clothes. Her mother was wiping her hands on her apron and heading across the room where she kept the birch switch hanging on the wall. She came to Sarah holding it before her, her mouth pulled into a tight line.

When Sarah saw her mother's arm raised, she put her head down, leaning against the playpen, trying to protect her face. As the searing blows fell across her back and shoulders, Sarah squeezed her eyes shut. She would not scream even though a rage of tears flowed. Again and again the switch snapped at her, the pain tearing through her body.

When her mother finished and turned away, Sarah loosened the buttons of her dress to ease the pulling against her painful shoulders. She wiped her wet face on her apron, rinsed a rag in warm water and washed the shit from Winfield before he smeared it into the sores on his arms. When the boys were clean, she started making the bread. While it baked in the oven, she dropped eggs into hot syrup her mother had set aside for her and fed them to the pair in the playpen.

The time passed slowly and the only conversation was feelings of anger.

Shortly after noon, Beatrice returned, breathlessly describing her experience. She told about the somber processional, the mahogany coffin with gold handles, the flowers banked all through the church, about talking with Dr. Montgomery afterwards.

"Now that his mother's gone," she said, her words rushing, "he needs someone to keep house for him…for just a few hours each day."

"What concern is that of ours?" asked Lillian.

"I could do it. We would have money coming in to buy clothes and blankets…"

"We weave our own cloth, sew our own dresses."

"We don't have to."

"Beatrice! Enough!"

"It would give you time to rest. You work too much as it is."

"No!"

Sarah watched the sparring back and forth between her sister and their mother.

Beatrice threw back her head, defiantly. "I told him I would start Saturday," she said.

"You will not."

"We're poor. I'm tired of being poor."

"You don't know what poor is," Lillian said, furiously.

Sarah held her breath, waiting to see if she would reach for the birch switch, but she didn't. Her mother and sister were so much alike, making quick, irrevocable decisions. Except Beatrice was usually cheerful and laughing. And nobody was laughing now.

Lillian stood to a self-righteous height. "The doctor is a rich man because he lives in sin…he makes money from sickness. It's mental quackery to make disease a reality…"

"Mother, the only reality is our need for money. With money, we could pay to have the hay cut and stored, the wagon hitch fixed so we could get our own wood..."

"The men in the town always bring us wood. It's the neighborly thing to do."

"We don't do anything for anyone else."

"Watch your tongue!"

Beatrice shrugged. "I'm going to work for the doctor."

"You're too young. He can find a girl in town."

Beatrice ignored her. "We could send away for new furniture from the Sears catalog. After I've worked a year, we could buy a new dining set. We could get two beds so Sarah and I could sleep separately." She talked excitedly, her eyes shining.

"You have to go to school."

"I'm going to do it." Beatrice slammed her spoon on the table, got up and left, shutting herself in the bedroom.

Sarah watched her mother warily. Had Beatrice gone too far?

Lillian furiously scraped the leftovers out beyond the back porch for the chickens.

Sarah knew there would be silence for the afternoon while her mother's anger smoldered and Beatrice sulked. Sarah cleaned and fed the boys for the second time that day and began preparing the baked beans for the evening meal.

At dinner, Beatrice finally came out of the bedroom and, except for the banging of forks and spoons, nothing was said. When they were finished, Lillian turned to Beatrice. "You're right. We could use more money. Sarah can work for Dr. Montgomery. She's finished with school."

Sarah's first reaction was terror. "I don't want to."

Her mother glared at her. "You'll do as I say."

"No. Beatrice agreed to the job."

"I said you'll do it. You can keep some of your earnings."

"Mother," said Beatrice, evenly, "That's not fair. I want the job."

Sarah had already adjusted to the fact that she would be doing house work for Dr. Montgomery. "Who'll do my work here while I'm gone?"

"It will be here when you return in the evening."

That night in bed, Beatrice tried to make a deal with Sarah. "I'll help with your chores if you give me some of the money."

Sarah turned her back angrily.

"Please, Sarah. Just a dime a week."

"No. Why should I pay for your mistakes and give you money besides?"

"Don't be mad, Sarah."

But Sarah was mad, so mad she was shaking.

Just before Beatrice dropped off to sleep, she said, "You're not being fair, Sarah. I said I would go to work for Dr. Montgomery."

But as always, it was neither of their decision.

Chapter Three

The first day that Sarah started her new job, she hurried through her morning chores at home, milking the two cows, feeding them hay, bringing in logs for her mother's stove, cleaning Winfield and Elbert.

Then she went to her room and put on her second dress, the one that didn't have blood stains from the boys, and hurried down the hill, past the General Store and the Congregational Church. She had to wait at the railroad crossing as the morning 8:12 Central Vermont passenger train moved slowly, gaining speed from the train station it had just left a block away. As she waited, she worried that she would not measure up as Dr. Montgomery's housekeeper.

As soon as the train passed, she rushed across the tracks, along the street, until she reached the private road leading up to the doctor's house. His was the largest home in town, a two-story colonial painted an elegant blue with white shutters framing the windows. The large central house had a smaller section at its south end. On the north end, set back from the street, protected by hedges and grass, was the huge porch entrance to Dr. Montgomery's offices. Although he was not ostentatious, his patients waited on the finest sofas and chairs done in heavy brocades, furniture his parents had spent a lifetime collecting and which Dr. Montgomery felt should be put to good use.

It was eight-twenty in the morning when Sarah stepped into the house. The waiting room was already crowded with patients to see the doctor. She wasn't sure what to do, but when the doctor finished with a patient and came to call for the next, he spied her and greeted her cordially.

"Good morning, Miss Morgan." He shook her hand gently, and his hand was warm. He had a quick smile. His eyes seemed to bore through to her soul with that one, rapid look.

Dr. Montgomery excused himself to the other patients and led her through his office into the main house, escorting her past the living room, the hallway and his bedroom. He explained her duties as he gently steered her from room to room. They paused longest in his dead mother's bedroom immediately across the hall from his.

"This room is to be kept exactly as it is," he said. "Please keep it thoroughly cleaned and dusted and replace the lavender sachets in the drawers when necessary."

Never had Sarah seen such luxury. Imagine, a lone woman having a double bed covered with a quilted spread that looked new and unused. On the dresser rested a sterling silver-handled comb, brush, and hand mirror, ivory pill-boxes, powders, perfumes in crystal bottles, pictures in gold frames. The windows were curtained with lace. Her mind could not take it all in before he was leading her upstairs to more rooms, spare bedrooms and storage areas.

If Dr. Montgomery knew that she was not Beatrice, he never let on. But it was possible he didn't see a difference. The sisters eyes were the same velvet blue, their expressions were similar although Beatrice had a narrower face, her cheeks not as full.

As Sarah followed him, she couldn't help noticing his black hair, streaked with gray, reaching to his collar. He turned toward her when he spoke, and his mustache brought up a long-ago memory of her father. Dr. Montgomery looked at her with such sincerity and compassion that she was glad her mother had chosen her for the job instead of Beatrice. Already she knew that she would clean his house better than anyone else possibly could.

She understood why he was adored by the townspeople, why his waiting room was busy with patients. But she did not understand the unfamiliar stirrings he had awakened in her.

After he left her to return to his patients, she went at the job of cleaning his house with such vigor and speed that she amazed herself. Such a contrast, enjoying the work, rather than the drudgery she resented at home.

Before the week was up, Dr. Montgomery was calling her by her first name and confessed that he'd known all along that she wasn't Beatrice. On Friday when he handed her four dollars for the week's work, her hand tingled and shook. When she gave all but fifty cents of the money to her mother, Lillian seemed to have a change of heart and Beatrice was told to assume some of Sarah's chores.

But a few weeks later Beatrice balked and told their mother that her studying was too heavy, she had no time for added duties.

That night in bed, Beatrice told Sarah the real reason why she'd complained. "You were supposed to give me a dime every Friday and you never have."

"I never said I would. Anyway, Mama would know."

"Not unless you tell her. Just for that, you can do your own chores."

From then on, Sarah's life became doubly hard. She would do chores at home before going to Dr. Montgomery's and again on her return. The only thing that stayed the same was that she didn't have to feed lunch to Winfield and Elbert or clean their messes in the afternoon. Her mother did the work.

At the doctor's home, she had her routine established. First she cleaned the kitchen, the bathroom and then his room. He was a man of economy. In his closet were three suits, two pairs of shoes and slippers. She could tidy his rooms and wash his clothes from the previous day in less than an hour.

Then she would move on to his mother's room, dust the furniture, carefully picking up each treasure from the dresser. In the beginning, Sarah studied the figure in the photographs. They must be pictures of his mother when she was a child, then as a young woman, finally with the doctor's father, and a single large picture of her in her bridal gown. Sarah was struck by the similarity of the shape of her own eyes and his mother's.

Each day she smoothed the lingerie that filled the drawers. After making sure that no one was watching, she self-consciously held up one of his mother's satin slips to herself and looked in the mirror. It would be a perfect fit. She had a brief tinge of guilt, quickly returning the slip to the drawer.

When she'd been working for the doctor for almost six months, he interrupted her one morning to assist him with a patient, a small boy with a shock of red hair who needed a stitch taken in a lacerated finger. At first, Sarah hesitated, knowing that her mother would disapprove. But how would Lillian ever know? Sarah had plenty of experience holding Winfield and Elbert and she deftly held the squirming, howling boy while Dr. Montgomery sutured the finger.

Later he thanked her, saying he'd never had a more able assistant. It was the first time she could remember receiving such a compliment and she swelled with pride, working even more diligently to please him.

Soon, she was helping him more in his office than with the housework. And he raised her salary another dollar a week.

Her mother barely acknowledged the added money she received each Friday. Sarah's main fear was that she might find out that she was involved with doctoring. If her mother knew, she would make Sarah quit her job, no matter how important the money had become to her.

Sarah never let on, especially to Beatrice, that she had learned to take temperatures, blood pressures, had listened to her own heartbeat with the doctor's stethoscope, had smelled evaporating piss he was testing for sugar over a bunsen burner, and had seen red blood cells under his microscope. He had a Materia Medica for Nurses that he let her read when she had a spare moment. How she would have loved to take the book home!

An idea slowly formed in her mind. What an exciting and forbidden thought - to be a nurse!

Of course, the thing that saved Sarah from her mother ever learning about her activities at the doctor's house was Lillian's aloofness. Accustomed to being shunned because she had those defective kids, Lillian never talked and barely looked at the townspeople when she went down the hill to the post-office or general store. The only reason she even went to the post-office was her hope for a letter from her sister, Elizabeth, living in Boston.

The hardest part for Sarah was that she could no longer believe in her mother's religion. She came to trust Dr. Montgomery's work more and more. He could help people with his hands and mind while her mother could only use her mind…and Sarah knew that the hate her mother had in her mind made her unsuitable to help anyone.

"*Hatred and its effects on the body are removed by Love*," Lillian would quote from her bible to Sarah, but lived a lie herself.

If her mother ever had loved, it had gotten lost, locked in the musty attic of her angry feelings.

It seemed almost no time at all that Sarah had worked for the doctor for almost two years. It was now January, 1926 and the country was beginning a depression. Although the doctor's income was less, he paid her the same amount each Friday. She had saved most of her nickels and dimes and was finally able to buy a nice dress and shoes for herself. Once she bought new cotton cloth for strips for Winfield's and Elbert's hands and arms. When she was cutting the cloth into strips, her mother turned on her furiously.

"Cutting new cloth! How can you do such a thing? That's a waste of money."

"Mother, the old rags are so worn that they only last a few hours until they chew through them and eat their own flesh. By afternoon, their arms and hands are bleeding again…"

"*…blood never gave life and can never take it away…*"

Sarah was silent in her disagreement, and she never bought new cotton again. But then she wondered, what difference did it make? There was no evidence that more money was coming into the house. Her mother never spent the money she'd saved from Sarah's earnings.

Even though Beatrice would yearn over the furniture in the Sears catalog pleading for their mother to order separate beds, she never did.

It didn't bother Sarah, though. She could see beautiful furniture every day at Dr. Montgomery's house. By now she knew his place almost better than her own; every corner and crack that needed washing or dusting, the nicks on the kitchen sideboard from years of chopping vegetables and slicing bread, the scald marks on the window-sill where Mrs. Montgomery must have placed hot pies.

Although Sarah dreaded the idea, she knew she couldn't continue with the doctor forever. After all, she was seventeen and of marriageable age. Her figure had matured. She was slim-waisted with full, round breasts, and long, firm legs. It was only a matter of time before one of the young men in town would ask for her hand in marriage, that is, if there was one who was not afraid of her retarded brothers.

When Sarah was at the doctor's house, she let her hair hang loosely around her shoulders, only piling and pinning it up in the severe style that met her mother's approval when she was ready to leave for home in the evening.

It was after the first winter snow that her life suddenly changed and it had nothing to do with her growing beauty.

Nineteen-year-old Winfield became sick. One Friday morning when she got out of bed, her mother was sitting on the floor holding him while Elbert lay in the playpen, screeching. Winfield was having convulsions, one after another. All that showed were the whites of his unseeing eyes rolling in his head. His weak neck tightened until the veins bulged and his face became purple because he wasn't breathing. His body would stiffen and then suddenly relax.

Sarah was terrified. "Mother, please…let me get Dr. Montgomery."

"Don't be afraid, Sarah," Lillian said calmly.

"I can't help it. Look at the sweat running off his body." She felt his clammy skin. "He isn't even biting himself because he's so sick." Sarah's heart pounded at the thought of what could happen.

"The cause of all sickness is fear," said Lillian, wiping Winfield's wet body and cleaning between his legs where he had soiled himself. "Sarah, why

do you live your life in fear? Being with that doctor has made you forget that *life is God and God is all*."

"Stop it, Mama! Winfield doesn't understand that!"

"He doesn't need to."

Lillian and Sarah took turns throughout that day and next night holding Winfield as his body stiffened and twisted and went limp. At the first light of morning, Lillian said she needed a letter posted.

"I'm telling Elizabeth to send a practitioner from Boston."

"That will take too long," Sarah said fearfully. "Besides, it's expensive."

"What is expense when it may mean your brother's life? And I have the money."

Sarah froze, knowing where the money had come from. It was the money she'd spent hard hours earning, hanging over buckets of scalding water to scrub walls and floors, fighting through terrible seasons of weather to get to the doctor's house.

"I don't think that money should be used for a practitioner," she said evenly, with a determination she seldom expressed. "You saved it when it could have been helping us, and now, you're going to throw it away on religion."

Her mother's hand which had been hurriedly scratching with the old quill pen stopped. She stood and went to the wall and pulled down the birch switch. Sarah knew what was going to happen. Still she could never have anticipated the rage that accompanied the act.

Her mother came at her, her eyes angry slits, the switch in her clenched fist. With the first snap of the switch, Sarah threw her body over Winfield to protect him as the blows seared her one after another to the sounds of her mother's animal-like grunts. The maddened frenzy continued and then stopped and her crazed mother was pulling her up by the hair. She swung Sarah around and threw her against the wall.

It was the excessiveness of the beating that finally freed Sarah. She suddenly turned on her mother, beating at her breasts and body, screaming hysterically over and over, "I hate you! I hate you!"

Thrown off balance, her mother dropped the switch trying to defend herself. The cruelty that had glazed her eyes turned to fear, fear that finally stopped Sarah.

Horror shot through her. What had she done? The throbbing in her head, her face, her aching body…

Their fighting had awakened Beatrice who stood in the doorway, crying.

28

Shaking, Lillian returned to the desk and quickly finished writing the letter and shoved folded money between the pages. She licked the envelope and handed it to Beatrice. "Go post this…immediately!"

Sobbing, Beatrice dressed and ran from the house, down the mud-slick driveway.

With her mother's anger simmering and her own turned to remorse, Sarah was appalled at what had happened. Never before had she turned on her mother. Never in her life had she imagined that she could subdue her mother.

As Winfield lay gasping in the playpen, Sarah decided that she would go and get Dr. Montgomery against her mother's wishes. She had no right to let Winfield suffer this way.

It was as though Lillian guessed her move for she went into the girls bedroom and brought back Sarah's worn coat, throwing it at her. "Get out! Get out! I never want to see you again! Never! Ever!"

Sarah was stunned. Never! Ever! Years before, those were the words her mother had said to Sarah's father.

She put on the coat, took a last look at Winfield laying flaccidly next to the screeching Elbert and ran from the house. She headed down the hill, the icy air knifing through her coat and across the switch marks on her back.

As Sarah passed the post-office, Beatrice came out.

"Why do you always fight with mother?" Beatrice asked, accusingly, walking away quickly, not waiting for an answer.

Chapter Four

Sarah had hoped to slip into Dr. Montgomery's office and see him immediately, but it was impossible. The examining room door was closed which meant Dr. Montgomery was not to be disturbed. She took the last available waiting room chair and could feel eyes furtively examining her swollen eyes and cheeks. As soon as he emerged from his office, giving a patient last minute instructions, Sarah hurried past the others. Seeing her, he quickly closed the door.

"Your face…what happened?"

Tears were streaming down her cheeks. "I don't want to talk about it. Dr. Montgomery, you've got to see my brother, Winfield," she pleaded. "He shakes and then lies still as though he's dead." She told him what had happened, how her mother was sending for a Christian Science practitioner. "But that's not going to save him. He'll die without your help."

He seemed disturbed and she didn't understand his confusing emotions. "I've never seen your brother, but I've seen others like him…"

"You have?" she said, never suspecting that there could be others like Elbert and Winfield.

Yes." He pulled his chair close to hers and took her hands between his. "Sarah, my dear, I can't help Winfield, not even if your mother would let me."

New tears gushed and spilled. He took her in his arms to comfort her, caressing her hair. She winced from the pain where her mother had yanked at it. "Please don't touch my head or back," she begged.

He pulled up her blouse and looked at her back. "She switched you, didn't she?"

"Yes," Sarah sobbed. "She told me never to come home again."

Dr. Montgomery let go of her, shifting back in his chair, contemplating her. He crossed his legs and twirled the ends of his mustache as he so often did when he was making decisions about his patients.

"You must stay here."

She collapsed in relief, crying even harder. When her sobs had subsided, he led her from the office, past the curious but silent patients and left her in his private living room. While he saw the other patients, she rested.

That afternoon, after the office was emptied, he came and told her that he had to make a house call to Mr. Miller whose broken leg was not mending properly. It was crushed by a falling tree weeks before. "I hope to be back before dark," the doctor said, "but he lives a ways out of town so it may take awhile."

She heard him gallop off on his horse. Since she felt stronger after her long rest, it seemed only proper that she should fix his dinner so she gathered eggs for custard, made a pork meat pie with vegetables and a side dish of baked beans and corn.

She set a single place at the table for him, but, three hours later when he returned, he would have none of it, insisting that she set a place for herself. He seemed pleased with the steaming meat pie, and she swelled with pride watching him breathe in the delicious smell.

"I haven't had a meal this exceptional since…" He stopped, his eyes reflective and distant.

After that, they ate in silence and finished as the grandfather clock chimed ten pm.

When he was satisfied, he stood. "Sarah, let me show you where you will sleep." He picked up the kerosene lamp from the table and motioned for her to follow him. He led her to his mother's room and lit the kerosene lamp resting on the dresser.

He paused and observed her. "Did you bring any extra clothes?"

"No." Embarrassed, she clasped her hands in her lap and stared at the floor.

He opened a dresser drawer and took out a warm pink nightgown with lace at the neck and wrists. Although Sarah had folded and refolded the fine gown dozens of times, she never dreamed she might one day wear it. Maybe it was her imagination, but Dr. Montgomery seemed agitated as he handed her the gown. But it was not her imagination that he first held it to his nose to breathe in the lavender sachet smell.

Something kept her from accepting the garment so he dropped it on the bed.

"When you're ready for sleep," he said, "call me and I will come douse the lamp."

"All right," she said, anxious for him to leave.

The doctor turned away and crossed the hall to his own bedroom. Quietly, so that he wouldn't hear, Sarah closed the bedroom door and quickly dropped her dirty, bloodstained clothes to the floor. She turned and looked over her shoulder to see her back in the mirror. Angry red welts crisscrossed her flesh.

As she slipped on the pink gown, the thought of sleeping in his mother's bed tormented her, somehow seeming wrong. She thought back to the day two years before when the stream of townspeople had converged on the church to attend the old lady's funeral. That was the day that Beatrice had agreed to clean his house and now, here Sarah was climbing into his mother's bed Even with her fear, she was still grateful to the doctor. Where else could she have gone tonight? She knew of no other place, unless, possibly her father's home in Burlington where he lived, or, so her mother said.

Instead of calling Dr. Montgomery to darken the lamp, she turned off the wick herself and found her way to the bed in the dark, lying on her stomach under the warm quilt because her back was too painful.

She couldn't fall asleep thinking about Winfield. Had his fever dropped? Had his convulsions stopped?

Tears welled in her eyes, spilling over and dropping to the bed sheets, mixing with the lavender aroma of the nightgown. She felt so helpless, unable to help her beloved brother. Now that she was alone in the night, she could give in to her grief.

It seemed as though hours had passed when she heard the doctor's footsteps in the hall, the handle of her door turning, the light from his lamp throwing eerie shadows across his face and the room. He placed the lamp on the dresser and came to the bed.

"You didn't call me," he said, and his voice had a strange huskiness.

"I didn't want to bother you."

"I wanted you to." He sounded different. His speech had an odd intensity, a pressured quality that she had never heard before. She turned on her side to look up at him. His face did not look the same. It had an unnatural shine, an almost mask-like tautness. His mouth quivered, his eyes were glazed and fixed on hers. He was not the same Dr. Montgomery.

"I thought you'd never come back," he said, his mouth sounding dry. He cleared his throat, reached for the bedcovers and started to lift them from her.

She drew back. "What are you doing?" She moved away, clinging to the covers, pulling them tightly under her chin, suddenly afraid of him, her heart pounding.

"Don't do that," he said quietly, gently pulling the covers from her and throwing them on the floor at the end of the bed.

She wanted to scream, but fear froze her throat and no sounds came.

"It's all right," he said softly as he moved in beside her.

But in her heart she knew it wasn't all right and she was on her back and the sheets were rough against the cuts. The room was deathly quiet and his breaths were short and hard. But the strong smell of sweat was sickening. She was sure that something even more sickening than sweat was to follow. She could feel her body tighten and she hated to show her fear. She wanted to be strong and in control. How dare he violate her but she knew it was coming...and then it did.

She turned her face away and felt her jaw tighten as his hand slowly slipped between her legs to touch what no man had ever touched. He gently caressed her and that scared her, too.

"That's good, isn't it, Mama?" He continued to caress her. "You always liked this, didn't you?"

"No," she screamed. "I'm not your mother. You're a mad man." Her heart had quickened and she tried to kick him away but it made her move on the bed and the searing pain on her back was unbearable. He was patient and she knew he had more plans. It wasn't going to stop there. He would go farther and farther until there was no turning back. She pushed his hand away and tried to climb down to the end of the bed.

"Don't fight, Mama," he begged as he grabbed her gown and pulled her back flat on the bed, pushing the gown up.

She whipped her head from side-to-side, to escape his frenzy as his tongue searched her breasts and kissed her nipples, then nibbled his way up her neck and kissed her passionately on the mouth. It was nauseating.

Then he whispered, "It will be good again, Mama. Just like always."

She tried to relax, wanting desperately to believe him. But it could never be good. His hand slipped between her legs again and he was caressing her.

He whispered something. Had she heard him correctly? The echo of his words came back to her. "I've made you ready, now you make me ready." And he pulled her hand over his penis. "Just like you used to do when I was little, remember Mama? You used to fondle me until, one day, it got stiff as a stick. We used to laugh and we called it a boner. Then one day you slipped it inside you and it was so wonderful. Give me a boner now, Mama. Make it wonderful again."

Now, totally repulsed at the thought that she was his mama who had done that to a child, she pulled her hand away and screamed, "I told you I'm not your mama. Now stop!"

But he quickly straddled her as he held her arms out to the sides. Her back was painfully raw with his every movement. She struggled to get free and he promptly flattened her, forcing her legs up and apart, then pushed his hardened penis against her. But the opening was small and she was dry and tight. So he put his hand down there and moved his finger around in the opening and slowly pushed and she screamed.

"No, no, please don't…"

"Now you can put it in," he said softly, wrapping her hand around his penis, moving her hand to the opening and shoving his penis inside. She yanked her hand away and he lay on her. Then he started to moved in and out faster and faster and the pain was excruciating.

"Please stop," she begged. "I'm not your mama."

"Of course, you are. You smell like lavender. You are my mama." He pushed harder and harder until she feared he would tear her apart.

"OK. I'm your mama," she shouted. "Please stop. Please. It's over. You got what you…"

And he pressed his mouth against hers, and she couldn't talk anymore. She started to cry and make guttural sounds hoping that she could distract herself from the evil thing he was doing to her.

But he wouldn't quit, until finally, after a few more deep pushes he grunted and collapsed with exhaustion dropping his head on her chest.

Her legs were still pushed to the sides and it was painful. Slowly, she began to slide out from under him, thinking if she was very quiet she could get away. When her legs were free, she slipped off the bed.

He was crying with his head buried in a torn piece of his mother's nightgown. "I didn't mean to frighten you." Then he quickly turned over and looked up at her standing at the foot of the bed. His eyes still had that glassy look. "Wasn't it nice again?"

"No. How could you?" She quickly reached for her clothes. As she slipped into her panties, she noticed blood was seeping through and down her legs.

He had done it to her. He had torn her virtue from her in a horrible way and she hated him for it.

He leaped out of bed. "What are you going to do?"

"Leave," she said.

"No."

"You can't stop me." She pulled her dress over his mother's nightgown and put on her coat. When she turned around, he stood between her and the bedroom door.

Again he had changed. He was firm, with the kindness that his patients understood to mean that they would do as he said.

"Sarah, you can't leave. You have no place else to stay." She shoved him aside with the same ferocity she'd used on her mother hours before. "I'll find a place."

She ran to the front door, fighting to unlock it, ignoring the pain that ripped her body, the wetness that coursed down her legs. She ran out, racing down the hill to the main street of town, slipping on the icy road leading to her mother's house. After she reached the front door, she waited until her heaving chest quieted. When her breathing calmed so no one could detect her, she would enter, find a cloth bag, gather her few clothes, get her savings, and leave Riverfork...forever. She knew the train heading south would be arriving in less than an hour.

She shivered in the cold and touched the freezing door knob. Thankfully, it was unlocked. She heard the grandfather clock chiming in the living room. The sound would conceal her opening the door. She went into the darkened house, stumbling against a wooden object in the living room. She felt along its edges to determine what it was. It was oblong and then she realized...a coffin!

She covered her mouth, stifling a scream. She listened for Winfield's cries, the wet gurgling as he tried to chew his fingers, but there were no sounds, The worst must have happened. Shaking, with tears streaming, she felt her way to her bedroom to get her clothes. When she pulled them from the dresser drawer, they came out in strips, torn strips of material. At first it didn't make sense. Then her sadness turned to anger. Her vengeful mother had cut her clothes into strips to use to bind the boys arms and hands. Her clothes weren't new cloth. It was as though her mother had torn her apart piece by piece. Why, oh why would she do that? To be completely rid of her?

Sarah shuddered. In a fury, she threw the strips to the floor, her mind exploding with silent screams of rage. She stopped when she heard Beatrice turn over in bed.

Far away outside, echoing her inner turmoil, she could hear the mournful cry of the Central Vermont Railway train that would stop in Riverfork just long enough to pick up passengers and collect supplies, drop off and retrieve mail. If she hurried, she could make the train.

She fumbled for her money tied in a tobacco bag that she kept hidden between the mattress and springs. Beatrice never stirred.

Then she tiptoed out, over the strips of cotton, avoiding the coffin in the living room, now visible with the first light of day.

She could hear Elbert chewing in his sleep as she slipped out the front door. In spite of her pain, she pounded down the road, her hair flying.

The train was just pulling away from the train station as she reached it. The conductor held out his arm and leaned over to help her. Just as he was about to catch her hand and she was ready to leap to the step, he pulled back, disgust written on his face.

"Please...please..." she cried, chasing alongside the train.

He turned around and went into the moving train, slamming the heavy door behind him.

Chapter Five

Shattered by his rebuff, Sarah slowed to a walk catching her breath, too stunned to feel anything, her legs numb from the cold. She took in the long stretch of railroad tracks that would guide her steps, her feelings crushed, knowing she'd not get help.

She had never been out of Riverfork and had no idea how far Burlington was, but people always said that the railroad tracks would lead you there. She set out, prepared for a long walk, determined to find her father.

She walked all that day and on into the night. Sometime after dark, her clothes stiff from the cold air, she paused and stripped, dropping Mrs. Montgomery's stained nightgown to the ground. Just being rid of it made her feel cleaner. Then she put her only dress and shabby coat back on. Still, hard crusts of dried secretions scraped her inner thighs as she walked.

It was nearly noon of the following day when Sarah reached the outskirts of Burlington, her feet raw from the iced gravel along her journey. Before her was a canyon with a raging river at the bottom. On the other side of the chasm, she could see houses, impossible to reach. But it gave her hope. Exhilarated, she quickened her pace and began to run, her coat and dress whipping against her legs, her breath leaving a trail of frost.

The railroad tracks suddenly veered left, traveling along the Lake Champlain waterfront. She ran past industrial buildings. The blast of a train whistle startled her and she hid in brush as the chug of quickening metal came closer. A Central Vermont Railway train rumbled by, heading north along the stretch of tracks she'd just passed.

She resumed her pace and in less than ten minutes reached the Burlington Union Station Ticket office, her heart racing in anticipation. How would her father react when she found him? How would he feel when he saw that his small Sarah had grown into a woman?

The train station was empty except for the station master working in a wood paneled office. He sat at his desk, bent-over, leaning on his elbows, sipping from a cup, blowing steam away, steam that clouded his glasses. A huge railroad clock hung on the wall over his head.

Sarah interrupted him. "Excuse me..."

"Yes..." he scowled over his glasses.

"I'm looking for my father," she stammered, afraid of disappointment.

"Isn't me. Do you see anyone else around here?"

"I just thought you might know him."

"What's his name?"

"Spencer Morgan."

He grimaced, disgusted. "Miss, do you know there are fifteen-thousand people in this town? No, I don't know your father." He turned back to his desk, dismissing her.

She backed away, embarrassed. Near the station entrance was a phone directory. She checked the names, but her father's was not listed.

Disheartened, she left the station and began walking up the hill to the business district. Was she wrong about his whereabouts? Just because her mother received letters from him with a Burlington postmark didn't mean that he lived here. Was he still in lumbering? Or had he changed occupations?

She passed the Vermont Pawn Shop, the Strand Theater where the movie "Anna Christie" played starring Greta Garbo; The Flynn Theater showing "All Quiet on the Western Front"; the Arcadia restaurant, a drug store, lawyers' offices. By the time she'd gone four blocks, she'd seen several doctors offices and shuddered at each one.

Even though the sun warmed the air, Sarah knew darkness would bring freezing cold again. The sidewalk was slippery with ice and her coat gave her little warmth.

A clock in a store window read 2:10. At the most, there would be less than three more hours of daylight before she had to have a place to stay. She turned off several blocks farther to Willard Street which was lined with maple and oak trees. Huge multi-storied gothic, federalist, colonial and Queen Anne homes loomed like disapproving relatives.

In house after house discreet signs hung advertising for "Guests". She walked another two blocks before deciding which house she preferred and settled on a domed Colonial with gleaming, white columns before the entrance.

She knocked, and a woman answered. She was dressed in a long skirt and wiping her hands on an apron. She smiled, but her face lost its friendliness when Sarah asked for information on lodging.

She excused herself, bringing back a man she introduced as, "The mister...Mister Garvin."

He invited Sarah into the parlor, furnished with flowered couches, matching overstuffed chairs, a rocking chair, an end table with a Philco radio. He motioned for her to sit.

"What is your reason for needing a room?"

"I'm looking for my father."

"Oh." His eyebrows raised. "Where is your home?"

She became evasive. "It is far from here." Then she told the truth. "I have no home."

The couple exchanged glances, their meaning secret from her.

"Where will you be working?" Mr. Garvin asked.

"I'll look for work as soon as I have a place to stay."

"There's a depression on...people all over looking for work. There aren't any jobs," he said, discouraging her.

"I have money. What is the price of a room?"

Mrs. Garvin spoke: "Five dollars a week. Double that if you want breakfast and dinner."

Sarah computed that her money might last several weeks with meals. In order to accept this place, she would have to have a job. "Thank you," she said, rising. "I'll let you know."

"Would four-dollars weekly be satisfactory?" Mrs. Garvin asked quickly.

"With a meal, yes."

"No, I'm afraid that's impossible." She shook her head. "For the room only."

With that, Sarah left and knocked on the door of the next house with a "Guests" sign hanging above the porch. She was turned away. No reason given. The landlady at the following house told her they would allow her to stay one week only for fifteen-dollars with no meals. Several others were blunt. "We don't rent to a woman alone." Or, "You're too young."

Other signs read: "For Gentlemen Only."

In all, she made eleven fruitless stops before darkness came.

She had to stay someplace for the night and thought of the train station. By the time she reached it, her hands and feet were numb from the cold.

The same station master was there. She huddled on a bench hoping to escape his attention.

"No more trains tonight," he said, not looking up.

She didn't reply or move.

"You can't stay here unless you're waiting for a train."

"I'm waiting for the morning train to St. Albans," she lied.

"Tomorrow's Sunday. Doesn't run on Sunday."

What could she do? Why wouldn't he just leave her alone?

Suddenly he produced a ticket. "Here…Montpelier. Two dollars and twenty-five cents. Leaves early."

She took the ticket and then changed her mind. "Please, just give me one more day. I have to find my father."

He waved her away.

Her heart sank, and she paid for the ticket. He left her alone for the night to do as she wanted, so she stayed on a bench against a wall where he couldn't see her. Now and again, she dozed.

The next day, after dropping the unused ticket in the trash, she checked every lumber company in town for her father. She asked at the W & DG Crane lumber company. They'd never heard of a Spencer Morgan. The answer was the same a block away at the Edward's Lumber Company.

She finally realized that she'd come to Burlington on false hope. The telephone directory told the story that first day. And yet she hadn't believed if and now she couldn't give up.

There was one more place on College Street. Even though she feared it would be futile, she stopped at the Shepard & Morse Lumber company.

The manager checked his books. "Yes. We have a Spencer Morgan."

Sarah's heart raced. Finally, after so long…"When will he be here?" Her voice was a whisper.

"After the thaw in about four months. He's in the Green Mountains with a lumbering gang."

Four months! That was a lifetime. "Please…please…help me get in touch with him."

The man shrugged. "Almost impossible."

"The men must get mail."

"They do. Maybe once a month."

She begged for pen and paper and he agreed to send off her letter. As soon as her father knew she was in Burlington, he would certainly quit the lumbering crew and rush home.

She wrote: "Dear Father: I'm in Burlington waiting for your return. Your loving daughter, Sarah." She drew symbols for love and kisses and handed the letter to the manager, but then wondered, what address could she give for her father to contact her?

"Can I have him send his reply here?" she asked, paying for the stamp. "I'll stop by daily until I've received an answer."

He nodded and took the letter. After she left the lumber company she went back to the Garvins place. At their quoted price, she would be able to have lodging nearly until her father returned.

She hurried up the hill to their home. They raised the price to twelve dollars a week with one meal.

She stayed two weeks, but after that, with no job prospects, her situation was impossible. Her dress was blood-stained and her coat tattered. Without new clothes, she would never find employment.

She asked the Garvin's to dispense with the meal and they lowered her rent to nine dollars a week. She paid for two more weeks. Half of the rest of her money went for a second-hand dress, coat and shoes.

That left her four dollars to last until she had a paycheck.

Every morning she went out and searched for work, returning each evening to her room with its single bed, chest of drawers and chair. Her stomach churned at the dinner smells wafting up the stairs from the first floor kitchen. While the Garvin's ate stews and hot breads, she survived on Quaker Oats mixed with hot water. She bought a can of maple syrup to vary the taste.

Finally, after several days, she replied to an ad in the "Burlington Daily News". It was for a position staying with two young girls at night while their mother worked. The woman was vague about the kind of work she did, however, her house was nicely furnished and the children well-dressed. Best of all, the refrigerator was stocked and Sarah was allowed to eat.

But food was all she got. After two weeks, when there was no salary paid and she asked questions, the woman fired her. She found herself back on the streets, reading the want ads once again.

She begged the Garvins to let her stay on and gave them her last few dollars. They seemed to genuinely like and feel sorry for her, giving her soup and bread every evening, but after a week with no signs of employment and her funds gone, they evicted her.

It was January, one of the coldest years in Vermont's recorded history and Sarah walked to keep warm, staying awake all night, huddling on the doorstep of a deserted building by day.

During a terrible snowstorm, she lay in an alley under old newspapers.

It was several days before someone found her and she was thought to be dead. She barely breathed. Her clothes hung on her. Her hands, feet and face were blistered from the cold, her body on fire with fever. When they moved her, she became delirious, crying out for Winfield and her father. She dreamed of his arms warming her, his voice soothing her.

She pushed her fists against her ears to try and stop the ringing that kept interrupting her father's words. That's the way she was when she awoke in a strange room and a man was hovering over her. She drew back when she saw his white coat. He wasn't her father.

Dr. Montgomery had found her! She began to scream and somebody took her hand, reassuring her with a strong, comforting grasp. As her vision cleared, she realized he wasn't Dr. Montgomery. She read his name from a lapel pin.

Warren Hollis
School of Medicine
Class of 1929

Behind him, a man was speaking: "Congratulations, Warren. It looks like her pneumonia is resolving. I believe you've saved her."

She had no idea what he meant, but she was caught by the concern in Warren Hollis' deep-set, blue eyes. Her heart flickered as she lapsed into unconsciousness again, but not before she had memorized his features. A straight, prominent nose, strong brow, a mouth drawn in concern. Dark, slightly curly hair, cut below his ears.

Later, when she awoke again, he was gone. Only a vague impression of him remained.

During the days she spent regaining her strength, he came by each morning accompanied by his physician mentor. They held hushed conferences in the hall and she knew they were discussing her. Eventually, Warren Hollis told her that he was a third year medical student from the University of Vermont affiliating with the Margaret Ward Hospital where she was recuperating.

After he left each morning, her day was as good as over for she spent the hours looking forward to the next morning.

Against her will, her heart quickening, she could think of nothing other than anticipating his visits. Even though she said she'd never trust another man, her resolve gradually vanished with thoughts of Warren Hollis.

After three more weeks, he told her she could leave at the beginning of the next week. "Why has no one come to visit you?" he asked.

How did he know? Had the nurses told him? "I don't know anyone here."

"Where have you been staying?"

She broke into tears and told him her story, about her father, losing her lodging because she ran out of money, the hopelessness, the not knowing. As soon as the words were out, she was sorry. Confessing problems was not her nature. It went against family pride. "Please forgive me for telling you...it is not true," she lied and he solemnly accepted her apology.

On the morning of her release from the hospital, Warren Hollis came to say goodbye and pressed several bills in her hand. "This should keep you until your father returns."

"I can't accept it," she said, dropping the money on the bed.

"You have no choice," he said. "I'm prescribing it for you."

She couldn't speak for her throat ached and tears came.

Warren Hollis turned away and left.

"I'll pay it back," she called after him. If he thought her promise idle, he was mistaken. But he was not mistaken about judging her needs. He had given her one-hundred and fifty dollars.

She dressed, slowed down by weakness, and took the bus back to Willard Street, offering the Garvins' sixty-dollars for six weeks lodging with meals. At first they acted as though they were going to refuse, but when they saw she had more money, they agreed. She prayed it was the last time in her life that need would dictate to her pride.

After several weeks, she found a job ironing shirts at night in a laundry. The pay was meager and she immediately began saving to repay Warren Hollis. She was always tired from the after effects of the pneumonia and sleeping poorly during the day.

As the end of April neared, she began stopping each morning at the Shepard and Morse Lumber Company to see if her father had returned from the mountains.

Each day, the answer was no.

Then, one day, it was yes.

Chapter Six

Sarah could hardly contain her excitement. Perhaps he had not received her first message for he'd left no reply. She left him another. Surely this one would reach him.

She spent anxious days listening for a knock at the front door at the Garvins' but there was none. Then she realized, maybe the man at the lumber company had not given him the message. Maybe her father couldn't connect with the message and put it in his pocket…or the waste can. She would trick them. She would wait at the entrance to the lumber yard while the men came into work.

As soon as she finished at the laundry, she would head for the waterfront, smugly waiting on the bus bench as the men went through the heavy gates. When the moment finally came, there was no mistaking his identity. It had been almost fourteen years since she'd seen him, although it was his gait more than his appearance that she recognized. His hair was graying, his serious face was the same, but with deeply etched lines.

She ran from the bench, shoving him off balance as she threw her arms around him.

He stiffened, but Sarah dismissed it as the fault of her exuberance. "Father, Father," she cried, first a shout, then a choked whisper as tears burst forth.

He held her, almost impassively, and then he put her at arms length looking her over. "Well, if it isn't my Sarah…" He smiled widely, but she saw no joy in his eyes.

Her heart plummeted. After so long, why was he so distant? Didn't he want to see her? How could that be possible?

When they had both regained their composure, he took her inside the lumber company and properly introduced her to the manager, Mr. Meehan.

"A persistent one," Mr. Meehan chuckled. "Been around here looking for you since you first went to the mountains. Almost delivered her messages to you myself even though the mails are good around here."

Spencer Morgan frowned. He quickly collected his salary, led her back to the street and helped her into his carriage. She sat next to him, stealing glances at him as the horses clopped along the maple and spruce tree-lined streets. It reminded her of the time they had ridden to Aunt Ethel's house, the night Elbert was born. Only now, she was no longer sure she was important to him.

He asked her where she was staying, what she was doing. By the time they reached town, she had reviewed the major events of her life, editing out the troubles with her mother, Dr. Montgomery's rape, and her near death from cold and starvation.

At the bakery, he pulled the horse to a stop and went in, returning with a brightly decorated cake. "To celebrate your arrival," he said, placing it on her lap. "No licking! You have to share it with your step-mother and brothers."

She went cold. He had another family. There had been a time lapse for her but not for him, she realized sadly. He had a new life and the hope was gone from hers.

Was this why her mother had turned into a real bitch? When she had learned that Spencer had taken a second wife and bore him sons? Why had her mother never told them? Did she assume her daughters would never seek out their father? Then again, maybe her mother never had a clue and just couldn't find any joy in her life at all.

Before long, her father stopped in front of a huge Victorian house not two blocks from where she'd been staying for more than five months. It was the most beautiful home on the street and the sparkling white, organdy curtains showing through the windows told her it must be a happy home.

The front door flew open and a dark-haired boy dashed out to meet them. "Dad, who did you bring?" the young boy asked, jumping up and down excitedly.

"Careful, careful," laughed Spencer Morgan, climbing from the carriage and helping Sarah down. "This is Potter," he said, introducing the boy. Her father took the cake so she could shake Potter's hand.

"Are you coming to work for us?"

Spencer laughed even harder. "No…she's your sister." And in an aside to Sarah, he explained. "Hannah, our maid, is always threatening to marry and leave."

"Sister!" Potter howled. "When did I get a sister?" In spite of his protests, Sarah could see his chest expanding with pride. And then very solemnly, he said, "I'm seven. How old are you?"

"That's not your concern," said their father. "Come into the house."

Potter ran up the walk before them. Sarah noticed similarities between him and her sister Beatrice. Their instant friendliness, inquisitive chatter, the impish grin. He bounded up the steps, holding the door open for them, at the same time calling, "Mother, Mother, Benjamin, Father's brought home a sister."

A dark-haired woman quickly came into the living room, her face drained of color. Except that her mouth was fuller and she had a cleft in her chin, she could have been a double for Sarah's mother, Lillian. And the small blond boy at her side could have been Sarah when she was younger. He clung shyly to his mother.

"Carrie," Spencer put his arm around the woman. "This is my daughter, Sarah."

"How do you do," Carrie said, her voice hardly a whisper. She wiped her hands on a towel hanging at her waist and extended her hand to Sarah.

"And this is your brother, Benjamin," said her father, identifying the blond boy. "Well now," he said, as they all stood looking at one another, speechless in the shock of the moment, "We'll just have to put one more place setting on the table."

This seemed to nudge Carrie as the color returned to her face. "Yes, yes, of course."

"And here is our dessert." He handed the cake to his wife and she retreated into the kitchen, her son clinging to her skirt.

"Do you want to see my room?" Potter was as excited as the first moment he'd seen Sarah.

"No, no, she's not interested in your room," their father said, taking Sarah's coat and steering her to the couch.

She was interested in Potter's room, but said nothing, and tried to adjust to the fine surroundings in the living room. A mahogany hutch holding crystal, gold and silver pieces; a matching desk polished to a high gloss; comfortable chairs covered in needlepoint; a huge, hand hooked rug protecting the wood floors; the starched organdy curtains she'd seen from the street.

It was certainly a finer home than she'd grown up in, but even if they'd had a nice home, it would have been dirty because of Louise, Winfield, and Elbert. Not even six maids could have kept it this neat or clean.

Potter sat beside her, drawing closer.

Their father sat in an overstuffed chair facing them, his hands clasped in his lap. "You told me a little about yourself," he said, "but not why you're in Burlington."

It had been years since she'd seen him. If she told him the truth, would he side with her mother? She wasn't willing to take that chance. "I'd rather not discuss it," she said, not wanting to sound disrespectful, yet frightened that he might press her.

"Of course, as you wish." He was plainly flustered and seemed to be thinking of something else to say.

She wished she could somehow retrieve the childhood bond she remembered having with him. If the bond hadn't been there, then why had she yearned for him since he'd left their home, and acutely these past months when she'd searched and waited for him? Now they were strangers with another family between them.

"How's Beatrice?" he asked.

"Fine."

"Who is Beatrice?" Potter demanded.

"Another sister. Now hush." Their father was irritated. "And Winfield?"

Sarah hesitated. Did she dare tell him with Potter present? Did her father know that Louise had died, too. Deciding for her was Carrie who tinkled the dinner bell. This wasn't a good time to tell him.

They moved to the table and Sarah briefly glimpsed Hannah, the maid, a slight girl, barely tall enough to reach to the center of the table to place the steaming soup tureen on the hot pad. Before retreating to the kitchen, Hannah gave Sarah a sweeping look. It hardly took a second, but Sarah knew she'd been measured, evaluated and compared.

Spencer Morgan said grace, filled their bowls with creamy watercress soup, dished out the delicious-smelling beef and pork stew, a baked apple side-dish, and finally, the cake that Sarah had carried on her lap.

Except for the pinging and clatter of forks and spoons, the meal passed in silence.

When they were finished, Carrie turned to her husband. "Will you be taking Sarah home?"

Sarah spoke before he had a chance to reply. "I don't have to go home. It's my night off from work."

Her father and Carrie exchanged glances which seemed to decide his answer. "It would be best if you went, Sarah. The spare room isn't readied. The next time you come..."

It was barely one in the afternoon.

Carrie quickly laid down her napkin and disappeared into the kitchen with Benjamin right behind her.

"Can I ride with you to take her home?" Potter was insistent.

"I can walk," she said. "It isn't very far."

"I won't have that," her father said, pulling back her chair as she stood, getting her coat for her. "Yes, Potter, you may come."

As they rode in the carriage, Spencer Morgan tried to make conversation, but Sarah felt it was meaningless, words to fill the air. When they neared the Garvins he assured her he'd be getting in touch with her shortly. "We'll plan better, spend more time together, maybe go to the Lake, ride in the countryside..."

She wanted to believe him. "I'm sometimes off on Wednesdays, too," she said.

"Wednesdays it will be."

He pulled the horse to a stop before the Garvins' without her telling him where she lived. He already knew. He helped her down and hugged her. "You didn't tell me about Winfield," he said.

She backed away from him, her head down. "He died," she said, "and so did Louise."

Her father did not respond. The only sound was the light rustle of leaves on the maple trees as she turned, hurried down the walk and went into the house. It seemed forever before she heard the horses clopping down the street, their sounds fading away as cleanly as her dream of a father she'd once known.

And, she decided as the weeks passed, if it had been up to him, she probably never would never hear from him again.

Gradually, her disappointment became resignation and she turned her mind to other matters. She concentrated on earning and saving the money to return to Warren Hollis, depriving herself, placing the nickels and dimes in a cigar box in her bureau drawer.

Her eighteenth birthday came and went, forgotten.

By late August, she had the full one-hundred and fifty dollars, folded it, hid it in her purse and boarded a bus going to the Margaret Ward Hospital.

The hospital bustled with people and the ether smell permeating the halls made her nauseous.

On her way to the medical director's office, she passed the superintendent of nurses' office. Outside, on a bulletin board was a photograph of the latest graduating class, eight girls wearing stiff, white uniforms with leg-o-mutton sleeves. On their heads were starched, white caps with a black stripe along the brim. Sarah looked at the girls for a long time, admiring their professional appearance and calm pride.

She paused long enough to read the announcement of the new class which would begin later in the month. The entrance fee was ten dollars. Applicants must be high-school graduates, in good health and between the ages of eighteen and thirty-five. The training period was three years.

She turned away. After her experience with Dr. Montgomery, she never wanted to be near medical procedures or a doctor again.

But then there was Warren Hollis. He'd been different.

She asked for him in the medical director's office, but Warren was gone and would not be returning in the fall. She was told to write to him at the University of Vermont.

With this unexpected dilemma, Sarah went home.

Waiting for her were two letters. The first, an announcement of a new laundry seeking experienced ladies to iron. She ignored this letter. The second one was from Potter inviting her to his eighth birthday party. He had made the invitation himself, cutting paper figures and placing them in a silver airplane. An arrow pointed to a girl riding in the plane bearing Sarah's name.

She sent him an acceptance note, replying that she would be "flying" to his party. For his gift, she bought a wooden model airplane kit with dozens of pieces to glue together.

On the day of his party, she went without sleep after working all night at the laundry. Shortly after noon, she walked to her father's house. Carrie met and kissed her. "I'm so glad you could make it, dear. I'm sorry but your father is away, working at the lumbar yard."

Benjamin was clinging to Carrie. Potter put a party hat on her, and told his friends that she was a special sister. They played party games, and blew party whistles that curled in and out.

Noting that Carrie was doing all the work, bringing sandwiches, milk, cake and ice-cream, Sarah asked about Hannah.

"She left to be married."

Sarah immediately rose from the table to help, removing used plates, lighting the birthday candles on the cake, helping the boys wash their hands and faces, cleaning up the gift wrappings from the presents.

It was three hours of noise with Potter having the best time of all, playing drop-the-clothespin-in-the-bottle, throwing darts at the donkey tacked on the wall, playing cowboys and Indians on the front lawn in the afternoon heat.

At five p.m., Spencer Morgan returned from the lumbar yard. Carrie called a halt to the party, sent everyone home, and dropped in to her husband's arms. "I'm exhausted. Sarah was such a help...she can heat the beef stew for you."

He grinned and pulled Sarah to him, holding both of his women tightly. Carrie quickly extricated herself and went upstairs.

"This house is too much work for her," Spencer said later as Sarah placed the heated stew before him.

"Yes," she agreed. "If it would help, I can stay. It's my night off from the laundry. I can do the heavy cleaning in the morning."

"No. You've done enough. I'll take you home now."

Her heart cried out. Didn't he understand that it wasn't the work? She needed a family, to be with him, her brothers, that her life had no latitude from one day to the next other than working, sleeping, eating...worrying, loneliness.

But she kept her feelings to herself and accepted his ride to the Garvins'. As before, their parting was strained.

As she left him, a bitterness began to fester in her. Not only with him, but with the Garvins. They seemed careful around her. On the first day of September, she learned why.

"You'll excuse us, Miss Morgan," said Mrs. Garvin taking the rent money. "We'll be needing the room by the first of October. The mister's old mother is coming...too feeble to live alone another winter."

Knowing that she would have to search for living quarters once again, Sarah sighed, instantly depressed. As she read the want ads, she found an ad her father had placed for a housekeeper, offering a salary plus room and board.

She responded, again to disappointment.

"We can't be passing money between relatives," said her father, refusing her the position.

Why not? Suddenly, she was sure she knew the truth. Why can't you be honest? she thought, anguished. You don't want me around. Am I an embarrassment, a reminder of another, less happy period of your life?

"Do you understand why I say that?" he said, breaking the awkward silence between them.

"Yes, I think I understand," she said, not understanding at all. "I won't bother you anymore."

He just stood there with a flat expression even though his eyes looked haunted.

Sarah left, hurrying back to the Garvins' where she got some of her money. Then she took a bus across town, to the Margaret Ward Hospital School of Nursing, and paid the ten dollar enrollment fee.

When she got word of her acceptance, she packed her few belongings. The Garvins didn't say goodbye to her and stayed away from the house on her moving day.

As she rode to her new beginnings, she mentally wiped her father from her life as she had done with her mother.

Whatever she got out of this life, she would have earned on her own.

Chapter Seven

After a month in the nursing program, Sarah felt like she'd been a student nurse probationer for a lot longer than four weeks. The onslaught of new experiences, rules and regulations, and, yes, regimentation made her wonder— what had happened to the world she'd known before she entered the doors of West Vermont Hospital?

Today, in the hospital lobby, volunteer ladies were putting up Halloween decorations, witches and goblins hanging everywhere, from the ceiling and walls, ghosts where a space could be found. People smiled as the fun found a holiday mood. Somehow, cheer seemed to touch patients and visitors alike during holidays…any holiday.

The same could not be said for the student nurses because, for them, there were no holidays. In the basement where they started each day, there were few smiles either.

Their first event of the day was meeting the superintendent of nursing for morning inspection. It took just one session to know that they would adjust to the ramrod straight Miss Edwina Bradford's morning inspection. Her welcoming expression was so flat that it was up to the students to guess what was on her mind. This ritual would continue every day of their three years in training when they were on duty. Otherwise, the only freedom they would ever get from the morning drill was when they were away on affiliation at the Greenbridge Hospital for the Insane or Tuberculosis Preventorium at Pittsford.

The two hospitals were supposed to provide varied experiences, different from those available at West Vermont. On the surface, the hospitals were different. Underneath, it was hard to find any difference at all.

At West Vermont Hospital, at precisely 6:20 each morning, the fifteen probationers filed past the formidable Miss Bradford, who stood outside the door of the basement dining room. Anyone who had her power could be expected to be large and overbearing. But Miss Bradford was slight and thin. It was her manner that had authority. Her right hand held a sterling-silver handled walking stick which she used to point out deficiencies in the students' dress. The movement of her fingers and hand told more about her mood than her facial expression which stayed as wooden as the stem of the walking stick.

As with a well-trained corps de ballet, each girl performed the routine automatically. As she passed before Miss Bradford, each student raised her arms to prove there were no underarm rips in her uniform. A quick flounce of her skirt revealed four garters holding up black stockings. And with a saucy flip of the right hip, each fanny was turned towards Miss Bradford so that she could see the bandage scissors hanging properly from a skirt loop. Naturally, with her first look, she had inspected their hair net that, if not properly applied, could allow escaping hairs to touch a collar.

Sarah was seventh in line, never taking her eyes from the walking stick. With little imagining, the stick became a birch switch, and Miss Bradford invoked all the apprehension once brought on by her mother.

"Miss Read," Miss Bradford's clipped, quiet voice stopped another student, interrupting the flow of the line of girls. "Your shoelaces are twisted and uneven." The stick jutted out, probing the tops of Miss Read's shoes.

"Yes, Miss Bradford." A mortified Emma Read quickly moved out of the line and bent down. The girl, the only out-of-stater, from Bristol, Connecticut, got up an hour earlier than anyone else to prepare herself, hoping to avoid this very disaster. She tried to please, and yet, it seemed impossible. She was terrified of Miss Bradford who was proving to be as easily dissatisfied and tyrannical as Emma's father, a precision watchmaker.

By the time she finished straightening the offending laces and headed for the dining room, four more girls had passed before Miss Bradford's critical eyes.

"Miss Barnett, your hair could be done more tightly. I see strays on your collar..." This time the stick remained still at Miss Bradford's side.

"Yes, Miss Bradford." Dutifully, Jane Barnett stepped from the line and took bobby-pins from an inside pocket of her uniform which held other items of an emergency nature; a safety pin, extra garter snaps. She pulled loose her mouse-brown hair and quickly twisted it properly.

Jane was the daughter of a proud man, a bookkeeper at the Lyman Coal Company located on the waterfront of Lake Champlain in nearby Burlington.

She had learned early that cooperation and obedience were the passwords to being a good girl. For Jane, manipulating others and situations became instinctive. As the youngest of four girls in her family, it had meant survival.

Finally, anchoring her cap correctly, Jane proceeded to the dining room as Miss Bradford gave her a second, probing inspection.

One more student and then it would be Sarah's turn. Suddenly, the cane flashed out at the girl directly in front of her. Susan Caldwell's progress was instantly stopped and Sarah saw her shoulders tighten.

"Miss Caldwell, I believe this is the second morning I've had to remind you that your right cuff is incorrectly attached to your sleeve."

Miss Caldwell faced the superintendent. "The stitching is crooked. I've not had time to take it off and move the snaps…"

Miss Bradford cut her short. "Excuses are not acceptable."

That was not all. Neither was talking back to the superintendent of nurses.

"Miss Caldwell, if you don't have time to do it right, when will you find the time to do it over? Might I remind you that you are privileged to be at this school of nursing. We do not need you. You need us…"

It was the refrain they'd heard from the day they'd entered the school.

"I can't sew…" Miss Caldwell's voice shook.

"You are dismissed to your room to learn to sew. I will expect you in my office within the hour, cuff mended."

Susan Caldwell spun out of line and hurried from the dining area. It was possible that the cuffs would always appear uneven for Miss Caldwell's arms were short, her hands had stubby fingers, the nails bitten to the quick.

Miss Bradford had given her until the end of probation to stop this filthy habit, but Susan's nails looked worse than on the first day of training. The harder she tried to stop, the more impossible it became.

She was not an attractive girl and she wondered what difference her nails made overall. Bent on supporting herself, she had the proper look for any occupation of her choosing, be it a nun, nurse, schoolteacher or secretary. As it happened, she chose to be a nurse.

Apparently, to Sarah's relief, her own blue uniform, white apron and belt, collar and cuffs, black stockings and shoes, taut hair net, met Miss Bradford's approval for she said nothing to her. But Sarah was tense until she was well out of reach of the walking stick. It was often a matter of timing. Just when you thought you were safe, the hand would suddenly charge the point of the stick at your heels or the back of your legs. There was no escaping the super's capriciousness.

And why did Miss Bradford have the stick at all? Some said she took it up years ago after returning to her Burlington apartment one evening to find her nurse roommate murdered. Others said that she used it following a skiing accident in which her lower leg was shattered. Indeed, scars did show beneath her calf-length skirt.

Whatever the reason, its original purpose was gone. Even so, she was never seen without the stick except when she was on the hospital wards. During those times, it stayed in her office, a triumphant survivor of dozens of intimidated students with crooked hems, torn sleeves, and uneven collars.

Sarah's relief was too soon for she was not out of reach of the walking stick after all. The cane rapped painfully at her heels.

"Miss Morgan, your stocking seams are crooked enough to derail a train."

Her heart pounding, Sarah moved aside to straighten the disgraceful seams.

Behind her, Miss Bradford was admonishing Laura Upton whose one solace had become food, or so most everyone thought. If that were true, then why, at the last monthly weigh-in, had the girl lost five pounds? Laura cried at night longing for Wes Jensen, her high-school sweetheart, whom she was forbidden to see until she passed probation.

"Miss Upton, in the past month you have loosened your belt two notches. I suggest that you forgo everything except your juice and oatmeal. Refrain from using cream and jams."

"Yes, Miss Bradford."

Immediately after breakfast, the girls filed into Miss Olive Gibson's third-floor classroom, a long ward with eight beds down either side, beds once used for medical patients and now brought to the classroom. A window was thrown open at the head of each empty bed to let in fresh air. It was in this room where the student nurses learned the practical aspects of caring for patients' environments; arranging and watering flowers, clearing bedside tables, sorting the contents of drawers, scrubbing and making beds, sweeping and washing floors, dusting windowsills.

"Always sweep before you dust," reminded Miss Gibson, the instructor, insistent on the proper order of duties. She was dumpy with short legs and waist and outsized breasts. Yet, her uniform was impeccably starched and her stocking seams were arrow straight, surely meeting Miss Bradford's approval.

For the morning exercise, Sarah was paired with Jane Barnett whose heavy lidded eyes made her appear tired. But this look was deceptive, for Jane was vigilant, seldom missing a word or nuance. She made it her business to be informed.

Quickly the partners went into action, each taking a side of the bed. They scrubbed the bed, from top to bottom, although the metal still gleamed from yesterday's scrubbing. Then they washed and flipped the mattresses, made the beds, their hands racing, throwing on a sheet followed by a rubber protective pad which they covered with a drawsheet pulled taut across the center.

Sarah glanced at others making nearby beds. Keeping up was not enough. They had to stay ahead.

Her roommate, Abbie Kirley, working down the line, winked at her. It was luck that they had been put together on the first day of school for there certainly was no plan as to which girls would room together. They were assigned in the order of their arrival at the school.

Shortly after Sarah had settled in, Abbie arrived with her grandmother. Sarah listened to Mrs. Kirley's lecture on deportment which ended with an admonition to right-all-wrongs with the Lord.

But Abbie's thoughts obviously weren't on the Lord. "What if I don't like it here?"

"Never you mind. Just do your business properly, get yourself to confession and church and the Lord will do the rest."

Abbie Kirley, a fair-skinned Irish-Catholic with heavy, coal-black hair was born in Rutland, Vermont. Her great-grandparents had migrated there from Boston in 1845. Her father worked at the Procter Marble Quarry, barely able to eke out an existence for his wife and seven children.

According to her father, Abbie's mother had died in childbirth. After her mother's death, Abbie went to live with Grandmother Kirley in Burlington, six miles from West Vermont Hospital.

Among the student nurses, Abbie quickly became popular with her combination of honest compassion and wit. This morning, her reassuring wink was a signal to Sarah not to take too seriously the impossible schedule of work the girls faced.

"Faster…faster…" urged Miss Gibson, who darted among the beds and students.

Of the three instructors, Miss Gibson was the only one who could muster up a smile or cheerful remark. Twenty-eight years old, she had graduated from the Margaret Ward School of Nursing just four years earlier. The hospital was the only real home she'd known for she had been an orphan brought up by a succession of uncaring foster parents. The first person who'd ever believed in her was Miss Edwina Bradford. Over the years, the superintendent had encouraged and guided her career, first as a student, then as a graduate and, finally, as a nursing instructor. What Sarah and the others saw as Miss Gibson's friendliness had recently turned to frustration, often bitterness, in her private life. She did not always appreciate Miss Bradford owning her soul…and more.

Lately, to escape her stifling attentions, Olive had taken to spending time with her arthritic sister and her family who lived in Waterbury.

But that was on days off. Now Miss Gibson was strictly business, scrutinizing the industrious students.

Sarah hurried with the bed-making and as she folded the spread back to make the last triangular corner, Laura Upton, working on a nearby bed, slumped to the floor.

No one noticed, until her partner, screamed. Miss Gibson spun around and rushed to the stricken girl. Sarah followed and the others quickly formed a circle around the three of them, watching helplessly.

Laura Upton was moving her hand across her forehead.

"What's the matter?" asked Miss Gibson, feeling the girl's pulse at her wrist.

"I'm dizzy," Laura said weakly.

"I'll get a wash cloth," Sarah said. "Maybe she's hungry. Miss Bradford had suggested that she eat less."

"Miss Barnett, go to the kitchen, bring back orange juice and a roll," Miss Gibson ordered.

While they waited for Jane to return, Sarah placed the wash cloth on Laura's forehead and Miss Gibson raised her to a sitting position, meanwhile admonishing the students hovering around the scene. "Get back to work. It doesn't take a classroom of gawkers to handle an emergency. Besides, you are so close you are taking away her air for breathing. If this is the way you behave in a minor emergency, how will you act in a major emergency?"

The girls hurried back to their bed-making, pulling at corners, tugging at draw sheets that would never be used by patients.

When Miss Upton had recovered sufficiently, Miss Gibson sent her to her room for the day, accompanied by Miss Barnett.

No one in the class had to be reminded that Miss Upton would be making up the lost time. The penalty for dizziness would certainly not be less than an evening working alone, making every bed in the classroom.

When the others had completed their beds and units, they stood with their hands clasped in front of them, the signal that they were ready to have their work inspected. Miss Gibson moved among the beds, her hand running along the edges of the mattress tops, her touch so conditioned that she felt the slightest out-of-place crease or lump.

She pulled back the top covers of the bed Emma Read and Lucy Austin had made, and pointed accusingly at the bottom and draw sheets. "A feather would never bounce on this…certainly not a coin." She freed the draw sheet and snapped it to a tautness that looked as though it would tear the sheet in half. Then she dropped a penny and the awed class watched as it struck the sheet and jumped into the air. A ten-pound weight would surely have bounced on Miss Gibson's finished product.

"Six beds!" she ordered Emma and her partner. "Remake this bed six times and I will check the draw sheet each time."

The girls stripped the bed and started over. Sarah sighed for them and absentmindedly smoothed the bedspread she had just completed. Miss Gibson's quick eye caught her move.

"Miss Morgan! Never smooth a bed. If you have made it properly, the bed will be smooth. Unnecessary motions are wasteful and unprofessional."

Sarah was mortified that she had been so careless. "Yes, Miss Gibson."

Miss Gibson ran her hand along the spread. Half way to the bottom of the bed, she stopped as though she'd touched hot coals. "There is an extra crease in the bottom sheet."

Sarah waited for her to add the inevitable word, 'unforgivable,' but she didn't.

"Please practice by remaking the bed a dozen times." Miss Gibson stood back, smirking. "Make that a baker's dozen."

Sarah was embarrassed as Miss Gibson laughed delightedly. But she did as she was told, pulled back the top sheet and spread and could not find the offending crease. Nevertheless, if Miss Gibson said that it was there, it was there. By the time Sarah had made the bed for the eighth time, the classroom was empty of students who had been dismissed for lunch. Only Miss Gibson remained with her.

"You are doing very well," she smiled. "I believe you will be one of our best students."

Sarah continued more swiftly, her spirits soaring by this unexpected encouragement. "Thank you, Miss Gibson."

The instructor stood on the other side of the bed as Sarah remade it for the ninth time. "I think you have done enough," she finally said.

"Thank you, Miss Gibson." There was no denying her relief to be done with the tedious, repetitive task.

Miss Gibson came around and encircled Sarah's shoulders, drawing her close to her. Sarah had a strange feeling of being comforted, yet, the closeness frightened her. Was that Miss Gibson's intention? Her fingers were around Sarah's upper arm, pressing against her breast.

"Miss Morgan, do you recall when you said that Miss Bradford suggested to Miss Upton that she eat less? I don't think that was any of your business. You overheard a private remark which you should not have repeated. You must be careful about the assumptions you make."

Sarah began to shake, her cheeks on fire.

"Do you understand?"

"Yes, Miss Gibson."

The instructor released her. Her lips were curved in a half-smile and there was no amusement in her eyes.

Chapter Eight

Sarah followed Miss Gibson from the classroom, too terrified to eat even though hunger pangs gripped her stomach. Besides, Miss Gibson had kept her so long that the dining hall was closed and she just barely made it to Dr. Palmer's anatomy class on time.

All the other girls were seated when she slipped into her chair, just seconds before the doctor strode in, his hands sunk deep into his lab coat pockets. In its open front could be seen the gold chain attached to a large pocket watch, which he dutifully pulled forth and examined and then tucked back into its proper place. When he reached the lectern and faced the class, he placed his stethoscope on a table to his left.

Sarah followed his movements, sure that the stethoscope picked up the pounding of her heart that surely came through to Dr. Palmer's skilled ears like the bongs of a drum. She took quick glances at her classmates, positive that their experiences were identical. But his remarks had nothing to do with the heart flutters of student nurses.

"As you know," he began, his large voice a rumble, "your examination is one week from now. Today will be devoted to review."

Sarah was not alone in her infatuation of Dr. Palmer, although, from the students perspectives, he was an old man. They guessed he was in his late thirties since his hair had shimmers of gray. That was the only clue to his age for there was not a spare ounce on his sturdy frame.

His dark, probing eyes swept over the girls and his lips moved slightly. He seemed to be counting.

"Who is missing?" He frowned.

"Susan Caldwell is with Miss Bradford and Laura Upton is sick," several voices chorused.

"Ummm…" he said.

If Sarah and the other girls had fantasies about him, he, too, had his fantasies about them, the untouched, young ladies he could only dream about. They were the finest, purest that Vermont had to offer, their skins smoother than the smoothest Grade A maple syrup.

He lectured to them, finding it very difficult to keep his mind on the subject because, at the same time, he was mentally stripping them of their cotton uniforms, aprons with bibs, and long black stockings until they were transformed into luscious, naked nymphs. The chairs and tables became forest trees and ground cover and he chased after the nymphs, always letting them stay ahead so he could gaze at their desirable, round rumps. Then he would narrow the distance until those and their firm breasts were just a few arms length from him, just waiting.

When he realized that his thoughts had wandered into forbidden territory, he would shake his head. He had to get hold of himself and not allow his mind to stray.

Although his thoughts had strayed, the rest of him was strictly home-based, absolutely safe from the pursuit of extra-curricular activities. He was a staunch Presbyterian and good to his beloved wife, Mildred. Unfortunately, she expressed her disappointment in him and their miserable lifestyle. Yet, he wondered, what was so distasteful about living in a nice house on the grounds of the West Vermont Hospital with a husband who occupied the prestigious position of medical director?

As far as he was concerned, nothing at all. Why couldn't she be satisfied with their circumstances, rather than berating him for his lack of ambition, reminding him that they could move to a prominent home in Burlington or Montpelier? After all, Mildred insisted, a private practice would be so much more financially lucrative than his present salaried position. He hinted that money wasn't everything.

"Maybe not, but at least it can be placed in a savings account," she fumed.

Why couldn't she understand the rewards he got right here close to academic medicine?

Now it was hard to hang on to his arguments with Mildred because the student nurses were bombarding him with questions. And Laura Upton's empty chair bothered him. She usually sat in class, a dazed, wistfulness distracting her from the subject of anatomy. A few times, she had stopped after class to ask him to fill in missing spots for her, lost during the hours that her mind must have been engaged elsewhere.

She was an ordinary looking girl, but her affect was sad as if she were burdened with deep, unspeakable feelings. He was touched by this…and her voluptuous hips.

At the very moment he was thinking about her, Jane Barnett whispered to Sarah, "Curious that he should ask about Laura. Do you suppose it has something to do with her condition?"

"What condition?"

Dr. Palmer glared at Jane. "Name the twelve cranial nerves, Miss Barnett."

He had heard the whispering and this was the punishment. To himself, he recited the same jingle that each student memorized to remember the cranial nerves. He was proud that it, if nothing else, stuck to his brain cells.

"On old Olympus towering top, a Finn and German viewed some hops…" Miss Barnett said carefully, leaving plenty of space between each word, the first letter being the start of the next cranial nerve which she stated while Dr. Palmer nodded in approval.

Shortly after, the class finished and the exhausted students returned to the nurses residence to prepare for dinner. Susan Caldwell, who didn't learn to sew in one hour, was weeping and lugging her suitcase down the hall, her mother at her side. "Never you mind," Mrs. Caldwell was saying, "This isn't the only school of nursing in Vermont. We'll enroll you in the Mary Fletcher Hospital or Fanny Allen, maybe St. Albans…I never approved of this place from the beginning."

The girls said self-conscious goodbyes. All except for Lucy Austin, an unwilling student since her first day. "I wish I could trade places," she said as the front door slammed behind Mrs. Caldwell and Susan. "If only I didn't have parents to please, I'd tell Miss Bradford I couldn't continue and I'd fail Dr. Palmer's final exam."

The next week, Lucy passed the anatomy exam, but Laura Upton didn't even though she felt better. Dr. Palmer decided to take her aside for private tutoring.

Prudently, he first outlined his plan to Miss Bradford, aware that the appearance of compromise could be as dangerous as compromise itself.

The following month, Jane Barnett failed the next anatomy exam and Dr. Palmer added her to his very private class of two students.

While receiving a first class education, it never occurred to the private students that Dr. Palmer would have failed his own anatomy tests. He covered up his own inadequacies by unique teaching strategies. He delighted in rattling a real skeleton, "Homer", for the students. With him in the classroom or his office, "Homer" was his constant teaching companion. You knew when Dr. Palmer was on the move for you could hear the bones banging against each other as he carried the skeleton down the corridors.

He referred to "Homer" as his wife. "Not too many brains," Dr. Palmer would say, chuckling at his joke.

Although he could almost name the bones of the body, the muscles were beyond him, their sites of origin and insertion a mystery. He couldn't tell the difference between smooth and striated muscle, but did know that only the heart had cardiac muscle.

Oh well. What difference did it make anyway? He never did claim to be a Vesalius and the student nurses certainly didn't need to be. When they were scrubbing bedpans and floors, did it matter where the frontal and temporal lobes of the brain were located? Nevertheless, he was proud that he had taught all of them the cranial nerves. "On old Olympus towering top..."

For several weeks, Dr. Palmer had taken Laura Upton to his study for a late afternoon private anatomy session, realizing that not everyone learned at the same rate. Perhaps a little extra help could make the difference between success and failure. And if it were up to him, Laura Upton would pass his class and receive the nurses cap that she would wear every moment of her on-duty time for the rest of her nursing life.

He set his skeleton, "Homer" next to his massive mahogany desk in the dimly lit office, lined around three walls with books and book shelves. He sat Laura next to the skeleton and, with a pointer, he reached out from where he sat comfortably in his leather chair, directing the wooden stick at a bone. In the beginning, he named the bones along with Laura. Gradually, in later sessions, he only pointed and almost immediately she would come up with the right answer.

It disturbed him that she only seemed to come to life during his drilling sessions and then she would lapse back into a depressing silence. This afternoon, he could tell that she'd been crying. Still, he proceeded with the same routine they'd adopted weeks before. Nervously, he rattled Homer into place and collected the pointer where it stood between two book cases. As usual, he directed it to the easy bones first.

Laura answered quickly. "Humerus, femur, radius, ulna..."

But there were catches in her voice. He studied her, trying to think of something to say. She certainly wasn't desirable by his standards, but she was pretty in a homely way. He could see that she would be a comfort to patients because she spoke softly and had an air of sympathy. It was as though she could get into others' thoughts, while hers remained elusive.

"…tibia, fibula…"

Then he pointed to the parietal bone of the skull. When she didn't say anything, the tempo of the exercise and his thoughts changed. Her hands were folded in her lap, her shoulders slumped, her face devoid of any expression that he could interpret.

And then, suddenly, her eyes overflowed with tears.

Impulsively, he laid the pointer on his desk, turned to her and gathered her in his arms. His emotions were so strong that he was unable to speak. How pitiful that anyone could be this distraught…so young…away from her family, working too hard…Miss Bradford wasn't the easiest of women..and Miss Gibson, not the most sensible. It must be terrible to feel so helpless, at the mercy of everyone in the hospital and the school of nursing.

Yet, he could hardly tell Laura his thoughts. Gratefully, he realized that words weren't necessary and her sobs gradually subsided. He stroked her fine hair and started to give her his handkerchief, but thought better of it.

"What is it, my dear?" he asked, when he felt she had calmed enough.

The tears rushed again.

"Are you homesick?"

"No."

"Then, what is it?"

"I can't talk about it."

"Do what you think best, but if you want to tell me, I'll help you…if I can."

It seemed an eternity before she said anything, as if she were debating her choice of words or whether she should even reveal the basis of her sorrow. Eventually, she did, however, and the tale that poured through her sobs was the very last he'd expected.

When it became clear to him what she was telling him, he found himself doubting his wisdom. She told him about her last night with Wes Jensen before coming into nurses training, her nausea since, her belt tightening. When she'd finished her story, he understood the reason for her weeks of distraction in the anatomy classes. Indeed, he did.

And yet, he knew, there was nothing he could do to help her. But her helplessness, her youth, his sadness at her plight…all his feelings came together and he hugged her to him more tightly, consoling her, holding her head against him. The bun in her hair was falling and he freed it from the hair net and pins, letting the strands drop to her waist as he stroked and kissed them. She was far from beautiful and, yet, at that moment...

"I'm sorry, my dear," he said, his throat aching. "I wish, for your sake, that it hadn't happened."

He had no idea how long they stayed like that, but eventually he became aware of another figure standing behind them. He relaxed his hold on Laura and turned in his chair to identify the intruder.

There stood Jane Barnett, her expression horrified, her mouth dropped open, very much like his skeleton, Homer. The difference was that Homer was a silent witness. Unfortunately, he couldn't be that sure about Jane. Dismayed, he took his handkerchief and handed it to Laura.

"I think that you've studied enough for one day," he said, quickly standing her on her feet and escorting her out the door.

After he regained his composure, he addressed Jane. "Perhaps we should postpone our session until Laura is feeling better."

"But Dr. Palmer, I always have a private half-hour with you.. .alone."

"Next time, you will have an hour," he said, firmly showing her the exit, too.

The following Friday, both Laura Upton and Jane Barnett received perfect scores on the anatomy test, even though Dr. Palmer hadn't bothered to review their exams.

And Sarah Morgan was grounded for impertinence to Miss Gibson, the length of the sentence dependent on her performance. The penalty was to scrub the men's ward daily before going to her regular assignment.

Chapter Nine

On her way to the men's ward to begin her penalty, Sarah, on this otherwise ordinary Tuesday morning, passed through the main hospital lobby, stopping long enough to read the "Burlington Daily News" headlines and front page:

GOOD NEWS! DAM HOLDS!

The story started, "Despite the heavy runoff of melting snow..." That was enough to reassure her that even though the weather had warmed and it had been raining for four days, there was nothing to worry about.

She had no time to read more for she had to get to the ward. Her day started at four-thirty in the morning when she got out of bed. She was on the ward scrubbing the floor by five so she could be finished for morning inspection. Then fifteen minutes for breakfast and on duty at seven.

It had been almost a month since her penalty had started and Susan had been dismissed. She trusted Jane even less than before and was still numb from experiences as were many in her class. Finishing training had become an obsession while they feared their fate would echo that of their departed classmates.

The hospital had recently suffered an influx of flu cases and everyone worked too long and too hard. Heavy on their minds was the memory of the 1918 epidemic and the millions of people who died. Mercifully, the current epidemic was finally in decline and the students were being reassigned to other wards throughout the hospital.

Sarah and Lucy were working women's surgical. They were expected to have the eighteen to twenty patients bathed, beds changed and treatments given by nine a.m. Since it was impossible, their assigned two-hour free time was spent finishing the work. Then it was a quick lunch before lecture classes started at one in the afternoon.

After classes, Sarah dragged herself to her room and slept through dinner and was back on duty at seven in the evening for another four hours.

One afternoon, Miss Bradford summoned her to her office.

"Miss Morgan," she said, rapping her walking stick against Sarah's chair. "It has been brought to my attention that you are not going to the dining room for dinner."

"I'm sorry, Miss Bradford. I'm just too tired…I don't have time to eat and sleep."

"Miss Morgan," the superintendent said, dryly; "*If sleep were sold over-the-counter for silver and gold, how many people would wail and weep because they couldn't afford to sleep?*"

It took Sarah some time to decipher her meaning. "Miss Bradford, I will go to dinner from now on."

"Indeed, you will."

So, instead of her craved-for rest, Sarah went to dinner. That evening, when she and Lucy returned to the ward, Miss Severn, the senior nursing student in charge of the ward that shift, ordered them to put old Mrs. Reynolds into a wheelchair and take her to X-ray in the basement.

"Her arm may be broken. She caught it in the bed rail. She's very restless. Please, both of you go with her."

They tied the confused woman into the wheelchair to keep her from falling forward. Then they took her in the elevator to the basement. Except for the rain beating against the building, the basement was quiet. Most of the work in those departments was done during the day shift and the people were gone. Because it was quiet down there, sleeping quarters were set aside for the on-call doctors.

In X-ray, Mrs. Reynolds complained of being cold. "Let me rub your feet," said Lucy, kneeling before her.

Sarah wrapped the old woman's robe more tightly and called to the X-ray technician. "How long do we have to wait?"

"Maybe an hour. There's four ahead of you." He was testy, "What's your hurry?"

"Never mind," said Lucy. Under her breath, she muttered, "Jerk."

"Honey, I'm cold," the old woman complained again.

"I'm going back to the ward and get another blanket," said Sarah. "We should have brought extras with us."

"Close the door behind you," said Lucy. "The draft from the corridor is coming in here."

"No, you don't," warned the X-ray technician. "I get claustrophobia."

Lucy shook her head.

Sarah went to the elevator and waited, listening to the steady rain. The light above the elevator showed that it was on the fourth floor. She day-dreamed as the elevator came down slowly, stopping at the second floor.

The elevator had started down again when it happened.

Without warning, a giant force rocked the hospital and she felt that it was being lifted from its foundation and was going to topple. Bricks crushing her flashed through her mind bringing panic. A short eerie silence followed when all she could hear was the pounding of her heart. The building was too quiet. Then there was another monstrous jolt and a tremendous crash as the doors at the east end of the basement bulged and snapped inward. There was a roar as a wave of water poured through the hall.

Sarah turned to run for the stairs, but she was too late. The hospital lights went out, the water knocking her down. She rolled and tumbled along the corridor, hitting her head, feeling her mind go black, coming to, fighting to the top, gasping for air before going under again. The few times she was able to get her head above the water and heard others screaming, she knew that she was going to die.

Something hard stopped her rolling and she struggled up. As suddenly as she'd been pushed under, she was freed from the wall of water. She stood, getting her balance, the water churning at her legs and feet. Shaking, she felt along the wall and realized she'd been dragged to the other end of the hall, past X-ray and the lab, and when the water reached the opposite wall, it veered down the stairs to a sub-basement that housed the heating system for the hospital.

The building had stopped moving. And she knew why. It must have been shoved off its foundation and slid down the hill, coming to rest in the Winooski River whose waters were flowing through the building.

She groped for and found the stairs leading to the first floor. Something struck her legs. She staggered under the force, caught herself, reached down and felt a body. By the size of the body, she was sure it was a man. She grabbed a shirt and struggled to get her arms under his shoulders.

At first, he was dead weight and she hauled him up a few steps until his head was above water. Suddenly he came to life, coughing, vomiting, fighting and kicking to get away from her.

He did elude her once, but she caught his shirt again as he tried to stumble back into the churning waters.

"Stop! Stop!" She ordered. "Don't fight me."

And then he went limp, falling against her. She forcibly held his head above the water while he regained his senses. After a long time, he reached for her, put his arms around her waist trying to stand, but couldn't.

"Wait until your head clears," she said.

He retched and she supported him wondering if he was a patient or an employee. From his firmness and strength, she guessed he was young.

She could hear the trickling of water down the corridor, but otherwise, it was quiet. There were no more cries.

He shuddered and lay against her. Then he shocked her with a casual, "Hi…"

She regained her wits. "Hi, to you, too."

He tried to stand, but couldn't without her help.

She began to shiver from the wet and cold. Gradually, the two of them worked their way up the stairs, leaning against one another.

As they neared the top, he thanked her for saving his life which made her feel good. There was something about his voice, something strangely familiar.

When they got to the first floor, it was dark and the floors wet, but the building seemed level, not crooked as she'd expected if it lay in the river bed.

They headed towards people huddled in a group beaming flashlights, talking rapidly.

A sense of danger returned to Sarah as she remembered the people in the basement, the patients in X-ray, the sleeping doctors, Lucy Austin.

"There are people trapped down there," she told them.

Somebody trained a flashlight on her. "Forget it," a man said. "We don't have diving suits."

Her grip tightened on the man she'd saved. Where had she seen him before? The answer eluded her searching mind.

Somebody brought a blanket and threw it around her shoulders.

Her mind went back to another time when she was in a haze and very sick and a man watched over he as she lay in a hospital bed.

Then she remembered. The stranger was Dr. Warren Hollis. It seemed that everything in her stopped and she felt her head spin.

The next morning, the Burlington Daily News added a bulletin to its published paper.

SEVEN DROWN IN HOSPITAL FLOOD   An ice-
floe, up river from the hospital, acted as a dam. The floe
finally succumbed to the extra pressure of water run-off
caused by the highest temperatures recorded for fall in 60
years. The water missed the bend east of the hospital,
careening across the hill into the basement and first floor of
the West Vermont Hospital. All drowning victims were
found in the basement.

Drowned in the disaster were: A laboratory technician; five
patients and a student nurse trapped under an over-turned
wheelchair.An X-ray technician miraculously lived and
gave credit to the Lord, saying, "It just wasn't my time."

Names of the dead are being withheld until notification of
next-of-kin.

At first, no one understood why the November fourth flood happened at
all. People had quickly learned about the ice-floe acting as a dam at the north
end of the Winooski river. But the story actually started several days prior at
the end of October.

It had been unusually warm and a two day spell of heavy rain sent water
furiously pouring down the mountains into the river. The weight of the water
built up pressure behind the ice floe which broke loose under the strain until
the whole thing gave way, with water overflowing its banks to the hospital
and the many villages below.

The hospital was lucky being on a hill about ninety-five feet above the
river. Even so, its basement was inundated with mud and water. The first
floor suffered some damage although the water receded rapidly. Everyone for
miles around the hospital was isolated wherever they happened to be at the
time of the flood.

The flood caused the worst disaster in Vermont's history. Man-made
barriers gave way to water which swept away bridges, dams and buildings.
Water, a necessity to life, killed. At least fifty-five people and an estimated
fifteen-thousand livestock drowned; whole towns disappeared; the Central
Vermont Railway was destroyed from Essex Junction to Barre; a house
moved a half-mile to rest on the railroad tracks at Bolton.

A dreaded typhoid epidemic was sure to follow.

But for Edwina Bradford, even with a possible epidemic, her life had returned to normal. After all, she had a school of nursing to run and Dr. Palmer had sent for her. The increased and demanding needs of the crisis gave her the comforting feeling that only she could accomplish the necessary tasks efficiently to the satisfaction of everyone.

Still, even a terribly busy day required personal perfection. Edwina stood before a full-length mirror and checked her uniform for creases. She turned her back to the mirror and looked over her shoulder, lifting her skirt ever so slightly to see the back of her legs, peering at her stocking seams, adjusting them ruler straight. She fluffed the edges of her hair under the hairnet, and then, satisfied that she was presentable, she reached for her walking stick and tapped her way to Dr. Palmer's office, wondering, whatever did he want her for?

On the way she passed a pair of senior nursing students who respectfully stopped for her. She nodded as she sailed past them, her heart swelling with pride at how professional they looked and responded.

In the main corridor, two first-year students were rushing up the stairs. Edwina checked her watch. Three minutes after eleven a.m. They were late reporting to their assignments. She made a mental note to speak to the two at tomorrow's morning inspection.

But who were they?

From the back, the students all looked alike except for the color of their hair and their height.

She sighed. How could she possibly keep up with all the disciplinary problems the students presented? After all, she was only human.

She rapped on Dr. Palmer's door and was instantly invited in.

He sat at his desk, smiling broadly, his hands clasped over a piece of paper before him. "Sit down, sit down, Miss Bradford," he said, waving her to a chair. He placed his pince-nez glasses on the bridge of his nose.

She couldn't help thinking of Teddy Roosevelt, but the similarity ended there. Roosevelt might have been a big game hunter while the biggest game that the doctor seemed to bag were young student nurses, too innocent to protect themselves.

He looked over the rims at her. "Let me read this to you."

"Dear Dr. Palmer: I wish to express my gratitude to Miss Sarah Morgan, a student nurse for saving me from drowning in the recent flood. But for her, I would not be alive to be attending to my duties today. Even though in danger of drowning herself, she responded to my need for help and pulled me from the raging waters.

I have thought of approaching her to thank her myself, but feel it more appropriate for this to be done through your office.

I remain, Sincerely yours, Warren Hollis M.D."

Edwina Bradford smoldered. Why was Sarah Morgan in the basement at nine in the evening when all patients were in bed on the wards? Lucy Austin was the only student she knew of who had been in the basement with a patient and they had both drowned.

"My, my, how lovely," she said, drawing up the corners of her mouth in the semblance of a smile.

"Yes," beamed the doctor. "She must be quite a remarkable young lady. I imagine she gives superior nursing care."

"I should hope so. We expect that from our students."

He held up the letter.

"I would say that this goes beyond the call of duty."

"Perhaps," Edwina murmured, thinking, not 'perhaps', but 'it most certainly does'.

"I think that we should commend Miss Morgan in some way. Is there an honorary award we could give her? If not, then we can make one for this occasion." His eyes shone with excitement. "We can call in the reporters. Wouldn't that make excellent publicity for the hospital and for the school of nursing? Wouldn't this act of bravery, this heroism, impress the townspeople?"

My, she thought sarcastically, it was as if he were already presenting the award. "That is an excellent idea, Dr. Palmer," she agreed. "But I wonder if you would allow me to first speak with Miss Morgan about it. Our students are naturally shy and modest. Such an award might overwhelm her."

"Of course," he said. "We wouldn't want to upset her."

She reached out her hand. "Dr. Palmer, I wonder if I might show her the letter."

"Certainly." He handed it over.

Edwina stood. "I will get back to you when we have settled the details."

He stood. "Fine. I can see the comments already…" His eyes had a faraway look.

She left him to his dreams of publicity. She certainly wasn't going to be a dupe in his public relations schemes, his need for a ceremony to remind others as to his importance.

She folded the letter and placed it in her uniform pocket Back in her office, Edwina Bradford wasted no time in summoning Sarah Morgan. She knew if she delayed, she would be too angry to control herself.

When Miss Morgan came in, she looked worried, as well she should. Edwina knew that just the thought of being called to her office was frightening to the students. "Miss Morgan, it has been brought to my attention that you were in the basement of the hospital the night of the flood."

"Yes. I was with a patient."

"Really? What patient, might I ask?" Surprising that Miss Morgan should lie so readily...she didn't seem to be of dishonest character.

"Mrs. Reynolds, the woman who drowned with Lucy Austin."

"Then why were you so fortunate as to be spared? In fact, why did it take two students to accompany her to X-ray?"

The student seemed to have difficulty finding an answer. "I was going back to the ward to get the patient a blanket because she was cold. I was standing at the elevator. After the water came and the lights went out, I almost drowned. When I was finally safe, I was struck by a man's body. I pulled him up the stairs..."

"Tell me the truth, Miss Morgan. You didn't save anyone. More than likely, he saved you." She spat out her contempt. "You were with the doctor the whole time."

"Doctor?"

Ah hah! She had been trapped. "Please do not act bewildered for my benefit. Surely, you must remember a certain Dr. Hollis."

The girl seemed frightened and confused as though wondering how Miss Bradford could possibly have learned this. "Do you know, Miss Morgan, I don't believe a word you've said. It's incredible the extent to which you students will fabricate in order to be with men."

The girl began to weep. "Believe me, Miss Bradford, I've told you the truth."

"Miss Morgan, please give me the credit to recognize the truth when I hear it."

The student reached into her apron pocket for a handkerchief and wiped her eyes.

Miss Bradford continued: "The capping ceremony is less than a month away. You will proceed with the ceremony and, immediately after the ceremony, you will return your nurse's cap to Miss Gibson. Is that clear?"

"Yes, Miss Bradford."

"Also, you will be grounded until the end of May. Is that clear?"

"Yes, Miss Bradford."

"You may return to duty, Miss Morgan."

Sarah turned to leave.

"One more thing, Miss Morgan."

The student stopped but did not turn around.

"Face me, please."

Sarah turned to face her.

"Have you slept well these past few nights."

"Yes, Miss Bradford."

"That will be all."

As soon as the girl had left, Miss Bradford took the letter and smoothed it out, placing it under the blotter on her desk. If Dr. Palmer didn't ask for it, after a suitable time, she would destroy it. And the chances of his asking for it were slim because he never kept his mind on one thing for very long.

Something bothered her though and that was the look of hatred Sarah Morgan threw at her as she left the office. That girl certainly could not hide her feelings. Deplorable for a Margaret Ward student. She would know better by the time she graduated, if she was lucky enough to reach that day.

* * *

Sarah was much too distraught to return directly to the ward. Instead, she went to the nurses residence to regain her composure. Maybe if she washed her face, changed her uniform, thought for a few moments, she would feel better.

Her mind was plagued with questions. Who had turned on her for saving the doctor? Who had misread the situation? Would it have been better if she had come forward at the time of the flood and told of the near-drowning herself? Had the doctor been chastised for being with a student nurse? Or had he even mentioned it?

Possibly, she decided. Then again, probably not. At any rate, Dr. Hollis had a right to know what had happened to her today.

Sarah reached under the mattress for her secret envelope. She counted the bills, still thirty-dollars short of what she owed him. Did she dare go to him with less than the full amount? Or did he even remember that he'd loaned her money? Discouraged, she decided against seeing him. Her problems with

Miss Bradford were of no concern to him. And Sarah could not face him again until she could make payment in full.

Instead, she dressed, stepped out to the hall and headed down the back stairs. As she reached the bottom, she saw two figures embracing in the corridor before Miss Gibson's door. Indeed, one of them was Miss Gibson. And with a start, Sarah recognized the other girl. Emma Read.

Quietly, Sarah turned and walked back up the stairs to the second floor, hurriedly went to the other end and went down the stairs leading to the front entrance. As she did so, the shock of what she'd seen turned to fear. Now, she wondered, how would this play out? What would knowing about the two women cost her?

Chapter Ten

Five days after the flood, the fears of the public health authorities in Burlington were realized. When the flood's erratic path disrupted sewage lines, water supplies became contaminated. On its travels through the hospital's basement, the water had picked up contaminated wastes and swept along dirty linen.

The Burlington Daily News headlined instructions for the prevention of infection from bacteria-laden water by sterilizing it for drinking. But for the first victims, the newspaper instructions came too late.

Overnight, typhoid cases bombarded the West Vermont Hospital. The first day brought thirty-two, more than half of them children. One ward filled within hours and was quickly closed to any other type of case and a second ward opened.

The students knew that the next two months would be grueling. The illness lasted from four to six weeks and complications didn't even begin until the second or third weeks. And those complications, hemorrhage and perforation of the bowel, were often fatal.

Again Miss Gibson paired the five students assigned to the children's ward. Emma and Sarah worked together, Mary Drury with Catherine Livingston, leaving Jane to work alone. When Emma was called away from the ward, Sarah and Jane worked together. Otherwise, Miss Severn, the senior student in charge, doing the last months until her graduation, helped Jane. Sarah could see Jane's resentment building. Her sullenness and curt manner with the children underscored her feelings.

As usual, the students were expected to have the twenty-one patients bathed and beds changed by nine am. And, as usual, they ignored morning work breaks and continued on into lunch to finish their duties.

One day during the third week of the epidemic, when they came on duty, Sarah heard Jane address one child. "Hello, I'm Miss Barnett. What's your name?"

"Potter.. ."

Sarah froze, her back to the conversation as she tended another child.

"Don't you have a last name?" Jane was being sarcastic.

"Morgan."

Her heart pounding, Sarah excused herself from the child she was with and went to the bed where the brown-haired boy lay, his eyes feverish. Without thinking, she reached down and took him into her arms, hugging him. He didn't respond until she said, "Potter, I'm Sarah."

Then his weak arms encircled her neck and he clung to her sobbing and sobbing. "I want Momma and Poppa."

"No, darling..." her voice caught. "Not until you're better. But I'll take care of you until then."

Jane was glaring at her. "Sarah, you broke technique. You were with another child and didn't change your gown."

"Sorry...you're right."

"And you should never hold a contagious child close to you."

"He's my brother."

Jane stood back, looking from Potter to Sarah. "I thought your brother was dead."

"That was a different brother. I have more than one..."

"Benjamin isn't dead," Potter interrupted.

"I know," Sarah said, soothingly, although furious with Jane for saying such a thing before him. He'd probably never heard of their father's first family, other than for her. She insisted on helping bathe and change Potter's bed, barely making it to lunch before the kettles and pans were removed from the serving table.

The assignments for the next several days continued the same. Even though Sarah asked to be assigned to Potter, Miss Gibson refused. But after a few days, she relented. The boy needed her.

As the days wore on, a pattern emerged. Shortly before noon, Miss Gibson would relieve Emma Read from duty and then Sarah would again work with Jane.

Finally, Jane's resentment boiled over. "Miss Gibson, why do you always allow Emma to leave before the rest of us? It isn't fair."

"Miss Barnett, when I need your comments or opinions, I will ask for them."

With that, Miss Gibson hurried out with Emma who kept her eyes averted, avoiding her classmates accusing glares.

Jane furiously threw a sheet on an empty bed. "Something is going on between those two," she said.

"Such as…?" Sarah asked, preferring not to know more than she already did.

"I don't know…yet."

They hardly had time to finish making the bed before Frank, the male orderly, brought in a new patient with typhoid.

"Got a bed in the corner?" he asked. "No one's going to want to see this one."

The child was concealed under a blanket. Miss Severn, who hadn't had a day-off since the epidemic began, looked under the blanket. Silently, she pointed to a crib in a far corner, her hand visibly shaking. "Sarah, add her to your assignment."

As Frank placed the child down, the small girl began to cry, a high-pitched, nerve-shattering screech. Overwhelming dread hit Sarah as she looked into the crib.

It was as though her whole childhood had returned, the years with her mother at Riverfork, the nightmare days and nights listening to screaming, blind, retarded children. The child in the crib before her could have been a twin to Louise, Winfield, or Elbert.

She covered her eyes, trying to rid herself of the memories, hardly able to believe it could happen again. Someone came towards her and then she felt a comforting arm on her shoulder.

"What's the matter?" It was Jane.

Sarah couldn't speak.

The two looked down at the crying child. She thrashed around, biting her lips, grabbing for her bleeding fingers.. Instinctively, Sarah hunted for bandages, binding the small hands, anchoring her arms to her sides so she couldn't reach her mouth, yet, doing it in such a way that she could still move in the bed.

"You've done that before," noted Jane, her tone respectful.

"Yes," Sarah said, filled with sadness. Even though Dr. Montgomery had told her he'd seen other children like her brothers and sisters, she hadn't believed him, until now.

As she bathed the child's feverish body, releasing one arm and leg at a time, someone came to the bed. She looked up.

Dr. Warren Hollis. Her heart raced.

As he gazed at the child, obviously stunned, his face drained of color, his eyes were fearful. What thoughts did he have? Or was it simply the initial response to something shocking?

Compassionately, he reached down and stroked the small child's leg. "It's a shame…," he said.

"Yes," she agreed.

"I never thought I'd see another…" he turned to her and stopped. Then he broke out in a broad grin. "Hi, swimmer."

"Hi." He did remember her.

He looked down at the girl again, his seriousness returning. "What curse hangs over families of these children?" His eyes clouded. Then he spoke again, more to himself than to her. "Is it fair to cure this child of typhoid only to let her continue a life of pain and suffering? Or would it be better to let the illness free her?" Shocked, she wanted to blurt out: "Do you have a choice? You're a doctor?" But it would be improper to speak to him like that, and so she kept her thoughts to herself.

He turned away, saw other children briefly, wrote orders in several charts and left the ward.

When Sarah reviewed his orders, he had spelled out the same regimen for the deformed girl as for any other typhoid patient. The name on the child's chart was "Marie". There was no last name.

Sarah stayed on longer that day, past dinner, giving the children the love that their parents could not during the period of contagion.

Late in the evening, as she dropped her last isolation gown into the hamper for that day, she saw two heads peering into the room from the door window. But the light shining on the glass acted much like a mirror, obscuring their faces from her. She waited before stepping into the hall so they could move out of the way of the swinging door.

She'd had one shock that day and wasn't expecting another. But it was expecting her. As she opened the opened the door, she walked right into Carrie and her father.

Her father grabbed and hugged her. "Sarah, why didn't you tell us where you'd gone?"

She felt crushed and lifeless under his gruff strength. And, at that moment, her feelings were just as lifeless, buried months before.

He released her, and asked, "How is Potter?"

This gave Sarah a chance to regain her professional composure. "His fever is still up. We bathe him with cool water and that makes him feel better. We give him ice-chips for his dry, sore mouth."

Carrie pressed Sarah's hands warmly. "With you caring for him, we know he'll soon be well."

"I'm working very hard," she said, and caught herself before confessing to them that she loved Potter desperately, his sweetness, his gentleness, his innocence, his love for her.

Quickly, she hurried away from them, knowing that they watched her every step down the hall. Tears fell against her will. Angrily, she resolved to never again stay on duty so late. Never again would she encounter those two if she could possibly avoid it.

* * *

Unknown to Sarah, Miss Bradford called Jane to her office the next morning. There were several offenses that she would not tolerate and insubordination was at the top of her list.

"Miss Barnett," she addressed the unsure girl standing before her. "It has been brought to my attention that you consider the ward assignments unfair, that you feel Miss Gibson favors a particular student."

"Yes." Jane agreed with more defiance than Edwina expected. "Favoritism in more ways than one."

Miss Bradford was taken aback at the girl's frankness. She had never considered Jane Barnett outstanding in any way, more as a backdrop to the more colorful students. Was this the basis of her resentment? "Favoritism in what way?"

"I must work by myself and Sarah is assigned to work with Emma Read. Yet, every day, Miss Gibson comes to the ward about an hour before lunch and takes Emma away. That leaves the two of us to finish all the work. This has been going on since the typhoid epidemic started. I don't know what they do together..."

Fury rose in Edwina, the fury of the betrayed. She glared at Jane. "What are you insinuating?"

Jane Barnett backed away, frightened. Edwina saw the student's eyes dart towards the walking stick and this made her even angrier.

"Nothing, Miss Bradford." The student's voice shook.

"I beg to differ with you. You are insinuating a great deal." She crashed her fists against her desk. The girl cringed, backing towards the door.

"Miss Bradford, please, I didn't mean anything."

"I hope you didn't. You have been here several months. I would think during that time, you would have learned one lesson and that is to mind your own business. Your only function in this school of nursing is to obey orders and become an exceptional nurse." Her voice rose as her anger escalated until she shook with rage.

"Yes, Miss Bradford." Jane's eyes never left the superintendent.

"I never want to hear your name in connection with any offense of prying, digging into others' affairs, making judgments as to your assignments..." She stopped although she could have strung out the list of possible violations indefinitely. She cracked the walking stick against the desk. "You may leave."

"Yes, Miss Bradford." Jane was gone from the office before finishing her words.

Edwina slammed her office door and pounded the walking stick on the desk, the top, the sides, making dents, repeating over and over with each new depression in the wood: "God dammit! Son-of-a-bitch! What kind of a hell is swallowing me?" This went on for several minutes, until she fell exhausted into her chair contemplating the badly bruised desk. She sat there for hours and by the time the afternoon had finished, she had made a decision.

* * *

Jane Barnett went to lunch, so scared she couldn't touch her food. Sarah, down from the ward, tried to draw her out, but Jane was mum.

"I can't talk about it...ever...not to anyone..."

In five minutes time, Miss Bradford had turned the character of Jane Barnett from one of conniving manipulator of people, to that much like a frightened animal, fearing for its life.

Her transformation was complete and permanent and would last the rest of her life. Regardless of what she might learn about others, for the most part, her lips were sealed forever. That night, she started a secret calendar, marking off the days to graduation—more than two years away.

* * *

Other than their being overworked, the next two weeks were uneventful for the students. The City Waterworks had repaired the sewage system and the typhoid hospital admissions began to wane.

The basement and first floor of the hospital still smelled musty from mildew and the dampness that could not be completely dispelled. X-ray, which had been shut down, reopened, and the lab moved back from its first floor temporary quarters.

Whenever Sarah went down to the basement, she relived the horrible night of the flood, being swept down the hall in dark waters, coming up, finding her footing, feeling Warren Hollis' body knocking against hers, reaching for him, leading him out as he gasped for breath.

Her worst imagined nightmares were minor compared to that night.

Now Dr. Hollis came on the ward each morning to visit the children, but he never referred to the flood. She wanted to tell him about her confrontation with Miss Bradford, but could never get up the courage. As drained as she was from the work, it gave her strength to see how the children responded to him. Oh, how they loved and trusted him, even though most were too weak to respond beyond a wan smile.

Only five children were left in the ward which would be shut down for fumigation after the last child was discharged, which was expected to be within three weeks.

Miss Gibson reassigned Emma Read and two other students to men's medical.

Potter had now been confined for twenty-two days and was desperately homesick for his parents and brother, Benjamin. "Please, Sarah, when can I go home?"

"Just as soon as you're well."

"How long will that take?"

"A week. I promise you, not more than a week." She prayed that she wasn't lying to him.

"That's too long," he pouted, crying a little.

She could forgive him for wanting to leave. He was so frail and pitiful. He had lost weight and was tired from his long ordeal. His eyes were listless and he was so weak that he could hardly turn in the bed.

He refused to eat lunch. She closed the blinds to give him semi-darkness, hoping that sleep would come and revive him.

That evening, after he awoke, he seemed even more tired and talked strangely. Sarah tried to feed him dinner, but it was no use. She left the ward at shift's end. Surely he would be better in the morning. But he wasn't. His temperature raged and his eyes were glassy.

Sarah was terrified, not even sure he saw her when she came on duty. Warren Hollis was with him.

"What's wrong?" she whispered.

Dr. Hollis met her glance, but said nothing, his expression more eloquent than anything he could have said. "His parents have been waiting all night…" was all he offered.

Her heart quickened.

She could see that Potter's mouth was dry, his tongue brown. His muscles were twitching, he was picking at the bedclothes and imaginary objects in the air. Sarah brushed away her tears with her sleeve, reaching down to him.

"Don't touch him," warned Dr. Hollis. "It will only aggravate his condition. Keep him lightly covered. His fever must be brought down."

She looked at him helplessly. "Just a careful sponging," she suggested, knowing that it meant touching her brother.

"I suppose that would be all right."

With that, Dr. Hollis was gone.

She was so upset that she could hardly remember which supplies to gather for Potter's sponge bath. She got a basin and filled it with tepid water. The other children were feeling better and laughing. One wadded his pillowcase and threw it at her as she passed. Water spilled over the edges of the basin.

At that moment, she hated all of them. Her mind was obsessed with Potter, who lay, gravely ill.

When she reached his bed, she smelled a new odor, the most fearsome of all odors. The worst complication had happened. The typhoid lesions that riddled his intestines had eroded through allowing blood to flow freely inside his abdomen. His pulse was faint and rapid, perspiration speckled his forehead. He cried weakly, saying that his stomach hurt and he couldn't breathe.

She put down the basin and hurried for Miss Severn. "Potter Morgan is bleeding internally," she whispered, desperately. "Please call Dr. Hollis."

As she said this, she saw her father. He and Carrie rushed in to the room. They must have been watching at the swinging doors.

"What is it?" Carrie demanded.

Sarah stood mute, holding them back.

It was up to Dr. Hollis to tell them. He arrived almost immediately, running past them to Potter's bedside. When he saw the boy's condition, he allowed the parents to come and be with their son. Sarah helped them into isolation gowns, her knees shaking. They stood at their son's bedside, their faces ashen.

Carrie fell into prayer. Spencer Morgan just looked stricken.

Potter Morgan had lapsed into unconsciousness.

Warren Hollis sent for a surgeon and ordered Potter be given a very small dose of morphine to insure absolute rest his intestines. But Potter was beyond the help of any surgeon. Within the hour, he was gone.

It took them all several minutes to realize he had died. Carrie fell into Spencer's arms, sobbing and sobbing.

Sarah stood at the bedside while Dr. Hollis led the parents to the hallway to console them.

After a long time, Miss Severn told Sarah that she should go off-duty for the rest of the day. Her comforting arm guided Sarah away.

In the hall, her father and Carrie were clinging to one another. When Carrie saw her, she screamed, "You got your wish. You wanted him to die. You couldn't be a part of our family so you made a pact with the devil to take our son away!"

Her stepmother caught Sarah off-guard. She broke loose from Miss Severn, ran down the hall, and out, across the grounds to the nurses' residence, where she fell numbly to her bed.

The next morning, after a sleepless, tearful night, devastated by the accusation, she was called to Miss Bradford's office.

"I am very sorry about your brother," the superintendent said.

Years later, Sarah would think back to this act of compassion from Miss Bradford and doubted that it had ever happened. All she could remember were her relationships with certain women and her walking stick.

Chapter Eleven

Of course, Sarah never learned of the letter from Dr. Hollis and she never found out the nature of the traumatic event that caused the drastic change in Jane Barnett.

Such intrigues had gone on at the Margaret Ward School of Nursing since its inception forty-five years before. The faculty easily forgave their own transgressions while insisting that the student nurses uphold lofty standards. Unknown to the young idealists, the golden font of preachments made of fool's gold was badly tarnished.

Perhaps not all students knew, but the faculty surely understood that at the final accounting, the loftiest goal for the students was survival.

For the real Margaret Ward, born in 1896, survival was never more than a hope" and that for only a few hours. She came into this world with a heart unable to do its job.

The school of nursing was born of grief, endowed with money which no longer had material meaning for the distraught parents. It could not buy them a child. Nothing could, for in the years that followed, the parents suffered the same fate two more times.

Tiny Margaret Ward's brief life was carried on in the memory of every student who passed through the nursing school named after her for she was part of the indoctrination process. If for no other reason, the profound respect people have for the innocence of babies, kept even student nurses on the right track. Especially babies who didn't have a chance.

That meant that Margaret Ward affected at least twenty-five to thirty budding nurses each year.

After graduation, some of the nurses stayed on at the school to train other students. Inbreeding eventually gave each graduate a "Margaret Ward" stamp of excellence. They could be depended on to have a certain starched dignity and high level of performance, sacrificing for their calling in the one-hundred-fifty bed hospital and anywhere else in the world where they chose to practice.

That they would have to maintain this image forever was not lost on the current probationers. In less than a month they would know if their image was up to snuff by being accepted into the school of nursing to complete the last two-and-a-half years. Passing morning inspection and anatomy tests were only the beginning. Their future hinged on every move they made, deportment, compliance, and performance.

In addition, they had to keep a B grade-point average.

If they made it, the ceremony where Miss Bradford placed the linen cap on their heads would be remembered by many as the most important event of their life. Even more important than their eventual graduation.

It was cold that January of the capping ceremony. The snow covering the walk between the nurses residence and the hospital one-quarter of a block away was cleared each morning at five a.m. so the nurses could get through. It used to be that the nurses and students entered the hospital on the second floor because the basement and first floors were built down the slope of the hill. This meant that, on the river side, the two floors built just below ground level gave a spectacular view of the river.

In the hospital basement were the ancillary services that patients and visitors never saw; the linen room, kitchen, X-ray, morgue, pathology lab, and sleeping quarters for the on-call doctors who affiliated from the University of Vermont, five miles away. The flood, two months previous, damaged the basement so badly that it could not be used for a year. A line would forever show on the walls where the angry waters finally ended their rampage.

On the first floor was the admitting area, emergency room, ambulance entrance, business offices, and the Medical Director's office. Most significant to the students was Miss Bradford's office located at the end of the corridor, giving her the utmost privacy. It was difficult to know what went on in its interior, but it contained fear-wrenching memories for generations of students. For an unknown reason, her area sustained little damage.

Surgery, recovery room, labor and delivery, and the surgical patients were on the second floor. The third and fourth floors housed pediatric and medical patients.

In this year, with a deepening economic depression in the country, with Hooverville ghettos made of cardboard and tin shacks springing up like weeds throughout the United States for the poor and unemployed, where liquor could not be used as an antidote for despair because prohibition was in effect, people in hospitals were almost the fortunate ones.

At West Vermont Hospital, patients on the north side of the hospital could watch the Winooski River tumble and roll down the valley, cutting between the freezing snow banks and proud trees bearing the heavy weight of winter. It might be the most comforting medicine these patients would ever know.

For the student nurses who toiled ten hours a day from seven in the morning to seven at night with a two-hour break somewhere in between if there was time, the river was a faded backdrop and not a happy memory. Students had no time for the beauty of any scenery. Especially the probationers who could never think of anything but their work.

The awe-inspiring capping ceremony finally came for Sarah and her classmates on a finger-stiffening cold evening, the last Friday of the month. It was held in the classroom where the students had learned to make beds, give baths, enemas, and take rectal temperatures, using each other as patients.

The ceremony proceeded with time-honored precision and sameness. The end of the invocation was Miss Bradford's cue to begin her performance. She had purchased a new uniform and white-shoes for the occasion. She stood at the rear of the classroom like a bride about to be given in marriage and turned regally to Miss Mabel Sheridan, one of the three instructors, who otherwise served as a night supervisor of the hospital. It was Miss Sheridan's function to light the Nightingale lamps.

At the instant the wick of Miss Bradford's lamp caught fire, a well-rehearsed Miss Gibson also standing at the rear of the classroom, snapped off the overhead lights and plunged the room into darkness.

The drama brought a gasp followed by a hush from the students' families seated along the sides.

The single flickering light guided Miss Bradford to the front of the classroom, her walk straight and unwavering. When she reached her destination, she set the lamp on the table where the new linen caps were placed in perfect rows. Then she turned to face the audience, her face expressionless, her hands clasped before her.

This was the signal for the students to imitate her performance. One by one, the girls proceeded to Miss Sheridan who lit the candles in their lamps. Then each student walked forward, stopping before Miss Bradford who presented the caps.

When Miss Bradford placed the wide-brimmed starched cap on Sarah's head, she was not prepared for the rush of emotion that overcame her, a feeling of pride and achievement. Even so, her heart was heavy. There was no one present from her family to share her accomplishment.

She had purposely withheld sending an invitation to her father fearing that he would not come and she didn't want the burden of wondering why.

Abbie Kirley had told her she was being dumb. "Why wouldn't he come? It should be a relief to him that you'll be self-supporting someday."

She doubted that her father would be concerned with that. "I'll send an announcement after the ceremony."

"No, Sarah, ask him to come."

Tears welled in her eyes. "Abbie, there are some things I just can't talk about."

Abbie looked ashamed and apologized.

Now, during the ceremony, the two exchanged glances while Miss Bradford finished placing the hair pin in Sarah's cap anchoring it to her head. This done, Sarah looked directly at the superintendent while she carefully centered the cap. Sarah was caught by the unexpected softness and compassion in her eyes during that brief moment, an expression that she'd seen one time before.

As she moved away, Laura Upton took her place.

When the fourteen girls had their lamp candles lit and the brand-new caps on their heads, they faced their families and recited the Nightingale pledge.

"I solemnly pledge myself before God and in the presence of this assembly, to pass my life in purity and to practice my profession faithfully. I will abstain from whatever is deleterious and mischievous, and will not take or knowingly administer any harmful drug. I will do all in my power to maintain and elevate the standard of my profession, and will hold in confidence all personal matters committed to my keeping and all family affairs coming to my knowledge in the practice of my calling. With   loyalty will I endeavor to aid the physician in his work, and devote myself to the welfare of those committed to my care."

This done, the student nurses recited the twenty-third psalm, their candles flickering as if as a symbol of hope to their families. Then the overhead lights were turned on, the girls doused their lamps, placing them on the empty table to be used again by the next class in six months.

As the girls filed past Miss Gibson, she handed them each a rolled scroll of the Nightingale pledge that she had painstakingly penned in Old English script. It had taken her months to make up enough for each girl in the class. Rolled inside the scroll were three one-dollar bills, a gift from the medical director. When Sarah reached Miss Gibson, her hands trembling, she removed her cap and set it on the table.

After the ceremony, the girls could go home for two weeks. Their families rushed to them, hugging them, laughing, taking pictures. Laura Upton's father was the loudest, whooping for his daughter, who'd already adopted the sedate demeanor the girls were expected to exhibit when in uniform. There were whispers between Laura and her father.

"You're coming home for a vacation," he said.

"I can't," she said, her voice wavering. "I have to make up my sick time. Miss Bradford just gave me my cap so I could be with the class."

"Then right after..."

Sarah was swept aside by the exuberant relatives and, after accepting a cup of tea from Miss Bradford, she slipped away to her room.

She stood before her bedroom mirror. She didn't feel different, but she looked different, except without the white cap she was not completely dressed in uniform. Gone were the ugly black shoes and hose, replaced by white shoes and hose. Even so, she was elevated from the level of the lowliest of beings, the probationer. Her mind wandered over the magic of the moment.

Deep in thought, she was startled when Abbie came in to the room.

"Examining your new prison garb?" Abbie asked.

"Not bad, is it?"

"No, considering that you'll be wearing it for the last two-and-a-half years of your sentence."

They laughed, but Sarah noticed the care with which Abbie removed her own cap and placed it in a hat-box in the closet. Then she threw some belongings in her suitcase and slammed the lid.

Sarah watched longingly. Abbie was going to her father's home for part of the vacation while Sarah would stay at the hospital for she had no place to go.

"Why not meet me at my grandmother's next week?" asked Abbie. "I'm spending the last week in Burlington."

"Maybe," said Sarah. "I don't know what I want to do yet. Call me in a week."

"All right, hermit." Abbie lugged the suitcase out of the room.

Sarah could not sleep that night. The residence seemed huge and eerie with so few people remaining. The only students still around were Laura and Jane Barnett who wanted to work during the two weeks rather than go home.

Miss Gibson was given the two weeks off, but she wouldn't be leaving until the following Friday when Mrs. Dunning, the perpetually worried housemother, returned from her daughter's home in Shelburne.

At no time were the student's allowed to be in the residence without supervision.

Although Miss Bradford would be staying at the hospital in her own quarters, she had never been known to come to the students residence and certainly did not accept responsibility for them during off-duty hours.

Within the residence, privacy was based on trust because the bedrooms were never locked. At ten p.m. the doors to the outside were locked and Mrs. Dunning or Miss Gibson would patiently answer the back door for students returning from late duty.

But, for two weeks, Sarah wouldn't be going on duty. In fact, she doubted very much that she would be going anywhere.

Sometime before midnight, terrible loneliness overcame her and she began to cry. At first, the tears were few and then suddenly they poured and she sobbed for what seemed like hours. She missed her rejecting family terribly, even her mother's favorite, Beatrice, with whom she never got along; her father who turned out to be weak, always deferring to his second wife's wishes.

She couldn't help thinking about Potter, their dear, eight-year-old son, now gone from all of them. She thought of him blowing out his birthday cake candles and the Nightingale lamp she had blown out earlier that evening, both rituals of change.

She reached for the Nightingale scroll to read it again and held the three dollars. The money seemed warm in her hand, and suddenly, Warren Hollis' face loomed in her mind.

She got on her hands and knees and reached under the mattress, retrieving the envelope with the balance of the money he'd loaned her. She added her three dollars from the ceremony, counted the bills...and calculated how many months it would take to replace the rest. Dismayed, she realized that if he returned in the fall, she still would not have enough.

Oddly, after thinking of him and her predicament, she felt better. At least worry had replaced loneliness. Worry was something she could take care of.

She decided to shower, put on her robe and headed for the second-floor bathroom at the opposite end of the corridor. When she opened the door, she heard retching. Laura Upton was leaning over the commode. Sarah rushed to help her classmate. When Laura stopped vomiting, she leaned against the wall. The two looked at each other, at first unsure, then they both started to laugh.

"Your eyes are as red as tomatoes," said Laura, still choking. "How come?"

"It's been a bad week."

"Just a bad week? To me, it's been a bad several months."

Suddenly, the bathroom door flew open and Jane Barnett, whose room was directly across the hall, stormed in. "Can't you two shut up? I have to get up early to be on duty."

They apologized, and after Jane slammed the door, the two began to whisper. "Come to my room, Laura. We'll be alone and can't bother anyone."

In the long hours between two and five in the morning, they exchanged secrets they might not have shared at any other time. Shamefacedly, Laura confessed of her last, careless night with Wes Jensen and began to weep.

"We love each other so much. Our parents made us promise not to marry until we're older. And now this…he doesn't know about it which is just as well, because I've made a decision."

"What's that?"

"I'm going to get rid of it. I'm not going through life an unwed mother with a bastard child. My parents would be disgraced. It would be better for them if I were dead."

"Don't talk like that." Sarah pleaded with her. "Please, Laura, you can adopt the baby out."

Laura laughed derisively. "It isn't that simple. I can't be pregnant. I have to finish training."

Sarah was at a loss for words or even as to how she really felt about Laura's dilemma. But Laura terminated the discussion with her grim pronouncement.

"I don't know how I'm going to do it but, when classes start again in two weeks, I won't be pregnant."

* * *

The following morning, after breakfast, Miss Bradford went to her first-floor office in the hospital, still reliving the success of the capping ceremony the previous evening. As in the past, she knew her performance had been so triumphant that if she ever had trouble with a student, the parents would back her in any counseling or disciplinary action.

She smiled at the needlepoint wall-hanging above her desk that read:

"It has been said and written scores of times, that every woman makes a good nurse. I believe, on the contrary, that the very elements of nursing are all but unknown."

Florence Nightingale

She unlocked the desk drawers and pulled out the papers she used to plan the students learning sequences and rotation schedules. It wasn't only the newly-capped students that she had to plan for, but the entire student body. The second year students would be away for the most part, either doing psychiatric affiliation at the Greenbridge Hospital for the Insane or learning how to care for TB patients at the Tuberculosis Preventorium at Pittsford. The third year students had finished most of the lectures and would be full-time on the wards, doing principally evening and night duty.

Her thoughts were deep into curriculums when she was interrupted by a rapping on her door. "Come in," she said, prepared to blast the intruding student.

It was Dr, Palmer.

Edwina Bradford stood quickly in deference to his status as a physician.

He acknowledged her and motioned for her to sit down, but she waited until he was seated. His visit was most unusual and she couldn't remember when he'd last been in her office. Perhaps, ten years ago. Generally, if he wished to speak with her, he summoned her to his luxurious, well-appointed study.

"Please excuse my interrupting your work," he began.

She demurred. "That's quite all right."

"I regret that I must bring a most unfortunate incident to your attention." He cleared his throat. "I have reason to believe that one of the probationers cheated on her final anatomy exam." He leaned very close and whispered a name.

"My goodness," said Miss Bradford, surprised. "I wish I'd known this before the capping ceremony…"

"I wasn't positive and I didn't want to spoil the ceremony for everyone."

"Of course."

"But, now I am quite sure."

"In that case, I will handle the matter. After all, honesty and integrity are primary virtues of our students."

"Thank you," he agreed, turning to leave and then reflected. "It's a shame…she seemed so sincere…"

"Dr Palmer, people are not always what they appear to be."

"That is true," he agreed, closing the door behind him.

Miss Bradford scanned her papers with the students schedules for the next six months. She took a ruler and penciled a line through Laura Upton's name. Dismissal was the only way to deal with a student who violated the nurses' code of ethics.

The superintendent sighed. The least she could do would be to spare telling the girl during the vacation period.

Chapter Twelve

Every day, Sarah and Laura went to meals together in the nearly deserted dining room. On Friday, Miss Gibson had taken her bags and left for vacation which meant Mrs. Dunning must be back. Saturday afternoon after going to Catholic confession, Abbie would be returning for Sarah.

When Sarah was alone with Laura that first week, she listened to her making plans to rid herself of the unwanted baby. But, since so much time had gone by and Laura had done nothing, Sarah decided it was just talk.

Saturday, at breakfast, had been no different with Laura's plan to get instruments from the obstetrical floor, sterile linens and other items she considered necessary. Sarah only half listened, but around ten am when she was reading in the residence study room, Laura passed by with a loaded shopping bag.

A few minutes later she returned, empty handed. "Will you help me?"

Sarah hardly looked up, terribly threatened. "No! I can't do something like that." She hadn't meant to speak so sharply.

Without a word, Laura left.

Shortly after, the residence door opened again and Jane Barnett entered. Her eyes watered and she was sniffling. "I'm too sick to stay on duty," she told Sarah. "Miss Bradford said you must report in my place this afternoon."

"I can't. I'm on vacation. Besides, I'm leaving today."

"I'm sorry. That's what she said."

"Why did you tell her I was here?"

"I didn't. She knew."

As Jane left for her room, Sarah stared at the door in outrage. Didn't private lives have any value? She tried to think of a way to avoid the assignment, but knew she couldn't. Furious and resigned, she dressed for duty.

As she passed Laura's door, she stopped to apologize for being harsh with her earlier that morning.

Laura barely opened the door.

"Is everything all right?" Sarah asked.

Laura looked at her shamefacedly.

"I can't find the hole..."

"It's just as well," Sarah said, relieved.

Laura glared at her. "It's easy for you to say because it isn't your problem. I never should have told you." With that, she slammed the door.

As Sarah left the residence she remembered Abbie. Quickly, she ran back, penned a note and tacked it outside her own door. It read: "I'm working. Wait for me in Laura Upton's room."

If Laura was depressed, company would surely help her.

* * *

When Abbie arrived by bus that afternoon to get Sarah, she saw the note. Dismayed, she was sorry that she hadn't called first. Should she go back to her grandmother's and return for Sarah the next day? No, buses didn't run on Sundays?

Abbie knocked on Laura's door. When there was no answer, she went in, surprised to see her classmate in bed. She was breathing rapidly and seemed to be in pain.

"What's the matter?" Abbie knelt beside the bed.

"Nothing."

But it was plain that something was wrong.

Laura kept gritting her teeth and moaning, her fist pressed against her mouth. She rolled from side-to-side drawing her legs up. Her hair was wet on her forehead.

"Tell me what's wrong," Abbie cried, frightened.

"Nothing. It'll go away."

Abbie stood. "I'm getting Mrs. Dunning..."

"No.. .no.. .please, no."

But Abbie ignored her and ran to the housemother's room, knocking desperately. There was no response. She went to Miss Gibson's. No response there, either. Why didn't they answer? One of them was supposed to be in the residence at all times.

There was no one to call so she went back to Laura.

Laura's face was contorted, her neck veins bulging. When she saw Abbie, she turned her back to her, crying, trying to stifle groans. After several minutes, while Abbie waited helplessly, Laura gave a sudden, sharp cry and then was quiet. From a frenzy of pain, she had grown silent.

Abbie didn't know what to make of it. She pulled back the covers and was paralyzed by what she saw. Something slimy lay between Laura's blood-soaked legs.

Abbie shrieked. "What is it?" Even as she said it, she knew. It was a baby, a tiny, perfectly formed baby. A long ago memory flashed through her mind of a time when she'd seen something like this with her mother. Her mother had moaned and later had thrown back the bed covers, and Abbie had seen a baby in the bed. Her mother said it was dead and a few days later, her mother had died. Abbie knew that, somehow, it had been her fault.

She shuddered. It had been a boy baby, the same as this one lying in Laura's bed.

Abbie began to scream, shaking Laura. "Don't die! Don't die!"

Weakly Laura took hold of her hands to quiet her. "Shhh, don't let anyone hear you."

Abbie realized this was not her mother, after all. "What shall I do?" she asked, frantically. "You've got to make him breathe?"

"No, he's dead."

Abbie watched, stunned as Laura sat up and separated herself from the infant, tying and cutting the cord. Then she lay back on the pillow covering her eyes with her hands, crying.

"What shall I do?" Abbie whispered, terrified, unable to take her eyes from the grey-blue child.

"Take it away."

"How? I can't touch it." She trembled, her teeth chattering.

"Yes, you can," coaxed Laura. "Get a towel…"

As though Laura guided her, Abbie brought back a towel from the bathroom, but she couldn't bring herself to touch the baby.

Tears streaming, Laura sat up and lifted the tiny boy, wrapping him in the towel, turning over the towel edges until he was wrapped tightly.

She handed the bundle to Abbie, but she backed away, her hands behind her. "No…no…"

"Take it!"

Abbey obeyed.

"You have to bury it. Get a big spoon from the kitchen, dig a hole near the edge of the river. Go…"

In a trance, Abbie concealed the towel-wrapped baby under her coat. She went to the kitchen where Jane Barnett was brewing tea, her eyes watering.

"I have a terrible cold," she said.

"I'm sorry," said Abbie, searching for a spoon in the drawer with her free hand. Dazed, Abbie Kirley took the baby outside in the spine-freezing January weather and ran down the hillside, slipping and sliding on the icy snow. Her knit hat was pulled down over her ears, but there was nothing to protect her face from the biting wind. She would have to get nearly to the river's edge before the snow would be shallow enough to dig through to the earth.

She set the towel with the baby down by the snow-laden sticks of a winter bush, not six feet from the Winooski River. She dug with the spoon, eventually getting through the hard, almost impenetrable ground. Before the hole was finished, there were icicles on the towel edges. It was strange the way it nearly blended in with the snow making it difficult to see…except for the red spots of blood.

Digging took her longer than she'd expected and as the hole deepened, she became convinced that there was no baby in the towel. For some crazy reason, she had been reliving a childhood nightmare that had gotten out of hand. It was behind her. She was a grown woman. It was the nurses training, the strain, the exhaustion, the fatigue which hadn't let up during the first week's vacation.

Anyway, she had only come back to the nurses residence to pick up Sarah. She felt the towel with something hard inside. How had she gotten down by the Winooski River to be digging a hole for a rock wrapped in a towel? Was God punishing her for some forgotten sin?

She picked up the towel by one corner, planning to throw it in the river. The rock rolled out in the shape of a baby. It rolled once and then lay on its side, its frozen legs drawn up, its arms folded in a supplicating position, its mouth blue and gaping.

Abbie started to scream uncontrollably, screaming words from the Catholic part of her mind: *"Oh my God…wash me from my guilt and of my sin cleanse me."* In a frenzy, she picked up the stone baby by its legs and flung it into the raging waters where it disappeared, sinking in the white swirls. Then she dropped the towel into the water and it floated along downstream.

She ran around and around in the snow, tamping the earth where she had dug, desperately chanting the act of 'reconciliation. *"Oh my God, I am heartily sorry for having offended thee. I detest my sins because I dread the loss of heaven and the pains of hell. But most of all because they offend thee, my God..."*

She rubbed snow on her arms, her legs, her chest, her face, hysterically crying over and over, *"Thou shall sprinkle me with hyssop and I shall be cleansed. Thou shalt wash me, and I shall be made whiter than snow."*

In the hospital where Sarah was passing medications, she saw several patients with their faces pressed against the window overlooking the river. She went to see what they were watching. Like a dark speck dancing on white, a figure down by the river was jumping up and down and running in circles. Sarah could see that it was a girl and the flying hair reminded her of Abbie Kirley.

Quickly, she asked permission to go down to the river's edge to see what was happening. She bundled up and ran down the hill. By the time she reached the girl, she was still, lying in the snow and being covered by a light snowfall. It was Abbie. Her eyes were closed as Sarah called to her.

"Abbie...Abbie...what are you doing out here? It's freezing."

Abbie jumped up, suddenly alert. She looked at Sarah in terror and began running up the hill, wailing. Sarah caught up with her, pulling at her clothes to stop her. But Abbie was possessed with incredible strength and broke away. She ran into the nurses residence and flopped on the living room floor, covering her head with her hands.

Sarah followed and knelt beside her.

Abbie took her hands away and looked at Sarah, her eyes tragic, beseeching: "I'm snow. ..I'm snow.." Then she began to scream again.

Mrs. Dunning rushed from her room and Jane Barnett followed seconds later at the sounds of Abbie's wailing. The housemother shook the distraught girl, but it did no good.

".. .whiter than the snow.. .snow...I'm snow." She threw herself from side-to-side on the floor, her eyes showing her terror.

Sarah could not explain what was wrong. Mrs. Dunning sent Jane for Miss Bradford who came and took the hysterical girl back to her office on the first floor of the hospital.

Abbie kept rubbing her body, repeating over and over: " ... snow... snow. . . snow. "

Miss Bradford helplessly tried to comfort her and failing, she put in a call for Dr. Palmer who came immediately and sedated the student. Between them, the doctor and superintendent concluded that, for whatever reason, she had been taken over by insanity.

The bromide took effect shortly and Abbie sat dazed and speechless in Miss Bradford's office.

Miss Bradford phoned Abbie's grandmother, asking her to come for the girl, for they didn't have the facilities to care for a mental case at the hospital.

When her grandmother arrived, the terror came back and Abbie threw her arms around her, wailing all over again. "See...I 'm snow, I'm white. I'm snow.. .snow."

Her grandmother clamped her hand over Abbie's mouth.

Miss Bradford apologized. "We don't know what happened. Why don't you take her home? Perhaps in a day or two when she is calmer..." Her voice trailed off.

*   *   *

Everyone was so upset over Abbie's breakdown that Laura Upton was completely forgotten. It wasn't until the next morning that Sarah remembered that she was in the residence and went to check on her. There was no answer to a knock on the door and when Sarah went in, there was silence and an odd smell.

Laura was lying in bed, nearly hidden under the covers.

"Laura. .." said Sarah, at first quietly and then loudly. "Laura!"

The girl didn't move. Alarmed, Sarah pulled the covers from her and turned her on her back. Her eyes were sunken and closed, her mouth slack. She was white, burning with fever. The sheets were blood-soaked.

Sarah shook her and Laura moaned, her head flopping helplessly to one side.

"Laura, Laura, talk to me."

But there was nothing more than a fluttering of her eyelids. Sarah felt her weak pulse and knew she'd lost too much blood.

Frantically, she ran to Mrs. Dunning's room, but the housemother didn't answer. So she pounded on Jane's door, hardly able to get the words out, pleading with her to go for Miss Bradford. For some reason, Jane obeyed without her usual curious questioning. She really had changed. Spooky, this couldn't be the real Jane. She didn't much like the other Jane, but at least she was real.

When Sarah got back to Laura, the girl was shaking, so she covered her, and watched her anxiously, fearful that she could do nothing but wait for help.

It seemed forever, but shortly she heard the familiar staccato of the walking stick on the wooden floor in the hall. Miss Bradford quickly assessed the situation and decided that Laura was sick, very sick, indeed. She quickly began cranking the bed so Laura's head was lower than her feet.

"Please get Dr. Palmer," she ordered Sarah. "You'll find him at his home." Already Miss Bradford had set aside her walking stick and was attending to the ill student.

Sarah tore out the back door, across the hilly expanse to the far side of the hospital grounds where the doctor's two-story white Georgian mansion was located. The doctor answered the door himself. Quickly she explained the emergency and together they rushed back to the nurses' residence.

When he saw Laura, his hands shook and there were tears in his eyes. He didn't seem able to function, just stood there with a faraway look. Sarah wanted to scream for him to do something. Miss Bradford, too, was studying the doctor.

Eventually, Dr. Palmer recovered from his shock, reached under the covers to feel Laura's abdomen and quickly pulled the covers away, took a look, then dropped the covers.

"We must get her to the hospital," he said. He turned to Sarah. "Get a stretcher." And because she didn't move fast enough to suit him, he shouted, "Immediately!"

Even Miss Bradford jumped. Sarah flew down the walk, her feet snapping the crunchy snow and brought back a stretcher from the emergency room. Then Miss Bradford, with surprising strength, Dr. Palmer, Sarah and Jane lifted the limp, unresponsive girl to the stretcher and pushed it back across the long walk to the hospital.

After they had Laura on the emergency room table with proper supplies and skilled nurses taking over, Sarah and Jane returned to the residence to clean the room, gathering together the blood-stained, soggy sheets and blankets. Sarah took the bundle out behind the building and tossed it into the trash.

In the emergency room, Dr. Palmer was examining Laura. He had the surgical lamp illuminating her genital area as he dabbed a sponge at her cervix. It had terrible lacerations as if it had been stabbed and torn numerous times. He was perplexed as he packed her with yards of bandage. If she had been pregnant as she'd said, why was there no baby? Was she imagining these things all along and told him of her supposed condition hoping for sympathy. And then done this horrible deed to herself?

He shook his head. It was little wonder girls did bizarre acts. A few months with Edwina Bradford and Miss Gibson could cause anyone to take leave of her senses. Could this poor student have been so destroyed that she chose to mutilate herself to escape?

He felt her pulse, perceptibly weaker. Quickly, he listened to her barely audible heart with his stethoscope. She was near death.

Dr. Palmer panicked. He hadn't stopped the bleeding. He put out a frantic call for an obstetrician. Even as he did so, Laura Upton died, her features relaxing and turning wax-like.

Stunned, he stared at her. Miss Bradford moved closer and stood with her hands clasped before her, her head bowed, said nothing, and soon left.

On his way home, Dr. Palmer agonized over his treatment of the girl. It was disastrous, he realized. But by the time he reached his front steps, he had convinced himself he had done all that could have been done.

When Miss Bradford knew that Laura Upton had died and the grim task before her, she went to her office to find the phone number of Laura's father. Gathering her courage, she began to dial, but changed her mind and decided to return to her private quarters. She also needed to make another phone call and she did not want it going through the hospital switchboard. Besides, she had to get up the courage to talk to Laura's father.

Both phone calls proved upsetting.

Within the hour, she had completed her sad mission and brought Laura's school record back to the office.

There on the floor, hidden in the alcove beside her office door was a folded towel. She picked it up and it fell open. Inside was a pair of scissors with bits of flesh hanging from it, a catheter, and a speculum.

It was a terrible sight. At first, Edwina Bradford didn't know what to make of it. It was probably a hoax. Somebody wanted to make a fool of her. Laura Upton had not been pregnant.

Dr. Palmer had said so.

Over the next several days, she watched the investigation into the student's death. An autopsy performed on the girl showed a macerated cervix and punctured uterus, either of which could have caused the severe bleeding that led to her death. The uterus was enlarged so that the pathologist concluded the girl had been pregnant. The police, detectives and medical examiner were puzzled. They couldn't understand the reason for the brutal mutilation. Could it really have been self-inflicted?

They questioned all the principals they suspected might have knowledge of the case.

Sarah Morgan explained how she had found Laura bleeding and that a week earlier, Laura had told her that she was pregnant with Wes Jensen's child.

Jane Barnett knew even less, only that she had helped Sarah clean the room after Laura was taken to the hospital.

Dr. Palmer gave his version of the self-destructive act. He testified that Laura Upton probably never had been pregnant and that he had helped her as best he could with what medical science had to offer.

Miss Bradford did not know anything. She decided to withhold the evidence she had until she did some investigating on her own. Somebody was holding back. So would she.

Chapter Thirteen

The sun glistened on the quiet snow the next Sunday afternoon when they buried Laura Upton in her hometown of Winooski. Miss Bradford could hardly take her eyes away from Laura's fiance, Wes Jensen, grieving, wringing his hands, finally throwing himself on her casket when it was about to be lowered into its grave. Family and friends pulled him away as he cried that his life, too, was over.

After the burial, Miss Bradford took the reins of the horse and drove Miss Gibson, Sarah and Jane back to the hospital by sleigh. The snows from the last two nights made it impossible to drive in a car or carriage. The quartet was bundled in woolens, mittens, coats, scarves, with blankets tucked across their laps. Miss Bradford guided the horse expertly, his mane flying smartly as he trotted the miles.

During the ride back, no one spoke, but there were sniffles and dabbing at tears. Miss Bradford's determination hardened, remembering Wes Jensen's agony and her mistake in waiting to tell Laura of her pending dismissal. Perhaps she would have made a different decision if she had known the truth. Even so, it was not right that the student had died so senselessly from a criminal abortion.

When they reached the hospital, Edwina let the students out at the entrance to the nurses' residence and then she continued on to the shed where she and Miss Gibson tied up the horse, fed, watered, and threw a blanket over him. Edwina gave the horse an affectionate pat and casually spoke to Olive. "Please come to my room. I have something to discuss..."

"Of course." Olive Gibson, ordinarily enthusiastic, seemed distracted which could be forgiven. It had been a difficult day.

Contrary to their usual custom, they proceeded together to Edwina's quarters. Generally, they went separately. Then when Edwina was ready to see Olive, she would pass on a message to her by way of a student or a phone call. The message was always the same: "Please come to my office to discuss a scheduling matter." In these cases, her office referred to her private living quarters and the scheduling matter referred to her personal needs.

Sometimes there were scheduling matters two or three times in a week, sometimes not for a week or more. It all depended on how Edwina felt. If the hospital had had too many admissions, or time consuming problems, if there were situations with the graduate nurses or students causing her sleepless nights, if a new class was about to enter, then Edwina did not see Olive. Personal needs received no priority at all. The hours were simply too jammed to permit a spare activity, even a pleasurable one.

In fact, as the two women trudged through the snow, it occurred to Edwina that she and Olive had not really seen each other more than half a dozen times in the last five months. But tonight, she did not plan to discuss scheduling matters…not that she ever had.

They hurried to Miss Bradford's suite in the hospital, a secluded area that few knew existed. Of all the nurses quarters, hers was the finest for she was particular about her surroundings. After all, this was the one place where she could be completely herself; no airs, no professional demeanor to contend with, where she shared only what she chose with whom she chose.

The visitors who had seen the inside of her suite could be counted on the fingers of one hand. And the only one other than Olive Gibson who had seen her bedroom in the last four years was the cleaning girl.

Besides the large bedroom, the suite consisted of a sitting room, bathroom and alcove. The alcove was intended as a dressing room, but Miss Bradford had fashioned it into a makeshift "kitchen".

She had no facilities for a stove and made do with a hot plate, toaster, and waffle maker to indulge her taste for sweets. Of a Sunday morning, nothing pleased her more than to heat maple syrup and butter to pour over steaming waffles for herself and Olive after they had spent the night together. They would talk until the clock reminded Olive that she must go to church.

Edwina would stay behind, straightening her quarters, quietly reliving the ecstacy of the hours just passed.

The women always covered their rendevous' by Olive's excuse to Mrs. Dunning that she would be at her sister, Flora's, until Sunday church services.

Which was precisely the problem this morning.

The funeral weighed heavily on Edwina's mind as she and Olive went up the back stairs to her suite. Once inside, they removed their coats, boots and wool scarves, placing them on the rack just inside the door.

As usual, Olive headed for the bedroom and Edwina followed, stopping at the door. Olive turned to look at her and quickly sensed that something was wrong. "Today has been upsetting for you, hasn't it?"

"Yes, and several days last week."

Olive, her eyes filled with concern, asked, "Why didn't you send for me?"

Edwina turned away, to conceal a troubled expression.

The two went into the sitting room and settled on the couch.

"I tried to reach you at your sister's..." said Edwina, dreading the unpleasantness bound to follow.

"We were almost never home."

This stopped Edwina cold: Olive was lying.

But it hardly seemed to bother her for she went into detail about the week, as to how she and Flora battled a snow storm to get to a potluck supper, taking homemade meat pies which Flora had made despite the agony of moving her arthritic finger joints. Olive laughed as she talked about an afternoon quilting bee where everyone was sewing squares for a wedding that would be taking place in the spring.

Edwina sighed, her heart heavy with despair. "Olive, I am very tired. I believe I need to be alone today." She stood, her manner clearly indicating that the visit was finished.

Olive looked crestfallen, found her coat, and left quickly.

As it happened, there was no unfortunate scene. For, although she never told her, Edwina knew that Olive had not spent one night of that week at her sister's home. Flora had told her so and, obviously, had not reached Olive with the message.

And she never discussed her second reason for having Olive come to her room. Olive's glib duplicity had so unnerved her that further topics had been out of the question. She had wanted to tell Olive of her doubts about the outcome of the investigation into Laura Upton's death. As the superintendent of nurses, Edwina felt it her duty to get at the truth. She knew she shared a secret with at least one other person and she was determined to learn that person's identity. She had hoped for Olive's help.

What had been the point in leaving the instruments of an abortion in front of her office door? Were they planted as a decoy? Was Dr. Palmer being honest when he said there was no baby? That the girl had not been pregnant?

Whoever did it must be waiting for a signal of acknowledgment. How was she supposed to react? She could have used Olive's advice, but under the present circumstances, how could she have asked for it?

* * *

On Monday and back from vacation, the students were quiet during morning inspection, stunned by the news of Laura's death. After breakfast when the students had started their ward assignments, Edwina sent for Sarah Morgan.

Sarah arrived at her office immediately. She was an appealing girl, sometimes with a touch of shyness, but her large eyes clearly indicated fear, common enough with the students and very annoying.

She tried to calm the student. "Miss Morgan, there is no need to be afraid just because I have sent for you. I know that the unfortunate death of Miss Upton has shocked you. But since you were in the nurses' residence with her last week, tell me what you know."

"I've already answered those questions for the medical examiners."

"Don't be impertinent! I have no way of knowing what you told them."

"I'm sorry. Miss Bradford. I found her bleeding," Sarah answered, quickly.

"Did she confide in you? Had she ever told you that she was worried about something?"

"She was worried about being pregnant."

"Oh." Edwina feigned surprise. "Did she have reason to believe it to be true?"

"I think so. Just before she came into training, she and Wes Jenson…" Sarah stopped, as though embarrassed.

"Yes, yes, I understand," said Edwina. "Did she tell anyone else?"

"I don't know, Miss Bradford."

"Tell me, Miss Morgan, did you help with the abortion?"

The girl's face turned white. Her voice shook. "No, I would never…"

"Miss Morgan," Edwina forced herself to patience. There was a murder to be solved and this wasn't the time for emotional theatrics. "Miss Upton could not have aborted herself and removed the evidence."

"Why couldn't she, Miss Bradford?"

"Miss Morgan, I ask the questions!"

But the disturbed girl blurted out: "What about Abbie Kirley?"

"What about Abbie Kirley?" Edwina shot it right back to Sarah.

"She must have known something. Why was she down by the river?"

"The two incidents are unrelated." She studied Sarah, wondering how she could get the truth from her. "Miss Morgan, I have one final question for you." She watched Sarah's face for the terror that would surely appear and did. "What did you do with the baby?"

Sarah dropped her head, sobbing, "Miss Bradford, please believe me. I had nothing to do with an abortion. I don't know anything. I never saw a baby."

Edwina waited for the girl's sobs to subside. Whatever she was withholding, she concealed it well. Further interrogation would probably be useless. "Miss Morgan, you are never to discuss this conversation with anyone. If I ever learn that you have, you will be discharged from the school."

Sarah lifted her head proudly, a hint of defiance in her quivering chin. "Yes, Miss Bradford."

"You may leave."

Next, Edwina sent for Jane Barnett. Miss Barnett came up to the desk and stood with her hands respectfully clasped before her, curiously studying Miss Bradford.

This student certainly had her share of self-confidence, perhaps more than her share. Edwina intentionally left her standing. "Miss Barnett, you were one of the two students in the residence with Laura Upton during the last week of vacation. What do you know about her activities?"

"I was too sick to know anything. I saw her with Sarah Morgan a few times. I would go down to make tea for my cold and I would see them coming and going. Once Abbie Kirley came into the kitchen looking for a large spoon."

"What for?"

"I don't know."

Edwina dismissed the information as trivia. "Miss Barnett, how well did you know Laura Upton?"

"Not very well. I took private anatomy lessons with her from Dr. Palmer."

Yes, Edwina recalled that Dr. Palmer had mentioned this. "What can you tell me about those lessons?"

"Only that each of us spent a private half-hour alone with him and then an hour together."

"Why did he give you a private half-hour?"

"Laura was having trouble learning bones and I was having trouble with muscles."

This questioning was frustrating. Edwina wondered how she could get at what Jane Barnett really knew without telling her something she might not know. She decided she would manage it the same way she had with Sarah Morgan. Secrecy with the threat of dismissal. "Was Miss Upton pregnant?"

"I don't know."

"Well, she was…"

Miss Barnett seemed stunned by the information. After a long time, she said slowly and thoughtfully, "I wonder if that's why I saw her crying in Dr. Palmer's arms. He was saying that he wished he could help her, but he couldn't."

So that was it. Was Dr. Palmer more evil than she had imagined? Had he impregnated an innocent eighteen-year-old girl, later claiming that she had cheated on an anatomy test so that Edwina would dismiss her from the school? And then he murdered the student with an improperly performed abortion? Of course, the answer of the missing baby was obvious. He had gotten rid of it.

Could she prove it?

"Thank you, Miss Barnett. Please remember that this conversation has been confidential. If it ever gets back to me that you have discussed it with anyone else, you will be dismissed from the school."

The student broke down. "How can I ever work with Dr. Palmer again?"

"It will be a good test of your understanding of nursing ethics, Miss Barnett. You cannot allow personal feelings to interfere with your working relationships."

Jane Barnett nodded agreement and left the office.

Edwina knew this would test her own tolerance of nursing and medical ethics…to the limit. Before she was through, she was going to bring down Dr. Palmer. He was a dangerous man. But could he have been so stupid as to leave those instruments outside her office door. Now she had someone pinned down to the crime. There was still at least one other person involved.

That afternoon, Miss Bradford received a very upsetting phone call. Abbie Kirley's father called to say that she would not be returning to nurses training. Her hysteria had advanced to the point that her distraught family had to send her away to the mental hospital. It was doubtful that she would ever recover for her mother had been hospitalized for the last fifteen years.

"It is a family curse," Mr. Kirley said, bitterly.

"Sadly, these misfortunes seem to run in some families," Edwina murmured, sympathetically. Meanwhile, she knew that if Abbie ever did recover, she would be barred from the school for it forbade students with mental histories.

Prudently, she decided to keep the information about Abbie from the rest of the faculty, students and medical director. It would suffice to tell them that Abbie Kirley admitted she wasn't cut out to be a nurse and withdrew voluntarily.

Abbie's circumstances were unfortunate, but the change in the student roster gave Edwina an opportunity. She called Miss Gibson and Mrs. Dunning to her office and informed them that there would be room reassignments in the students dormitory. "I think it would be best if Miss Morgan roomed with Miss Barnett."

Both women concurred with her decision.

Edwina rested well that night knowing that, in spite of their promises to her, in the dark hours of the night, the girls would confide in one another. The information would eventually get back to her. It always did.

Chapter Fourteen

The flood wasn't forgotten. Laura Upton wasn't forgotten. And neither was Abbie Kirley. It had been a harsh winter, even by Vermont standards with many nights of sub-freezing temperatures.

On a Sunday, the Congregationalist minister announced that even with all of their troubles, god was fair and the towns in and around the Winooski Valley had paid any dues owed many times over.

At the Margaret Ward Hospital Training School, Sarah and her classmates had been beaten by life's winter in the last six months. Sarah didn't feel that god was fair at all. She still hadn't recovered from the superintendent's accusation that she was responsible for Laura Upton's abortion. Naturally, she dreaded further encounters with Miss Bradford, for she was unpredictable.

It was Monday and the girls were passing through morning inspection and reading their posted ward assignments.

The typhoid epidemic was over and now pneumonia cases were coming in. More than half of them were dead within twenty-four hours. As quickly as a bed emptied, it would be filled with a new case. It particularly hit the very young and very old.

The school of nursing quickly adapted to the increased needs for nursing care. Days-off were eliminated for the students and no set time schedules were given. Instead, students reported for duty at 7 am or 7 pm and left after twelve hours—if they could be spared.

Sarah was assigned to days while Jane was given nights.

"Please, trade with me," Jane pleaded.

"Sure, if you get permission," agreed Sarah.

Of course, no such change would ever be requested and Sarah knew it. It was part of a students training to accept assignments cheerfully with no fuss.

The work was exhausting. The girls were soon putting in fifteen to twenty hour days or nights with hardly any time left for sleep after they'd eaten, bathed, and laid out clean clothes for their next shift.

Even though the residents of Burlington were staying indoors to avoid catching the terrible malady, the pneumonia cases increased.

On the third morning of almost non-stop duty, Miss Bradford conferred with Miss Gibson. Steps would have to be taken to protect the students whose susceptibility would be compromised because of their fatigue. Isolation techniques were quickly instituted, although Dr. Palmer laughed, claiming them useless.

Nevertheless, Miss Gibson made the girls change into isolation gowns before entering the ward and they wore face masks all shift.

Many of the students were assigned to the men's ward which had twenty beds, ten along each side with the heads flush against the window sills. The well-lighted room belied the gloom that persisted in the beds. There were at least four students on duty at all times and they worked at a relentless pace.

Still, the work was never finished; turning patients who were allowed no activity; adjusting oxygen tents; changing sheets sopping from the heavy condensation inside the tents; carrying and adding ice to the demanding containers through which the oxygen passed to be dried and cooled; giving cold baths to patients delirious with fever; applying cold compresses, sometimes warm poultices or mustard paste to chests aching from coughing; setting up steam inhalations; holding patients in an upright position so that Dr. Palmer and his colleagues could tape painful chests; holding an arm still when a bloated, livid face indicated the need for a venesection to relieve dyspnea. The students gave liberal injections of codeine and morphine to ease the agony from constant coughing.

The ward was an endless chorus of hacking, rasping coughs, some dry, some wet, interspersed with moans of helplessness.

The work was draining while the students watched the fever charts, anxiously hoping for the raging fever to peak which meant the crisis had come and the patient would begin to get better. Many times, there was no crisis and, when death came, mocking silently, the students took it as a personal failure.

Praying that they wouldn't be caught, Sarah and the others would go off to cry alone when a patient they'd worked especially hard for died. In the days caring for them, the students learned their family histories. They met the spouses and heard about the children, the kind of farm the family had, even the number of cows and sheep they reared, and this time of year, the number of maple trees producing sap.

On the seventh day of the epidemic, Sarah, Emma Read and Hannah Davis were working with the men. Miss Gibson supervised. All of them were exhausted. It was late afternoon when the lull that came just before darkness pervaded the ward. It was extra quiet, coughing seemed less.

Sarah had just finished helping Hannah bathe Mr. Tobias, a thirty-eight year old father of four, who was in the fifth day of a high fever. It had been hours since he'd made any sense, fighting the staff to be free from restraints. But with their ministrations, he had grown quiet, and both students hoped that the crisis was beginning and his fever would soon drop.

Hannah went to the kitchen to get more ice while Sarah went back to her assigned patients.

Suddenly, she heard a clattering of metal and looked up. Mr. Tobias was climbing over the bed rails. Quickly, she yanked up the side-rail of her patient. It jammed and wouldn't lock in place. She pulled at it, crying for help.

As she did so, Mr. Tobias fell to the floor, but quickly got up. With a strength he summoned from someplace, he ran across the room and leaped on another patient's bed and climbed to the window sill. Without warning or stopping, he smashed through the glass and plunged out the window. Sarah screamed, unable to reach him in time, visualizing the fall his body made. There was no sound when he struck the hardened snow.

Hannah Davis ran in. "Oh my god!" she cried out, when she realized what had happened.

It wasn't long before the ward was filled with superiors investigating the incident. Hannah collapsed when they told her that the patient had died.

The first year students were dismissed and senior students brought in to work the ward.

Sarah and Hannah were summoned to Dr. Palmer's office where Miss Bradford waited with him. Dr. Palmer asked for a statement from each of them, telling them that the police would be by later to record their versions for the official record. After each of the girls finished speaking and Dr. Palmer had taken notes, Miss Bradford broke in, unable to withhold her anger.

"Miss Davis, did you leave the patient unattended without restraints when you knew he was delirious?"

"We'd just finished changing him. He'd been quiet. I thought he'd be all right." She was crying.

"As you can see, you thought incorrectly. We have procedures to prevent errors in judgment."

"Yes, Miss Bradford," said the grief-stricken student.

Miss Bradford turned to Sarah. "How could you have prevented this?"

"I don't know, Miss Bradford." God knows, she had tried. Her head was pounding from the hours and days with no rest and, then, this final nightmare. At this point, Dr. Palmer interceded. "Miss Morgan, how long have you been on duty?"

"Since yesterday morning."

"And you?" he asked Hannah.

"I don't remember. One day…two days.."

"When was your last day off?"

"Day off?" She seemed puzzled. "I don't remember."

He turned to Sarah again. "When were you off?"

"Eight days ago."

"When did you eat last?"

"This morning."

Hannah couldn't remember when she'd last eaten, but supposed it had been that day since all students were required to be at morning inspection and, from there, proceed to breakfast.

He addressed Miss Bradford. "I do not wish to minimize the seriousness of the unfortunate incident that has occurred, but I feel that these girls have been pushed beyond human limits. They must have rest."

"Dr. Palmer," Miss Bradford snapped, striking her walking stick against the floor. "The nursing care of the patients must come before personal considerations. A patient has died from neglect and you are rambling on about meals and days off."

If Dr. Palmer had been a student nurse, he would have been instantly dismissed from the school. He backed off. "I am only stating my personal opinion."

"I would appreciate it if you would allow me as the superintendent of nurses to run the nursing department. You can make all the judgments you wish about medicine. Nursing decisions are mine."

Sarah was mortified at Miss Bradford's anger at the physician with them present.

But Dr. Palmer held his own. "Miss Bradford, regardless of your position in this hospital, might I remind you that a doctor's judgment, even that of the newest intern, outweighs yours as a nurse."

She glared at him, her eyes narrowing. "Pathetic, isn't it!" She spun on her heel, rapping her stick. "Come, students. Follow me to my office."

Sarah and Hannah followed their superior, sure that their fate had just been determined. Sarah weighed the options on the basis of disciplinary measures she'd seen handed out. Surely, she would be dismissed.

Miss Bradford made her wait outside the office while she gave Hannah Davis the verdict. The girl came out of the office, dazed, mouthing the word, "dismissed".

Then Sarah went in.

"You can thank Dr. Palmer for keeping you in the school," said Miss Bradford, hostility underlining his name. "You will be given three months to improve your performance, especially obedience to rules. If you do not improve, you will be dismissed." She paused as though weighing her further choice of words. "You will eat all meals regularly." Then, sarcastically, she added, "As you heard Dr. Palmer say, meals are important for keeping up strength."

"Yes, Miss Bradford." Sarah's knees were shaking.

"You may leave."

She left the office, quietly closing the door. It wasn't as bad as she'd expected.

But how could it have been worse? Her thoughts dwelled on the man who had leaped to his death, about Abbie whose mind had gone, about Laura Upton…and she lapsed into a depression that was to last for weeks. At that moment, if she'd had any place to go, she would have quit nursing school. No one would have to dismiss her.

The next morning when she went to scrub the floor of the men's ward, a new patient viewed her with feverish, pained eyes. It was Dr. Palmer, hospitalized during the night, another victim of the virulent Type III pneumonia.

Chapter Fifteen

When the student nurses heard that Dr. Palmer was hospitalized, they fought for the honor of caring for him. Miss Gibson organized them into teams. Jane Barnett was brought to days and paired with Clara Sherwood, an only child, whose parents never left her thoughts; Mary Drury, the youngest student in the class, was teamed with Eunice Thompson, a perfectionist on sheet corners just like Miss Gibson.

Sarah was assigned to work with Emma Read who complained, "Draft horses don't work this hard."

Sarah and Emma Read were not the first to care for Dr. Palmer. They came on duty the second evening of his illness. Mrs. Palmer, the envy of the nursing staff, was just leaving after her daylong vigil.

Regardless of the time of day, she was impeccable in appearance. Her gray hair shimmered, always looking freshly coifed, and her fine clothes never appeared mussed. It was as though she'd just been got up at the Royal Dress Shop and Vogue Millinery down on Church Street in Burlington.

Sarah greeted Mrs. Palmer shyly as she said goodnight to her husband. He was so desperately ill that he hardly seemed to recognize her.

The students wore isolation gowns and face masks. Dr. Palmer was restless, unmanageable and rapidly becoming dehydrated from a raging fever that had stayed at one-hundred-four degrees since the previous day. His eyes were glassy and he thrashed in the bed. Keeping him confined inside the oxygen tent was almost impossible.

Sarah prepared a basin of tepid water to sponge him down, hoping to reduce his fever. During this time, the students removed the oxygen tent and lowered the side rails. As taught, they began sponging his face, before moving down his body.

As soon as Sarah finished sponging his perspiring forehead and brow, sweat formed again, immediately. When she began wiping his mouth, he turned his head and gave her hand a loud, smacking kiss. She pulled it away, startled. He winked, teasingly. Dr. Palmer! Who would ever have thought…but she quickly regained her composure.

They washed his arms and his chest. Then the two heaved him to his side. Emma Read stood on the other side of the bed, propping him, while Sarah applied cooling alcohol to his back and rubbed along his spine and hip pressure points.

Suddenly, Emma let out a scream and jumped. "Quit it!"   With one hand, Dr. Palmer had a firm grip of her breast, his other hand grabbing her fanny.

"Stop it! Stop it!" she cried, trying to free herself without dropping him to the floor.

Sarah and other students rushed to her aid. Sarah pried his fingers loose against his incredible strength. The whole time they wrestled with him, Emma wept, outraged and humiliated. When she was free, the students turned him on his back and covered him without remarking to him about his actions.

"Why did he do that?" Emma cried.

Nobody could give her a good answer.

In truth, the instructors had never mentioned that patients personalities sometimes changed during illness. Although not violated by Dr. Palmer, memories of Dr. Montgomery rushed back to Sarah and she had a sudden feeling of nausea and lightheadedness.

Dr. Palmer began fighting again. Somebody must have gone for help because Miss Gibson came into the room. The students were trying to tie restraints on his wrists and to the bed but he would have none of it "As a doctor, I am ordering you to stop!" he yelled.

"Do as he says," said Miss Gibson, quietly.

They stood back from the bed.

When he heard her support of his position, Dr. Palmer relaxed, and the students resumed sponging his feverish body. Shortly, Miss Gibson left.

"Doctor," said Sarah, firmly, not trusting him for an instant. "Please put your hands across your chest so I can sponge your stomach. We must get your fever down…" He obeyed as she pulled the sheet down below his waist, careful to avoid any improper exposure.

As she sponged him, she saw his arm creeping down, coyly touching her hand. She paused, prepared if he should suddenly take a vise-like grip of her.

"You're beautiful," he said, his speech thick from his dry mouth.

"Thank you, Dr. Palmer." She continued sponging his stomach in smooth, circular strokes, as she'd been taught. He had his hand on top of hers. She was embarrassed because he kept staring at her face.

Suddenly, he flexed his knees against his chest and kicked off the sheet, his feet narrowly missing Sarah. She held her hand on him at arm's length, just in case he kicked again. Emma protected her face with her arm.

"Honey," Dr. Palmer's voice was hoarse. "Wash that." He pointed to his erect organ.

Sarah yanked up the side rail, grabbed a sheet from the linen pile and threw it over him. Right then, they stopped sponging him. For all Sarah cared, he could burn up. After all, there were limits…what an old, ugly buzzard!

The students were glad that their turn caring for him wouldn't come up for three more days. And they debated, should they warn their classmates? Would they believe them?

Over the next several days, Dr. Palmer exposed himself many times and made personal remarks to other students. Clara Sherwood, away from home for the first time in her life, recorded his outrages in her diary for her parents to read. Eunice Thompson left the case early, complaining of severe abdominal pains. Dr. Palmer took a swipe at Jane Barnett. Without thinking, she slapped him.

He screeched.

Clara Sherwood stared at her dumbfounded. "You shouldn't have done that."

Jane grimaced, judging her witness. Already, she could see the notation in Clara's diary. If Miss Bradford found out, Jane would be dismissed on the spot. Jane gave the doctor an injection of morphine and then led Clara to the locker room. Jane removed her face mask, dropped it into the linen hamper, then turned to Clara, saying, "You didn't see anything, did you?"

"Yes. I saw you hit Dr. Palmer."

Jane knew that there would be no explaining to this self-righteous daughter of a god-fearing Methodist minister. And, at that moment, she knew that Clara Sherwood had control of her entire future in nursing. Jane started to cry. "I'm going to tell you something very confidential," she said, after a long period of sniffling. "Dr. Palmer is an evil man. He fathered Laura Upton's baby and she died because he gave her a bad abortion."

Disbelief clouded Clara's face. "Are you serious?"

"Yes. I hate him." Jane covered her face, sobbing.

That night, the damning confession was duly recorded in Clara's diary. By the next afternoon, every student in the school of nursing had heard the rumor about the doctor and Laura, as Jane had hoped.

She was not surprised when Miss Bradford called her into her office that evening to ask her if she'd started the rumor.

"No. Yesterday, Clara and I were bathing the doctor and he was saying terrible things to her..terrible things" Jane hesitated. "I just couldn't repeat them."

"Such as," Miss Bradford said, dryly.

"He told her that if she would have relations with him, he'd give her an abortion the same as he had for Laura Upton."

Miss Bradford's expression did not change.

Jane shrugged. "I know Clara didn't mean to do it. But Dr. Palmer frightened her and she hit him…" She waited for the impact of this to settle on Miss Bradford.

Still, Miss Bradford's expression did not change.

Jane began to cry. "Oh, Miss Bradford, Dr. Palmer isn't the same man anymore."

It was as though she hadn't heard this last. "Did anyone else see her hit him?"

"No."

"Thank you, Miss Barnett. You may leave."

Miss Bradford sat in her office for a long while considering the implications of Jane Barnett's story. Just before nine that evening, she called Clara Sherwood to her office.

"Miss Sherwood," she said, grimly. "It has come to my attention that you have spread a rumor about Dr. Palmer. You are well aware that violating a patient's confidence is a serious infraction of nursing ethics."

Clara stood before Miss Bradford, nodding her head in agreement, her eyes fearful.

Miss Bradford continued as though she'd only completed half a thought. "Therefore, you are being dismissed from the school."

"But Miss Bradford…" she protested.

Almost instinctively, Miss Bradford reached for the walking stick and rapped it sharply on the floor, quieting the girl. "You will be gone in the morning. Now, get out!"

The stricken girl backed out of the office.

Wisely, Edwina had refrained from mentioning Clara's hitting Dr. Palmer. If that were to be known, it would involve an investigation by others outside of nursing, an embarrassment she preferred to avoid. She only hoped he'd never report it himself.

The superintendent realized she would have to calm the students who had heard the story about Dr. Palmer's involvement with Miss Upton, and assure them that it was unfounded. It wouldn't be easy, because Miss Bradford also believed it to be true. Within the hour, word of Clara's dismissal swept through the nurses' residence like a fire storm. Sarah was unable to sleep thinking about it. She knew that Jane was awake, too, because she tossed and turned in the bed against the opposite wall.

Something bothered Sarah about the reason for Clara's discharge. Laura had once told her that Wes Jensen was the father of her baby, yet the rumor of Dr. Palmer's involvement had come up more than once.

"Jane, where did Clara hear that rumor about Dr. Palmer?"

"From him, while we were bathing him."

Something didn't ring true. "Why do you want to get even with Dr. Palmer? What did he ever do to you?"

"It's none of your business," she snapped.

Next morning, still shaken by Clara's dismissal, Sarah reported for duty with Emma. Mrs. Palmer was already at her husband's bedside. After several day long vigils, she varied her pattern, coming twice each day, once in the morning and again in the evening. The doctor lay unresponsive, breathing through his mouth, blowing a foul odor. He had gone beyond his behavior of the previous two days. The few times he did arouse, his words made no sense.

Sarah worked discreetly around Mrs. Palmer. Even though she must be under terrible strain, it only showed in her eyes. She seemed to be occupied in memories. She said nothing to the students and it wasn't clear if she understood her husband's critical condition.

But it was clear to Sarah that Mrs. Palmer was the dutiful, proper wife who might well join the parade of mourners grieving for a loved one who died from the pneumonia.

The pneumonia ward was a somber place. Always a family weeping in the outer hall, always a patient gurgling his last, always a death.

Chapter Sixteen

During the last week of March, the situation was so desperate at West Vermont Hospital that the acting medical director recalled all medical students from their rural assignments to help during the crisis.

After Sarah's day of caring for Dr. Palmer, Miss Gibson sent her to the pediatric medical ward for an indefinite period. Children were coming in with pneumonia. Tiny Marie was still there because no one came to take her home.

She was almost thankful that she was assigned to care for Marie, the deformed and blind girl, weakly biting her fingers and arms. While she cared for the girl, Sarah was acutely aware of someone coming to the crib. It was Dr. Hollis.

He acknowledged her and studied Marie, reaching down to pick up a tiny hand, his face registering concern. Sarah had been watching Marie, numbly seeing in her the cardinal signs that meant the end was near.

The two waited as the intervals between the child's shallow breaths became longer and more uneven, until there was a final, nearly inaudible sigh and nothing more.

Although prepared for the death, Sarah was not prepared for the avalanche of emotions that followed. Forgetting the demeanor required of a student nurse, she leaned against the crib rails, dropped her head on her arms and cried.

Dr. Hollis comforted her, his arm around her shoulders. She reached for a handkerchief and, when she opened her eyes, she saw the doctor gently stroking the child's still arm.

As sad as it was, she knew that Marie's suffering was over. Blessedly, she would never again chew at her scarred fingers and torn lips, that frustration wouldn't have her in a never satisfied frenzy. Pneumonia had liberated her from a living death.

As she and Dr. Hollis stood silently at the bed, the capable strides of nurses shoes moved across the creaking, wooden floor towards them. The steps had a muffled sureness about them that every student nurse had imprinted in her mind. The rhythm of those steps belonged to Miss Bradford.

Following behind the superintendent was charge nurse, Miss Severn.

Miss Bradford spoke: "Miss Morgan, when you have finished your morning's work, please come to my office."

Tears blurred Sarah's view of the two women standing on the other side of the crib, their eyes boring at her as though the male arm comforting her was the devil's pitchfork.

Sarah tried to free herself from Dr. Hollis, but he held her firmly. "She's not ready, yet," he said quietly, but with authority.

Miss Bradford opened her mouth to speak, but didn't.

The two women marched out of the ward and in spite of the tragic situation, Dr. Hollis smiled at Sarah. "This is obviously not the place for a discussion, but I want to help you work this through...perhaps some afternoon."

She could hardly believe she'd heard accurately.

He scribbled a note and shoved it in her apron pocket. "Let me know when...," he said.

Her work was finished after she'd wrapped and taken the small child's body to the morgue. After she returned the empty crib to the ward, she headed for Miss Bradford's office.

"I trust that your education has been enhanced by the golden words and concern of Dr. Hollis." Miss Bradford's lips curled in scorn.

Sarah waited.

"Miss Morgan, you are being grounded from now until fall. September twenty-third, to be exact, one year to the day since you entered the Margaret Ward School of Nursing."

Sarah's heart plummeted but quickly recovered. Then she asked herself, what was this all about? She'd already been grounded—twice before.

"You will report to Mrs. Dunning each morning by six a.m., even when you are not working. Again at noon, at four p.m. and eight p.m. You will have no privileges."

She didn't have privileges now. Somehow, Sarah thought Miss Bradford had a better memory and was more organized with her paperwork.

Miss Bradford continued lambasting her, as if she couldn't chastise her enough. "You will sweep the carpet in the nurses' residence daily and will carry all soiled linen to the laundry room. You will scrub every pot in the kitchen so that the bottoms could serve as mirrors for vain students."

Suddenly, she seemed to run out of ideas. She raised the wooden walking stick and rapped the floor. "You are dismissed."

"Yes, Miss Bradford." Sarah shook her head. This lady had a very short vocabulary; dismissed, grounded, and a global list of unreasonable work assignments—anything to make the experience miserable.

As she left the office, she muttered to herself. "I hate her…I hate her…I hate her," over and over all the way to the nurses' residence. And then she laughed. The penalties didn't mean anything anymore. She'd personally keep track of the penalties Miss Bradford handed out and give her the list at graduation. On second thought, why bother? She didn't need the last word.

When she entered their room, Jane was just falling out of bed for she had worked the night before and had to get ready for afternoon class. She had flipped on the radio to Cole Porter's song, "Just One of Those Things".

How true, how true, ran through Sarah's mind. She removed the metal brads from her uniform buttons, put those and the pearl buttons on the dresser and slipped out of her uniform. Just as she was about to drop it in the laundry, she remembered the note from the doctor and pulled it from her pocket. It said, "Theater, Sat. 2pm. Hold July 4th…for Battery Park." and then he'd added his mailing address.

He was asking her to the annual fireworks display and regatta to be held on the shores of Lake Champlain! Four months away. That was too far away.

As soon as she recovered from her excitement, the shattering reminder hit her that none of it was possible. She had no privileges.

Dressed in clean uniforms, Sarah and Jane went down the back stairs. When they reached the first floor, Emma Read still had her hand on the knob of Miss Gibson's door, closing it. She fell into step beside them and the three continued on to class.

That night, as Sarah penned her regrets to Warren Hollis, she asked Jane: "Why was Emma at Miss Gibson's door this noon?"

"Was she? I didn't notice." Jane pulled up the covers around her shoulders and turned her back to Sarah. "In fact, in a week, I will probably have forgotten that I saw her at all." Her voice trailed off, sleepily.

Sarah stared at her roommate. What happened to her curiosity, her meddling? The change in her was unbelievable.

The next morning, Sarah sent her reply to Dr. Hollis. Two days later, she received a second message. "Won't you reconsider?"   What was there to reconsider? She replied: "Theater, can't. July 4th—maybe."

At the beginning of June, she yearned even more to see him. Perhaps it was because the weather was warming, that spring was turning into romantic summer. Perhaps it was because the class work was ending for a month. Perhaps it was the excitement of students preparing for their two-week annual vacation.

Whatever the reason, Sarah decided to appeal to Miss Bradford to suspend her sentence for just one day in July. She would tell her a plausible lie that she was going to Abbie Kirley's home in Burlington.

So what if Miss Bradford denied her request and became angry. What other chores could she pile on her?

Immediately after breakfast, Sarah went to the Super's office. She took a deep breath and raised her hand to knock on the door, but voices in the office stopped her.

There was an urgency in their tone, and suddenly they were yelling. Sarah drew back. She recognized them; Miss Gibson and Miss Bradford.

The only words she clearly understood were, "You won't get away with it". But she wasn't sure which of the women said it. She hurried away.

It took another two days to get up the courage to try and see Miss Bradford again. But now her office was locked and dark. Sarah asked around. No one had seen the superintendent.

On Monday morning, it was Miss Gibson who stood before them to conduct morning inspection. Not a word was mentioned of Miss Bradford's whereabouts or when she would return.

Sarah was desperate for permission to attend the July fourth activities. Still, there was only one other person who could grant her the privilege.

That day, she was working a split shift from seven in the morning until seven in the evening with four hours off in the middle. At eleven a.m., she went off duty and headed toward the residence, stopping at Miss Gibson's door. A radio played softly. The song was, "Night and Day".

She knocked. No answer. She knocked harder. Because none of the doors in the residence were ever locked, she suspected Miss Gibson was at her desk, concentrating over a lecture or similar project.

Determined that she would have her answer so she could write Warren Hollis, Sarah opened the door quietly.

Miss Gibson was deep in concentration, but not at her desk.

In the single bed, two bodies were intertwined in passion, kissing and fondling one another.

Mortified, Sarah quickly closed the door, ran down the hall to the steps at the other end, and hurried to her own room. She lay on her bed, staring at the ceiling wondering…Emma Read. So that was why Miss Gibson favored her.

Shaken, it took her awhile to remember why she had gone to Miss Gibson's room in the first place. And, rather than ever make such a mistake again, she resolved she'd not ask anyone for permission to leave the hospital on July 4th. She'd just go.

Her hand shook as she wrote her acceptance note. It hardly mattered or occurred to her that half the students in the school of nursing might be at the park that day and that fraternization with a doctor or medical student was grounds for immediate dismissal from the school.

* * *

On the fifth day of Dr. Palmer's illness, while Miss Gibson and Emma Read were caring for him, he came to life once again, taking a swipe at Miss Gibson. But her years in nursing had taught her a measure of discretion and wisdom in dealing with patients who abused their freedom.

"Keep your hands to yourself, buster," she muttered under her breath, leaning over close to his ear so that only he could hear. Smiling, she took hold of his wrist under the sheet with both of her hands, twisting his skin in opposite directions.

Dr. Palmer shrieked, and gave her a look as of one betrayed. He lay back, meek and compliant.

"Next time I'll do it to something else," she said, again, for his ears only.

From then on, he obeyed her every command, issued with the utmost respect. When she said, "Doctor, we're going to turn you over," he did not resist. When they sponged him down, she told him to keep his legs still and his hands to himself and he did. When she told him to use the bedpan, he did. When she told him that they were putting the oxygen tent back over him and that he wasn't to bang at it, he obeyed.

The students, especially Emma, were impressed. How was it that Miss Gibson could get Dr. Palmer to do exactly as she wished when the rest of them had to cajole, beg and plead with him? Without revealing her secret, Miss Gibson's answer was simple. "When you've been around long enough, you'll figure it out for yourselves. Patients recognize experience and they see it as power. Never forget that."

Overnight, Dr. Palmer began failing again. On the sixth day of his fever, the nurses were sure they were losing him and they called Mrs. Palmer and the minister to his bedside. The students and Miss Gibson withdrew to a respectful distance for there was nothing more they could do for him. His fate was in the hands of the Lord.

The Lord must not have been ready for him. Miraculously, on the night of the seventh day the crisis came and Dr. Palmer's fever dropped. By morning, he had undergone a striking metamorphosis. Before the day was out, it was hard to imagine him as the terminally ill, recalcitrant patient he'd been. Even though he was extremely weak, his former dignity had returned.

He called all the nurses to his bedside and other doctors who were in the hospital at the time. He commended the beaming nurses, especially singling out Miss Gibson and Miss Morgan for their exceptional nursing skills.

Even so, every student nurse present saw him with two sets of eyes and mind frames; as he was now and the way he'd been during his illness. In spite of his glowing speech, they would never forgive him for what he'd done to Laura Upton, and secondarily, to Clara Sherwood.

That same night, Emma Read came down with the dreaded Type III pneumonia and Miss Gibson quickly took charge of her nursing care, spending every available moment with her for the next ten days.

Emma nearly died, and many believed that it was Miss Gibson's determination and compassion that saved the girl. That included Miss Bradford.

As soon as Emma was able to leave the hospital, Miss Bradford sent her home to recover despite the objections of Miss Gibson who wanted to care for her in the nurses residence. Perhaps Olive Gibson did not get Edwina's whole message which was meant to accompany this decision. Of all the traits that Miss Bradford valued, loyalty was at the top of the list. It seemed that Miss Gibson had misplaced her loyalties. More than once.

Chapter Seventeen

For Sarah, the months leading to July 4th were slow to pass. When the holiday finally arrived, she left early in the morning to wait for Warren Hollis where the bridge crossed over the Winooski River. The train running on the tracks alongside the river was the only sound breaking the quiet. She carried a sack loaded with picnic supplies that Mrs. Dunning had wondered about.

"Are you going out for the day, Miss Morgan?"

"Yes."

"You have no privileges. Did someone give you permission?"

Sarah was ready for this. "Yes…Miss Gibson."

"Where are you going?"

"To a birthday party."

"With picnic supplies?"

"It's going to be at the park." She gritted her teeth, quickly signed out and hurried away. What did the housemother expect? The truth didn't help around there, so, if Sarah had to lie, then she'd lie.

"How clever of you," Sarah heard her say as she closed the door.

Yes, it was clever and the basket was filled to the brim with chicken and ham sandwiches, potato chips, bottles of apple juice. When she had bought the food, she'd felt guilty—very briefly—because the money had come out of the stash she owed him.

When she reached the bridge, he was already there, standing by his car, watching for her. Just seeing him took her breath away.

He smiled at her, and, in that moment, there was nothing or anyone else in the world that mattered. Only him.

"You look lovely," he said.

"Thank you," she said, pleased with his admiration. He looked pretty good himself.

He took the basket and helped her into the car. "I can't get over the change in you with your hair down and no uniform.. ."

"We're not supposed to be attractive in uniform." She tried to check her excitement, self-consciously patting the skirt of her cool, summer dress.

"You do all right," he said, searching for a parking place near Battery Park. He parked and carried the basket past hoards of picnickers, their radios blaring popular tunes "I'm Getting Sentimental Over You," and "Brother, Can You Spare a Dime." which echoed the despair of the times.

When they reached the western edge of the park, he put the basket down. This was the place where cannons had forced back three British ships intent on invading the United States in 1813.

At that time, four-thousand military men had been camped on the spot. Today, it seemed there must be almost that many people commemorating the event.

She laid out the red-checkered gingham cloth in a small space on the grass and arranged the luncheon.

"This must be old stuff to you. Since you live here, you must come every year," he said.

"No, I don't live here. This is my first time."

He seemed surprised. "I took it for granted you were from Burlington."

"No, a small town northeast of here called Riverfork."

"What a coincidence."

He was sitting beside her, sending thrills racing through her.

"We're practically neighbors. I'm from Milton."

It was her turn to be surprised. "Yes, we are neighbors. As close as it is though, I've never been there."

"You've got plenty of company," he laughed. "It's a quaint town with one store, a combined grocery-hardware, the big attraction as you drive into town; the library has plaques listing all the locals who've served our country in war. Even though you've never been there, if you and I were to search our family records, we would probably have common ancestors." He paused, "You know about those travelers and bundling boards."

She looked up. His eyes were teasing. "I've heard tales."

People were crowding in front of them and Warren stood to see what was happening on the lake. "Boats are lining up. I don't see how they'll sail with so little wind."

It hardly mattered to Sarah whether the boats moved or sank, she was so engrossed in Warren Hollis. Her stomach fluttered making it nearly impossible to touch the sandwiches or apple juice.

"It'll be awhile yet," he said, sitting down beside her again. "Time enough for you to tell me about Riverfork."

Censored, of course. She began with her first childhood memory, her father taking her by the hand and running down the hill from their house with her. "My legs were too short and I couldn't keep up with him, but it didn't matter, because he always laughed and encouraged me on. When I stumbled, he swooped me up. In those days, he always saved me."

"Reminds me of my father," said Warren, "except that he was always behind me, pushing...pushing 'Son,' he would say, 'you daydream too much. You don't keep your mind on what you're doing or the promises you make'."

"What promises?"

"I don't know. I suppose little things like taking books back to the library on time, raking leaves." Then he quickly changed the subject. "I see your legs did get longer."

Embarrassed, she pulled her skirt down to her ankles. "Yes, but by then, my father had left. He couldn't stand being with my mother and the backward kids..."

"Backward kids?"

"Yes, my brothers..." She didn't mention Louise.

Suddenly, he was quiet, slowly eating his sandwich, obviously deep in thought. Then he was aware of her again, broke off a piece and told her to open her mouth. He plopped the sandwich on her tongue, as seriously as if he were examining a child.

They both laughed and he hugged her. She closed her eyes, savoring the moment, wishing it could last forever.

The crowd was getting noisy.

"It must be time for the race to begin," he said, pulling her to her feet. They gathered the picnic supplies and he maneuvered them through the people until they came to the bluff overlooking the lake. They were crowded among hundreds of others sitting along the bluff, and it was possible to see most everyone else on the curving perimeter.

A gunshot went off, the signal for the race to start, but the boats were guided more by the enthusiasm of the spectators than by the wind. The race was over from the beginning. The boaters waited for the breeze that never came.

After awhile, Sarah, bored with the boats, shifted her position and looked at the people. From several yards away, she saw binoculars trained in her direction. Then the owner dropped them to her side. Sarah recognized her. Jane Barnett. Next to her was Emma Read.

Sarah's heart sank. She carefully removed Warren Hollis' arm from around her. "We have to leave," she said.

"Why?"

"We've been found out. Other student nurses are here."

"So what! Remember, they have to work with me. They'd better keep quiet."

She wasn't sure that mattered, but she gave in and stayed, her afternoon ruined. When it was over, he drove her back to the hospital, letting her off a block away in the protection of overhanging trees.

"I'll call you soon," were his parting words.

If I'm lucky enough to be around, she thought, heading for the hospital with the empty picnic basket.

*   *   *

That evening, Miss Bradford returned to the hospital after spending time alone in a Montpelier Hotel for a few days. Quickly reviewing activities during her absence, she looked at the record of student checkouts from the nurses residence. She was furious when she saw Sarah Morgan's name and called her to the office at once.

"Miss Morgan, you were not to leave the hospital grounds for the entire summer. Yet, I see you disobeyed yesterday. Who gave you permission to leave?"

"Miss Gibson."

"What was your reason?"

"To attend Abbie Kirley's birthday party."

"You should not have asked for any exceptions to your being grounded. You are, of course, aware that your behavior is cause for immediate dismissal."

"Yes, Miss Bradford."

"You are already grounded for several more months which puts me in a difficult position." She stopped, thinking. "Miss Morgan, you could be dismissed but I'm not considering that at this point. The very least that you can be given is a two-week suspension, time you will have to make up before graduation."

She opened Sarah's file on the desk before her. "I will notify your parents that you will be going home." She dialed the Morgan home in Burlington. To her surprise, Mrs. Morgan said, "Sarah is not welcome in our home," and hung up on her.

"When did you have a falling out with your mother?"

"She's my stepmother."

"Your parents are divorced?" She didn't wait for an answer for she had already decided that an unstable home life must be part of Sarah's rebelliousness.

"Then I will call your mother."

"I can't go there either."

This situation was more complex than Edwina had expected. "Why not?" She had a way of raising her voice on the final word, giving it more emphasis.

"I can't talk about it."

Since when could a student withhold information from the school of nursing? But she chose not to pursue the subject just then, not sure that she really cared. "Very well. In that case, I am extending your time without privileges to the end of the year."

"Yes, Miss Bradford."

"You may leave." She watched as the shaken girl left her office, wondering why she would use such an improbable excuse as Abbie Kirley's birthday party. On the fourth of July? Something else amazed Edwina. How had Abbie's secret been kept from the students for so many months?

She had another question, one much less amazing. Had Sarah also lied about Laura Upton's activities just before she'd died? Perhaps Sarah did know the whole story, the never found baby, the obstetrical instruments before Edwina's office door. As time went on, she was easily the most likely suspect for both.

Surely the student would eventually break down and reveal what she knew before the first of the year. Confinement had a way of curing students of secrets. Interesting, however, that Jane and Sarah must not have compared notes regarding Laura Upton. Nothing had ever come back to her.

Above all, Edwina prayed that Sarah would give her no reason to dismiss her. After all, the students had to staff the hospital and take care of the patients. And the number of students had decreased dangerously low to accomplish the mission.

* * *

As soon as she saw Jane, Sarah confronted her. "Did you tell anyone that you saw me at Battery Park?"

"When did I see you at Battery Park?"

Sarah stared at her. What was going on with her? She was like the three monkeys, see no evil, hear no evil, speak no evil.

Sarah dropped to her bed, defeated, reliving the experience in Miss Bradford's office. Why hadn't the Super mentioned Warren Hollis? Or was she saving that information for a latter time?

* * *

As Miss Bradford predicted, the fall months were miserable for Sarah. Warren Hollis was going to graduate from medical school in December making it even worse for her. She was lonely and waited and waited for a call or letter from him. But none ever came. Just to hear his voice, even if she couldn't see him. She never got away from the hospital or its oppressiveness, almost worse than her home during her growing-up years.

Along with the humiliation of being grounded were the daily reminders of a student's unimportance; standing at attention for doctors, instructors, graduate nurses and senior nursing students; always listening to instructions, never asking questions, expected to obey with no talking back. Hardly ever a kind word from the instructors, certainly to their minds, never an unnecessary word; having to get up to attend class during the day after working a twelve-hour shift the previous night; going to class on days off which meant no visits to town for shopping or the movies. Oh, how the students prayed for a Saturday or Sunday off when the doctors and nursing instructors weren't teaching.

But all of the students suffered the same schedule so it wasn't considered personal.

Being grounded was personal. Sarah was a prisoner with no outlets from work or study. It was during this period of deep gloom that she finally heard from Warren Hollis. He sent her a gold-engraved invitation to his graduation from the University of Vermont. She debated what to do while she ran her finger across the fine engraving, feeling the exquisitely raised letters.

She checked her calendar. His graduation would be December fifteenth. Of course, there was never any doubt as to her reply. She couldn't attend and she had too much pride to tell him the reason. So, it was with a heavy heart that she penned her regrets stating that she would be working that day.

She feared that she had let him down and that this would be their last correspondence. But following his graduation, he wrote a glowing letter while traveling in the Mediterranean, part of a two-month cruise given him by his parents.

He continued to send her letters during his travels which she concealed under her mattress along with his money. At Christmas, he sent her a Currier and Ives card of an elegant sleigh being pulled by high-stepping horses. In it rode a couple. That card was a terrible reminder of the day Miss Bradford rode them to Laura Upton's funeral in a similar setup.

After his return, he sent her a letter during his internship at the Greenbridge Hospital for the Insane. He wrote that as long as he lived, he hoped to never be in such a deplorable place again. Once he finished there, he was going to erase the place from his mind, forever.

And that was the last she heard from him. Every day when she checked the mail, it was as though her heart stopped while she reviewed every envelope, but none was ever from Warren Hollis.

Had he changed? Was there someone else? After all, her relationship with him had been one of the moment surrounding the tragedy of her brother's death. What other ties did they have to hold them together? Their day at Battery Park must not have been enough.

Sarah decided that she had best try to forget him. She was so conflicted. After all, the relationship had been complicated, too much on and off like a light switch.

On the fourteenth day of January, 1929, when she checked the morning assignments, there was an asterisk beside her name as well as four others. At the bottom of the page was the notation: "To Greenbridge until April fifteenth."

One day's notice before they were to leave for their psychiatric affiliation at the Hospital for the Insane. Nobody could have been as happy or excited as Sarah. There was no way that Miss Bradford could keep her grounded so far away.

And contrary to her plans to live and forget him, all she did was to forget that she'd ever had such a stupid idea. For, after all, Greenbridge was where Warren Hollis was assigned.

Chapter Eighteen

The four girls hardly slept that night after a frantic evening of packing and notifying their families. Early the next morning, Mrs. Dunning drove them to the bus station, fussing and worrying over them until they left for Greenbridge.

Even though the Hospital for the Insane was less than a hundred miles east of Burlington, the rainy weather made the journey difficult. There were places where the bus had to wait while a snow plow pushed aside the white fluff that had fallen in the night. The windows steamed as the bus lumbered through and over the white-blanketed Green Mountains. They passed through Morrisville and Hardwick, moving very slowly over a ice slick bridge above the Lamoille River, finally reaching the town of Danville where they turned off to Greenbridge.

A car from the institution met them and drove them to the hospital. It was located a mile outside town, on acres of snow-covered hills. A dozen desolate, brick buildings, united by brick-walls, loomed like black shadows in the twilight. A church spire pierced skyward from within the compound. There were no visible exits from the property.

Without signs of life, the scene was oppressively quiet. This changed as soon as the girls lugged their suitcases into the lobby.

Student nurses from other affiliating hospitals were already there, waiting in clusters. Soon the students were escorted to the dormitories by an orderly who carefully unlocked and locked each door they passed through on the way. The girls from Margaret Ward were dumped in one room which they would share for their three-month stay.

For all its internal security, Sarah and the others had heard many tales from classmates returning from the experience. They knew that Greenbridge was almost without restrictions during off-duty hours except for a ten p.m.

curfew. Dartmouth medical students also affiliated there, giving the girls a rush comparable to the opening of hunting season.

Best of all, the stories usually did not reach Miss Bradford.

That night the exhausted girls didn't even talk and fell into bed early. The next morning, Miss Markey, the nursing supervisor at Greenbridge Hospital, met them, her manner unusually calm, not with the tight control they were used to from the instructors at Margaret Ward. Miss Markey taught them the fundamentals of moving about in a psychiatric setting, rules concerning all hospital keys, locking and unlocking doors. She took them for a tour of the facilities and then she left them in the conference room with Dr. Maynard Whittemore, Chief Psychiatrist.

Sarah had a preconceived notion of the doctor for previous students had told of their experiences in his lectures. He was not handsome, his forehead too broad, his hair line receding. But his eyes were mesmerizing, nonjudgmental yet penetrating and he seemed to miss nothing. He slouched comfortably in a heavy leather chair, puffing contentedly on a pipe. For the rest of her life, the smell of slightly sweet pipe tobacco would bring back memories of Dr. Whittemore and the Hospital for the Insane.

The students had filed into the conference room and, when all were gathered, he gave the signal for them to be seated. They sat properly on the edges of their chairs as he began lecturing to them. After a few moments, he abruptly ordered them to relax, bringing them to frightened attention. When they realized he meant it, they leaned back in their chairs, imitating his casualness.

"Everything you will see in these mentally ill patients covers a hidden meaning that we try to identify," he said. "Sometimes we can only make suppositions but, for the most part, I think we are usually right."

His low tones, his quiet delivery, his eyes moving from one student to the next, set hearts on fire. This was something else Sarah knew. Student nurses became infatuated with him. But not her because she compared each man to Warren Hollis and they all came off wanting, second best.

After Dr. Whittemore finished his presentation, he signaled Bruce, a male orderly, a giant of a man whose arm muscles were as thick as his neck, to bring in the "cases" for that morning.

While Bruce went for the first patient, the doctor gave the students a preliminary picture of him.

"His name is Stewart. According to his parents, he stopped talking when he was nine-years-old, set their barn on fire and tried to immolate a younger brother, fortunately, without success. His family became afraid for their lives. They would tie Stewart to his bed at night and to a post in the yard during the day, but he often escaped. In desperation, they brought him here when he was eleven-years-old. He hasn't had a visitor in twenty-eight years…"

The story sent shivers through Sarah. Twenty-eight years…no visitors for twenty-eight years. A lifetime. She couldn't imagine such isolation from family, except, when she thought about it and if the last few years were a glimpse into her future, it could happen to her.

Bruce brought in Stewart. One of his legs was shorter than the other. His hair was gone from the right side of his head where he had pulled it out. He moved constantly, feeling the doorway, snaking his hands up the jamb, jumping to try and touch the ceiling. He moved along the wall, systematically spitting, Bruce keeping close watch on him, following wherever he went.

Stewart didn't seem to be aware of the students seated around the table. He passed behind the doctor who swivelled his chair around to face the patient.

"Stewart," the doctor said, getting his attention.

At first, Stewart looked at him as though he were another object and then a change came over him. "Cigarette, cigarette, cigarette," he repeated maniacally, jumping up and down, holding his grimy, yellowed fingers out to the doctor.

Sarah held her breath, wondering if the doctor would oblige, and if he didn't, how would Stewart react?

Dr. Whittemore reached into his pocket and handed Stewart a cigarette. After the doctor lit the cigarette, Bruce hurried Stewart from the room. "Miss Mitchell," said Dr. Whittemore. "Stewart will be your case for the next three months. He has a treatment program which you will monitor and do alongside him. You will take him to the dining room and eat meals with him. You can exercise with him in the gymnasium. You make whatever he makes in occupational therapy, and so on. At the end of the day, write notes about your day's activities."

Then the doctor spoke to the total group of students. "At the end of this month, each of you will start assembling your notes and at the end of your experience, you must turn in a paper describing your patient's behaviors and your reasons explaining the behaviors. You probably understand very little at this point. In three months, you will know a lot."

The conference room door opened again and Bruce brought in Alice, a slight, sullen woman who suddenly smiled when she saw the students in their crisp uniforms and caps. "Got a new bunch, eh, Doc? Giving them the full bullshit?" She laughed, delighted that she'd shocked them. Her hair appeared clean, but it was as wild as a bramble bush, her legs were banged and bruised. "He's full of it," she confided to them. And as if they didn't know what she was talking about, she spelled out bullshit carefully and then clamped her hand over her mouth in mock horror. "Oh, excuse me, Doctor Whittemore. We must be proper, mustn't we?" She tweaked his chin and pecked a kiss on his cheek.

He smiled as if he'd been through this routine before and knew what to expect.

After Alice had left the room, he explained to the students; "As you can see, Alice is hyperactive so we try to keep her busy. She's in charge of the clothing room, issuing clothes to patients who don't have their own. It isn't too demanding a job because the clothes are all the same, either men's shirts and pants or ladies dresses. Because of her manic-depressive illness, we know that she will become even more agitated, never sleeping. Then she will plunge into a depression and be sent to the ward for 'disturbeds'. She will be given hydrotherapy and the drug metralazone."

Sarah was assigned to Alice. A summary of the coming months flashed through her mind. How would she handle Alice when she became difficult? The thought gave her the willies.

When the doctor finished assigning patients, Miss Markey took the students to the examining room to explain procedures. She showed them the sensation tray used for neurological tests. It held bottles of solutions; salt, sugar, acetic acid, and quinine to test exactly what the patients could taste; peppermint, clove and camphor to check their sense of smell; cotton balls, tuning fork, a long pin to check skin feelings; an ophthalmoscope and flash light to examine the light reflex of the eyes; a percussion hammer to test reflexes, and a blue pencil for marking the skin; finally a pencil and pad for notes.

Miss Markey called for Bruce to bring in a patient. The orderly came back with a patient identified as Mr. Hudson, a intense man who cooperated with Miss Markey, tasting, smelling, obediently closing his eyes while she lightly pricked his skin.

When she finished with Mr. Hudson, she told Bruce to take along Aurelia Mitchell, a student nurse, and bring back Stewart. He came easily enough, but when Aurelia reached toward him with a cotton swab, he batted it from her hand and screamed obscenities, spitting, kicking, until the orderly locked him in a hold. Aurelia stood back, shaking.

Miss Markey smiled: "It appears that Stewart isn't going to cooperate today. He may be taken away. Miss Morgan, please go with Bruce and bring back Alice."

Aurelia Mitchell also went with them and they left Stewart at occupational therapy. On the way, they passed dozens of disheveled patients, some soiled with excrement, some pacing, some lying on the floor curled in on themselves. Some played supervised basketball, billiards, or ping pong. Some played at small table games in the gymnasium; dominos, checkers, or backgammon. When they saw Bruce, the patients viewed him warily and Sarah knew they were afraid of him. Bruce led her to the clothing room. They watched at the door while Alice threw gowns in a corner, pants on a table. She had neatly folded and shelved several garments.

They waited until she finished what she was doing. "Alice, will you please come with us?" Sarah asked.

Alice stuck up her middle finger. "Fuck-off!" Sarah turned to Bruce. "What do I do?"

Without a word, he reached over the half-door into the clothing room and picked Alice out. She scratched him as he plunked her on the floor. She threatened him with a clenched fist. "Watch it, Alice."

"You're not going to get no cooperation," he told Sarah, stating the obvious, as he shoved Alice along the hall.

In the examining room, even with Bruce keeping her arms pinned to her sides, the neurological examination was a disaster.

"Miss Markey's up to her malarkey," Alice chanted, over and over.

Disgusted, Miss Markey dismissed Alice.

When the ordeal was over and each student nurse had tried to examine her assigned patient using the sensation tray and failed, the supervisor summarized, smiling but not with the cynicism they would have seen from Miss Bradford.

"As you probably noticed, few mental patients follow our rules. You must learn your limitations with each patient and the methods to cajole him or her to your side. The skillful student can usually do that."

Sarah looked at the sensation tray, neatly rearranged to appear as when they first started the session. She realized it was nothing more than a front for a hopelessly custodial operation. Greenbridge was made up of chronics who never saw a sensation tray or anything else different except when new and dumb student nurses came to the hospital.

At mealtime, each student had an assignment in addition to her regular patient. At lunch time, Sara got tunnel duty. Her job was to move the patients along to the dining room. Aurelia was on tray duty. Mary Drury fed the disturbed chronics restrained by camisoles, jackets that pinned their arms to their sides. Eunice Thompson passed out silver to those who could have spoons.

Sarah had hoped that she would be in charge of directing Alice's care, but before the day was up, she knew that Alice was in control of both the situation and her.

That night, the girls dropped into bed, too exhausted to think of the boys from Dartmouth.

In the dark, Aurelia confessed that she was afraid of Stewart.

What false reassurances could they give her? They were all afraid of their own patients.

The next day, Sarah took Alice to breakfast and then to the clothing room where Alice dispensed garments as she pleased; pants to a woman, dresses to the men. "If you don't like it," she laughed raucously to one bewildered patient, "shove it up your ass." He threw the dress at her.

In spite of her rudeness, Alice seemed grateful when Sarah gave her assistance. Shortly before lunchtime, Sarah took Alice for a walk in the buildings. They went to the gymnasium where at least fifty women milled about, wandering around, some shouting, few seemed to have any purpose to what they were doing.

Several orderlies stood along the wall, scanning the crowd for trouble, ready to move in and restore order.

All Alice wanted to do was have a cigarette. She smoked, dropping ashes on the floor, paced back and forth with Sarah trying to keep up. As they walked around the gym, Sarah saw a figure sitting on the floor against a wall. Her black hair was matted and snarled. She had her face cupped between her hands and she rocked from side-to-side. She looked strangely familiar.

Sarah moved away from Alice to see the girl. When she got closer, she froze, barely able to form the name on her lips.

There was no mistaking. The girl didn't notice her and she moved closer, fearfully, and leaned down. "Abbie," she whispered.

The girl looked at her with no sign of recognition.

Sarah knelt beside her. "Abbie...it's me, Sarah."

The girl continued weaving back-and-forth.

"I'm snow. ..snow..." she repeated, idiotically.

Sarah reached out to embrace her, and Abbie grinned, escaped her grasp, got up from the floor and ran away.

One of the orderlies stopped her at the door and she sat down at his feet.

Sarah was aghast that she had provoked the sick girl. She turned back to where she'd left Alice who had seen her advantage and disappeared. Sarah panicked. She'd done the inexcusable, taken her mind off her own patient.

Desperately, Sarah went from building to building searching for her and found her in the last place she would have expected, the clothing room. But instead of folding and issuing clothes, she had opened the window and cold Vermont air blew into the room.

In a frenzy, Alice was tearing and heaving clothes out the window—pants, shirts, dresses, camisoles.

"Goddam son-of-a-bitchin' clothes," she yelled, scrambling for every last item in the laundry room.

Sarah ran to get Bruce who put Alice in restraints.

"Bastard...bastard...bastard," Alice singsonged. "Bitch...bitch...bitch..."

They dragged her to the section where the disturbeds were locked away. For ten hours that day, Sarah listened to Alice's obscenities and by nightfall, was sure that she, too, was insane.

Later, secure in her own dorm bed in the dark of night, she realized why Miss Bradford knew she had not been with Abbie Kirley on the fourth of July. Miss Bradford knew that Abbie had been at Greenbridge all along. She flushed with embarrassment at how she had blamed Jane Barnett for turning her in. How wrong she'd been.

The next morning at psychiatric conference, Dr. Whittemore spoke: "Yesterday, one of you agitated a young girl who tried to escape from the gymnasium. It is better that you stay away from patients who are not assigned to you since some cannot tolerate closeness."

Sarah knew he referred to her.

He smiled at the students and puffed on his pipe. "The patient does have an interesting history though. As you probably know, she was once a classmate of yours. But when illness took over, unresolved conflicts came to the surface in a distorted fashion.

"She always felt that her younger brother had taken their mother's affection from her. She expresses it in a very odd way and the few times when she breaks from her repetitious, 'I'm snow...I'm snow...', it's only to say that she threw her baby brother into a river." He paused. "Of course, that is an unfulfilled wish, but she suffers unbearable guilt as if she had actually done it. Now she feels that her mother died and abandoned her for being evil. Unfortunately, this poor girl doesn't know that her mother is in the Vermont Hospital for the Insane at Waterbury. Perhaps mental disease runs in her family."

The girls were stunned by the doctor's story and interpretation and that mental disease could be hereditary. But Sarah was stunned for another reason. Abbie's real story was more accurate than his interpretation. She finally knew what had happened to Laura Upton's baby and who had done it.

Chapter Nineteen

For the next ten days, Sarah took care of Alice in the "disturbed" unit. Alice berated her all day for keeping her a prisoner. It was very difficult for Sarah to keep her mouth shut for she was just as much a prisoner. Alice had to be spoon fed and, often, she knocked the spoon from Sarah's hand.

"Use persuasive techniques," Miss Markey had said in lecture.

Persuasive, indeed. If Alice listened, she ignored every word. She paced around the room, empty of furniture save for a bed and one chair, designed to cut down stimuli that might increase her agitation. And yet, it was hard to imagine her any more agitated.

Within an hour of coming on duty each day, Sarah was a wreck. She pleaded with her patient. "Please, Alice. Just let me bathe you. Let me cut your fingernails. Lie down Alice and I'll give you a massage. Why don't you be quiet, stop talking? It will relax you. Just for today, Alice, please don't bite or spit."

She exhorted her patient. "No, Alice. You get one cigarette an hour, if you're good. If you're not good, then you'll have to wait another hour."

Of course, Alice was not good and she wouldn't wait another hour. Waiting only increased her agitation. Sarah gave in and got rid of the rule about being good.

Alice lost weight and so did Sarah. She was told that Alice never slept, while she fell into a near coma as soon as she hit her own bed.

When she had first come to Greenbridge, she had dreamed of finding Warren Hollis, but she had never seen or heard of him there. Now he was the farthest person from her mind. It was only Alice, Alice, Alice.

After ten days of their wretched togetherness, Dr. Whittemore conceded that Alice was not getting better and ordered hydrotherapy.

Alice protested and went kicking and screaming, dragged from the quiet room to the baths by a determined orderly. "Okay, Alice. We're doing it my way." Alice wouldn't do it his way.

Sarah hurried along with them, carrying the bathing supplies. When Alice had been stripped of her dress, the orderly held her while Sarah rubbed her with lanolin, heavily on her hands and feet. Then she put a gown on her, stuffed cotton in her ears, a bathing cap on her head. When Alice was ready, the orderly locked his arms around her and put her in the hammock inside the tub, restraining her with a sheet.

Then Sarah turned on the water which would run continuously. It was Sarah's job to watch the thermometer so that the temperature of the water stayed at a constant ninety-eight degrees.

"Cigarette...give me a cigarette, you purple cunt."

"No cigarettes while you're in the bath..."

"Fuck yourself, fuck your mother, fuck your father, fuck, fuck, fuck..."

Sarah wondered if cotton in her own ears would shut out the obscenities, language she'd never heard in her life. She sat next to Alice through the long day, encouraging her to drink water. For a change, Alice cooperated, drinking all that was offered.

After the longest day of Sarah's life, she went off duty. When she returned the next morning, Alice was still in the tub. They took her out, but she was just as agitated, so they put her back in.

It took four days of treatment before Alice slept.

At night, Sarah's roommates wanted to talk, but she was too exhausted to concentrate on their problems. Eunice Thompson was piling up the squares she'd crocheted with her patient. Mary Drury had put her toilet articles on a small loomed mat she'd made.

Each night, Aurelia Mitchell brought another religious clay figure that she'd sculpted with Stewart that day. They'd finished "The Last Supper" and were working on figures of god, as Stewart interpreted god.

"Stewart doesn't like me," Aurelia said, adding the figure to the dresser top.

Sarah lay on her bed, a cool wash cloth to her forehead, trying to relieve the terrible headache she had at the end of each day from the tension of being with Alice.

"Maybe Stewart doesn't like anyone."

"He doesn't pay attention to anyone else. Only me."

"That means he respects you."

"No. He tells me to go away." She came and stood over Sarah. "I'm really afraid of him."

Sarah sat up, holding the washrag. "Aurelia, he's been here for years and he's never done anything. Dr. Whittmore wouldn't assign you to a dangerous patient."

"I'm not so sure."

Seeing her classmate's worried expression, Sarah made a decision. "Let's get out of here. Dwelling on these patients is making us just as loony." She put on a fresh skirt and blouse.

"Let's go to the dining room."

As they ate, Sarah could hear whispers behind them and suddenly two men sidled up and slid into chairs at their table.

"Hi," said one, leaning over to shake hands. "Are you willing to suffer the companionship of two dynamic, magnificent Dartmouth medical students?"

The two men bowed ceremoniously.

The girls stood as they were expected to do when superiors were around. The men weren't bad looking although, as far as Sarah was concerned, neither compared favorably to Warren Hollis. Too slick, too confident, too corny.

"But of course," said Aurelia, matching his continental air.

"Terrific. Let me introduce myself. I'm Malcolm Randall and this is Jonathan Hathaway." He turned to his colleague.

Within minutes, the girls had agreed to accompany them to a dance hall on the edge of town. Excitedly, they rushed back to their room, changed clothes and met the men in front of the main building.

Sarah expected they would have a car. She drew in her breath. What a car! A shiny, black Packard sedan. Imagine riding in such luxury.

It seemed a random pairing. Jonathan with Aurelia, Malcolm driving with Sarah beside him. He tore out of the long drive, accelerating as fast as possible, taking the turns on the dirt roads on two wheels, throwing them from side-to-side, laughing. It was crazy, but no more crazy than the month they'd already spent at Greenbridge.

Malcolm slowed down as they reached town, driving carefully through the small business so as not to attract attention from the police, past the post-office, grocery store, American Legion hall, the library. When they were out of town, Malcolm laid on the accelerator once again.

Before long, they came to Hayes Cove, a dance hall. They went in and could hardly see for the cigarette and cigar smoke giving an other-world mist to the room. Juke box music blared Fletcher Henderson's "Wabash Blues". Girls dressed in high heels and short skirts, some with sleeveless tops, danced with partners wearing wide-legged pants with key-chains draped from a pocket.

Although President Franklin Roosevelt had changed Prohibition's Volstead Act to allow the sale of beer, no hard liquor was allowed. But it was plain that patrons were drinking more than beer.

Jonathan railroaded a table for them and disappeared to get them drinks. He came back with four glasses, daringly balancing them and placed them before the girls with a flair suitable to a well-trained butler.

They yelled "Cheers!" to one another over the din, clanking glasses all around, laughing.

What a release to be away from the mental hospital with normal people having fun. Sarah relaxed for the first time in weeks, the daily episodes with crazy Alice seemed remote.

They laughed, they drank, they danced to "Fidgety Feet", and then switching partners, to Louis Armstrong's trumpet playing, "Keep a Song in Your Soul". When Sarah questioned the odd taste of her coke, Jonathan told her that it was a taste peculiar to Greenbridge.

The smoke in the room was making her giddy. A thought occurred to her. "Have either of you ever heard of an intern by the name of Warren Hollis?" she asked.

The medical students looked at each other. "From what medical school?"

"University of Vermont."

Malcolm smiled tolerantly. "Hardly. We're from Dartmouth, remember?"

She let his sarcasm pass, checked her watch, barely able to focus on the hands. Aurelia, getting into the spirit of the crowd, accepted the first cigarette of her life, puffed hopelessly, choking until she got the hang of it.

Sarah was dizzy. "I've got to get out of here. The air is making me sick."

"It'll pass," said Malcolm, dragging on his cigarette, playing with his glass.

"Please, take me back. It must be nearly curfew."

"So…"

She didn't like the tone of his voice. "If we're late, we'll be suspended."

"Nah, do you really believe all that stuff?"

"Yes." The room was going around. Aurelia was leaning against Jonathan, dreamily allowing herself to be dragged around the dance floor.

"I'm leaving." Sarah stood and had to brace herself against the table. The room whirled and whirled. She staggered to Aurelia. "C'mon. We have to leave." Aurelia opened her eyes and stared at Sarah vacantly. "Just a few more minutes." Her speech was slurred. They'd never get past the house matron in their condition.

She yanked Aurelia away from Jonathan. "We'll wait in the car for you," she said, pulling Aurelia through the crowd.

As the girls got out the front door, a car was stopping. Two men stepped out, passing them in the nearly dark parking lot. Sarah held her breath as they went by and then helped Aurelia into the back seat of the Packard. She closed the door, shivering from the ice-cold night air.

She lay back against the seat, her head foggy, watching the entrance of Hayes Cove for a sign of the medical students.

Suddenly, the front door of the dance hall flew open. People came running out, pushing and falling over one another, racing down the street, leaping into cars, an urgent silence accompanying their getaways.

Malcolm was among them, leaping into the Packard and gunning off without waiting for Jonathan. "Raid," he muttered, slamming the accelerator to the floorboard. She had been right. There was more than beer being served.

This time, Malcolm didn't bother slowing down as they passed through town. Sarah was sure she was going to be sick. When he came to the turn-off to the long road leading to the hospital, they hit something and the car buckled. Malcolm slammed against the steering wheel, grunting when the breath went from him. There was a terrible roar from outside. Sarah fell to the floor.

Aurelia asked over and over: "What happened?"

When Malcolm had recovered his breath, he jumped out of the car. Sarah and Aurelia followed. They knew they'd hit an animal because of its screams.

Sarah retched when she saw the huge beast, its side split open, blood splattering on the snow and the front of the Packard, dark speckles on the lights showed as they were trained on the crying animal. The cow, throwing her head around in a frenzy, tried to stand and couldn't. Sarah released a rope from around the cow's neck that had caught on the car's bumper. The cow scratched the ground and pulled herself away from the car. She struggled to the roadside, where suddenly, she stopped moving and was quiet.

Malcolm examined the cow. "She's dead," he said, kicking the broken animal.

Seeing him brutalize the dead cow cleared Sarah's head from the drugs she knew they'd poured into her drink, and she began beating on Malcolm's chest. "What kind of a bastard are you, anyway?" Alice had taught her something, after all.

"Get away!" He gave her a shove.

She hauled Aurelia out of the car. "We're walking back to the hospital."

The two ran and stumbled along the snow-covered road. Behind them they could hear the engine of the Packard turn over, but they never heard if it started.

When they reached the hospital, Sarah knocked on the locked door and the matron opened it.

"Sorry, if we're late." Sarah held her breath. "We were out walking and went farther than we thought."

The matron didn't give them a second glance as they sailed past her and hurried down the hall. Was it possible they were safe? They would never have gotten by with this at Margaret Ward with Mrs. Dunning sniffing the students and checking their eyes.

The next day, the news was all over Greenbridge Hospital: the raid at Hayes Cove; the medical student who was rounded up and thrown in the St. Johnsbury jail and another medical student who had wrecked his father's car when it killed a cow on the road leading to the hospital.

The medical students were suspended from Dartmouth and the laughing stopped.

Nothing was said about girls being present.

As upset at the cruelty, as disappointed as she was with the medical student, he made her think of Warren Hollis. He would never have been so dishonorable and heartless, angry with a cow he'd injured, stupidly taking advantage of her. For what?

And with all the questions as to who the medical students might be, Sarah got up the courage to ask about Dr. Hollis. Miss Markey said Dr. Hollis had left weeks ago. To where, she did not know.

* * *

By the end of the month, President Roosevelt introduced the New Deal, a string of policies and agencies with alphabet soup titles, that were supposed to bring the United States out of its economic slump.

For Sarah and the other students at Greenbridge, it was the same old deal.

Sarah continued to care for Alice who had left the manic phase of her illness to become mute and profoundly depressed. Because she was no longer agitated and unmanageable, she was allowed out of the "disturbed" ward. She didn't even hold out her fingers for a cigarette. She had to be spoonfed, but would only suffer through the annoyance and tedium of a few bites.

Meanwhile, Aurelia watched Stewart eat everything on his plate and beg for hers. She complied, counting the hours when she would be through with him.

To the students, it seemed they'd been in nurses training for a lifetime, but they were just reaching the midpoint.

And they had gotten a secondary education in handling the roving students from Dartmouth who hung around like bees hunting for flowers to pollinate. Even though Sarah thought seriously only of Warren Hollis, she went to Hayes Cove dance hall a few more times. She loved jazz dancing and flapper clothes, and wore her short, chiffon-pleated dress and high heels.

After her disastrous first experience, she carried her own soft drink in her purse, never again risking the possibility of being drugged.

To insure their safety, the girls agreed that a date for one meant a date for all. So it was not uncommon to see the girls from Margaret Ward in a car with a lone Dartmouth student. The men complained bitterly that the girls were making conquests impossible to which they smiled demurely. Precisely the point.

On their last day at Greenbridge, there was an air of excitement. The patients were unusually high. There was a restless feeling running through the dining hall, recreation areas and occupational therapy departments, rising as the morning progressed.

All the affiliating nursing students would be leaving to be replaced by a new group the following week. Lunch was to be their last meal together. The Margaret Ward students would leave at one in the afternoon to make it back to West Vermont Hospital by nightfall. The drive would not take nearly as long as the trip coming, for most of the snow had melted and run off into swollen rivers.

Sarah took Alice aside in the clothing room to say goodbye to her. "I'm leaving today," she said, sitting across from the mute woman who looked up only briefly. "I hope you'll miss me just a little because I'll be thinking about you a lot."

Without warning, Alice reached over and patted Sarah affectionately and, although she said nothing, there were tears in her eyes. Sarah threw her arms around the patient, broke down and wept with her.

After a few moments, she wiped her eyes and lead Alice to the tunnel where it was time for Sarah to do tunnel duty, getting the patients to lunch. Patients were beginning to crowd through and for the last time Sarah urged them on.

"Come along…come along, there's no reason to stop here…move on.. .move on…"

* * *

In the occupational therapy room where Aurelia was putting the finishing touches on the last god figure she would have to sculpt, Stewart was nervous, walking in circles, around and around the room. He had just started a new clay figure that morning but left it after a few minutes.

At lunchtime, Aurelia put the figures away for drying and took Stewart by the hand to lead him down the hall. She could feel his tenseness. They reached the tunnel where dozens of patients pushed along to the dining room. She could hear Sarah's voice and repetitious refrain, "Come along.. .move on…"

It was noisy, but when there was a pause in their progress and movement in the tunnel stepped, Aurelia talked to Stewart. She couldn't put it off any longer.

"Stewart, I'll be leaving this afternoon. I've really enjoyed taking care of you." She lied, hoping there was some conviction of truth in her voice.

Stewart became more nervous. Was he distressed at losing her after their three-month almost daily relationship? Was she making a mistake and upsetting him? Would it have been better not to say goodbye? Or was he just upset with the crowd of people who prevented their moving forward in the tunnel?

As these questions spilled across her mind, Stewart turned on her. "You're lying. You're not really leaving. You've told me that before and you keep on following me anyway. You've been following me around all my life."

Aurelia was scared and didn't know what to say. Where had he gotten that idea?

Stewart rambled on: "You followed me from Nebraska. And then from Florida. Everywhere I go, you follow me, telling me the same lie, and now you're doing it again. You know I'm leaving to go back to Nebraska and you're telling me the lie so you think I won't know you when you come after me again. You're going to follow me, but you're not going to get away with it again."

He sounded so lucid and so crazy. She had never heard him say this much. "No, Stewart.. .I've never followed you." She could feel her throat tighten. She couldn't understand his irrationality. "I'm telling you the truth."

"No, you're not." In the crowded tunnel where everyone was jammed together, he shoved her against the patients pressing against them.

She lost her footing and tried to grab something, anything, to hang on to. But Stewart was her only support. He had fallen on top of her. They were both on the floor and he began screaming, horrible, guttural sounds coming from his drooling mouth, slobber running on her. At first she was confused, unable to believe what was happening, but as his hands became vises around her neck, she knew what he was going to do. She had never known such paralyzing fear in her life and she couldn't get her breath. With tremendous strength, she fought back, scratching and beating his arms and head. He wriggled around, trapping her arms under his knees and as she arched her back to relieve the pain in her arms, he pressed harder. Her neck was in agony and waves of nausea erupted and vomit forced up in her throat, falling back into her lungs. She fought and fought, choking and choking.

"Quit following me! Quit following me!" Stewart screamed wildly. Other patients were yelling, drowning him out. Aurelia tried to cry out, but nothing came because her throat was cut off. She battled in panic, her head feeling as though it were going to burst, her eyes pop. Black spots danced crazily before her, but there was no releasing his strangle hold. She had no more strength, not even for thinking. In the haze, she felt herself relax.

She heard Sarah crying hysterically: "Stop! Stop!"

Aurelia felt a numbness engulfing her, almost as if her body were disconnected from her head and neck. The colors she saw settled to greens and reds and yellows and a kind of peace came over her and she no longer felt the need to fight.

* * *

Sarah hadn't known what was happening in the tunnel, but suddenly the line of patients stopped moving and she heard terrible screaming. It sounded like Stewart. Over and over, he kept repeating, "Quit following me! Quit following me!" His voice didn't even sound human, more like the screeching of a crow. The other patients had caught his frenzy and were stamping and shoving each other in the tunnel. Sarah tried to force her way through them, pulling away first one and then another. There must have been two dozen of them flopped on one another, yelling, screaming, cursing, kicking.

Male orderlies were yanking the patients out of the pack and shoving them along in the tunnel. It took several minutes before order was restored. When all the patients were separated and heading toward the dining room again, a form lay sprawled on the floor of the tunnel.

Sarah screamed. "Oh, my god! Aurelia!" Her face was purple and her mouth hung open, drooping to one side. Her neck was black and blue from someone's hands and fingers.

Somebody brought a stretcher and placed the still figure on it, covering her. They hurried her to the infirmary. Sarah was sure she was dead, but when they got to the examining room and Dr. Whittemore came in, they found a thready pulse and Aurelia's chest moved slightly.

They worked on her, but it didn't seem as though anything helped.

In shock, Sarah completely forgot about Alice and lunch. Miss Markey sent her to the dormitory where Sarah packed her and Aurelia's clothes. When she had all their belongings in the suitcases, she lugged them to the lobby where they were taken and placed on the bus.

They left shortly after one in the afternoon, leaving Aurelia Mitchell behind, unconscious in the infirmary. The girls were told that her parents were already on their way from Waterbury to be with her and that Miss Bradford had been notified of the tragedy.

Sitting by herself on the bus, Sarah held a box of clay gods which Aurelia had made with Stewart. She didn't see the passing landscape for a veil of tears clouded her eyes.

Instead she saw the faces of departed classmates. Their class had started with fifteen students, the number which met with Miss Bradford's approval. After all, hadn't Miss Florence Nightingale's first class consisted of fifteen beginning students?

Beginning was far from the end at Margaret Ward School of Nursing and the original roster was now reduced by several. First to go had been Susan Caldwell who left after the first month, ostensibly because she couldn't sew. Then Laura Upton died and Abbie Kirley went insane. Hannah Davis declined to return after her suspension was up. And now Aurelia...

Sarah's grief turned to anger at the helplessness she felt, the senselessness of those lives changed or destroyed by their contact with nursing, with Miss Bradford, Miss Gibson, Dr. Palmer, Greenbridge, and patients like Stewart.

For the rest of the journey, she fiercely clutched the gods wondering why the crazy people had more control over others than the ones who were supposedly all right. She still had not come to terms with it when they arrived back at the hospital.

But for the time being, the subject was closed. For two letters waited for her that meant even more change.

One was from Warren Hollis saying that he missed her. His message was the news that he would be returning to study surgery at West Vermont Hospital. She could not decipher the postmark from where it was sent.

The second letter was from her sister Beatrice who had located her through their father. She hoped that Sarah would attend her wedding to Charles Parker, their cousin on their mother's side. Sarah had never heard of him.

She read the date of the wedding. It had been more than a month ago.

That evening she penned a reply, explaining why she hadn't been present. She took ten dollars from her secret hiding place, money rightfully belonging to Warren Hollis, and tucked it in the envelope with her note. She also added the hope that their mother was well and, of course, that she prayed Elbert was no worse.

Chapter Twenty

A month passed and Sarah still hadn't heard from Beatrice about the belated wedding gift. If she'd received it, had she doubted Sarah's excuse or been unforgiving as in the days when they were growing up?

Or was it their mother, Lillian, continuing to poison the sisters against one another? She could hear Lillian self-righteously reciting from the bible: *"Sin makes its own hell and goodness in its own heaven,"* while adding the usual, "There's nothing I can do about Sarah. Your sister is selfish."

Her mother's and sister's feelings and opinions of her mattered less now. Too much had happened. Too many tragedies had crossed her life since she'd last seen them for her to care about things when she couldn't help.

Besides, Warren Hollis, a good distraction, had come back into her life, unexpectedly, surprisingly. A week ago, after breakfast, when she had come out of the hospital cafeteria, there he was, behind her in the basement corridor. It seemed as if he'd come out of nowhere. After her initial embarrassment, she laughed, but when Jane Barnett looked at her strangely, Sarah quickly apologized and started to hurry away.

He grabbed her arm. "Hey…what's the hurry?"

"Not here," she whispered.

"Then where?" He spoke loudly.

She brushed him away. "I can't talk now."

Other passing students gave them curious glances.

Warren had the most evil grin. "Why can't you talk?" He knew. He knew. She wanted to pound her fists into him. "Dr. Hollis, I must go."

"Where?"

This was her chance. "Women's medical." He let her go.

Later that morning, he came to women's medical as she'd hoped and feared he would. He stood in front of her as she set up her medicine tray.

"We can't go on meeting this way," he said.

"You're right about that," she said, not looking up. With her luck, the head nurse or another student nurse might come about now.

Or, as it turned out, Miss Gibson. When she came in, Sarah gave Warren a beseeching look and he began firing orders at her as though he'd been at it for some time.

".. .when that is finished, place the patient on her right side. If the pain continues, notify me."

"Yes, Dr. Hollis."

With that, he left.

Sarah watched as the ward door closed.

Now, as if waiting for him to be gone, Miss Gibson spoke: "Good morning, Miss Morgan."

"Good morning, Miss Gibson." Sarah waited respectfully, but her instructor did no more than look over the tray she was preparing. She seemed to be planning to say something, but she didn't and, without another word, left.

Sarah was so rattled that she could hardly get through the morning's work. She couldn't keep running into Warren Hollis. Eventually, something would be said, because student nurses were not supposed to fraternize with doctors. There would be repercussions and a price to pay.

At the end of the day, she dropped a note in his box in the medical director's office, praying that the secretary would be too busy to pay any attention to her.

The note read: "Flynn's Theater. Two p.m. Saturday."

She left the office, amazed at her boldness. But who would know that she wrote it? She left no name, only the message.

She never slept Friday night from the excitement of her next day's plans. And also the fear that this would be 'Sarah's folly'.

She dressed in her finest skirt and sweater, snuck a pair of high-heeled shoes in her over-sized purse to exchange for her flats on the bus as soon as she was away from West Vermont Hospital.

She waited outside the Flynn Theater until the very last minute before buying her ticket and going in. She watched Marlene Dietrich in "Sign of the Cross" by herself because Warren Hollis never showed up.

She came out of the theater feeling humiliated and downhearted. It had been a mistake to be forward. A lady never made overtures to a gentleman. Now, what would she do when and if she ever saw him again?

She found out on the following Wednesday.

He came up to women's medical and held out the note to her. "Do you know anything about this?"

She turned away, blushing, opening a drawer to get matches to light her alcohol burner.

"Well," he said, very sternly.

"I'm sorry, Dr. Hollis," she stammered. "I'm very busy."

"You didn't say which Saturday."

She tried to reach the counter where her supplies were, but he blocked her way.

"Which Saturday?" he repeated.

She certainly wasn't going to tell him it had passed.

She looked squarely at him and lied. "I don't know what you're talking about."

"I'm talking about this note. It was in my box this morning."

"This morning?"

"Yes."

So that was it. He didn't pick up his mail very often. Her note had been there for days. "This next Saturday." She felt so stupid that she didn't know whether to laugh or cry.

It was a good thing she did neither for here came Miss Gibson.

Warren Hollis slipped the note in his pocket. "The patient certainly seems to be improving," he said. "Perhaps we can discharge her this coming Saturday, Miss..." He stopped and squinted at Sarah's name pin. "...Morgan."

She thought quickly. "I'll tell the charge nurse," she said, observing protocol for Miss Gibson's benefit.

After he'd left, Miss Gibson remarked, "That is the second time I've seen that doctor talking to you."

"Yes, Miss Gibson," she said. "He's very attentive to his patients."

"Indeed, it appears so. Even for patients who are not his. Miss Morgan, he has no patients on this ward."

"Really?" Sarah furiously poured the pills. "Then why does he give me orders for some of them?" As soon as she said it, she realized how lame her comment had been.

"I'm sure I don't know...if you don't," the instructor said dryly and left.

As the weekend neared, Sarah questioned the wisdom of going to the Flynn Theater. She was traveling a dangerous path and would eventually be found out. But as her reservations increased, so did her anticipation. Her heart cried out that any sacrifice or chance was worth just one minute with Warren Hollis.

Well, almost, she chided herself. Don't get crazy and ruin your life for just one minute.

They met in the darkness in the last row of the Flynn Theater and sat through two showings of Greta Garbo in "Grand Hotel," holding hands the entire time.

At first intermission, they parried.

"You are very mysterious," he said, "leaving unsigned notes."

"You are even more mysterious, not answering them for a week."

"A week?" His surprise was genuine.

"Yes. I should be used to it though. You send me postcards with no dates or return addresses. I never know when I'm going to hear from you or when you're suddenly going to show up again."

"Sometimes I don't know myself."

"You were supposed to be at Greenbridge Hospital when I was there, but I learned that you'd been gone for weeks."

"I couldn't stand that place. I thought I might like mental diseases, but I hated every day of it," he said. "One morning, I got out of bed and said, 'forget it', resigned and left. Before I knew it, I was on the bus and never looked back. It's a pity that I didn't know you were going to be there. I might have stayed on a little longer."

"It's just as well you didn't. It was a sad experience." She told him about Aurelia Mitchell. Sarah knew it had affected him because he was thoughtful, drawing her closer to him. "Do miserable people have the right to destroy us?" he asked.

She didn't have an answer and the movie came on the screen again. All she could think of was that Stewart was happy sometimes, especially when he had a cigarette.

In May of their third year, the students received their last formal classroom lecture from Dr. Palmer. When they had started training, the class required two rows of chairs. Now the students who remained sat in a single row facing the doctor.

Sarah was sure she detected a tremor in his voice and a misting of his eyes as he announced to them that he had enjoyed their time together.

"So many changes," he sighed, looking over the group. But he didn't go on to describe the changes.

When the brief lecture was finished, the girls filed from his classroom.

* * *

For almost a year, she and Warren met in Flynn's Theater. She'd take the bus to downtown Burlington by herself, pay her way into the theater, and would protest when he insisted on reimbursing her. It was ironic when she owed him so much. As it was, the money usually came from the fund she was saving to repay him.

With him at her side, she fell in love with Gary Cooper in "Farewell to Arms," sure that he bore a resemblance to Warren Hollis. Was it possible to be in love with two men at the same time, she wondered?

They adopted a ritual. Just before the lights in the theater went on, he would kiss her. She dreamed for that moment when he touched his lips to hers, caressed her cheek, buried himself against her neck sending waves of passion through her. Oh, she wanted him so...oh, for the day when they weren't held back because she was a student nurse.

She never allowed him to take her to dinner or walking, insisting that it was too dangerous.

He teased her. "Let me take you to the Black Cat Cafe for a late meal."

"No, we'd be seen."

"Whoever saw a black cat at night?"

She pretended to hit him, picked up her purse and left him in the theater, knowing that he would be smiling to himself at his outrageous teasing. He probably thought she took the schools rules and regs too seriously. Oh, what he didn't know.

A fantasy formed in her mind, a fantasy she hoped would eventually come true. Someday, he would ask her to marry him. Her happiness spilled over into her work. Her self-confidence zoomed, her nursing skills became expert. Before, she had resented the senior students who ordered her around unreasonably so that, in a morning, she might do eighteen bladder instillations, a dozen catheterizations, or thirty injections.

Always, the seniors gave the same excuse, "You need the experience."

Now it didn't bother her. She flew through her work, massaging the bodies of the patients delicate from illness, never allowing a reddened area of skin to break down. She sterilized water on the alcohol burner with the screw-in spoon used to mix the hypodermic solution, hardly aware of what she was doing, for her mind was faraway with dreams of Warren Hollis.

At the end of summer, he had changed his future course once again. After his stint of surgery ending in two weeks, Warren told her he was going to New York's Cornell University to study genetics. After that he would make a final decision about his life's work. He had narrowed his choices to surgery or genetic research.

Because she was upset at his leaving and contrary to her good sense, she agreed to meet him on the hospital grounds and they went for a walk down to the Winooski River, the water moving lazily in the humid August. She felt an indescribable emptiness when she realized they would be parting. He said goodbye as they sat on the river bank watching the crystal water. A large bush protected them from prying eyes and they idled away the time until she had to get back to the residence and change into her uniform for afternoon class.

Warren poked at the water's edge with a stick. "I'll come back for your graduation," he promised.

"There isn't any graduation. One day, after we've put in the required hours, we're finished."

"That's all right. I'll come back anyway."

"That's weeks from now," she cried, hardly able to bear the thought of being separated from him that long.

"The time will go by very fast," he said, the stick bumping against a hard object. He fished for it, retrieving it from the dirt he'd swirled, and washed it off. It was a large spoon and he handed it to her.

"This looks like one of the ladles from the kitchen in the nurses residence," she said, debating whether or not to save it. In the end, she tossed it back in the river.

She rested against him, dreading the moment when they would have to part. His feelings must have been similar for he gathered her tenderly in his arms and then began kissing her with such passion that it frightened her. She found herself pulling away from him. No, she mustn't let herself be caught up in anything this dangerous. After all of her fantasies of wanting him to control her, take her, now that the moment had come, caution came as a companion. And then she realized that it was her own passion that she feared.

He seemed to sense her feelings, for instead of urging her on, he let her go and impulsively took off his school ring. It was gold with a ruby in the center. He slipped it on her ring finger. "I want you to have this," he said.

It was much too large. They laughed as he moved it to her middle finger where the fit was better. She closed her hand to keep the ring from dropping off, kissed him, thanking him and quickly stood up for she could feel that she was about to cry.

"Please don't say goodbye," she said, a lump rising in her throat.

"Sarah, everything's going to be all right," he said, softly.

She hurried away from him, up the hill, with the unbearable sadness and the terrible thought that their partings always seemed so final.

She wiped away the tears as she entered the residence. When she passed the study, Emma Read and Miss Gibson were talking, seated side-by-side on the sofa with not an inch separating them.

Sarah rushed up the stairs, hoping they hadn't noticed her.

Chapter Twenty-One

Warren Hollis was only partly right about the next several months passing rapidly. For Sarah, it was true when she was working. But off duty, when she had too much time to dwell on her memories with him, it seemed an eternity since she'd seen him last or before she would see him again. She couldn't write to him because she didn't know where he was. Even though he'd sent her postcards from his travels in the past, he was just not a letter writer.

She prayed for her graduation date. For hadn't he promised to come back then?

After their last afternoon together, Sarah went back to the residence and straight to bed for she was to begin night duty for a month. From now until October when they would have enough hours to be finished, the students would be used anywhere in the hospital to round out their experience.

If Miss Bradford felt a student needed more emergency room work, she was sent there: If more scrubbing experience, off she went to the operating room. In reality, the assignments were not designed to meet the needs of the students, but, rather, the graduate nurses. It seemed that the girls either received assignments they formerly detested, or where the charge nurse wanted her back because the student had proved exceptional her first time through.

Also, something else had happened to change hospital nursing. In those days, a patient who wanted personal services or needed more than minimal nursing care automatically hired a private nurse. Since the United States was still in a depression, few people could afford the extra cost. So fewer and fewer graduate nurses were called in on cases which meant that they were out of work.

That didn't mean that plenty of patients didn't need private nurses as private nurses were defined in those days. It meant that the students added the hospital care that these patients required to their daily assignments. From then on, each student had too much to do, a situation that never changed, even when times were good. Forevermore, hospitals always hired too few graduate nurses to get the work done. Students were used to meet the hospital's service needs and not the student's learning needs. Eventually, years later, hospitals gave up their schools of nursing with the excuse that they were too expensive to run. This meant that hospitals no longer had student nurses to provide nursing care. Still, hospitals didn't hire enough graduate nurses.

In those days of economic depression, national crisis and poverty, illness as self-indulgence was hardly possible or acceptable. There were few "nervous" cases coming into a hospital such as people who needed respite from a hard life, the unemployed, a depressed husband and father, or a sick, pregnant wife and mother.

Sarah lost track of time. The weeks flew by and could be counted only by the stack of uniforms she took to the laundry each Monday and picked up the following Thursday.

Spring became summer and, without warning, Warren Hollis showed up in September. She had gone to breakfast at the hospital and he grabbed her in the basement hall when she came out of the cafeteria as he'd done before. Naturally, she was completely unprepared and flustered. After her initial shock, it was all she could do to keep from throwing her arms around him. Even though he was a month earlier than she'd expected, she should be used to his ways by now.

"Why didn't you write?"

"Because," he said, grandly, "I prefer to be the master of surprise."

"That you are."

He walked beside her down the hall. "I wanted to see you before I leave for California…"

"California…" She suddenly felt weak. "Why? That's so far away. It's like moving to another continent."

"It is, but I have been offered a research position there and I can also do surgery."

They were in the hall by the elevator, where fate had brought them together once before when she had saved his life. Her mind was a turmoil.

"I'm lost for words," she said, wondering if she should tell him the truth. He might as well be going to a remote planet touched only by stars. "Warren, this is a terrible shock." She shook her head in disbelief.

"I know." He was apologetic. "I was afraid it would be, so I've set aside the whole week to be with you. I'm hoping you can get the days off."

She tried to get time off but couldn't. They had to grab her free hours and cling to them jealously, getting double value in memories. Working nights made it difficult and she went without sleep to be with him, meeting him at Flynn's movie house in the afternoon, where they relived the past and the present. As before, they had to be discreet, careful not to be seen.

After the movie, they would walk down to the dock beside the Lyman Coal Company. They fell in love with the moonlight over Lake Champlain and they would sit on the beach, watching the orange glow settle across the channel on the Adirondacks over New York, the bright arms of the glow leaving sterling wrinkles on the lake.

They came to know every bend, bush and rock for two miles along the waterfront. They didn't always talk, but would hold hands quietly, walking back and forth along the lakefront. One evening, they would head north, the next evening, they would go in the opposite direction, their sights always set on the waters that, in a way, symbolized their present. One night, storm clouds came, and she had a premonition, pushing away the idea that their future would be heavy with dark clouds. She literally had to shake her head trying to get rid of the thought.

The evenings went by too fast and she would get back to the residence just at curfew.

Mrs. Dunning remarked as she noted the time in the sign-out book. "My, you do like movies...*"*

"Yes." Oh, how she liked movies. Mrs. Dunning could never know how much she liked movies.

The night Warren was to leave was a Saturday. He drove very slowly back to the hospital and just as he was about to let her off, she took hold of him. "Not yet. I can't bear the thought of this being the end."

Warren turned the car around and drove to their hidden area two blocks from the hospital. They left the car there and, holding hands, walked down the hill to the Winooski River to the place where he had given her his class ring, the ring that hung around her neck with a chain long enough for her to touch and hold the ring whenever she thought of him.

Even though it was dark, the sound of the river and light from the moon above led them to their special spot protected by heavy bushes. He spread a blanket over the grass at the river's edge. Gently, he took both her hands in his. "Let's sit for awhile and say our goodbyes."

"I don't like to think of goodbye," she said. "It scares me." She pulled her hands from his and began twisting her ring. "I've said too many goodbyes in my lifetime."

He went down to his knees, taking her down with him. Laughing, he said, "It's not goodbye. It's *au revoir.*" He had a special way of laughing, different than anyone else. His eyes would close and he'd toss his head back and make devilish throaty sounds. It always made her laugh, even now, when she was so nervous.

"I'll miss your...you," she corrected, tearing up at the same time. "I can't stand the thought of your being so far away. It's upsetting."

He cupped her face in his hands. "I haven't left yet," and kissed her tenderly on the mouth, then pulled her down on the blanket.

She buried her head in his shoulder as he stroked the back of her head. "I'll think of you every minute and write you everything that happens," he said. "Soon I'll send you train tickets and we'll be together again. It won't be long, I promise."

She lifted her head to look at him. "Will the tickets be my graduation present?"

He looked at her with soft, gentle eyes as he answered. "No. They will be our graduation present."

"Those are beautiful words," she said. As much as she wanted to believe them, in her heart, she continued to fear their separation. She turned over on her back and gazed at the stars. In the distance, she thought she could hear the crackling of fire crackers and it brought back memories of their picnic on Independence Day.

She hoped this wouldn't be her independence day. She didn't want to be independent. She wanted to cling to him forever. "Did you hear that?" she said in a very small voice.

"You mean, the firecrackers?"

"Yes. Somebody has the holidays mixed up."

"It's possible but I thought it was my signal to tell you that I want to give the rest of my life to you and know that I will always have you."

He rolled over on top of her and kissed her passionately. She readily responded, grasping him with both of her arms. "You'll always have me, Sarah," he promised. "There will never be anyone else."

His hand slipped up underneath her skirt between her legs and he caressed her outside her panties. She spread her legs further apart and pressed against him and then he slipped her panties down below her knees. She kicked them off along with her sandals as he continued to gently finger each fold hidden beneath her pubic hair. "I've wanted you for so long," he murmured. "Can I have you now?"

He barely heard her say, "Yes". But her movements told him she wanted him, too.

He slipped her dress over her shoulders. She removed her bra as he removed his shirt and pants. Then, for the first time, they were skin to skin. He kissed her breasts, slid down to her belly, then further to nuzzle his face between her legs. She gasped as his tongue began to please her. Eagerly, she opened her legs wider wanting more. And he gave her more, then made his way up and mounted her, slipping his penis into her moisture, pushing gently at first, then faster, sweeping both of their cares away as the quiet summer breeze brushed over them. To her, they were one, forever, as they climaxed together.

Quietly, they lay exhausted, still joined together. Sarah broke the silence as she whispered, "That was so beautiful."

"It's just our beginning," he murmured, "because, I love you very much, Mrs. Hollis."

She reached up and wrapped her arms around his neck. "And I love you with all my being, Dr. Hollis."

They remained quiet enjoying the sound of the river. When he rolled off her and on to the blanket, he took her hand in his and squeezed it. "We'll be together before you know it."

"Is that a promise, doctor?"

"That is definitely a promise."

She rolled over and kissed him. "Thank you."

He drew her to him saying, "Thank you…for being you."

And now she listened to her heart and knew she could trust him with her life.

She was crying and he caressed her face, kissing her cheeks and she could tell he, too, was crying.

"It will be all right," he said, his voice husky. "As soon as I'm settled in Los Angeles, I'm sending for you."

"When?" She wanted to know and, yet, she knew it was an impossible question.

"It will have to be a surprise."

She didn't want surprises. She just wanted to know that she would never lose him. She hugged him more tightly.

"Would it surprise you if I just came?"

His answer was a long, probing kiss. Just as she was about to sink into passion again, she caught herself. "It's time to go."

"Just a few more minutes," he said.

She wanted a few more minutes, too. She wanted to stay in his arms forever, but below them, the river had already said goodbye and above them on the hill was the hospital and her call to duty.

When she did get up, clocks were back in her life. It was well past ten and she knew the residence would be locked. "Warren, I lost all track of time," she said in a panic pulling on her clothes.

"Don't worry. You're too close to graduation for them to bother with a little tardiness."

"I wish…there's no such thing as a little tardiness…Miss Bradford says a 'rule is a rule' right up to the end."

They walked along the edge of the river until they were beyond the buildings before they went up the hill. It was an indirect route, but safer.

"Just go up to the door, pound loudly, and demand entrance," said Warren.

"Sure," she said, but she had to laugh in spite of herself. "I'll beg Mrs. Dunning to forgive me just this one time and tell her that it was Gary Cooper's fault. He made me miss the bus."

Warren took her along the back walk. Another student passed, but Sarah didn't care. The second-year student wouldn't dare say anything.

The idea of saying goodbye to him was more than she could handle and when they came to the back entrance of the residence, they stepped behind the hedge for just one, last passionate kiss.

This was the very last time they would be together in Vermont. Their next meeting would be in California.

There were the sounds of a scurrying animal in the brush and the lazy squeaking of crickets, drowning out any sounds she and Warren made.

She heard the back door open and clung to him, not daring to move, holding her breath. A figure moved swiftly past. It was a woman, her walk familiar, holding something over her arm that gave a silver gleam in the moonlight, until she disappeared into the hospital a half-block away.

"Do you realize how close that was?" she said.

"Go," he urged her on. "I'll call you before I leave." And then he, too, was gone.

She pounded on the back door and Mrs. Dunning sleepily answered, letting her in without a word. She hurried down the hall and heard the housemother throw the bolt, once again barricading them in.

It would be Miss Mabel Sheridan, a night nursing supervisor, who had a key and would let her out to go on duty, accompanying her to the hospital. She had been doing this for students as far back as anyone could remember.

At 11:15 p.m., Sarah came downstairs to wait for prim, starched Miss Sheridan. To Sarah's right, behind the stairs, was Miss Gibson's room. Directly in front of her, across from the stairs, was Mrs. Dunning's room. The hall seemed hot. Perhaps the night was unusually warm, or her passions still on fire from Warren.

At precisely 11:17, Miss Sheridan came down stairs and unlocked the back door.

"Miss Sheridan, I think I smell something burning. Do you?"

She sniffed. "No." She hurried down the walk, rapidly settling into the pace she would use throughout the night. Still apprehensive, Sarah looked back at the residence. An orange glow flickered from Miss Gibson's window.

"Miss Sheridan," she cried.

Miss Sheridan turned and saw the flames. They rushed back, Miss Sheridan using her key to get into the residence. They went to bang on Miss Gibson's door, but the heat drove them back.

"Fire! Fire!" they screamed. "Get out!"

Sarah pounded on Mrs. Dunning's door, and the housemother flew out in her nightgown.

The women were forced outside by the heat and Sarah ran to the hospital to have the operator call the fire department. By the time she returned to the scene, there was pandemonium. Medical students and doctors, staff and patients were standing on the lawn watching the blaze. The residence was engulfed and yellow and orange flames and black smoke swept across the second floor licking through the roof.

People were yelling. "Get the students out! Get the students out!"

Mrs. Dunning and Sarah rapidly named the students and determined that none were inside the burning structure. Those who weren't on duty had gone home for vacation or the weekend.

They stood back, Sarah seeing her room explode in orange, the money she'd saved for Warren Hollis a joke to the fire.

The Burlington Fire Department arrived and poured a hopeless stream of water at the building, concentrating on Miss Gibsons's room, the only person not immediately accounted for. Even as they did it, the fire captain said grimly that it would be a miracle if the occupant survived. "And frankly, I don't believe in miracles."

He knew what he was talking about. Hours later when the fire was under control, the residence gutted, firemen found their way into the rubble to Miss Gibson's room and pulled out her charred body.

Although she was unrecognizable, one thing was clear. Miss Gibson's skull had been bashed in.

* * *

The next morning, Warren Hollis came looking for Sarah when he read about the fire in the Burlington Daily News. They talked in the basement of the hospital, protected by people milling around.

"That fire was deliberately set," she whispered to him, "and I know who did it." The secret weighed heavily within her and yet she was afraid to reveal the information. If she told, she would be expelled, for she would have to admit she'd been out beyond curfew. And she could not bring Warren Hollis forward as a witness because that would be further grounds for dismissal.

"Wait until you've graduated," he advised. "Then you'll have plenty of time to decide what to do."

"Maybe I should tell Dr. Palmer now."

"Wait."

She said goodbye to him again and went upstairs to the first floor of the hospital. Miss Bradford walked past with her arm around someone whose head was bent forward, her body shaking from sobbing. Sarah recognized Emma Read, inconsolable over Miss Gibson's death.

Chapter Twenty-Two

Sarah had to keep her terrible secret for another month, at least. After the fire, the students moved into the hospital on the same floor where Miss Bradford lived. The unused rooms with single beds were quickly cleared out and cleaned for the students. For the first time during her training, Sarah had privacy, a room to herself.

It was a good thing. The fire and death of Miss Gibson left her so nervous that she was sick to her stomach most of the time. She'd awaken in the morning, retching.

Mercifully, her last six weeks were fairly light. Nearing graduation, Miss Bradford assigned her to special two cases. One, a woman who'd had her diseased gall-bladder removed. The other, Mrs. Peter Mac Neal, a first-time mother, who developed an abdominal abscess following a Caesarean section which required frequent wound care.

But it wasn't just six weeks. It was eight. In the middle of the next month, Miss Bradford summoned her to her office. Her message was simple, complete and as cold as the graduation pin she handed her. "Miss Morgan, you have completed your hours for graduation. You may now leave the school."

"Thank you, Miss Bradford."

After three years, that was her graduation ceremony, dispatched with the efficiency of punching a time card. She left the office, struck by the incongruity between her elation and Miss Bradford's cool presentation. She realized that, to the superintendent, students were nothing more than a totaling of hours and days and then she was rid of them. And to think she'd seen compassion in Miss Bradford's eyes at the capping ceremony and after Potter died. At least she thought she had, but maybe that, too, was a fiction.

Terribly disappointed, Sarah went back to her patients, feeling no different than when she'd come on duty that morning. The biggest obstacle now was getting employment. From here on, she had to be self-supporting. She could work at the hospital until the end of the month but, at no pay. And she would be required to pay room and board as long as she stayed.

The lady with the Caesarean was more than delighted to pay for her services. Sarah agreed to go home with her to St. Albans while she finished recuperating. Mrs. Mac Neal would be leaving in three days.

The time had come when she could no longer put off seeing Dr. Palmer. She made an appointment and met him in his office. The doctor was thoughtful while she talked, never interrupting with questions, but he had little reaction. "Thank you very much for the information. You will probably be contacted by the police after I speak to them."

"Dr. Palmer, I will be at St. Albans on a private case for the next several weeks."

"That's fine. If you're needed sooner, we'll bring you back."

"Thank you, Dr. Palmer," she said, relieved that she had finally told her story.

The doctor stood. "Miss Morgan, congratulations on your finishing training." He put out his hand to shake hers.

"Thank you, Dr. Palmer."

* * *

Dr. Palmer watched the new graduate leave his office. After all these years, she had given him the ammunition he needed. Finally, he would be getting his satisfaction with the most horrible, hateful woman he'd ever known.

Prudently, he waited until Sarah Morgan had left for St. Albans with her patient before calling Miss Bradford to his office. When he saw the walking stick, he said, "I wonder if you'd be so kind as to give that to me?"

She sat down. "Whatever for?"

He took it from her. His words were careful and measured. "I'd prefer holding the murder weapon."

She stared at him, her eyes narrowing. "What ever are you talking about?"

"I have reason to believe that you killed Miss Gibson and set fire to the nurses residence to conceal her murder."

"Ridiculous," she scoffed, her eyes registering indignation but her hands were shaking.

He didn't respond, letting silence do the work for him.

Miss Bradford gradually became more agitated.

Oh, how he was enjoying this. Within the hour, he would be through with her. Her time left as a superintendent could be counted in minutes. Only last week, he feared she would plague him for the next twenty years.

"You have no proof," said Miss Bradford, her face white.

"I have a witness."

"Who, might I ask?"

He debated telling her and then decided it made no difference. "Miss Sarah Morgan."

"Impossible."

She twisted her hands, brushed back her hair already fastened in a tight bun, adjusted her skirt as she fidgeted in the chair.

Finally, she became calm, her eyes shining. "Perhaps, Dr. Palmer, we can even an old score."

"Such as…"

"I have remained quiet on your behalf for a very long time."

"Really…what are you talking about?" He decided to be extraordinarily tolerant of the distraught woman. After all, as soon as he liked, he could terminate the discussion and send her on her way. If she wanted to belabor the time a bit more, he was agreeable.

"I am speaking of your murdering a student nurse, Miss Laura Upton."

It took him awhile to recall the girl.

Miss Bradford continued her well-rehearsed words, as if she'd saved them until the moment when they would be most useful to her.

"You fathered a student's child, aborted the student and destroyed her baby. Then you allowed her to bleed to death. At first, I thought it was ineptitude, but when I learned the truth, I realized it was intentional."

Now it was his turn to be agitated. Where did she get this crazy idea? Why had she harbored such misinformation? Why hadn't she come to him at the time with her suspicions? "Miss Bradford, when did your good sense leave you? You are terribly wrong."

"I don't think so. I, too, have a witness."

"Who, might I ask?"

"You would not ask if you were innocent."

"Certainly, I would," he said, angrily. "Because you have no witness. You're fabricating an outrageous falsehood."

"On the contrary. My witness secretly left the instruments of abortion outside my office door that very night."

He didn't believe her. And yet, thinking back to his examination of the student nurse, he'd had the same thought at the time, that she was the victim of a botched abortion. But who would want to set him up for this? He tried to recall and retrace those days. And they gradually came back to him. It had to be the very same girl who had stood in his door when Laura Upton sat on his lap, crying out her story about Wes Jenkins. She must be the one placing the blame on him. It took much probing into his memory to remember her name.

"I suspect, Miss Bradford, that you are speaking of a certain Miss Barnett."

"No, I believe we have the same witness. Miss Sarah Morgan."

Dr. Palmer was stunned. He and the superintendent had a long moment weighing the impact of their information on one another. She was out of her mind, as ruthless as she was hateful. Regardless of the truth, however, Dr. Palmer was a realistic man. Finally, he smiled and clasped his hands as a gesture of a man about to extend a confidence. "Do you know what I think? I think she is wrong about both of us," he said, as disarmingly as possible. "I always did consider that girl nothing but trouble."

She nodded. "Yes, Doctor. At least we are in agreement about that."

He handed her back the walking stick. "I'm sure you'll handle the matter quietly to the satisfaction of both of us."

"Of course, Doctor."

* * *

Sarah was never called by the police to give her story. It took more than three weeks before Mrs. Mac Neal began to get her strength back at home in St. Albans. For the first three Fridays, the family paid her regularly. On the fourth Friday, they told her they had no money.

"But we can donate eggs and milk to the hospital in your name…please stay on," the grateful, young father pleaded.

Sarah agreed to one more week. She could not afford to work longer for nothing. After all, her hospital residence room and board expenses continued. And she was anxious to find out if Warren Hollis had sent word to her from

California. She dared not admit her deepest hope that he might even have sent for her.

Besides, she needed time off, for she was always tired.

The following Saturday, she took the bus back to West Vermont Hospital, carrying several dozen eggs. She expected a change on her arrival. Perhaps the police were waiting for her return to talk to her. Perhaps Miss Bradford would already have been dismissed. But everything was the same and there was no letter from Warren Hollis.

Deciding to brave it out, on Monday morning, Sarah went to Miss Bradford's office to announce her return and say that she was ready to take on another case.

"I'm very sorry," Miss Bradford said. "With a depression and times difficult for everyone, there are no private cases to be had."

Sarah knew that private cases were scarce, but Emma Read always had one, Jane Barnett and Mary Drury each had new assignments.

"Perhaps, next week..." Miss Bradford smiled.

Sarah waited out the next week and then another. After three weeks, she had neither a private case nor word from Warren Hollis.

Why hadn't he written? Had he changed his mind about her? Was there somebody else? Was he unhappy? And then she thought about him and his habits. Hadn't he always been whimsical about contacting her? Nothing for a long time and then, suddenly, he'd be beside her.

In spite of her need for work and money, every Friday afternoon, a truck from St. Albans pulled up to the kitchen entrance of the hospital and unloaded dairy products, eggs and milk from her last case as the family had promised. She was in financial trouble and the eggs weren't counted towards her rent.

For that matter, the cook didn't know what to do with all that food.

Along with her worries and no money was another worry. Why did her stomach churn every morning? She wasn't that hungry. Worse yet, when she checked the calender, she realized that she'd missed her menstrual period.

Now she had a good reason to be desperate to contact Warren Hollis. She remembered the name of his home town, Milton, seventeen miles north of Burlington, but could find no phone number listed under his name. On a hunch, she took the four-ten afternoon train arriving at Milton fifty minutes later.

If she could locate his family, perhaps they could tell her of his whereabouts. She got off at the station, walked down the long hill, a street lined with sycamore trees, quiet, large, with many stories, past a church with a cemetery behind it, until she came to the corner drug and hardware store. She couldn't find anyone on the first floor and decided to walk up creaky old stairs to the second floor. There she found the owner working among fishing gear, sorting spinners and flies.

She asked him where she could find the Hollis residence.

The man peered at her thoughtfully. "Been a long time since I heard that name. Family used to live here years ago. Two sons, one retarded. One day, they packed up and left. Heard they went to Boston."

That couldn't be Warren's family. "Perhaps there's more than one Hollis family…"

"Then you know more than I do." He glared at her. "If you're so smart, why did you come bothering me?"

She blushed.

"Don't think much of it," he apologized. "Some folks just can't take it when something's wrong in the family. They don't talk about it, especially to strangers. Afraid of a black mark against them."

* * *

Realizing that her situation had become impossible and not likely to resolve itself, Sarah promised Jane Barnett to secrecy and told her what had happened. Jane offered her a loan which she accepted. Without telling anyone else, she took the bus to New York and boarded a sleeper train to Los Angeles.

She was going to find Warren Hollis. There was no more denying that she was pregnant with his child. If he knew this, surely he would be as ecstatic as she. And, yet, why should he be? She hadn't heard from him since he'd left and she was left with the oldest conflict ever—facing life with an illegitimate child.

* * *

The head housekeeper told Miss Bradford that Miss Morgan's room seemed to be vacated and that no one had seen the graduate nurse for five days.

Miss Bradford thanked her for the information and went to her office. After jiggling the door to be sure it was locked, she emptied the paper-clips from a never used very large ashtray that rested on her desk, a souvenir that

Miss Gibson had bought for her during a one day Coney Island rendevous. Oh, that had been such fun.

Then she lifted the large blotter and pulled out a handful of letters with Los Angeles postmarks, letters that had arrived regularly from Dr. Warren Hollis to Miss Sarah Morgan and which Miss Bradford had intercepted.

As she tore the letters apart one-by-one, she glanced at the contents before ripping them to pieces and flinging them into the ashtray. The letters began with his excitement over his new position, his finding a place to rent, preparing it for her. One letter contained a train ticket. She tore that up, too.

Finally, there was a letter with the plea: "Did you receive the train ticket? Why haven't you written? I am nothing without you."

Grimacing as she ripped it to pieces, Miss Bradford took a match to the lot. Incineration was the method she preferred when getting even with others who had displeased her.

Chapter Twenty-Three

The size of Los Angeles was beyond Sarah's credibility. For some reason, she had expected there would be one or two hospitals, churches, and homes laid out on quiet streets, a larger duplicate of a New England town. But Los Angeles was busy with dozens of everything and without meandering streams or covered bridges. The city sprawled with no beginning and no end, stopped only by the desert and ocean with mountains in between.

After Sarah got off the bus, stiff and exhausted from the long journey, she found a phone booth, and checked every directory for Warren's name. He wasn't listed. Perhaps he'd not been here long enough to be included. She checked with information and the County Medical Association with no luck.

Disappointed, she asked for directions to the YWCA and spent her first few nights there, hoping to get her bearings and a job. She interviewed for a nursing position at Hollywood Presbyterian Hospital, the Hospital of the Good Samaritan, St. Vincent's, and Queen of the Angels, hospitals central to the city.

At her first interview, the superintendent of nursing looked her over sharply without even reviewing her application. "I'm sorry, we have no openings."

At the second hospital, the Super, her white uniform starched stiff as cardboard, cited Sarah's lack of local experience or, for that matter, any graduate experience. "You should have stayed at your home hospital and developed references."

At the third hospital, the smiling Super asked questions, slowly and thoughtfully. "Your name, please?" She jotted it down. "Your husband's name, please?"

"I'm not married."

The Super put the pen down. "If you don't mind an observation, perhaps you should be."

At the fourth hospital, the reception was the same. Sarah's face burned with embarrassment as the Super looked her over.

"I'm sorry. We have no positions," she said, terminating the interview.

Even though her belt was tight, Sarah was surprised that she showed. As she left the office, she felt the round hardness of her belly. Obviously, her pregnancy and not being married were going to stand in the way of employment.

She got on the electric red car with all of her belongings in a single suitcase and rode to the end of the line which turned out to be in Santa Monica. She walked down Ocean Front drive, escaping to the beach. She wiggled her toes in the water, and swirled the sand, wishing this were Vermont and Warren was beside her. She grew pensive thinking of him, their hours of walking along the sands of Lake Champlain. The beauty of the Pacific Ocean dropped into a empty chasm inside her without him. And then came the grief of betrayal. Today, she was going to satisfy herself that he wasn't in California, or, couldn't be found by ordinary means in the state.

She stood and continued walking towards the pier. When she reached the boardwalk, she found a phone booth and read the names of area physicians and surgeons. He wasn't listed. The information operator couldn't help her either.

She heard music coming from the carousel at the pier's entrance and hurried towards the sound. Excited children riding brightly painted horses grabbed for the elusive gold ring with each revolution of the merry-go-round, laughing even when they missed. Wistfully she watched. Someday…

At the far end of the pier, she watched fishermen cleaning fish, throwing scraps to a striped cat, viciously gnawing the pieces, devouring scales, eyes, entrails. As she watched this performance, the predators devouring the helpless, she thought of the interviews she'd had with the hospital superintendents and the way they'd dismissed her.

Why hadn't she lied to them? Where had honesty gotten her? They didn't care about the truth, only that she met the criteria and appearance of the proper nurse.

A plan came to her as quietly as the fog moving in over the bay. She decided to settle in the beach city. Looking for Warren Hollis was proving futile. If she wasn't going to find him or the search was long, she might as well be in a place she liked. For she knew she'd never return to Vermont.

She found a motel room, took a quick shower, freshened up, and headed for the local hospital, quaking inside as she asked to see the superintendent of nurses. Before she could be interviewed, she needed to complete an application. The superintendent scanned Sarah's papers. "I see that you are a new graduate."

"Yes."

"And that you've just married."

"Yes."

"Please, what brought you to California?"

"My husband. He's a doctor with a research position here."

"I see."

The Super seemed to be thinking while she reviewed papers she'd pulled from her drawer. "If you're willing to scrub nights in the operating room, you can start work immediately."

"Yes...I can..." she said, hardly able to contain her excitement.

"Very well, Mrs. Stanhope," said the Super, standing. "You may report for duty on Monday."

It was strange being addressed by the fictional name of Mrs. Stanhope, a name she'd remembered from a cemetery marker in Vermont. And the fiction had brought her a real job.

She wasn't just Mrs. Stanhope. She was Mrs. William T. Stanhope. Before long, the fiction seemed real.

Exhilarated with her new job and first paycheck, Sarah rented a small apartment within walking distance of the hospital.

The work was hard. She would scrub on surgery cases that kept her standing all shift, dropping into bed as soon as she got home in the morning.

She was at a loss to explain what had happened to Warren's love for her. It just didn't seem possible that he would forget her. She could not summon the energy to continue searching for him and was almost convinced he wasn't in Los Angeles at all.

Had he lied to her, a nice lie to keep from hurting her? The same way she'd lied about being married out of necessity? But what reason could he possibly have had?

Meanwhile, her belly grew and grew and the baby inside her was very active. She never made friends at work for fear they might learn the truth about her. After the baby was born, she would think about relocating with a new fiction, the divorced or deserted young mother.

In her seventh month of pregnancy, the Super told Sarah she would be terminated the following Friday.

She should have known this was coming. Even her obstetrician had advised her to quit sooner. But she needed the money. It was quickly apparent that she wouldn't have enough to pay for a private delivery. She would be a charity case which meant having her baby at Memorial Hospital of Los Angeles.

So with her last pay-check, she counted up her bills and budgeted for the next three months, after buying clothes for her baby.

On an afternoon in early May, a month before she was due, she felt pains in her lower back and noticed a pink discharge. Calmly, she took her suitcase, packed with baby clothes, a nightgown, a book, and took the bus to downtown Los Angeles. Her belly was huge and the bus driver looked at her apprehensively. She took the back seat where she could put her legs up.

Three hours and two bus transfers later, she reached Memorial. From a distance, the hospital seemed like a fortress. Up close, it was more friendly, a huge Spanish-styled structure with ivy-covered walls.

She lumbered up the steps pulling herself with the hand rail, stopping when the aching pains forced her to wait until they passed.

She was quickly admitted and whisked upstairs to the labor and delivery ward. Once there, it was like being in a maternity store for babies, with mothers in various stages of labor, some crying, others moaning, all waiting for the checkout line to the delivery room.

A doctor examined her, a nurse prepped her and, before long, the labor pains came on hard. She labored in a four bed ward. About once each hour, a nurse wearing a green scrub gown would come in to check her progress. Despite the agony, it seemed the baby just wouldn't come.

She remembered when she'd been a little girl and her terror at her mother's pain before Elbert was born. Her mother had been stirring the dinner and she'd dropped the spoon during a hard contraction. Now Sarah knew what it must have been like for her.

After many hours, she was writhing and begging. "Please, how much longer." She clenched her teeth and the tears came, but no relief from the pain.

They gave her an injection which dulled the pain slightly and she lost awareness of time between the contractions.

Suddenly, she was taken from her bed, placed on a gurney, and whisked into a brightly lighted delivery room. There, under the impersonal eyes and help of strangers, her baby came. She heard the doctor say she'd had a girl and then she lapsed into sleep, hardly aware when she was placed back in a bed and darkened room.

Around noon, she awoke, anxious to see her baby. The nurse brought her in and Sarah clung to her. She was so tiny, so perfect, so helpless. She lay quietly looking at her mother with the bluest eyes imaginable, almost violet. Her tiny hand reached out and grasped Sarah's finger. Sarah placed the baby to her breast where she sucked eagerly, her eyes closing, her long lashes curled against her cheeks.

Sarah stroked her fine hair, kissed the tiny hand and named her. "Judith...," she said, and then, pleased with the sound, repeated it. "Judith...Judith. It fits you my sweet baby, my child of worthy praise."

Judith looked just like her father.

Chapter Twenty-Four

In her hospital room that evening, Sarah penned a note to Lillian telling her that she was a grandmother. She described the delicate but strong child with flawless skin and dark hair touched with red, her deep-set, blue eyes. She omitted details of her own private life other than her mailing address. Perhaps time had dissipated her mother's anger and she would send news of Elbert, Beatrice and her husband.

Next, Sarah wrote a letter to Jane Barnett, relating the fictional story of her new identity, asking for her understanding and hope that the truth would never cross Jane's lips. If her daughter, Judith, ever needed help, she asked, would Jane be there for her?

Jane wrote back, saying that she would love the responsibility. She also enclosed a copy of the Alumni Bulletin listing the nursing positions of the new graduates. A smiling Miss Bradford was pictured welcoming Miss Emma Read as the newest member of the faculty.

Was Miss Bradford repeating a pattern with Emma, also taking her on as her lover? Sure of the inevitable ending, Sarah set the bulletin aside, at least comforted by Jane's promise that Judith would never be left alone. It was no surprise to her that her mother, Lillian, never responded.

The years passed in a frenzy of work. Most of Sarah's salary from her job as a surgical nurse went to pay for baby-sitters.

Sarah became overprotective of Judith, giving the child all the love that she, herself, had been denied. She sheltered her daughter with rules and acceptable companionship, never allowing her to know the problems that dominated Sarah's every waking moment.

On Judith's second birthday, Jane Barnett sent the child a gift and a copy of the Alumni Bulletin for Sarah. Two items were starred: One showed a beaming Dr. Palmer handing Miss Bradford a scroll and plaque in honor of her twenty-one years as Superintendent of Nurses, presented at her retirement dinner; The other item, on the back page of the bulletin, was an obituary. "On April 2, the body of Miss Emma Read was found in the Power Plant Gorge in her hometown of Waterbury, Vermont.

Police speculate that she lost her footing during a heavy rainstorm and plunged into the Winnoski River, fracturing her skull on the rocks below."Miss Read was a graduate of the class of 1930 and gave distinguished service on the nursing school faculty.

Miss Bradford extended condolences to her family on behalf of the hospital."

Sarah's thoughts went back to the past, seeing the gleaming sterling-silver handle of Miss Bradford's walking stick hanging over her arm as she hurried away from the nurses residence the night of the fire. She could imagine the walking stick crashing into Miss Read's skull during impassioned anger, the same as it probably had with Miss Gibson. Had the superintendent gotten away with murder again, for at least the third time?

* * *

As time passed, Miss Bradford and the school of nursing faded from Sarah's memory. The years rolled over one another, 1933, 1934, and finally 1936 when Judith entered kindergarten. It was a harsh awakening for the child, being exposed to so many other children all at once, squabbling, asking frank questions.

They asked about her parents. Judith wanted answers from her mother. When Judith had been very small and asked about her father, she would just be told, "Never you mind."

But that answer didn't satisfy a five-year-old's curiosity. Sarah tried to stall her. In truth, she had no idea about Warren Hollis for she'd never sought him out after Judith's birth, believing it futile, underscored by her lack of time and money.

The children in school asked Judith other questions which she brought home. "Are you and daddy divorced?" she asked Sarah.

"No."

"Then, why doesn't daddy live with us?"

"Because he doesn't know where we live."

"Why don't you tell him?"

"I don't know where he lives."

This seemed to satisfy her, but Sarah knew she would eventually have to lie to her daughter. That day came unexpectedly.

Although Judith was old enough to understand the meaning of war, she had no idea of its personal cost. The United States had entered World War II sending lives into upheaval. There were air-raids and blackouts in Santa Monica and rumors of German submarines in the waters off the once serene California coast.

Just before Judith's eleventh birthday, Sarah, anxiously following the accounts of the war action, picked up a copy of the Los Angeles Times.

On the front page was the headline: "Doctors Wave Goodbye to Wives," over a picture of doctors in Air Force uniforms.

Sarah stared at the picture. In the front row stood a somber Warren Hollis, hardly changed from when she'd last seen him. He was waving in the direction of a petite woman holding up a handkerchief, smiling bravely. The caption said that Dr. Hollis was temporarily leaving his research position at Memorial Hospital of Los Angeles to join the war effort.

It was the very hospital where Judith had been born. After the initial shock wore off, she wondered if he had been nearby at the moment of his daughter's birth. Then she decided, he could not have been there for she would have surely felt his presence.

Why was he not listed in the Los Angeles telephone directories or with the medical association? With that newspaper clipping went any slender hope Sarah had of ever seeing Warren Hollis again. He had found someone else and probably had children.

She clutched the school ring that she still wore on a chain around her neck, looking again at the initials inscribed inside. …WTH.

That night after Judith was asleep, Sarah went through every item from her past and destroyed anything with a reference to Warren Hollis, everything except the ring.

She waited a few months and then one day told Judith: "You can be very proud of your father, darling. He was a doctor and went off to the war. I've just been notified by the War Department that his plane was shot down over Germany. Judith, your daddy went to heaven."

With that, she gathered the weeping girl in her arms, crying herself.

She took the precaution of preserving the falsehood by writing to her family telling them about her fictitious husband, Warren Stanhope and his death, receiving a letter of condolence from Beatrice. It had been more than eleven years since Sarah had heard a word from her family.

Dearest Sarah:

We were glad to hear from you even though your news was terribly sad. Vermont, too, is an unhappy place. Elbert died several years ago and, although I have tried, I have never been able to bear a child. Just when it seems that we will have success, I lose the baby, months before it is due. Sarah, you are fortunate to have your beautiful daughter, Judith.

Mother's health is bad and she cannot live alone. She stays with us, but will have nothing to do with my husband. We send our sorrow at your tragedy and hope that Judith remains a well, happy child.

Your loving sister, Beatrice

The return address on the envelope was the same as always, Sarah's childhood home. So it was not that their mother lived with Beatrice and her husband. They lived with Lillian. Beatrice, too, found it necessary to lie in order to give proper appearances.

Sarah destroyed the depressing letter.

The years were not easy, but the love and dependence that Sarah and Judith had for one another seemed to make up for the hardships. As Judith grew up, she created fantasies about her father and eventually decided she, too, would become a doctor.

"I'm not sure your father would want that for you," said Sarah. "It is too much work."

"That's all right," said Judith, with her usual conviction.

Sarah blamed herself for her daughter wanting to emulate Warren Hollis. For Sarah had always told her that it was the insurance money given to them by the government following his death that made it possible to buy her the special things; her own bicycle, fine Easter and Christmas dresses, visits to the hairdresser for haircuts and perms, when it was actually Sarah's working double-shifts, nights and weekends that provided these extras.

In the ninth grade, Judith announced that she wanted to take geometry and Sarah didn't object when the school counselor enrolled the girl in a home economics class instead.

"It's just as well," said Sarah. "It will help you more when you get married. Until then, you can teach school or be a nurse."

"Never!" cried the outraged teenager. "I'll never be a teacher and I don't want to be a nurse."

Sarah sighed. "I don't expect you to be realistic at your age." Someday, Judith would understand the wisdom of her mother's guidance.

Indeed, she did change her mind about wanting to be a doctor, deciding to become an actress instead. She would go to the Santa Monica public library to study, and began to read theatrical biographies and plays, forgetting the Dr. Kildare novels and her homework.

"How will you have time for drama with all of your other schoolwork?" asked Sarah.

"Mother," she said, exasperated. "Let me try."

But Sarah was worried. "I don't want you at rehearsals after dark and I have no way to come get you."

"I'll take the bus, the same as I do during the day."

"No, it's too dangerous."

Judith shot back. "That pleases you, doesn't it? You always go against my wishes, never letting me do what I want. You keep me caged while other girls date. All I want to do is join a little theater group. What's so unrealistic about that?"

"What good will it do you in the future?"

"What difference does the future make?" Judith stamped her foot.

"Don't you ever do that again!" Her daughter's defiance brought back swift memories of her own troubles with Lillian, and how unfair her mother had been with her. Was it possible Judith saw herself in the same position? Sarah realized her own teeth and fists were clenched even though she would never strike her daughter.

"Why can't you just let me be?" Judith was crying. "You let me do the safe things, joining the Girl Scouts, taking swimming lessons. Now I want to do something different."

"Acting may be different, but it's a second-rate profession." Sarah hated the way she sounded which was just like Lillian, opinionated with no real justification for what she was saying.

"Oh, is it? And what is a first-rate profession? Nursing?" Judith laughed derisively.

Sarah was stunned. "Yes," she said, proudly. "Nursing is a first-rate profession."

Judith scorned her. "I wonder if my father would agree with you. Surely, medicine is, but not nursing."

It was the first time Judith had ever used the father she'd never known against her.

Sarah felt her cheeks burning. Had she finally lost her daughter? The girl was a teenager and disdained her mother's life work.

Against her mother's wishes, Judith joined drama classes, but withdrew after one semester because her mother couldn't provide the costumes.

"If we can't afford to buy the costumes, then sew them, Mother. Please sew them," Judith pleaded.

"I can't cut a piece of cloth straight," she lied, even though she mended her own worn dresses again and again. "But you took sewing in the seventh grade. You can sew your own."

And yet, it seemed to be impossible getting together the money to purchase the material.

Judith cried in desperation. "What do you want from me?"

"I want you to be happy."

Judith's eyes shimmered. Happy, such an easy, such an empty word. "What is happiness to you? Is it my obeying?"

Sarah had no answer, as confused as Judith as to the breakdown of their relationship. From then on, it seemed that Judith argued less, was quieter and more withdrawn. She had a brief infatuation with a boy in her class, but she was never allowed to see him away from school and the interest died. Academically, she returned to her former desire to become a doctor.

Not fully aware of her own deceit, Sarah steered Judith in the direction of nursing once again, telling her she'd need the same courses for medicine. Two years of Latin, science and algebra.

In Judith's graduation year from high school, Sarah received tragic news from Vermont.

It was a letter from Charles Preston.

"I am in sorrow at the loss of my wife Beatrice, and our son, Roger. He was born with an affliction common in your family. In a fit of depression, Beatrice took her own life and that of our only child.

I am writing to tell you that your elderly mother is no longer in her right mind and cannot live alone. I am not willing to stay with her since she has caused me much suffering and I must get away soon.

Because you are her only remaining family member, I am handing you this problem and will await word from you as to its resolution.

I remain your devoted brother-in-law."

When she finished reading the letter, Sarah went down to the ocean alone to think, walking along the water's edge, the only place where the world ever made any sense.

She relived her childhood years and how she had resented Beatrice. It was impossible to believe that her sister had had a tragic life. Beatrice who had been so full of life, who always made the best of every situation, at least for herself; Beatrice who had been resilient and seldom accommodating, brought down by a child like Louise, Elbert and Winfield.

Sarah was overcome with guilt that she had spent so much time involved with her own plight and keeping up social appearances that she'd never tried to make amends with her family, always telling herself that it was up to them. After all, hadn't they turned her away?

But that excuse was no longer valid. As much as she hated her mother, she could not allow her to be abandoned, old, senile and alone.

Finally, on the beach at Santa Monica, the answer as to what she should do settled out from the possibilities.

She went back to the apartment where Judith was curled up on the couch reading a book. Sarah told her about the letter. "Judith, we are going back to Vermont to be with your sick grandmother."

Judith dropped the book and after a time said quietly, "I'm not going. I'll stay here by myself until you get back."

"It isn't that easy."

"Mother, nothing is easy."

"It could be years…"

"Years…" Judith seemed stunned.

"Yes."

"I'm still not going. I'll be all right."

"I can't leave you here alone."

"Why not? I'm old enough to take care of myself."

"Judith, this is not the time for dreams. I can't afford to keep the apartment. You must decide whether you are coming with me or…" She looked at Judith a long time before she said it.

"…going into nurses training." She was dressing for work, taking her cap from its storage box. "You must make a decision."

Judith attacked her. "You know I want to be a doctor and you've discouraged me. Now you're back to that nursing thing again. Why would you want me to be a nurse? With all the hell you've been through, double-shifts at peasant wages…"

186

"It's been worth it." Sarah knew she was being defensive—with her own daughter.

"I don't think it has. Believe me," Judith declared, "no daughter of mine will ever be forced into something she doesn't want. If she wants to be a doctor, she'll be a doctor."

"The study of medicine takes a lot of money," she said. "I'm sorry, but I never had that kind of money."

"Then why did you lead me to believe you did."

"Did I? I shouldn't have." She turned away from her angry daughter.

"Why did you betray me?" Judith shot out.

"I didn't think I had."

In the end, Sarah made the decision. Against her daughter's wishes, she enrolled her in the nurses training program at Memorial Hospital of Los Angeles, the only school in the area which gave the students a monthly stipend, albeit small.

It was with a feeling of sorrow that Sarah took Judith to her new home in the nurses quarters of the huge hospital. Her daughter kissed her goodbye and marched into the nurses residence, not asking Sarah to accompany her.

"Wait, wait," Sarah called after her, quickly scribbling Jane Barnett's Vermont address on an envelope. "If you ever really need anything, she's expecting to help you."

Judith angrily stuffed it into her pocket.

"Judith, please," she begged. "Everything will be all right."

The girl glared at her, her chin quivering. "Who is going to make it all right?" Then she went back into the residence.

As Sarah watched her daughter's retreating figure moving swiftly down the hall, she worried that this was more than a brief misunderstanding. For some reason, she had a terrible feeling of dread for her daughter's future and didn't know why.

BOOK II

JUDITH

1952—1984

Chapter Twenty-Five

Life has many accidents. For starters, more boys than girls are born. By one year of age, their numbers are equal because five boys have died, a failure rate of almost five-percent.

In 1952, student nurses had a far higher failure rate than biology would have permitted. And it was not due to accidents of nature, but to the perversity of human nature. That is to say that the gods are kinder than humans.

At Memorial Hospital of Los Angeles, the failure rate was more than sixty-six percent for the graduating class of 1955. Of the one-hundred-five girls who started nursing school, twenty-six were gone in the first six months. Thirty-three marched out with the black stripe on her cap three years later.

Judith Stanhope had grown up scarred with doubts about herself and unanswered questions about her mother. Why was she so evasive about certain events in her life? And she was surviving doing something she absolutely did not want to do. It's a wonder that Judith turned out to be a warm and trusting woman, against the odds. It had to be genetic.

She was never sure if she would be one of the nursing school graduates or whether she cared enough. Even the most well adjusted could succumb to the paranoia nurtured in student nurses.

The instructors remarked that her bedside nursing was superior, but Judith found some of the classroom work miserably time-consuming when she was exhausted. It hardly seemed important or necessary to memorize all the bones in the body or the different types of bacteria on the microbiology plates.

But memorize them she did to become one of the seventy-nine students to pass probation.

During the capping ceremony, her class was reduced by one more unlucky student.

While Miss Gooding, the Director of the School of Nursing, read her prepared statement, midway through the formalities came the unmistakable clanking of metal. The students, their feet hidden, were shoving a heavy set of chains along the wooden floor while their eyes remained firmly fixed on the speaker. An embarrassing murmur spread through the crowd.

Miss Norton, who taught nursing ethics, hurriedly retrieved the chains and identified the perpetrator who was expelled following the ceremony. As the remaining students knew, Miss Norton was wrong because the girl was innocent. Establishing innocence or guilt, however, was not a primary target in Miss Norton's or the administration's system of justice.

It was finding a culprit.

The students were not living in a fairy-tale world. Each knew she was a potential culprit.

In a sense, the paranoia at Memorial was representative of a similar national disease. In Washington, Senator Joseph Mc Carthy was head-hunting, stalking "commies", real and imagined enemies of the United States. The Fifth Amendment of the Constitution became popular as witnesses to the Army-Mc Carthy hearings "took the fifth," not giving testimony for fear of self-incrimination.

At Memorial Hospital, students took the Fifth in a slightly altered form. They used the weapon of absolute silence which often worked and got a few girls through training.

There had been at least one improvement for student nurses in the previous quarter-of-a-century. "Training schools for nurses" were renamed "Schools of Nursing". As teachers reasoned, animals were trained, people were educated.

After the capping ceremony, more students resigned, voluntarily and involuntarily. At the end of the first year, only seventy-one were left.

Again, Judith made it, scraping through communicable diseases and neurology.

"This is hell," she often remarked to her two roommates. "Who has time for these hideous studies and working on the wards, too?"

Kate Armstrong, her wild, auburn hair hiding her features as she lay face down on her bed studying, agreed. Susan Ryan, normally slim had become scarecrow-thin, desperately trying to pass medical-surgical nursing. She just sighed. Talking was an indulgence with exam deadlines always before them.

Their lives were so intertwined during that first year, that an experience for one was an experience for all. They cried together over failed exams, their first exposures to death, and incredibly difficult ward assignments. They shared clothes, boyfriends, and deep secrets.

They were always tired and run down, sustained by the knowledge that they would have a vacation after the capping ceremony.

When vacation break finally came, the three drove in a broken down Hillman car to the Grand Canyon in Arizona. On a freezing February morning, they ran down the trail leading to Phantom Ranch at the bottom. Even though there was ice at the rim, before long they were hot, peeling off their outer clothing, and singing: "I Dreamt I went to the Grand Canyon in my Maidenform bra."

It was in this condition that they met a returning donkey caravan bringing up people who'd stayed at the ranch overnight.

Judith hastily pulled a sweater over her head. She caught Kate's smirk and Susan's embarrassment as she held a jacket in front of herself.

"It'll cost you eighteen-dollars and seventy-five cents each to be rescued and hauled out," advised the guide.

"Wise guy," Kate laughed, running past his caravan.

As it was, the guide was almost right. Twelve hours later, on the way back, Judith lagged behind, her leg muscles drained of strength, and finally, her mind of any desire to continue. Kate had gone on ahead, but came back for her.

"Kiddo, you're supposed to make it on your own." Kate got behind her and pushed.

"Sorry, I can't and it isn't worth it if I have to do it alone. I'm too tired to care."

It was well after dark before they pulled themselves to the ledge, their legs aching, their bodies protesting.

They made it, but the Hillman finally didn't. After staying in their cabin for three days until their legs would move again, they took off for the return trip to California. When they reached Yermo and the border check, the car died. A tow truck hauled the car to a mechanics garage.

Judith found four quarters, a nickel and two pennies in her purse and the others came up with two-dollars and thirty-seven cents, hardly enough for the car's repair bill.

They occupied themselves for the next ten hours wondering about the inevitable penalty from Miss Gooding.

"Have you ever heard of anyone surviving something this dumb?" asked Susan.

"I've never heard of anything this dumb," said Kate.

"I'm sure everything will be all right," Judith said, secretly fearing her mother's reaction if they should be expelled.

They played canasta all night and dropped money into the jukebox, hearing the same songs over-and-over: "Ebb Tide", "From Rags to Riches", and a Latin-American song, "Vaya con Dios".

By morning when they wired the school of nursing for money from the "mercy and sympathy fund", Judith was so sick of canasta that she took the deck of cards and sank it into a bucket of wet, oily rags in the mechanics garage.

After their return to the hospital, unbelievably, nothing was said.

Relieved and chastened, Judith returned to duty, wearing her new, starched broad-brimmed Memorial cap. Because each school of nursing had a distinctive and different cap, this would someday be her identifying trademark. No matter where she worked, other nurses would know her nursing heritage and she would be judged accordingly. For each school also had a unique reputation and Memorial, the second largest hospital in the Western United States, was noted for being hard. A graduate from Memorial knew her business.

Caps were not the only similarities between the students. When they were lined up, regardless of their height, each student wore the same white uniform and a ruler would be exactly six inches from the floor to the bottom of the hem. Although their physical features were different, their expressions were often identical, programmed into them by instructors with set ideas as to proper professional demeanor, designed to conceal personal feelings. The intention was that this training would last forever.

The students had tremendous responsibility in the hospital, each student assigned to care for as many as forty patients. Mostly, the second year students worked on the evening tour of duty, a few in the operating and delivery rooms.

During this rotation, Judith was assigned to the operating room. It was located on the fourth floor of the hospital and consisted of eleven operating suites.

One Tuesday morning, just after four a.m., Judith closed down surgery and was the last to leave. But first, she did a final check of the operating rooms to be sure all of the autoclaves were turned off, their doors cracked to let out the steam. The final surgical case had been an amputation and Judith picked up the severed limb and wrapped it in a sheet to take to the pathology lab. She locked the operating room doors behind her and got on the elevator. As the door was about to close, she realized she didn't have the identifying paperwork.

Since she was sure there would be no one taking the service elevator this time of night, she left the leg on the floor of the elevator and went back to the surgery suite, unlocked the door, retrieved the paperwork from the desk, and went over the ritual of closing up the operating room again.

When she returned to the elevator, the doors were closed. She watched apprehensively as the light moved from floor to floor, stopping twice, finally returning to her floor.

The leg was missing.

She got on, stopped the elevator at every floor, sure that somebody had just placed it outside the door but she never found the amputated limb.

How could she have been so stupid? Even though she was sure the mistake meant automatic termination, she reported her error to the night nursing supervisor.

The next morning, Miss Gooding called her in. She had Judith write an extensive memo, explaining the circumstances, what she had done wrong with suggestions as to how such situations could be avoided in the future.

Judith wrote all morning, fearing that each word brought her closer and closer to the end of her time at Memorial. When she was finished, she took the pages to Miss Gooding.

"What do you think the penalty should be for this offense?" asked the Director.

"I don't know."

"Miss Stanhope, surely you've thought this through. What do you think will happen?"

Judith looked down. "That I'll be expelled."

"Precisely."

Judith took the news without looking up, her chest tightening, her heart pounding.

"Miss Stanhope, I'm sure that you did not believe you were being careless at the time you left the leg on the elevator."

Judith didn't answer, her eyes fixed on her feet.

"Please look at me when I am speaking to you. Did you?"

"No. I thought it would be safe that time of night. I was wrong."

"You certainly were, however, I think you may have learned your lesson. Can you think of a lesser penalty?"

Judith could think of nothing except that this room was getting smaller and smaller and Miss Gooding larger.

"Well..." Miss Gooding sounded impatient.

"A month's suspension..." Judith stammered.

"That sounds fair enough, but a week makes more sense. You can make up that time by working on your days off," said Miss Gooding, rising, opening the office door and letting in a blast of cool air. "By the way, you showed good judgment in reporting your mistake. The limb was found."

She had no home to go to, so Susan's mother gave her a haven for the week. Judith wrote her own mother, fearful of the expected response. The return message from Vermont read:

Dear Judith:

If this teaches you to be more careful, it will be worth it. There is precious little room for mistakes in nursing. Be thankful that Miss Gooding kept you on. Students have been let go for far less serious offenses.

Your loving mother.

During Judith's suspension, she watched the proceedings on television as Joseph Mc Carthy's colleagues censored him for his witch-hunting activities, destroying him as rapidly as he had destroyed others.

After Judith returned to Memorial, she became more serious about her work, being extremely careful in carrying out orders on the wards, being attentive at lectures, never allowing her mind to wander, taking word for word notes in class, especially when the doctors lectured.

The students seldom saw the same doctor twice for each gave lectures in his specialty and the students weren't expected to know any one subject in depth. There was a kindly, older man who gave a pediatrics lecture, specifically on surgery for deformed children, the victims of accidents or birth defects. Judith was intrigued by him, his excellent presentation, his serious, deep-set blue eyes, his kindly expression. Somehow, it was as though he spoke to her personally. Perhaps it was because he discussed pediatrics, her favorite subject.

If he gave them his name, she missed it.

At the end of the second year, a second red stripe was added to the brim of her student cap.

By then, with classroom work almost finished, the rest of the students time was devoted to practical experience in pediatrics, psychiatry, and communicable disease nursing.

Although the Salk polio vaccine was being tested, it wasn't routinely used yet and four students contacted the dreaded disease this last year of their training. One died. One was paralyzed and could not continue in nursing. The others dropped out to recuperate.

In the middle of the third year, Roberta Becker, a winsome, quiet student, spent the first day of a four-day weekend shopping for a filmy green negligee. After she found one that satisfied her, she stopped at a florist's shop and bought a single lily.

On Sunday night, when her roommate returned from weekend pass, she found Roberta on her bed, an empty Nembutal bottle and half-filled glass of water neatly placed side-by-side on the bedside table. She wore the green negligee. Her hands, folded at waist-level, held the wilted lily. She was dead.

The entire student body went into a state of shock.

Roberta's death was no accident, but nobody could think of a motive for her suicide. She'd not signaled unhappiness and did not leave a note.

Her benumbed roommate moved in with another student. Roberta's room was closed up for the year, a silent reminder for those who passed by that life had failures which could not be predicted.

In the larger context, the suicide was no different than a lot of things that had happened to the students. It made no sense.

Nearing the end of her third year, Judith was assigned to a month in the nursery for deformed newborns. Not all students passed through here because they could not bear the sights: the unseeing eyes, the microcephalic heads where a light placed near the skull shined through an empty, mostly brainless ball; the hydrocephalics with heads the size of basketballs; the little bodies with missing limbs, webbed fingers or toes, the monsters indefinable as humans, the Siamese twins pathetically joined from the top of their sternum to their naval, a common liver making it impossible to ever separate them, and the borderline child with multiple deformities, his face split from eyes to chin, his intelligence a question mark. His parents had named him Matthew.

Judith hadn't slept for two nights after she'd first seen him and the other children and she could never eat until well into the evening when she'd been off duty for several hours.

This morning, she held Matthew, pinning his arms to his sides, while a consulting surgeon examined him. He gently shined a light around the gaping orifice where a nose and lips should have been.

"...a very large cleft palate..." the doctor said, more to himself than to her. He aimed the light into the boy's eyes. The child flinched. "He responds to light."

The doctor was so close to her that she could feel his breath, clean-smelling as of wintergreen mouthwash. The name sewed on the pocket of his lab coat read, Dr. Warren.

He examined the child's deformed nose, half of it missing, rolled into the hare lip. She marveled at the doctor's accepting attitude, his compassion.

"This will require extensive work," he said, straightening up, dropping his ophthalmoscope into his laboratory coat pocket.

He looked at Judith, started to speak, but stopped, studying her briefly. He cleared his throat and seemed momentarily at a loss, as though he'd forgotten what he'd planned to say.

Finally, he regained himself. "I think everything here is correctable." He reached down and took the child's hand and the tiny fingers grasped his eagerly. "He may have some intelligence so we'll see what we can do for this unfortunate baby."

For some reason, his conclusion gave Judith hope. Without thinking, her revulsion forgotten, Judith kissed and hugged the child.

The doctor continued stroking the tiny hand. "Everything will be all right," he said, as if the child could understand him.

His words sent a shiver through Judith, a reaction she could not explain.

"I want you to care for him after surgery."

"Oh, I can't do that, Doctor. Students never have special assignments."

"Hmmm..." He read her name tag and turned away.

She couldn't keep her eyes from him as he searched for the child's chart in the rack, his strongly muscled arms, his full hair, nearly reaching his collar. Something about him fascinated her.

He wrote in Matthew's chart as she placed him back in his crib, changing and feeding him with the duck-billed feeder that was barely suitable.

As she dripped the formula into the child's deformed mouth, she tried to recall where she'd seen the doctor before. Later that night she remembered.

More than a year before, he had lectured to the pediatric class. She'd had the same feelings about him then, his mysterious attractiveness, Something about his expressions were so familiar and she couldn't explain why. Still, she was being silly. He was a doctor, older, certainly not available for he wore a wedding band. And doctors were off-limits to students.

But dreaming was free and legal.

She didn't know how the doctor got permission, but she was assigned to care for tiny Matthew after his surgery.

Her fantasies about the surgeon increased ten-fold with each of his visits to the nursery. In fact, the better Matthew got and the closer it came time for his discharge, the more visits the doctor made on one pretext or another to view the child's progress, examining the stitches, the healing, his general condition.

And just before the baby went home, Judith noticed that the doctor's wedding band was gone. But after the first thrill of excitement, she knew he'd probably slipped it off while he performed surgery.

The morning Matthew left, the doctor said a quick goodbye to the child and his parents. He had to get to surgery to do grafts on a five-year-old girl who had been badly burned in an East Los Angeles apartment fire. He again asked that she be permitted to be the child's special nurse. Again, the school of nursing approved his unusual request.

She wondered why. Her pediatric instructor, Miss Vaughn, told her the reason. "You could never get a finer experience. He is the best plastic surgeon on the West Coast, possibly in the U.S. He won't even use his real name here because he's a very private person with more referrals than he can handle."

Judith was puzzled. "Why would he ask for me?"

The instructor eyed her sternly over rimless glasses. "Your looks probably have something to do with it. But we suggest that you not encourage the relationship. Students who stand out from the others usually do not finish training."

Judith had a moment of fear. "Can I refuse to take the assignment?"

"No. Your pediatric rotation will be over in ten days and he doesn't need to know it."

The implicit message was that she'd better not tell him, either. That meant she'd not be able to see the child all the way through her recuperation, expected to be at least a month.

But Miss Vaughn was wrong. The doctor was well aware of the date her pediatric experience ended.

On her last morning in the nursery, he came to her.

"Miss Stanhope, I wish to thank you for the care you've given to our small friend." He was wrapping the little girl's head with bandages, covering a fresh skin graft. After it healed, all that would be left would be a scar, hidden by her hair. "As you can see, everything is going to be all right."

Tears welled and she saw the two of them in a blur. They were tears of gratitude, for students were seldom commended. And coming from him, the compliment meant even more.

The doctor continued: "You have exceptional compassion when you work with the children. That, perhaps more than my work, makes for their recoveries. I've had no complications with the children you've cared for."

"Thank you." She could hardly speak.

"I'd like to see you again," he said.

He was looking at her and they studied each other longer than she felt proper. Why was it that whenever they had intense moments of feeling, he seemed so familiar?

"I'm sorry, but the school of nursing doesn't allow us to see doctors," she said, flustered, regretting every word.

"You mean, if they know." He winked. "I'm sure there's a lot they don't know."

She laughed. Oh, yes. What they didn't know. The student who peddled a phony cancer cure, a liquid medicine her grandmother concocted in her Pasadena home overlooking the Rose Bowl; the wine party at Mr. Agnelli's home to celebrate his recovery. Four student nurses consumed a gallon of his homemade wine and had million-dollar hangovers the next day; the crazy dance at Cal Tech when the guys had invited the student nurses as blind dates, a party that went on until dawn, in the bushes and in the back seats of cars in the Rose Hills; the students who'd been to an abortionist over in the Silverlake district of Los Angeles and whose secrets had been kept.

Yes, perhaps Judith could get away with going to dinner with the doctor. But then she thought about the elevator and the lost leg. Other students got by with misdeeds, but she'd be caught. And there must be good reasons behind the school's rule.

"Please, Doctor, I graduate in two months. Could it wait until then?"

"Of course." He took her hand and caressed it gently. It was only her hand but the thrill traveled through her whole body leaving every nerve in a state of shock.

Chapter Twenty-Six

It was a long two months. Judith finished training and a black band was glued to the brim of her white hat, replacing the two red stripes from her student days. Out went the tattered school uniform, later burned up in a wild class party. On went the white professional dress with the distinctive, school pin, her initials engraved on the back.

She set up residence in the graduate quarters, sure the doctor had forgotten about her.

Something inside her warned that it must be for the best. Life gives complications to test relationships and theirs had not had even a whisper of dust kicked up to cloud it. Perhaps she had been a passing thought for him which lost its direction the moment the road turned.

Oh, how wrong she was. Somehow, he knew exactly when she'd finally settled in for he called and asked her to go out to dinner with him.

"I can't," she stammered, doubts nagging her. Why had she led him to believe she'd see him again?

"Why not? You've graduated. The school of nursing doesn't own you anymore."

Did she dare tell him the truth? She drew in her breath and the confession rushed out. "I won't go out with a married man."

He laughed. "You have that right. At any rate, you don't have to worry about me."

"Aren't you married?"

"No. No children, no baggage."

She didn't know whether to believe him. Didn't all men say that? Should she take a chance?

After all, it was crazy. He was older. Her mother would never approve. He was experienced, a successful surgeon with a tremendously successful private practice, although she'd only seen the side of him that did charity work.

She was a nobody, a dumb new graduate nurse who had never really dated in her life. Just those crazy undergraduates from Cal Tech. And yet, her attraction to him rushed back so insistently that the uncertainties were lost in the crush.

Well..." he broke through her thoughts. "Will you?"

"Yes," she said, her hesitation and restraint satisfied.

In order to feel presentable, she spent an entire month's paycheck on clothes, an extravagance unlike her. She bought a cocktail dress with three-quarter length sleeves and a bubble skirt which made her waist look even tinier. She tried on a blue, full-length, clinging satin evening gown. The bodice had a deep V-neckline which she thought too provocative. She put it back on the hanger and just as quickly changed her mind again, adding it to her purchases.

He took her to dinner in Beverly Hills at El Morroco. He took her dancing at Ciro's, where the music seemed almost written for them. They waltzed to "Fascination", a song from a Gary Cooper movie about the love affair of a girl and an older man. Judith loved to dance, so involved with the music and the band that she and the doctor hardly cared or had time for conversation, but they did sketch in brief biographies for one another.

"I was born in the same hospital where you met me," she said, ashamed of the poverty that had made it necessary for her mother to deliver there.

He was guiding her in a slow tango. "Marvelous. Marilyn Monroe was born at County General, not far from there. California makes outstanding babies."

She could feel herself blush, inappropriately blurting out, "My mother was born in Vermont..."

"I knew we had something in common," he said, very seriously. "So was I. One way or another, we New Englanders find each other and cling together like oysters."

They stumbled around the dance floor, laughing at his outrageous humor.

Later she told him that her father had been a doctor, killed in World War II over Germany when she was very young. She said she could never remember having seen him. The doctor murmured his regrets.

Over the next several dates, she came to realize how wealthy he was. He often came to get her directly from a hospital where he'd been doing surgery. He had a chauffeur, by the name of Curtis. The doctor explained the unobtrusive man's presence: "I need every moment for preparation, reading, making notes. I can't waste time behind the wheel."

If nothing else, he was a practical man. And, she realized, very busy. Also, terribly romantic. They liked the same things, or was it possible that he knew her better than she thought?

He took her to the theater. They saw, "The Dark at the Top of the Stairs", and "Look Homeward Angel". He took her to the Philharmonic where they sat in loge seats while Alfred Wallenstein conducted Brahms and Mozart. She didn't tell the doctor that she and her roommate, Kate, had been there before using tickets donated to the school of nursing and she'd seen the stage from the last row.

Afterwards, Judith and the doctor discussed the concert.

"Who is your favorite composer?" the doctor asked.

"Between the two of them, I'll take Mozart, although my absolute favorite is Haydn. I used to feel stupid because I'm often confused by Mozart, Beethoven and Haydn. So much of their music sounds similar. It made sense once I learned Haydn was teacher to the other two."

"Yes," he said, in surprise and admiration. "I feel the same way myself. Haydn was the father of them all. The effect was as if history repeated itself."

That was only one of the surprises as they got to know one another. When he ordered for her in restaurants, it was always exactly what she would have chosen for herself.

He sent her books from Martindales, a Beverly Hills bookstore, and it was almost as if he'd seen those she already owned. None were duplicates, but they reflected her taste and subject matter; biographies, autobiographies, plays, books about the theater.

She lived for his calls, his visits, their dates. When he leaned over to kiss her goodnight, he held her for the longest time and she wondered if there would ever be more than kisses. And she dismissed it as impossible. After all, Curtis was always there, his racing form on the seat beside him.

She was wild with anticipation and desire for him and was ashamed of herself. Was it right to want him so?

She wrote her mother weekly, hardly mentioning the romance other than that she was dating, careful not to say that it was with one man, exclusively. Her mother would be upset, if she knew.

Kate found out about the doctor and admonished her. "Are you out of your mind? You've just finished nurses training. You need to work, make some money, do something with yourself and for yourself. Travel. See the world.

After all, you've just gotten out of one prison. Do you want another by tying yourself down to one man?"

"Yes," Judith said. "But he hasn't asked for any kind of a permanent relationship."

"Judith, be careful…"

Susan Ryan voiced similar concerns. "Get to know him better. Maybe you think you love him, but he may be taking advantage of you. After all, you're young and he's just gotten a divorce. He could be lonely and on the rebound."

Even if he were, what difference would it make? She knew she loved him and that it was more than a crush or infatuation. She spent every waking moment going over their times together, never thinking that she should doubt something that seemed this perfect.

After she'd been dating him for two months, he asked her to work in his Beverly Hills office and be his private scrub nurse at the hospitals where he did surgery.

"My scrub nurse, Marian, is retiring after sixteen years with me."

At this she hesitated, envisioning the complications.

"It would mean my moving again. I'd planned to wait until my mother came back from Vermont so we could get a place together."

"Do what you feel is best. But the offer is open to you for ten days. Marian wants time to train her replacement."

"I need more time than that."

"A month, then."

Over the next few weeks, she didn't see or hear from him. Was he avoiding her by not asking her out? Or was this his way of exerting subtle pressure? It was then that the head nurse on pediatrics told her that he had only come to Memorial once a week as part of his charity work except when Judith had been caring for his cases. Then he had come daily.

And for several weeks, he'd had no new surgeries there.

She missed him so, her heart aching from loneliness. Why hadn't she accepted his offer immediately? She wrote to her mother and asked her when she was coming back to California. Sarah replied that she didn't know, but that she might be in Vermont for several more years. So Judith, shocked at herself for welcoming her mother's decision, made plans for her own life without her mother.

She accepted the position with the doctor, rented an efficiency apartment on the bus line five miles from his office, packed her things and left Memorial. She mailed a change of address to her mother saying that she'd taken an office job for awhile. Her mother's return reply was that sometimes it was necessary to get away from the heavy hospital pace.

Within a week, Curtis and the doctor were picking her up on the mornings he did surgery, taking her to the different hospitals. As they drove, the doctor read charts, sipped coffee, and was generally distracted by his work.

He was a challenge. Two different men, the detached, absorbed professional during the day, the elusive romantic at night. She wondered how he could change so. And, yet, she couldn't imagine him being any other way.

Her happiness was nearly complete. She was doing the kind of work she loved, helping a man she cared for deeply...except that her yearning for him was indescribable and went beyond the hours they worked side-by-side in surgical masks, sharing a single thought as the time went by...zeroing in on what was best for the tiny anesthetized patient before them.

Before long, it was difficult keeping their working and private lives separate. One day, he stopped off at his Bel Air mansion after work to study a reference book. While he researched a problem, he told her to freshen up, if she liked.

She was overwhelmed by the size of the place, bigger than any home she'd ever been in. It had mammoth living, dining, and sitting rooms. The library alone was larger than her apartment. The maid led her to an upstairs guestroom with a sliding glass door that looked out over a huge expanse of green lawn. A pine tree's branches settled on the wrought iron patio enclosure outside the room. It was an awesome setting.

She languished in the roman-styled tub, feeling dirty afterwards when she had no choice but to put back on the same uniform she'd worn all day. This happened often enough that she got the sense to leave a small overnight case with an extra set of clothes in his car.

Gradually, it became a ritual, stopping at his place, being served refreshing drinks, showering, resting, changing her clothes before he took her to dinner.

At first, she was overwhelmed by the difference in their lifestyles, from her miserable apartment to the opulence of his electric-gated driveway, overhanging trees and sweeping lawns, the massive front door opened for him by his butler, Raymond, who bowed deeply to her. Yet, the doctor didn't seem aware of her discomfort.

Soon, he had the guest room specially prepared for her, always a robe available in her size, beauty supplies to match her coloring, her favorite perfumes and bath oils.

"This is more convenient," was his excuse.

One evening, she had just stepped from the bath and had a towel wrapped around her. When she went into the bedroom, he was sitting on the edge of the bed. She self-consciously wrapped the towel more tightly, but he held the robe out to her and it seemed natural to just take it and substitute it for the towel. She had a brief moment of apprehension when she was naked, but he seemed to pay no attention to her because he had gone back to studying a patient's chart he was reviewing. The thought occurred to her to close the sliding glass door for there was a very slight breeze. It wasn't necessary for the robe quickly warmed her.

He was talking about the day's consultations: about the newborn who died before they could get her to surgery; another with uncorrectable birth defects; the ecstatic parents taking their child home for the first time in his seventeen months of life. The doctor's eyes were distant and reflective.

When Judith was comfortable, she sat beside him brushing out her hair as he talked on, seeming to relax from the catharsis of free time to unwind. She didn't interrupt him in his monologue, but felt her heart speed up. She had difficulty concentrating on anything other than his being with her.

Suddenly, he asked her a question, a question she missed completely. All she heard was the last part. "...cases today?"

She fumbled for words and he turned to look at her. She was embarrassed, but he grinned, stroking her cheek.

"Not listening..." he said. Then he stopped and looked into her eyes and they held the look for the longest time, thinking, measuring each other and before long she knew they were thinking the same thing.

He took her chin in his hand, his palm resting against her throat and kissed her gently. Quietly, he put an arm around her and drew her closer to him. His hand traveled up and down her back through the robe which bunched crazily. She pulled away to straighten it, still holding it together in front. He placed his lips to hers again, encouraging her to open her mouth and his tongue went deep. She felt herself sinking with desire, desire that welled from deep within. His hands slipped inside the robe, his caresses moving over her breasts, making peaks of her nipples, and then the robe somehow slipped away and he gently kissed the peaks, there just for him.

She felt him smoothing her skin, his hands moving lower and lower down her body. She sank farther and farther beneath his spell and found herself slipping away from him and landed on the floor for they had been on the very edge of the bed.

He tried to keep her from falling, but he was too late. She giggled as he helped her up.

"Don't break the spell," he said, crushing her lips with his.

"Never," she tried to say, but it was lost in their passion.

He pulled down the covers and settled her against the huge down pillows before slipping off his clothes. Then he was beside her, caressing, kissing, driving her insane with desire and need.

With an abandon she didn't know she possessed, she gave into love-making, straddling him, astonished at her own aggressiveness. He lay quietly, allowing her freedom to explore him and then she dropped on him with only the rustling of the silver-dollar trees outside the window accompanying their ardor.

She aroused him completely, moving her hips tantalizingly, holding her hand around his throbbing penis, pressing it in circles against her genitalia, until he suddenly drew in his breath as he strained against her. He pulled away her hand and gently urged her to the bed, changing positions with her. His strength, her wanting to be submissive now, wanting him to take her, his teasing with his tongue, overwhelming her, making her wild, the frenzies inside her begging. And suddenly, his penis was pressing against her and she wanted him inside her so she reached down and held his organ against her vagina, raising her hips ever so slightly and before she knew it, he was inside her, filling her with breathless pleasure. His thrusts were slow and shallow at first, then they went deeper and deeper and stopped almost as though he were trying to delay the moment. He took his weight from her and held himself up with his hands against the sheet. She clenched her legs around him holding him tightly in her. And it was as if this was just what he wanted, because his thrusts suddenly came faster until she felt a tremendous burst inside her and then another, and then, too soon, it was over.

He kept her wrapped in the warmth of his arms, covering her with the comforter, caressing her to slowly end the passion that had overcome them.

He kissed her ever so softly, again and again. "I don't know why," he said, "but I feel as though I've…"

"…known you all my life." She laughed, finishing it for him.

"Don't be so smart," he said, pinching her.

"You devil," she squealed.

"There's a little of the devil in you, too."

The breeze and the rustling trees started all over again. But she caught herself, wrapping the sheet tighter around her. "Enough…"

As he got out of bed, she admired his firm body and she knew there would never be another man for her.

Two months later, he asked her to marry him. She'd known and loved him for more than a year and was sure of herself in spite of the warnings of Kate and Susan. "Don't tie yourself down. He'll expect you to give up nursing."

Too bad, and so what!

She wasn't sure how to tell her mother, fearing that it would only upset her because she couldn't afford to give Judith a wedding and probably couldn't get away from Vermont. So Judith decided to remain quiet. If, and when she married, she would surprise her mother. It would be the easiest way.

The doctor's surgery schedule was so heavy that they could never set a wedding date. Instead, one Friday, he canceled everything, took her to the jewelers, bought her a monstrous pear-shaped diamond ring, and said, "Anytime you're ready."

"How about yesterday?"

"That's gone. How about today?"

Impulsively, they had Curtis drive them to Las Vegas and he served as their beaming witness at the Drive-Inn Wedding Chapel, where they got out of the car just long enough to say their vows.

After they were married, her new husband asked her if she wanted to call her mother?"

"She has no phone...I'll write her." She hugged him. He was so thoughtful. Imagine, thinking of her mother first.

They drove back to Beverly Hills to spend their wedding night in his bed.

The next morning, she sent her mother a telegram.

Dear Mother: Surprise! You're a mother-in-law. His name is Warren Hollis, M.D. We send our love and wish you could have been with us.
Love always, Judith

* * *

Randall Thorne, M.D., his black hair more unruly than usual for he had just removed his surgical cap, was walking down the hall of Hollywood Presbyterian Hospital with his closest friend, Warren Hollis. They had just finished examining a severely compromised newborn.

"What do you think?" Randall asked. Even though he had one of the busiest obstetrical practices in Los Angeles, he had never adjusted to these tragic, unfortunate births..

"I could correct the facial defects, but the esophageal atresia is too extensive. The best we have to offer is a permanent gastrostomy. Without it, the child will die. I'll explain the possibilities to the parents and let them make a decision."

"No, Warren. I'll speak to them." Randall knew that parents vacillated with their abnormal children. With the shock of the unexpected, they might say, 'do everything at any cost,' a decision that they might quickly regret.

If he had a family who could not handle the extreme emotional strain of their defective newborn, he would quietly make the decision for them. They never knew the difference.

To him, quality of life meant a great deal. He questioned destroying the happiness of an entire family for the sake of a marginal life for one child, especially if the child could not relate to life in any meaningful way.

He tried to keep the emotional trauma of the family to a minimum. Just knowing that they had born a deformed child would forever change the way they viewed themselves, their lives and futures.

Randall didn't arrive at his philosophy overnight, but only after years of dealing with tragic situations.

Since his graduation from the USC School of Medicine, he'd seen plenty of nature's mistakes. In his years of internship and residency at County General Hospital, life-and-death decisions were made daily in these cases. Just the huge number of deliveries there guaranteed a statistical number of birth defects. But this tiny boy delivered in the night at Hollywood Presbyterian was one of the worst cases he'd seen.

"Warren, thanks for your opinion," he said, already knowing the decision he would suggest to the parents with the empathy that few people were able to give.

They'd reached the end of the hall and Warren stopped him.

"Randall...on a personal subject, I want to tell you something before you hear it from anyone else..." He paused.

"Don't tell me...I can guess. You've gone back to Evelyn."

"Not quite. I've remarried."

"Christ!" Warren had just divorced Evelyn. He hadn't even waited out the required year. Recovering from his surprise, he pumped Warren's hand. "Congratulations, old buddy."

It would take time to absorb the implications, but without a doubt, the marriage would affect his personal relationship with Warren. After all, Randall's wife, Denise, and Evelyn were close friends. This morning the two were playing tennis together. They both served with the same charitable organizations, even though Randall knew that the only way Evelyn would be able to keep up her Bel Air image would be with alimony. Sometimes he resented it because he wasn't the most fulfilled of husbands.

"Now that I have my wits back, who is she?"

"Her name is Judith. She's younger…in her twenties…a nurse. Of course, she isn't working now."

"What are you doing, robbing the cradle?"

Warren laughed. "Not really. It's more like robbing an old memory."

Randall let the obscure remark pass because he was visualizing Judith in his head. A doll-like bundle, probably cuddly and not-too-bright, something for Warren to play with between the sheets. Oh well, who was he to judge, he with his proper, rather dull relationship with Denise. They had been fooling the Bel Air and medical crowds for years who thought they were the all-round perfect couple.

But he didn't think Warren had been fooled for a long time. They'd been close, personally, in business and professionally and could usually second-guess one another. How had Randall missed this one?

Warren was talking: "I had my doubts, at first, until I realized I'd felt this way only one other time in my life."

"With Evelyn?"

"No, she was before Evelyn. I lost her and I never knew why. I searched for her, but she had erased all traces of herself. I still don't think I've gotten over her."

Randall didn't probe further. Obviously, that had been a painful time in his friend's life. "I just hope you'll be happy, Warren."

Inside, Randall wondered if the young nurse hadn't married Warren for his money. He had to be one of the wealthiest doctors in the country. And he deserved every cent with his amazing surgical abilities, the lives he'd rescued from despair and heartbreak.

"I will be. I wasn't taking any chances of losing her. In spite of our age difference and backgrounds, I know she's right for me."

"Good. When can we get together with the wives?"

"Anytime…"

Randall wasn't sure how Denise would take this addition to Warren's life. "Does Judith play bridge?" he asked, hopefully. Denise would tolerate anyone who could play a decent game.

"No. She hates cards, but plays a mean canasta when she has to."

"Canasta, it is."

* * *

After the first blush of love mellowed and Judith had settled down to her life as Mrs. Warren Hollis, she worried more and more about her mother.

Why was there a curious silence from Vermont? Why hadn't her mother acknowledged the letter telling her about the marriage? Judith had written two more letters, both returned unopened, stamped MOVED—NO FORWARDING ADDRESS She expressed her fears to Warren. "Something has happened to my mother."

"What makes you think so?"

She showed him the returned letters. "This doesn't make sense. Why would she move without letting me know? We both wrote regularly. We had letters going back and forth weekly, sometimes oftener. Now, these."

"My dear, I suggest that you go back and find her."

"I was hoping you'd say that." But before she could make definite plans, morning sickness attacked her and the idea of flying made her dizzy. As soon as it passed…

* * *

On a hunch, Judith rummaged through her things for a name and address. Her mother had given her the name of a woman to contact, in case…

She finally found the piece of scrap paper with Jane Barnett's name on it, and the original creases from when Judith had angrily crumpled it and shoved it in her pocket on her first day of nurses training.

She wrote a letter to Jane Barnett, asking her if she'd been in contact with her mother and signed the note, "Judith Hollis".

A reply quickly came back. *"Not for several years. But do keep in touch and if I hear anything…"*

* * *

211

The Hollis' and the Thornes' made numerous attempts at getting together but something always interfered. The first time, Denise had a cold. Then Randall was called out of town on a consultation. Warren had an emergency surgery that couldn't be handled by anyone else, and Judith felt lousy.

Of course, there was only one choice for her obstetrician. Randall Thorne and he refused to let her travel even when she felt better. The pregnancy was hard and she threatened miscarriage several times.

Of course, Randall was amazed when he saw that Judith didn't match his preconception. She was one of the loveliest girls he'd ever seen; flawless skin, blue eyes, almost the color of the morning glories that had grown over the fence of his childhood home. She had a maturity his own wife, Denise, didn't have.

Judith had already adopted Warren's habit of listening, nearly expressionless, so that it was impossible to tell what she was thinking. He couldn't help but admire Warren's choice. He was a fortunate man with excellent taste, even if his wife did look like his female counterpart.

Such narcissism, Randall thought.

Chapter Twenty-Seven

Five months into her pregnancy, Judith and Warren finally got together with the Thornes for the promised social engagement.

Although usually not concerned with clothes, Judith worried her way through a closet filled with maternity dresses. She settled on an Empire-styled, cream-colored lace gown. She pinned up the sides of her hair, letting the waves fall softly.

When Warren saw her, he took her in his arms. "Let's stay home."

She laughed, guiding him out the door.

It was a short drive to the Thornes, hardly a mile from their own home. Curtis only had to go around a few bends on Bellagio Road to reach the entrance to the sprawling Tudor estate with rich-looking, diamond-shaped windows. It was still hard for Judith to realize that these mansions would be a natural part of her life.

Her own friends, Kate and Susan, were cramped in an Alhambra bungalow just outside the city of Los Angeles, in quarters barely large enough to hold their old nursing textbooks and a few clothes, their closet mostly taken over with uniforms.

Judith could imagine the closets and clothes in the Thornes' magnificent home. So many, they must have to be catalogued.

Before she and Warren had a chance to get out of the car, Randall was out the front door to meet them, wearing tennis shoes, shorts and knee highs.

It was a jolt to her, used to seeing him in shirt, tie and lab coat during her office visits. She would have the same problem getting used to him without his hospital gear as she'd had with Warren.

Randall helped her from the car, put his arms around both of them and escorted them into the house. He hurried them into the den and mixed them drinks. As soon as they were seated on the plush couch, Denise, Randall's wife, swept into the room.

Her elegance stunned Judith. Denise had thick, blond hair, braided to her waist, high, glistening cheek bones, a classic profile. Her slim figure was accented by a skin-tight, cerulean floor-length gown. Dainty slippers revealed red toe-nails. If Judith had to guess, Denise must be around forty.

The smile she gave Judith seemed frozen as in a magazine ad. Her muscles and skin moved, but her eyes were dispassionate, almost cold. She accepted the drink that her husband mixed for her and arranged herself on the arm of the sofa next to him. Her every pose could be framed as in a well-staged photograph. This evening she had achieved a perfect Palm Springs effect. Even the miniature potted palm tree on the floor behind them showed to Denise's advantage.

Judith mentally slapped herself for the bitchy thoughts and moved closer to Warren. She could think of nothing to say and Denise did not extend herself beyond pleasantries.

Their husbands discussed mutual business ventures, the apartment and four office buildings they owned from Westwood to Venice, the new accountant they'd hired. When they moved on to medical business, hospital politics and interesting cases, Denise left the den, returning shortly to announce that dinner was about to be served.

It had been a two-drink lead-in.

As the group moved to the patio, Judith could smell charcoal and wood burning from an outdoor barbecue, a monstrous brick affair with preparation counters on either side. The sun had disappeared leaving an orange-brown glow. Candles floated on artificial lily pads in the pool. Lanterns were strung around the patio giving substance to the shadows.

They ate crisp salads to the crackling of the juices from the steaks snapping against the coals. As soon as their salads were finished, the plates were replaced by hot platters with perfectly grilled steaks, baked potatoes with chive and sour cream dressing, and broccoli dripping with a cheese sauce.

As they ate, Randall brought up the subject of the World Health Organization conference to be held in Geneva, Switzerland. "It's time we send in our reservations and get our plane tickets."

Warren kept eating.

"You are going, aren't you?" Randall asked.

"I'm afraid not. Perhaps next year." Warren reached under the table for her hand.

"Old buddy, we've been going to these conferences since their founding in 1948. We can't break our record."

"This year is out for me."

"I said Judith couldn't travel, but you aren't restricted." Randall was becoming insistent.

"I want to stay with her," said Warren. "This would be a good year for you and Denise to go together."

Randall looked at Warren as if wondering if he really meant it.

Denise smiled woodenly.

Then something clicked with Randall and he became enthusiastic, turning to his wife. "Sounds great. What do you think?"

From inside the house, they could hear a child screaming.

"I wish he wouldn't do that," said Denise. "He makes me so nervous."

"Ignore him, darling. Estella can handle him." Randall explained to Judith, his tone apologetic. "He's our son, Brian."

Denise laid down her fork and placed her napkin beside her plate and started to rise. "You know that once he starts, he won't stop," she said.

"Denise, stay here," Randall commanded.

She sat down again, picked up her fork and played with her food. When the men quickly returned to shop talk, debating who would be the next recipient of the Albert Lasker award for Rehabilitation Medicine to be presented in London, Denise unobtrusively rose and left the table.

The butler didn't bother to put dessert at her place.

Judith listened attentively as the two doctors discussed the Mexican children being brought to this country for Warren to correct their birth defects. He described a current case and sighed. "If I operated all day, I could never meet their needs. We have to get more surgeons involved."

The dessert dishes were removed and after dinner liqueurs placed before them. Randall asked the butler about Denise. He left and when he came back, they could all hear his whispers to Randall. "Mrs. Thorne says that she will not be returning."

They finished the liqueurs. The canasta cards that had been brought to the table remained, never shuffled.

After a time, Warren rose, shook his colleagues hand, thanked him for the fine meal and evening, and escorted Judith to their waiting limousine.

On the way home, his attitude was grim. "I hate to tell you this, but their kid, Brian, is nine-years-old. A rotten, spoiled brat. So much for canasta…and Denise."

Deep down, Judith knew that Brian wasn't the real issue. Denise didn't like her and wasn't making any false pretenses of friendship. She had to admire her honesty, if not her method. After all, she knew Denise was a close friend of Warren's first wife.

Over the next several weeks, they were asked out numerous times by Warren's other colleagues, but the reception was always the same. All of the encounters had the same lack of reality as at the Thornes'. Judith became very ill-at-ease, dreading new engagements. She became acutely aware that Warren's friends did not accept her.

He hardly seemed to care, even if he noticed. It seemed that his every moment went to making her happy. When he was away from home, he called her between surgical cases to be sure she was all right. He sent or brought her impulsive gifts. A gold bracelet with tiny jade Buddha charms. They laughed. Yes, she was beginning to feel like a Buddha herself.

He sent her flowers, dozens of bouquets, roses, daisies, potted geraniums, azaleas and tulips. He had nightgowns and robes delivered to her from Saks and I. Magnins, perfumes and soaps from Bullocks.

He expected her to pamper herself, lie around and do nothing. She hated the inactivity.

Near the end of her pregnancy, Kate Ryan came to see her. They hugged over Judith's big belly. "You're as big as this house," Kate said. "Are you miserable?"

"Yes, I am."

Her attention turned to the home Judith shared with her husband. "Do you give tours of this place?"

She showed Kate around the vast living room, movie screening room, den with full bar done in Western style, the one distinctive difference from the New England elegance throughout the rest of the house.

She showed her the baby's nursery decorated in blues and white.

"Optimist," said Kate. "Obviously you have this color scheme because you really want a girl."

"It can be changed quickly enough."

"Of course, with a snap of the fingers."

They passed the stairs leading to the second floor. "Up there are more bedrooms, a study and sewing room. I haven't been up there for at least a month."

They went through the kitchen, the pantry, past the maid's quarters and outside passed the tennis courts, never used, the water in the swimming pool quiet except where a bug had dropped in making ripples as it fought for its life.

They sat on the patio chairs and the maid placed pineapple coolers before them. Kate was quiet.

"I'm glad you came to see me," Judith said. "I miss you and Susan, Memorial, everything…"

"I'm glad I came, too. You haven't changed but, to tell you the truth, this kind of living is too much for me. Remember the days when we used to go to Alvarado Street to get a Tommieburger?"

"And across from Union Station to Phillipi's for a double-dipped French sandwich."

The two looked at each other for a long moment. Judith spoke first. "What are we waiting for?"

"Nothing." Kate bounded out to her Chevy with Judith lumbering behind.

They took Sunset Blvd all the way from Bel Air to Los Angeles where it ended, went to Phillipi's where the homeless could buy coffee for a nickle. In their favorite booth, the wooden seats were riddled with carved initials from many years. Their feet scrunched on the sawdust covering the cement floor.

"We've just returned to heaven," Judith sighed.

They spent the next two hours gossiping, catching up on the happenings of their graduated classmates, the job changes, marriages, moves.

Kate asked about Judith's mother and she had to confess that she hadn't heard from her since the marriage.

The longer they talked, the more Judith realized how much she missed her old friends and vowed she would see them on a regular basis. And she missed nursing, which was no longer a possibility for her to pursue. Warren felt it didn't suit her position as a doctor's wife and, compared to Warren's money, nurses wages were a joke.

Kate talked about hers and Susan's worries making ends meet. "We thought we would save money living together, but we don't. There's always an emergency with the car. If we lived in the graduate nurses residence at the hospital, we wouldn't need one. Then Susan got an infected tooth. Then we couldn't pay the light bill, so they were shut off."

217

"I'm sorry, Kate."

"I shouldn't be telling you. It's our problem."

It hadn't been too long since Judith had had similar worries, but now, she knew that the combined salaries of her friends wouldn't pay the light bill on Warren's Beverly Hills mansion.

Kate talked about her new job at County Hospital. "We thought Memorial was big. County is enormous. It takes weeks to figure out how to get in and out of the place. It's got underground tunnels that go on for blocks."

"Warren talks about it. He has charity cases there."

Kate looked at her oddly. "I've never thought of patients as being charity cases."

Judith felt her face redden. "You're right…Im sorry."

Kate shrugged.

On that note, they left Phillipi's. On the way to Kate's car, they had to pass by the residents of skid row waiting for handouts.

When they arrived at the mansion, Warren was pacing the front hall. He seldom came home before eight in the evening when their dinner would be served. It was only five p.m.

Judith could tell he was upset. "What's the matter, darling?" She kissed him.

"Where have you been?" His tone was sharp.

"Out for the afternoon." Embarrassed, she introduced him to Kate, who hung back, said a few words, and left hurriedly.

Judith apologized to her husband, but he didn't acknowledge it.

"I canceled surgeries when I learned you weren't home. No one knew where you'd gone. I called Randall…"

"I'm sorry, Warren. Truly I am."

"Don't ever do that again," he said, fear behind the anger in his voice.

She'd had no idea that a flash of independence would threaten him.

After that, he didn't have to worry because Judith was too uncomfortable to do much more than get up in the morning, shower, dress, walk the grounds, and lay on the couch watching television soaps.

She began to dwell on her mother until it became an obsession. They had been so close. Why hadn't Sarah contacted her? Was it because she hadn't been asked for her permission for the marriage? Still, her mother wasn't spiteful. She would have forgiven Judith by now. As Judith could never have imagined living the way she did today, she could never have imagined not hearing from or writing to her mother at least weekly. But there had been no word for almost a year.

On a hot August afternoon, Judith's labor pains started. She called Warren at Cedars, but he couldn't get away because he was involved in an emergency. She was heartsick. "Warren, I need you."

"Darling, I'll be there as soon as possible. Randall will be more help than I..."

Hardly, she thought, resigned to the fact that Warren's work had to come first.

Curtis, who said he was worried about this trip, drove her to the hospital where Randall met and tried to reassure her.

Judith was quickly settled in a private room with her own nurse, who was knitting afghan squares as she sat next to the bed, talking to Judith about her own children.

Judith was scared and wanted Warren, her fears increasing with the intensity of the contractions.

The labor went on for hours. And still Warren never came. Randall stopped by, examined her and told her she was doing fine. Then he left.

"I can't stand this pain any longer," she finally cried. "Isn't there something..."

The nurse put down her knitting, disappeared briefly, came back and jabbed a hypodermic needle into her, sending her into a world without time or awareness, where her mind only responded when her body was ripped apart with a contraction.

She never knew when the baby was born, only that she woke up in a quiet room and it was morning. An older nurse came in with a cheery greeting. "Good, you're awake. Now your husband can see you."

"Where is my baby?"

"Just be patient." She gave Judith a warm, damp face cloth and straightened the bed covers.

Judith had no reason to be anxious, but she was. It must have been hours since the baby had been born. Why hadn't somebody awakened her and told her what had happened?

Shortly, Warren came in, wearing a surgical gown and mask. In his huge arms was a tiny pink-blanketed bundle.

He presented her with their baby. "Our daughter."

Excitedly, Judith opened the blanket and examined every inch of the tiny body, counting the fingers and toes, watching the busy, searching mouth. She opened the top of her nightgown and helped the baby reach her breast, quickly feeling the warmth of the milk starting to flow.

She looked up at Warren. They both had tears in their eyes.

"Thank you," he said.

"She's perfect."

"And so are you."

"Us," she corrected.

"Terrible grammar." He could barely get the words out.

She urged him down to the bed beside them.

They watched the baby nurse and began discussing girls names for the first time, tossing around their mothers' first names. Her mother's, Sarah. Rejected as being too old-fashioned. His mother's. Ethel. Even worse. They agreed on Gillian.

She wanted to let her mother know about Gillian, so she sent another letter to Vermont. Maybe, by now, the post-office had been given a forwarding address. But it was futile. The letter was returned, undeliverable.

Judith was hurt and angry. If nothing had happened to her mother, she had no right to reject her this way. When she calmed down she knew that it had nothing to do with rejection and she had an obligation to learn the truth. Her mother would never reject her. Something had happened to her.

* * *

For the time being, it had to wait as Judith settled into motherhood, never so happy and content in her life, even though she could never completely get her mind off her mother. When Gillian was two months old, she told Warren of plans to go east.

"No, darling. Not just yet. When Gillian's a little older, we'll fly back together and search for your mother."

But when Gillian was a few months older, it was winter in Vermont, the worst blizzard in years locked the state to outsiders and it was no time to take a baby anywhere.

When Gillian was a year old, it was summer again, and Warren couldn't get away. His surgery and lecture schedules were too demanding.

Judith almost never saw him. Her main companionship was with Gillian and long phone calls to her friends. Kate and Susan would come for lunch, never seeing Warren. But Judith never left the house with them. There was that uncomfortable feeling of not wanting to upset Warren.

If her future could have flashed before her at that point, even a brief part of it, she might have done things differently. Except for the long absences away from Warren, she thought she had the perfect life, even though she felt vaguely dissatisfied as though something was missing. She had no way of knowing it, but she was as happy as she would ever be. In fact, the decline had already started.

Chapter Twenty-Eight

Judith waited until Gillian was fourteen months old before she made the decision. Over breakfast in early October she told Warren they had to go back to locate her mother before another winter came.

"I suppose you're right." That morning, he checked with his secretary and found that his schedule was jammed for months. He reviewed it, eliminating lectures, awards, delaying elective surgeries. All he gained were holes in his day like patches torn from a quilt.

"Darling, I don't see how I can possibly clear this schedule to go."

"Warren, you agreed more than a year ago that we had to do this."

"Give me a few days. Maybe I can put off more surgeries if the patients will agree."

"Why don't you just tell them?"

"I'd rather discuss it with them. Some have waited a long time."

"While you do that, I'm making travel arrangements. We must leave by the middle of the month." She couldn't ever remember being adamant with her husband and expected that he would snap at her. Actually, he never snapped, he was just very firm which meant no more discussion. This time, he did nothing as if to say the subject was closed.

He rose from the table. Curtis was waiting out front with the limousine idling. As he did every morning, Warren went to Gillian's room before leaving for the hospital. He awakened the sleeping child and brought her with her wet nightclothes to Judith. He hugged and hugged her, calling her "Daddy's little angel"—his pet name. He placed her in Judith's arms, handed her a stuffed bear, and the little girl promptly went back to sleep.

That would probably be the last time he'd see his daughter that day. He quickly pecked kisses on the two of them, grabbed his coat and briefcase and rushed out the door.

As soon as the travel agency opened, Judith booked plane and train tickets wondering as she dialed why Warren never had any free time. She'd heard the tales of doctors whose offices were closed all day Wednesdays, and all weekend starting from Friday noon. But not Warren's office. Except for the hours of sleep he required, he was working, lecturing, consulting, operating.

So much of his work was volunteering at County and Memorial Hospitals. Perhaps if he gave up some of that, they could be together more. Still, if it hadn't been for his charity work, she would never have met him. And those patients were just as important to him as his Beverly Hills clients who came in for expensive face-lifts, tummy and fanny tucks, breast and nose jobs. In fact, his children from Mexico and Korea meant more to him, but the Beverly Hills crowd made his work with the children possible. For them, he wasn't guaranteeing beauty, only the hope for a decent life.

The sacrifices left Judith ambivalent. When he was with her, they were so happy, with a contented kind of love. But she wanted more of those times. She longed for him, finding the long hours apart empty except for Gillian. Her life was on hold and she began to wonder, hold for what?

If he would just close his office for one day a week…They'd discussed it, but he could never get it arranged.

That night she told him: "Booking is for nine-twenty in the morning of the fifteenth. We leave from Los Angeles International."

"Fine"

He was tired. They went right to bed after a light supper, holding each other close as they always did.

"Warren, I don't see enough of you."

"We'll make it up in Vermont. I have some good memories of that place."

"Vermont isn't the rest of our lives."

"Of course not." He drew her even closer and then they were exploring.

"I must repeat," she said, giving in to his adoring caresses. "I don't see enough of you."

"Then turn on the light." He smothered her laughter with kisses.

* * *

Two days before they were to leave, he called her from the hospital. "Judith, can we delay for another week. A patient has gone bad…cancer eroding through a small neck artery. I've finished repairing it, but she'll be critical for at least four more days." I can try…"

223

"Thank you, darling." She changed the reservations. The best she could do was another two weeks or take a chance and standby. She took the reservation.

Three days before they were to leave, he called her. "Judith, remember that explosion in Burbank last month?"

She did.

"One of the men is in desperate need of skin grafts. I can't put if off until we return."

She pleaded. "Get somebody else to do the surgery."

"Judith, the family won't accept anyone else. I've tried..."

Would there always be an emergency, something he could not cancel? "Warren, it will soon be winter. We can't count on good weather after October. The first snows..."

"That's all right."

"You wouldn't go last year in the winter."

"No. It isn't a good idea."

Suddenly, an unfamiliar resolve took hold of her. "Warren, I'm going."

"I don't blame you for feeling that way, darling. Change the reservations and I'll go with you, no matter what."

She kept the reservations she'd already made and told him when he came in that night. "I want you to come. I want you to be with me. But I don't want another disappointment. I've lived with the delays so far Warren, but inside, it hurts. Sometimes I think my only chance is to be an emergency case..."

He seemed resigned. "I'm sorry, dear."

"Our bags are packed and we're leaving Thursday."

"We..."

"Yes. I'm taking Gillian."

His alarm was immediate, but he was low-keyed. "It wouldn't be safe to take her."

"Why not?"

"Please consider. It would be a new area for her with strange bugs, communicable diseases, possible flu. She's used to life here, her own room, familiar surroundings..."

"And her mother." Judith bristled. "What is all the rest of this worth to her if I'm gone?"

"We'll get a sitter..."

Warren, I'm not leaving my daughter with a stranger."

His eyes flashed. "You are not taking her to Vermont."

She was furious at his control over her. She wanted to scream at him to let her out of the cage he'd constructed around her. But she didn't have it in her. "All right, Warren, if that's your decision…"

In the end, she delayed her departure long enough to hire a live-in nanny. Her name was Annetta. She was French and spoke with a heavy accent. Annetta was comfortably in her fifties and had work references covering twenty years, but she'd only had two jobs.

"Why are you looking for a new position?" Judith had asked her.

"The children do grow up," she sniffed.

Judith sensed she was strong-willed which would be good for Gillian. But could she, herself, manage disagreements with her? "We'll try it for a month."

After a week, she hoped Annetta would stay with them forever.

The morning she left was not a good one for her and Warren. Their parting was strained. He was exceptionally tired, but going to the hospital anyway. And, even though he was exhausted, she couldn't find it in her heart to forgive him for never being available.

But she was so happy with Annetta that she began to see it almost as an omen. If he had not refused to let her take Gillian, she would never have looked for a nanny. Yet the idea of being away from Gillian for even a day was no less painful.

She flew to New York and took the overnight sleeper train into St. Albans in northern Vermont. It had been a chilly night and when she opened the window curtains the next morning, she was greeted with a fantasy of color. The maple trees had brilliant orange, red and yellow leaves, white birches had leaves in all shades of yellow and browns. The ash trees were a violet color and leaves dropping off looked like new silver dollars when they took up the sun.

At St. Albans, she hired a car and driver, a slender, older man who held an unlit pipe between his teeth, wearing it as though it were a set of dentures. She told him she wanted to go to Riverfork.

"Can't imagine what you'd be going there for," he said, placing her luggage in the trunk. "That is one dead town."

"My mother was born there."

"Some things can't be helped. So long's she had the sense to get away."

She hoped he was wrong about Riverfork.

They drove for several miles, eventually traveling alongside a river, wide enough to be a lake.

"The Winooski River," he said, pride in his voice.

They passed through lush countryside, passing gorgeous, autumn touched trees. Just after they passed a dam, they came into a small town.

"Riverfork," the driver announced.

There was a white steeple church, quiet streets of old homes with storm windows up on some, a sign of approaching winter.

The town was quiet as if it had settled all of its old scores.

The driver stopped in the business section of town, such as it was, comprised of a small store and a post-office. Judith asked for her mother at the post-office.

"Stanhope..." The postmaster thought awhile. "We got letters to that name and put them in the Morgan box...same house number."

Judith's heart quickened. "Where is their home?"

"A ways out. But they moved away. Put the old lady in a rest home in Burlington. The Stanhope woman went back where she came from. Supposed to have a daughter in California."

Judith was crestfallen. "How do I find their old home?"

He led her to an old, brown-edged map of Riverfork thumb-tacked on the wall. "Here," he said, pointing, "this is the place where they used to live."

He drew a quick diagram which she took back to the car and handed to the driver. As he drove the hilly streets in the quaint New England town, she recognized homes and buildings that her mother had talked about. The church with the cemetery behind it. The culvert running under the road at the end of the main street. The railroad tracks. Were those the tracks her mother had walked along when she was seventeen on the way to find her father in Burlington?

Some of the homes had large, screened porches, immaculate, as if they had been freshly painted. All except one corner house that could be beautiful, but showed terrible neglect. Shattered windows, crooked shutters, sagging roof. In front was a faded, broken sign that read, "Dr. Montgomery".

If only signs and buildings and houses could whisper their memories, Judith mused. What tales they must have.

Then they were away from the stretch of large homes and heading out in the country where farmhouses sat on small hills surrounded by farmland and maple trees.

The driver stopped, consulted the map sketched by the man at the store and drove up a nearby hill. Judith got out of the car and walked around the grounds. In the back of the main house was a maple sugaring house and a barn, it's door fallen off. On one side of the barn she saw small crosses. Were they old grave markers? There were no names on them.

She pulled at the board closing up the back door of the main house. It came loose easily enough. She walked inside and knew every inch of that house from the stories her mother had told. It was as though she'd been in it a thousand times before. Judith could see her grandmother, Lillian, bending over the stove, cooking. There was the downstairs bedroom off the kitchen with only a broken down bedstead and a rocking chair with the cane seat falling out like old straw.

Next to this was a second bedroom. This must have been the bedroom where Sarah slept with her sister, Beatrice. All the stories her mother had told her came back, how she and Beatrice fought, about Beatrice being the favored daughter, and then she eventually died by her own hand.

Judith opened a dresser drawer and picked out old dusty strips of torn cloth which she dropped on the floor. There was nothing else in the room other than an old bedstead with a ripped mattress. In the kitchen a soup ladle was thrown in one corner. She tripped over a pan with a missing handle. Nothing that was left in the house was any good or gave any clues about previous owners.

Obviously, she wasn't the first to have pried off the board from the back door.

Judith went back to the car. "How far is Burlington?"

"Twenty-five miles, give-or-take."

"Please drive me there."

"Ma'am, I have to get back to St. Alban's."

It took some persuading and money, but he agreed. Burlington turned out to be seven miles away.

He apologized. "Thought I knew Vermont better," he said. "I'm from down by Waterbury, myself."

She got out at a hotel on Church Street and he left. She was on her own, too tired to do any serious searching that day. She took a room, perused the telephone directory, but found no listing for Morgan. She called Warren who wasn't home, took a hot bath and went to bed. If he returned her call, she was asleep.

Judith awoke early and as soon as a decent hour arrived, she was on the phone calling every public agency listed in the phone directory.

She called all the retirement homes listed with no results, then all the hospitals, finally a medical and health care information center. She read off a list of the places she'd called to the receptionist. "Is there someplace I could have missed?"

"Yes." The receptionist gave her the numbers of two homes not listed in the directory.

As it turned out, the Home for Elderly Women had a resident by the name of Morgan. Nervously, Judith wrote out the address and sent for a taxi.

Mrs. Patterson, the woman from the home, who'd answered her call, met her at the door. She was plump with a good-natured laugh, and immediately took Judith to see Lillian Morgan.

Lillian was resting in a chair, staring out the window, her lap covered with a blanket. She was a tiny woman, frail, her hair yellowish and thin. And yet, Judith could see a resemblance to her own mother in this woman.

Mrs. Patterson introduced her to Lillian.

"Mrs. Morgan, your granddaughter has come to visit," she said, brightly.

Lillian glared at her with mean eyes. "You're not my granddaughter," she said, turning away.

Judith was stunned.

"Now, Mrs. Morgan," Mrs. Patterson intervened. You've forgotten. This is your daughter, Beatrice's, girl."

"No, I'm not," Judith interrupted. "I'm her daughter, Sarah's, girl."

The woman and Lillian glanced at one another.

"You must be mistaken," Mrs. Patterson said. "She had only one daughter and she died, tragically."

"No, she had two…" Judith corrected.

Lillian spat at her, angrily. "Don't make up my life for me. I had one daughter. Her name was Beatrice and she's dead. Now go away and leave me alone."

Judith left, shaken. Mrs. Patterson stepped out in the hall with her. "Usually she talks nonsense, because she's weak in the head. But the facts about her family are very clear to her. She is telling you the truth. Had you ever met your grandmother?"

"No."

"Obviously, someone has given you wrong information."

She went back to the hotel, called Warren and told him what had happened.

"Why would my grandmother deny her relationship with my mother?"

"Maybe the old lady's right and she's not your grandmother."

"Warren," she said, exasperated.

"Maybe there are family skeletons you don't know about."

"Maybe there are." Maybe something so dreadful had happened to her mother that her grandmother shut her out of her mind, denying she'd ever existed.

Besides, her grandmother's last name wouldn't be Morgan, would it? That was Sarah's mother's last name.

Chapter Twenty-Nine

After Judith returned to Los Angeles, she and Warren hired a detective to search for her mother. He went by the single moniker, "Coal", and his business card read, "We Even Find Them in the Dark". Although he worked diligently, spending several weeks in Vermont, he came up with nothing, not during the dark or the light.

"Your mother did a real good job," Coal concluded. "She plain doesn't want to be found."

But Judith wasn't ready to give up and pleaded with Warren. "We'll both have to go back. Give ourselves plenty of time next summer."

"If a detective can't find any trace of her, how can we?"

"I don't know."

They kept Coal on retainer just in case. Gradually Judith realized that he was right. Her mother didn't want to be located. Why else would she have so completely erased her tracks? If she were dead, there would have been a notice of it someplace. And Coal had checked as many records as possible. He couldn't even find a social security number.

Still Judith was positive that, someday, something would happen revealing her whereabouts.

Finally resigned to her mother's disappearance, Judith was more and more at loose ends. The head housekeeper kept the Hollis enterprise in Bel Air running smoothly. The lawns were mowed and the flower beds weeded by a crew of dependable gardeners. The cook took care of the shopping and meals. Judith took care of Gillian as much as she wanted, but Annetta, her nanny, clearly felt the little girl was her job except on her days off.

Judith expressed her dissatisfaction to Warren. "Our lives are so organized that I feel useless. Gillian is well taken care of and happy. This house hardly needs me and I don't see enough of you. I've got to do something..."

"Why?"

"Don't you know?"

"No."

"I'm bored senseless."

He was rational about it. "Boredom is a state of mind. You bring it on yourself, so you can cure it. Frankly, I don't see how anyone can be bored."

She tried to be equally reasonable. "Warren, you're too busy to be bored. You never let up which is also a problem. Why don't you take on a partner so that we can be together more."

"I've never found anyone who can meet my standards."

"Perhaps your standards are too high."

"In this business, that's impossible. I'm dealing with peoples lives, their futures..."

She turned away in frustration. If only she had half the decisions to make that he did. If she had just a tenth of his responsibility, but she had none.

"This resolves nothing," he said. "I'm happy. If I am, then I can't understand why you're not."

"I can't either."

It was an impasse, but taking in his comment about boredom being self-made, she decided to keep herself busy.

She volunteered at UCLA in the Guild.

The UCLA Hospital was about two miles from their Bel Air home and Judith walked there. When Mrs. Tremaine, head of the volunteers, asked Judith her background and interests, she told the organizer that she was a nurse.

"A nurse..." Mrs. Tremaine's eyebrows lifted, but she barely slowed down rearranging the gift shop magazines. "My, now nice."

Her icy, scornful tone was proof to Judith that it certainly was not nice. Even though she was proud of it, she never mentioned it again.

She was always introduced as Mrs. Warren Hollis, the wife of the brilliant, distinguished surgeon and generous humanitarian.

Never as Judith Hollis.

She became resigned to that, too, becoming aware that she had no important identity apart from Warren.

But hope that things would not always be that way kept her going. That and Gillian who was bright, inquisitive and a fast learner.

The little girl played the violin, starting on a cigar box model when she was tiny. Judith showed her how to hold it by laying on the floor on her back. It was play and Gillian loved it.

"Good thing you don't want her to learn the piano," said Annetta, pretending to hold up a huge instrument.

They hired a Suzuki teacher to coach the child in the imitative method of violin playing. Before long, she was playing Vivaldi and Bach, graduating to larger and larger violins as she grew.

By the time she was four, they knew she was a special child.

"Warren," Judith said. "Do you realize how lucky she is?"

"In what way?"

"She can be anything she wants. She has the intelligence. And she'll never have to worry about money."

"True enough."

The possibilities raced through her mind and she spoke them just as fast. "She could be an engineer, a scientist...the space program is going to be big...a chemist, doctor..."

"Why would you want her to be a doctor? You're always complaining that I have no free time. Do you want to wish that on our daughter?"

"Warren, it's a matter of choice. Remember what you said to me about boredom? You have no free time because you don't want any."

She knew she'd made him angry because he became tight lipped, not answering right away. When he did, she was humiliated.

"You'd like to think it's a matter of choice, but it isn't. I have a large office staff to support, Gillian, you, our home, our style of living. It hasn't been a matter of choice for a good many years."

"I'm sorry, Warren."

Her apology only heated him up.

"With you, your life can be a matter of choice. Purely. You can take exercise, art or cooking classes. You can go to afternoon matinees, spend time shopping. You can go to the Guild or you don't have to. You don't have to do any of these things or you can do all of them."

"Warren, I said I was sorry."

He stopped as suddenly as he had begun, his eyes softened and then he gathered her into his arms, kissing her long and tenderly.

"Darling," he said, "these arguments are ridiculous."

"Yes," she agreed. "Why don't I just go back to work as a nurse…where I have to punch a time clock, eat breakfast on the run…and all the rest that goes with the working life?"

"That, too, is ridiculous."

Actually, she didn't think so. When she had practiced nursing, she felt needed and that she was doing something worthwhile. She began to realize that Warren decided her choices.

* * *

They never again had an argument like that, but Judith often thought about the differences in their perspectives as she went about her job of motherhood, shared with Annetta.

Judith bought a station wagon so she could taxi her daughter around to various lessons, ballet, drama, modeling. She would take Gillian and her small friends on outings to the Saturday matinee at the Children's Theater, to Helm's bakery, where they were given donuts at the end of the tour, the Carnation ice-cream company where they got cones. They ran along the Santa Monica beach and the cool breeze tangled their hair. Then she would bring the girls home for swimming in the pool and dinner. Afterwards, they would watch cartoons in the screening room until their parents came for them.

Gillian's life was Judith's life and she had just about lost track of her two closest friends, Kate and Susan.

She got a post-card from them when they had taken a return trip to the Grand Canyon.

"It's not the same without you. Remember the Maiden-Form bras…and sore legs? This time, it's donkeys for us and sore you-know-what?"

She laughed and wrote back that she expected to be included the next time.

But Susan married and moved to the San Fernando Valley and Kate went off with the "Good Ship Hope" taking her nursing knowledge to less fortunate parts of the world.

Susan would call every once in a while, usually with the news that she was either pregnant or just delivered. Her social life consisted of an permanent affair with a washing machine. She would cry to Judith that she could never get the house clean and that it wasn't big enough.

233

They didn't have much in common any more. Judith went out to visit her and was overwhelmed with the stair-step children and huge Labrador dog. They talked about nursing.

"All the nursing I'll ever do is right here on Collins street with my family." Susan was folding diapers at which she claimed to be the world expert. She had a newspaper clipping taped on the refrigerator about a young mother who got so fed-up with washing diapers that she piled them all on the living room floor and set a match to them. "It keeps my sanity knowing I'm not alone," she said.

From then on, it was mostly phone calls and those not very often between the two former roommates.

Kate sent postcards from the various ports where the "Good Ship Hope" stopped. There were cards from South Africa, Peru, and Brazil. How Judith longed to spend just one day with her, teaching the mothers how to give basic baby care, teaching the reasons for immunizations, treating infected sores on their legs.

Instead, the only children she saw were patients at UCLA who passed her in the hall on their way to clinic appointments, the lab or X-ray while she headed for the Guild's office. She was given the job of cataloguing items for the December holiday sale, the hundreds of slippers, gowns, handmade pillow slips and scarves, the art work painted or drawn by the doctors. She sewed doll's clothes for the fund raiser and raffle tickets for the Rolls Royce that would be the main attraction.

She hated every minute of it. Busy boredom was just as boring as any other kind.

The self-assured women working alongside her seemed to enjoy what they were doing, often coming in wearing tennis outfits. They discussed vacation plans, shared recipes, most already tried out by their own cooks. They preened over their wifely roles, cultivating them as carefully as an ornamental Bonsai tree that had to be kept confined to its container.

They talked about the best schools for children in Westwood, Brentwood, and boarding schools, for the day when those would be necessary. They talked about the bargains they'd found at the garment district in downtown Los Angeles, their pilgrimages to Grand Central Market for fresh produce once a week, saving money in time-consuming ways when they had fortunes to burn.

And Judith's boredom barometer skyrocketed, clanging the red bell.

Mercifully, she was saved from a lifetime of it. When Gillian was enrolled in a special first-grade class for bright children on the UCLA campus, Judith found herself pregnant again. She couldn't think of a happier diversion to get her away from the guilds and boards of directors and parties.

Warren surprised her, no, amazed her. He was so delighted that he cancelled everything and took her to Hawaii where he pampered her for a week. He wouldn't allow one phone call.

She had never been happier than with his attention, even though the initial fatigue of pregnancy kept her down for hours every morning.

Randall Thorne must have gotten wind of the tryst, because on the fifth day of their stay, a package was delivered to them.

Warren opened the box which had written on the outside. PLAIN BROWN WRAPPER It was a rubber plant with various contraceptives hanging from the limbs like flowers. A simple card hung from it. "Enjoy, old man!"

Warren roared, setting it on the table before the opened sliding glass door of their suite overlooking the surf. "Too late for this stuff."

"Didn't you tell him?"

"No. When we get back, I'll give him the plant and tell him it failed."

They fell on the bed laughing, rolling and tumbling together, cooled by the night breeze coming in from the ocean. The air rustled the contraceptives on the tree and the lovers laughed and laughed at the spectacle, hardly able to stop long enough to consummate the reason for their playfulness.

They made love everyday until they could no longer count the times and the week went by too fast.

"Does this guarantee us a boy?" Warren asked at one point.

"It does," she said, solemnly.

* * *

When they returned to Los Angeles, it was back to the frantic pace, the surgeries, the emergencies, Gillian and the taxi service to school and various music lessons.

The fatigue of early pregnancy soon left. Except for the times when the baby moved inside her, she was hardly aware of being pregnant. It was much easier than the first time.

She knew Warren was excited, too. Annetta looked forward to caring for the new baby.

"It will be good for Gillian," she said.

When Judith neared term, Warren was extremely conscientious in letting her know exactly where he could be reached. He'd given orders that he was to be interrupted regardless of where he was, even if during the most delicate surgery.

He didn't want her to be alone this time. "I think I let you down last time. It won't happen again."

The pains started on a September afternoon.

A Santa Ana wind blew through the valley and over into Bel Air which was unaccustomed to the desert breezes. Forest fires crackled in the dry Topanga Canyon to the west of them. City swimming pools were jammed. School had just started for the fall semester.

It was the hottest day of the year.

Warren and Randall met her at Cedars of Lebanon Hospital. She was taken to a private room and her husband stayed with her. They were left alone except for the times Randall would return to check her progress.

It was an easier labor than with Gillian and in the late evening, they wheeled her into the delivery room. Warren went with her. She was given a spinal and placed in delivery position.

"It won't be long," Randall said, telling her to push.

She pushed and he said, "I see a head of dark hair." There was a wait and then his comforting voice told her to push again.

"Your baby's head is out."

She waited for him to tell her the shoulders had been delivered and finally the body. She waited to hear whether the baby was a boy or a girl, but the next thing that happened was a sudden flooding in her brain, something sweeping her away into unconsciousness.

* * *

She awoke hours later in her private room. A dim light was on. She slowly regained her bearings and realized that she'd delivered a child and knew nothing about it.

She pushed the buzzer and a nurse came in.

"Can I see my baby?"

The nurse looked away and became very busy, lifting up the covers to massage Judith's abdomen to see if her uterus was hardened. "I will call your husband. He wants to see you."

"Is my baby all right?"

The nurse hurried out, not answering. Terror ripped through Judith. Soon Warren came in. He was ashen.

She was so scared that she could hardly speak. "What's the matter?" An ache in her throat threatened to close it.

He sat beside the bed, just looking at her, as if he wanted to talk, but couldn't.

"Did I keep my promise?" she finally asked, to break the terrible silence.

"What promise?"

"Did I give you a boy?"

"Yes." There was no pleasure in his eyes, no life or happiness. Instead, he seemed haunted.

"Something's wrong…isn't it?" Every part of her body radiated fear.

"Darling," he took her hand, and for a moment, he couldn't speak. "Our baby has problems."

"What kind?" She was wary.

He turned away, reaching for his handkerchief.

Her stomach tied in knots, her throat ached, her head became light. "Is he alive, Warren?"

"Yes, he's alive. Very much so."

This gave her some relief. "Then what's the matter? What could be so horrible that they knocked me out at his birth, that the nurse avoids my questions, that you are holding back? What is it, Warren?"

"Our son has birth defects." He choked on the words, his eyes signaled tragedy.

After a brief moment of apprehension, she relaxed. "Thank God, you're a surgeon, Warren. You can help him."

"No. His defects go beyond the kind of help I can give."

He held her hand and she lay back, closing her eyes, trying to absorb the information, trying to understand what this meant to them.

"Warren, take me to see him."

"No."

"Warren, he's my son, too. Please."

"No." Overcome by emotion, he kissed and held her. She felt his chest move heavily as he sobbed and he quickly left the room.

They brought her some hot tea and toast. She couldn't touch either.

Randall came by the next morning and expressed his condolences. "I'm sorry, Judith. I don't know what happened."

"Just take me to see him. Seeing him can't be worse than not seeing him. My imagination has me in hell."

Randall made a phone call to the nursery to tell the nurse he was bringing Mrs. Hollis to see her son. He took her to the back of the nursery. The baby was in a bassinet away from the viewing windows, where he could not be seen by others.

He was sleeping and, at first, Judith couldn't see what was wrong, and then as she reached down to touch his cheek, stroking it ever so slightly, the irritation woke him up and he became a frenzy of movement. His eyes were too far apart, deep-set. She couldn't tell whether he could see or not. His head moved frantically as if searching for something and she saw that his lips were black and blue. He strained at the blanket that had his arms pinned to his sides, papoose style. His chin was receded and his ears were strange, like rose buds in the process of flowering. She had the ludicrous thought that he looked like a battered miniature fighter.

His mouth made frantic, biting motions.

She turned to Randall. "He's hungry."

"Yes, you're probably right."

She couldn't understand why he sounded relieved. She reached into the bassinet to pick up her baby and as soon as he felt her arm against his face, he turned on her ferociously, trying to grab her flesh. She stifled a cry of pain, pulled back, shocked. She quickly grabbed a bottle that the nurse handed her, but the child didn't know what it was and fought it.

"He doesn't know what he's supposed to do," she said, wondering what she should do.

Randall took the baby from her and handed him to the nurse. Judith fell against the doctor, burying her head against him.

"Will he ever?" she sobbed. "You didn't tell me."

"I don't know," he said, leading her away from the nursery.

* * *

It was one of the most heart-breaking moments of Randall's life. Now, he had to face the child's father. He went to his office where he met Warren, doubtful that they could keep their emotions under their usually protective professional veneers.

Warren was slumped in the leather office chair, dark circles under his eyes, the look of a tormented man. "Thank you for helping Judith."

"I don't think she fully understands yet," said Randall.

"It's just as well."

"Warren, I'm going to bring another pediatrician in on this case. I can't tell you what happened. I've never seen anything like it before."

"Don't bother. I have. I had a younger brother…lived to be fifteen. I was born in Vermont and Judith's family came from there. A few of the women passed the disorder on to their sons. It's genetic, sex-linked…"

"I'm sorry, Warren. I know how badly you wanted a son."

Warren broke down, sobbing shamelessly, Randall helplessly attempting to comfort him. What could be said? What words of condolence would be sufficient to the moment?

At one point, Warren regained his composure and said in despair, "Any son we have could be born with the disorder."

*   *   *

The hospital clerk stood by Judith's bed, holding papers. "We are typing your son's birth certificate. What name would you like for him?"

Without hesitating, she said, "Warren Thornton Hollis, Jr." After all, they had always said their son would be named after his father.

The clerk asked for verification of the spelling.

Suddenly, Judith thought better of the chosen name. "I think I'll discuss this with my husband."

"Okay. So long's we have a name by the time the baby leaves. Less problems with the paperwork."

The next morning, Judith readied herself to go home. She had showered and dressed in a new nightgown and robe, waiting for Warren to come for her. She rested on the top of the covers as the janitor came in to mop.

She idly watched the mop moving back and forth.

When Warren arrived, he handed her a bundle of baby clothes. She rang for the nurse to take them away to dress their son for the ride home.

"Warren, we must give him a name before we leave."

"Why?"

As soon as he said that, she was glad she hadn't made their son his namesake. "Easier for paperwork."

"You name him."

"No, Warren. He's your son, too."

239

He was thoughtful. Their only distraction was the floor man's mopping. Suddenly, Warren turned on him. "Must you do that now?"

The startled janitor froze.

"What's your name?" asked Warren.

The janitor panicked, shoving the mop into the bucket on wheels. "I'll come back later."

"What's your name?" Warren repeated.

"I didn't do nothin' wrong," the man said, almost child-like.

"No, no," said Warren, quickly. "Nothing like that."

The janitor relaxed, breaking into a wide grin. "Ed."

"Short for Edward?"

"No. Short for nothing. My dad calls me 'Ed'. My mother calls me 'Eddie.'"

"Good," said Warren. "That's good enough."

"You won't get me into no trouble…"

Warren shook his hand. "Certainly not."

The janitor hurried out.

Judith realized Warren's plan and when the clerk came in with the birth certificate, she watched, feeling her first distance from Warren over the baby.

"His name will be Eddie," he said to the clerk. "Is that agreeable with you, Judith?"

She gave her consent by silence, allowing Warren to sever the slim cord of identity to their son.

"Middle name?" the clerk asked.

"No middle name," said Warren, turning back to help Judith into the wheelchair for the ride to the car.

The nurse brought Eddie and placed him in Judith's arms. She was careful to place a small pillow between his face and her arm.

Judith threw the baby blanket over his face as Warren pushed her down the corridor to the elevator.

"New baby?" a curious woman asked. "Can I have a peek? I just love new babies." She reached for a corner of the blanket.

Judith grabbed for the blanket protectively while Warren grimly elbowed the woman aside, and pushed Judith into the elevator.

When they arrived home, Gillian came with her nanny to see Eddie.

Gillian studied her brother. "His face is funny."

Judith left the room, crying. Was this the way it was going to be with Eddie?

She regained her composure and went back to Gillian, determined to help her have a good beginning relationship with Eddie.

Annetta was looking out the window.

Warren stood near the door to witness this first encounter between the children.

"He knows me, mommy," said Gillian, excitedly.

"That's because you're his sister. His face is different, but you can love him just the same."

Gillian looked at her, puzzled. "But I do," she said.

Judith was ashamed of herself. She had turned a child's observation into something it hadn't been.

"Do you want to hold him?" she quickly asked.

Gillian sat on the round vanity chair and Judith placed Eddie in her lap.

He tried to bite his sister, but Gillian instinctively grabbed his chin, forcing his face away from her. She kissed his cheek and looked him over. "Does he see?"

"No," said Warren, leaving the room.

Judith's thoughts traveled with him. Would he ever accept their son?

* * *

The next morning, unknown to Judith, Warren had a vasectomy as she, whose love for him was endless, resolved that she would someday give him a normal son.

Chapter Thirty

Life with Eddie was a struggle from the beginning. Some of the decisions about him came easily enough. Others were forced on them with heart-wrenching necessity.

They didn't send out birth announcements. After all, Eddie didn't fit into the normal rituals that involved congratulations and hopes for a glowing, fulfilling future.

Judith had told Annetta that she wouldn't have to get up with Eddie in the night. After the first night with the boy, Judith was exhausted. Eddie screamed most of the time, seldom sleeping. Feeding didn't seem to ease his misery, whatever it was. He bit at his lips, his fingers, anything that he could grab. Judith spent hours trying to figure ways of covering and protecting his hands.

She could hardly wait until morning when Annetta would take over as soon as she'd gotten Gillian off to school.

At breakfast, Judith moved her chair so that it touched Warren's and she could lean against him. "I can't go through this night after night," she said. "I hardly got any sleep."

"Neither did I." He stroked her. "We'll put him in an upstairs bedroom where we can't hear him."

She felt her chest tighten. "No, Warren. I have to hear him. How will I know if he's all right?"

Warren was thoughtful. "I'll think of something."

Judith stared at her food, unable to eat, too tired to know if she was hungry. In a few minutes, Warren would say goodbye to Gillian and the both of them would soon be gone for the day. Annetta would take over Eddie's care.

When Warren left, Judith attended to Eddie one more time before falling into a hot tub, too tired to dress and put on makeup.

Annetta asked to speak to her. Judith was lying on her bed, her eyes closed, a warm wash cloth soothing them, but welcomed in the children's nurse.

Annetta stood at the side of her bed. Judith invited her to sit.

"No, I'd just as soon stand." Her voice shook.

An alarm signaled in Judith's exhausted brain. She took off the washcloth.

Annetta's hands were tightly clasped in front of her. She cleared her throat. "Mrs. Hollis, I can't take care of the new one. He scares me."

Somehow, Judith hadn't expected this. Annetta had such genuine love for Gillian. Eddie was not different. He just didn't understand. That was all.

"All right, Annetta," she said, wearily, sitting on the side of the bed, massaging her neck where the tension had built up.

"I can resign my position, if that suits you."

"We'll let you know," she said, her tone flat.

"If I stay, I don't want to see that boy. Hearing him is bad enough."

"That will be enough." Judith seethed.

Annetta left hurriedly.

Judith went to the window, hoping that viewing the quiet yard, the green lawn, the calm pool would translate to her over wrought emotions. She thought about her alternatives, but wasn't sure what they were. Her one hope was Warren who had said he would think of something.

She cared for Eddie all day, laying on the couch in his room between changing his diaper, feeding him. She was even becoming immune to his screams, almost able to sleep through all but the most piercing.

As the day progressed, she became even more angry with Annetta. How could anyone reject a helpless baby, no matter what kind of a problem he had? And then, there was the underlying current with Warren. Wasn't he also rejecting Eddie?

She clenched her fists in frustration, crying. Was this the way it would to be with Eddie? He couldn't handle frustrations either and fought out with the only weapon he had. His mouth—screaming and biting. Annetta and Warren used another weapon. Walking away.

When Warren came home that night, Judith was resting on the chaise lounge in their bedroom, waiting for him. She told him of Annetta's decision. "She doesn't have to resign," Judith said. "We can fire her."

"How can you even consider such a thing? Think of Gillian."

"I am. If Annetta rejects Eddie, what if she transfers her feelings to Gillian."

"You can't blame Annetta for feeling the way she does. It may be difficult getting anyone to care for Eddie. After all, people are afraid of deformities."

"Why? He's a tiny baby."

"I don't know. Basic biological response, perhaps. It's a Darwinian thing which prevents mating with abnormals so fewer are born. But that's only a guess."

"Don't be so theoretical, Warren."

"You asked."

"And Annetta says that she doesn't want to see Eddie if she stays."

"I already suggested that we move him upstairs."

"Warren! I won't do that."

He was patient with her, leading her to the bed and making her get under the covers. "I'm getting you hot tea. Tonight I'll take care of Eddie. Tomorrow, after you've had some rest, you can make a better decision, although I hope you'll agree with me."

She was too tired to fight her husband. Warren disappeared for a long time. She waited and waited, her mouth warm from the idea of the hot tea that he would be bringing to her.

She heard Eddie screaming, but she didn't get up. After all, hadn't Warren said he'd take care of the boy?

When she woke up, the sun glared through their window, a cup of cold tea sat on the bedside table. Warren was sound asleep.

She hadn't heard Eddie cry all night.

Judith leaped out of bed. Something must have happened to him.

But their son lay quietly in his crib, sleeping, long intervals between his even breathing.

When Warren got up, she asked him what he'd done.

"Phenobarbital. He needs something to reduce his central nervous system irritability."

"Warren, that's a terrible thing to do."

"No, it's appropriate. You slept, didn't you. He slept…"

"You don't really know anything about Eddie's condition. You haven't the background," she said, and watched as his expression hardened. "I mean…you're not a neurologist. I wish you'd have Eddie seen so we know exactly what we can hope for him."

"No." Warren marched out with his briefcase, angrily escaping to work.

That morning, Judith called in the movers and had two upstairs rooms rearranged. One for Eddie, one for herself and Warren.

He'd left in anger that morning and, that night, when he saw what she'd done, he was furious. "Why did you move us?"

"I don't understand your reaction. It was what you wanted."

"I said to move Eddie's room. Not ours."

"Warren, I have to have him near me."

"Why?"

She was dumbfounded. "How can you possibly ask that?"

"He doesn't care where he is."

"Warren, do you want him out of the way?"

"No." He was sharp with her. "You need to get away from him. You'll never get him on any kind of schedule, especially with those Dr. Spock books you read. You'll just have to program yourself. You don't need to be near him."

So they had two bedrooms. One downstairs and one upstairs which Warren never used. Only Judith did when she flopped down there on the nights that the phenobarbital didn't work as well.

How their lives had changed. Warren always seemed to be on edge. Eddie was barely two weeks old and the situation in their home had taken them from heaven to hell.

The only one managing at all was Gillian who cheerfully kissed Eddie goodbye every morning before she left for school. "It's all right, little brother," she would say. "Don't bite. I'm your sister. I love you."

Eddie would turn on her ferociously, but she would just work around his fighting fingers and mouth.

These daily exchanges between the children just about destroyed Judith, but gave her the hope to keep going. During the day, she checked on the baby a hundred times a day, changing his diaper, feeding him, rocking him which upset him more. Eddie couldn't tolerate any kind of external stimulation. It was as though he had too much inside already.

In the evenings, Gillian came upstairs to help her mother. Annetta and Warren never saw Eddie. Except at night, when Warren would give the baby a hefty dose of phenobarbital.

They advertised for live-in help, specifically to care for Eddie. The applicants would come, hear about the salary, be enthusiastic about the private room that came with the job. They would see Eddie and that would be it.

The excuses covered the map.

"I don't work with retards. I thought you meant he just had a little something wrong with him."

"Sorry, but I couldn't stand to look at him. But I wish you the best of luck. This is a nice place you got here. Pool and all…but looking at him would make me sick."

A middle-aged woman accepted. "Sure I'll take the job. But I need an advance to get me over…and I need every Friday off, sometimes Wednesdays…"

Judith grimaced, escorting her to the door.

She lost track of the people refusing the job. Finally, there were no applicants and Judith continued doing all of Eddie's care.

She and Warren never had time to themselves. "Darling, we'll get something arranged," he said. "Don't worry, everything will be all right."

Inside, she'd thought the same thing. But the day-to-day reality gave her doubts. Warren had never had any spare time before. Now it was almost a relief for both of them.

When Eddie was a month old, Susan Ryan called. "We've got to get together. I've got five kids and you've got two and we haven't seen each other more than seven times since we finished training."

"I can't get away, Susan. Eddie takes all of my time."

"That's a switch. I used to have that problem. Now, no matter what, I get out. I get a sitter when I go to the supermarket. It saves me money because the kids aren't there to drop junk into the basket. I never thought I would see grocery shopping as fun."

Neither did Judith who hadn't been grocery shopping for months. "The next time you're at the market, why not drop by my place?"

Within the week, Susan showed up for lunch. "Where is your little bundle," she said, hugging Judith.

Judith took her upstairs. Eddie was biting furiously.

Susan stared at him, her face contorting in disbelief and revulsion. "What caused it?"

"It? How do you mean?" Eddie was not an impersonal object.

"What is he?"

Anger and pride rose up in Judith. "What is he? He is our son."

"Judith, don't get me wrong, but he's got problems."

The two ate a hurried lunch. Judith couldn't bring herself to ask about Susan's kids. She resented the little monsters, and their mother whose biggest problem was deciding who got the shoes with the next paycheck.

As they said goodbye, Judith knew it would be the last time they'd see one another.

* * *

The day came for Judith's six-week check-up with Randall Thorne. She jammed Eddie's bassinet in the back seat so that it wouldn't move while she drove. She left through the Bel Air West gate and across to Westwood Blvd., passing by fraternity row near the UCLA campus. Water was running down the street from hoses the college students were using to wash cars. In between, they were spraying one another, drinking beer, while girls in shorts watched their antics.

How Judith envied the parents of the strong young men. Did they take their good fortune for granted? Their strapping sons were going to become successful corporate men, marrying, with no worries about their futures.

Suddenly, Judith got angry with herself. Ever since Eddie's birth, she'd been on one long roller-coaster ride feeling sorry for herself. It was to the point where she couldn't stand herself.

Somewhere along Gayley Avenue, on the campus perimeter, she resolved to stop her self-defeating, cry-baby attitude.

In the back seat, Eddie screamed the whole time, upset by the movement of the car. When she saw Eddie, Randall's nurse immediately took Judith into the inner office.

"How are things going?" Randall asked her.

"All right," she lied. "It's hard because we can't find anyone to live-in and help with Eddie. I just wish I really knew what was wrong with him, if he has any potential."

"Why not have him seen by a neurologist?"

She hesitated. After all, Randall was Warren's closest friend. "Warren won't give his permission."

Randall examined Judith, drew blood and checked her hemoglobin. It was down. "Judith, you've got to do something. You've lost too much weight." He prescribed her iron pills. "Get your blood back up where it belongs."

Instead of making her feel better, the visit to his office depressed her even more. She had enough to worry about without wondering if she would fall apart and no longer be attractive to Warren. Had she really given herself a good look in the mirror recently?

* * *

As soon as Judith left his office, Randall Thorne got on the phone and tracked down Warren.

"Warren, have you looked at your wife? She's a wreck."

"It's no wonder," Warren said. "She worries too much about the baby, hasn't been able to get someone in to take care of him. It's been a strain."

"Warren, why don't you give her a little peace of mind? Have the child seen by a neurologist?"

"Randall," he said, good-naturedly. "Mind your own business."

This made Randall mad. "When are you going to quit playing God? You stand aloof, above-it-all. You have no right to do that to Judith."

"I said, 'Mind your own business'". But it was more as a friendly put-off than with any anger in it.

"Okay, old buddy. When's for dinner?"

* * *

As Randall suspected he would, Warren had Eddie seen by a neurologist friend although Judith went alone with their baby. Harvey Fielding increased the dose of phenobarbital and referred the child to a pediatrician for a special formula. Judith learned that Eddie would never be any better, never grow much more than a five-year-old, if that much. He could live for two weeks, two years, two decades, depending on the quality of his care.

Chapter Thirty-One

When Judith arrived home from the day of consultations, a letter waited for her. It was from Kate on the "Good Ship Hope" anchored in South African waters.

Hi Judith: I have time on my hands. Lots of it. I've come down with malaria and look like a yellow pumpkin. I wanted to die several times. But we don't give up, do we Judith? I'm jumping ship for now.
Be back in L.A. end of October.

Judith wired her. "We expect you to recover at our place." She also mentioned Eddie.

Warren came in late that evening, a full day's surgeries behind him, another ahead of him in the morning. Judith tried to make his evening nice, making him comfortable, mixing him a double-scotch, handing him his robe. She had already given herself the bathroom once over, a head-to-toe examination in the mirror, bathed, brushed out her hair and splashed a light perfume on herself. Finally, she slipped into a silk caftan.

Maybe Randall Thorne thought she looked awful, but if Warren thought so, too, he didn't mention it.

"What did Harvey Fielding tell you?" he asked.

Her hand shook as she sipped a glass of wine. "Eddie could live to be twenty..." She couldn't go on.

Warren blanched, quickly downing the scotch. Had his previous self-assurance been a false front? Had he not really believed his own words until they were confirmed by someone else?

"Are you satisfied now?" He sounded defeated.

"Satisfied? No. Devastated is more like it. You were right about Eddie. He doesn't know anything. And he is blind and deaf."

"Maybe I shouldn't have told you. Maybe I should have left it to Harvey."

"It doesn't matter, Warren. It isn't something I ever wanted to hear from anyone."

He became thoughtful, his eyes glazing over, whispering, "Twenty years…"

Watching him, she realized that he hadn't known everything. "It's not two hundred years. He isn't going to shipwreck us."

"He al…" Then Warren abruptly caught himself. "Let's eat." He took her hand and led her to a breakfast room off of the kitchen, not the formal dining room, but one more suited to their mood.

As always, they ate by candlelight, with soft music in the background. Warren liked Lawrence Welk's champagne music, the innocuous sounds barely intruding. Tonight, she wished they would. She couldn't get her mind off Eddie or Warren's torment.

But he tried to bring some normalcy back to their situation. "Now that we're sure about Eddie, we'll have to focus more on Gillian," he said. "It's time she took up the piano."

"She's studying the violin, Warren."

He shook his head. "When did she start?"

"Five months before Eddie was born."

"Why haven't I ever heard her play?"

"She practices while you're at the hospital, Warren." She didn't realize that he didn't know about the lessons. Rather than add to their tension, she changed the subject. "Kate's coming back…going to stay with us."

"Good," he said, and it was obvious that his mind was elsewhere.

* * *

The afternoon when Judith brought Kate from LAX, Westwood was high with the excitement of the U.C.L.A. homecoming week. Stores advertised homecoming specials, the streets were filled with roaming students, honking cars. Banners reading, HOMECOMING 1958, were stretched above Westwood Blvd.

"If I don't do one other thing," Kate sighed, "I want to see the parade."

She had lost weight. In the past, she'd always complained of eating too much, but now, she barely touched her dinner. She was still jaundiced.

"The itching drives me crazy, but blood tests show I'm not contagious."

Still Judith had her doubts. "Kate, you don't have to concern yourself with the kids. If you want, you can stay in your room until you're well. Or walk around the grounds, sit in the pool…"

But when they reached home, Gillian bounded out to meet them. She and Kate took an immediate liking to one another.

"Come see my brother." She took Kate by the hand and led her upstairs. Judith followed.

When Kate saw Eddie for the first time, she didn't seem shocked.

He was wet so she changed him while his arms and legs flailed. And she asked to sleep in the upstairs room next to his. In spite of Judith's earlier remark, Kate insisted on caring for Eddie. "While I'm here, I'll take over."

Judith gave Eddie phenobarbital and Kate went to her room to rest.

Warren came home and welcomed their house guest. "If you have no objections, Kate, I'd like to do blood cultures on you."

Judith was embarrassed for Kate, but knew it was a sensible precaution.

"Please stay away from Gillian until the results are back," he added.

Kate slept twenty out of the next twenty-four hours, but got up with Eddie, changing and feeding him. It was the first relief Judith had had since he'd been born.

The next morning, Judith took Kate's breakfast up to her.

"I like the little guy," Kate said. "I just wish he could know me."

When Gillian came home from school, she couldn't understand why Kate could play with Eddie but not with her.

"Kate isn't playing with Eddie. She doesn't feel well," Judith said.

Days later, Warren said the cultures were clear. Kate came downstairs for dinner and Gillian was happy again.

The following Saturday night, Westwood Blvd. was closed off to traffic for the homecoming parade.

Judith pleaded with Warren to come home early and take care of Eddie so that she, Gillian and Kate could go to the parade.

He made the concession and was home before five.

Kate came down to dinner, but she wasn't dressed to go out. Gillian was excited and didn't touch her supper. Judith was ready, dressed in Levi's, and a U.C.L.A. shirt.

"I'm too tired to go," Kate said. "You and Warren take Gillian."

As badly as she felt for Kate, Judith had to admit that the idea of going with her husband and daughter was exciting. Warren agreed without an argument.

They drove from Bel Air and had to walk more than a mile from their parking place to reach the center of activity. Westwood Boulevard was jammed with people, but Warren was able to jostle Gillian to the front row where she jumped up and down, waving a Bruin flag, cheering the team when their float passed by. Judith and Warren held hands and she had to get on tiptoe to see some of the action.

"I can't get over how much Gillian has grown," said Warren.

Judith squeezed his hand. It was the first time she'd felt any serenity in months. Warren kept studying Gillian as though she were a new book that had been lying around the house for months, unread, and when he finally did read it, wondered why he hadn't picked it up sooner.

They were one happy family going home and putting Gillian to bed together. The little girl clung to her father for a long time until he agreed to read her a story.

Eddie was quiet upstairs and Kate's light was on, but they didn't disturb her.

Judith and Warren made love that night, with all of the old glow returning. They fell asleep exhausted and woke up in each others arms. It was still dark.

"One more time," she said, dreamily.

"Only one?"

She kissed him teasingly and he crushed his mouth against hers, leaving her breathless, finally taking her. It was as though Eddie had never happened.

Ten weeks later, Warren's schedule was busier than ever. One Monday evening, he had agreed to accept an award from the City of Hope for time he'd donated in his specialty. He didn't like the publicity, but felt he couldn't avoid the honor.

Because Kate was still with them, Judith was able to accompany her husband. She wore a simple, but elegantly designed suit for the occasion and didn't even try to contain her pride when he was given the award.

After the months of having Kate staying with them, bringing a special feeling of goodness to their home, Judith was ready to offer her anything to stay permanently.

She approached Kate.

"No, Judith. You have your lives to lead. It's time I get on with mine. I'll never be able to thank you enough for letting me come here to recuperate.

When my strength's back, I'm going back to work. Maybe at Memorial. Goddam, I hate being weak. It ties me down, makes me dependent."

Kate left two weeks later in early March. It was a sad day for all of them. Before it was over, Judith realized how much her friend had done for them. She had forgotten how demanding Eddie was.

The week after Kate left, he had his first illness. One morning, he was unusually crabby, his cry different, as if he was having pain. His little body was hot, his temperature raging at one-hundred-five. She feared he would have seizures, sponged him off, gave him aspirin, and put in a call for Warren.

A nurse relayed his reply to her from surgery where he was doing a face-lift. "Dr. Hollis will be home as soon as possible."

She debated calling the pediatrician, but decided to wait and see what Warren thought.

"As soon as possible" turned out to be the time he ordinarily came home. Nine p.m.

He hurried upstair's to Eddie, barking questions.

"When did he get sick?"

"Sometime last night?"

"What's his temperature?"

"It was down to one-hundred-two, but he feels hotter again." Eddie's skin felt like parched sand.

Warren examined the boy, too ill to scream while Judith held him. "His chest is noisy," he said. He peered into Eddie's ears with his otoscope. "They're a little red, nothing major."

"Are you going to give him antibiotics?"

"No, I think he has a virus."

"Warren, if Gillian were this sick, you'd give her antibiotics."

"Don't make comparisons, Judith. He has a virus. And you know antibiotics are not effective with viruses."

"How can you be sure without doing blood cultures.?

"Judith," he admonished. "Everything will be all right."

He left the room and Judith sponged Eddie again. She found herself looking around the room at the stuffed toys and the colorful chintz curtains that he would never see. The six-month-old boy was so sick that he hardly cried. He didn't grow tense as Judith changed his diaper and the sheets.

When she was finished, she found Warren in the den, draining a scotch on the rocks. When she came in, he poured himself another.

"Make me one, too," she said.

253

He obliged.

"Warren, I want to call the pediatrician."

"It's not necessary," he said. "I think you should trust my medical judgment."

She kept her thoughts to herself.

In the morning, she got up early. Eddie lay limply in his crib, diarrheal stool dripping down his legs, soaking the sheet and blanket. His temperature was up to one-hundred-five again. His eyes rolled and his dry mouth bled even though his aimless biting movements were few.

Warren had left for the hospital and Judith put in a call to him.

By noon, he still hadn't returned her call and Judith, disregarding his wishes, dialed Sam Chandler, their pediatrician. He told her to bring in Eddie, immediately.

After a thorough examination, Dr. Chandler prescribed antibiotics.

By nightfall, Eddie's temperature had dropped and he could sip water.

Warren came home, later than usual.

"Why didn't you return my call?" she said.

"When did you call?"

"This morning."

"I'm sorry, Judith, but the message didn't reach me."

Within three days, Eddie was better and Judith was exhausted.

She drove down to Westwood to pick up more of Eddie's special formula, deciding that she would request home delivery in the future. She passed fraternity row again, for the eighth time that week, and it was as though the message had been there all along and she'd been sent past the houses by design until she realized it.

It took her a few days, but she got the names and addresses of all the fraternities and the presidents of each from the public information office at U.C.L.A. She drafted a letter and sent it to a half-dozen presidents.

She received negative replies to every one, some formally by letter, others by telephone.

Not willing to give up, she went to the next six fraternities on the list.

One president wrote that his fraternity would like to consider the job of caring for Eddie.

Chapter Thirty-Two

Judith's first view of the fraternity president was when he rode his ten-speed bicycle up the drive to their home and parked it smack right in front of the door, not off to the side, but right in front of the door, so that everyone else would have to go around it or move it.

She opened the door to greet him with second thoughts. Was she doing something really stupid?

But the thought quickly blew away for she was greeted by a blast of cool March air. The president stood there, winded from his uphill climb. He offered her a wet handshake, smiling, the beads of sweat running along the creases of his forehead.

"Hi," he said. "I'm Burgess Selwyn...or Burger."

"Good morning. I'm Mrs. Hollis...Judith..."

She took him to the downstairs den where they could talk privately. Thank God, Eddie was cooperating. He had finally stopped his screeching and was sleeping.

She explained her needs to Burger. "Our son, Eddie, requires special care because he has neurological problems. He must be fed a certain way and be given sedatives to keep his nerves under control." She hesitated, not sure how much to tell Burger, not wanting to discourage him. "We are trying to get him on a schedule which hasn't been successful so far."

Burger took it all in, studying her, looking around the room, at the western bar with bull horns holding beer glasses, the pictures of Hollywood western stars, Gene Autry, Rudy Vallee, Roy Rogers. It was hard to tell from his expression what he was thinking.

"Burger, tell me something about yourself."

"Huh...yeh, sure." He related his growing years in Claremont, California where his parents owned an orange grove which went to encroaching home building. He was the only son with two sisters. He'd always known he wanted to be a doctor when he gave up being a second Captain Kangaroo. He studied hard and had always worked. "My folks always had it rough. Then my Mom got sick and it wiped out everything they had. You'd think the government would help poor, old people who've paid taxes all their lives, wouldn't you?"

He was so intense and sincere. "Yes, Burger. I think the government should help poor people." It hadn't been so long since she'd been poor, yet, she'd never felt in need. Maybe it was because she'd never wanted anything unattainable. And, then, maybe she didn't have much imagination as to her possibilities. For Burger, a medical education must be an impossibility. "Tell me, how can you afford UCLA."

"It isn't easy. Yeh, it sure isn't. I make tuition with scholarships and small jobs. Next year I go into medical school. U.C.L.A has accepted me…but there are problems."

He didn't go into these but gazed around the room. "Is that really Roy Rogers with his horse and Dale?"

She wasn't sure whether he was dubious or admiring. "Yes, really." If only Warren would realize that not everyone knew this room was a put-on. It wasn't Warren's taste at all. And certainly not hers.

"Great! The perfect All-American family."

She laughed. Already she liked Burger. "Let me show you Eddie."

They went upstairs and she took him to see the boy. He was so tiny and, sleeping, almost looked normal.

She waited for Burger's reaction.

"He looks all right to me." Burger reached down to touch him, but Judith quickly stopped him. "Don't. It scares him."

Burger apologized. "I'm sorry. I thought…"

"No, I'm sorry. I didn't mention that touch excites him. When you see him awake, you'll understand."

"Why doesn't he wake up to our talking?"

"He doesn't hear."

"Oh."

She knew he was awed by Eddie.

Burger fidgeted. "When can I see him awake?"

She thought about it. What point was there in waking Eddie when it would surely upset him? "Are you interested in the job?"

"Oh, sure. But I want to see him awake."

"All right." As gently as she could, she picked up Eddie. Almost immediately, he stiffened out, let out a scream and tried to grab at his own flailing arms, biting his lips.

Burger stepped back.

Her heart sank. Like everyone else, he was afraid.

But Burger quickly recovered. "Is it okay if I hold him?"

They stood close to one another while she handed the baby over. It took coordination because Eddie was like a squirming wet fish.

Burger held him tightly, clasping Eddie's jaw so that he could look directly at him. "It must be hard to calm him when he can't hear your voice. When he quits yelling, does it help him to see you?"

"He can't see."

"Oh." Burger held Eddie even closer trying to stroke the tiny forehead. At first, Eddie fought. And then, he seemed to became quieter. After awhile, with Burger holding him, Eddie relaxed as much as he'd ever done in his life. Judith went for his bottle and Eddie took the bottle from Burger. He knew how to hold Eddie so he would feel secure.

"You are really terrific," she said.

Burger beamed.

When Eddie finished his bottle, she bound his hands again and Burger put him back in his crib.

"What do you think?" She was almost afraid to ask.

"About what?"

"Can you do it?"

He studied Eddie as if he were a stalled car on the freeway that had to be moved. "Sure. I'll have to do some reading though."

"I don't think you'll find anything."

He shrugged. "Do you mind if I bring back my frat brothers? We've got to work out a plan..."

"I'll give you our plan."

"You said it didn't work."

Judith bristled. "At least you could try it."

"Yeh, okay. If it doesn't work for us and you insist on doing it your way, then we can forget the whole thing, friendly-like. Agreed?"

He waited for her answer. "No, please, no. Then you can try it your way."

He headed down the stairs to the front door. Gillian was just coming home from school. "Hi," he said to her.

Judith introduced them. "Gillian, I'd like you to meet Burger."

Gillian sparkled. "You mean like a hamburger?"

"Gillian!"

"Exactly," said Burger. "Spent a lot of years working at Mac Donalds. At least they didn't call me Big Mac."

Gillian giggled, covering her mouth. Annetta came to the foyer where Judith was saying goodbye to Burger. Judith introduced the two. Annetta gave a disapproving look to his tennis shorts and sneakers.

"Annetta, please take Gillian..." She waited until the two were out of earshot. "Burger, we haven't discussed salary."

"Too soon," he said. "Gotta wait until the frat decides if they want to handle it."

That night, in bed, she mentioned the plan to Warren.

"Fine," he said, quickly falling asleep.

After brewing over the situation, afraid Burger and his friends would refuse the job, and afraid they wouldn't, she finally fell asleep.

The next Thursday evening, the entire fraternity showed up. Judith watched as Burger took them quietly upstairs. There were about fifteen of them, short, tall, wide, skinny, dark hair, light hair, nondescript clothes. There was absolute silence for about four minutes and then they all trailed down the stairs again.

"Do you mind if we use the Roy Rogers room for a few minutes?"

"Go right ahead."

Gillian had come to watch the boys, fascinated. Judith steered her out. "Go back to Annetta." She did, dragging her feet, looking over her shoulder the whole time.

The boys hardly seemed aware of her. Judith started to lead them into the den, but Burger interrupted her, clearing his throat.

"If you don't mind, Mrs. Hollis, we'd like to talk this over privately."

"Certainly." She went into the kitchen, sitting on a high stool, surprised to find herself swinging her foot nervously. What if they decided they couldn't handle it?

The fraternity boys were cloistered in the den for a long time. Finally, as if he were the foreman in a jury trial, Burger came looking for her.

"We're ready to talk business."

She accompanied him back into the den. Only four boys remained. She hadn't heard the others leave.

He took over. "You were right about the literature. There isn't anything. Something close, but not quite the same...Lesch-Nyhan disorder. We'd like to take on the job."

There wasn't a word to describe her relief.

He introduced his four fraternity brothers. "Like you to meet Windy, he's an engineering major; Rex, another premed...there isn't going to be enough room for both of us in medicine..." The boys all laughed. "And Scranton, biology, Ace, psychology."

She shook hands with each of them.

"We've looked over your plan," said Ace. She could envision him already as another Freud, his stern features and domineering eyes belying his casual manner. "We're not sure we like it, but we'll give it a try. Do you mind if we finally work out our own routine?"

"No, no, of course not."

"With no interference."

"Well..." She couldn't make that commitment. After all, Eddie was her baby. "Let's try each other for a month."

Burger posted a schedule for Judith.

"We've got most of the bases covered," he said, "but there are holes."

"We'll fill in..." Judith said. Imagine having just one free hour in the day.

"If you could do it from six in the morning until noon, we can do the rest. We've got conflicts with our class schedules."

Six am was her busiest time, getting Warren off, having breakfast with Gillian. "Fine."

Ace, Windy, Rex or Scranton stayed with Eddie from noon to six pm when Burger took over until morning. He said very little when he arrived, taking his armload of books upstairs for the twelve hour night shift.

For the first week, Burger stayed with his fraternity brothers to help them get used to the situation. The quintet quickly became known as the Eddie Squad. They never asked Judith for anything.

When Eddie cried or needed feeding, the boys went to the kitchen and prepared the formula. They changed the baby's diapers, bathed him, kept him warm, tried to keep the external stimulation to a minimum.

Judith stayed out of it.

Warren saw the posted schedule. "What is this all about?"

"Remember. I told you about the fraternity that was going to handle Eddie's care."

"Oh, yes."

She knew he didn't remember a thing.

The experiment was a success. Once Burger got the Squad going, they showed up like clockwork, with never a call or an excuse. Plans to get Eddie on a schedule did not work. Not theirs or Judith's. Eddie wrote his own script and the program was different every day.

Judith hardly got to know the boys, because they were under Burger's authority and he'd instructed them to leave her alone.

Annetta had to pull Gillian away every day. She wanted to spend the whole afternoon with the fraternity boys, but was allowed to go up for only one-half hour each day when Eddie was awake. She helped the frat boy on duty. Annetta never went with her.

Burger sent word that somebody had to accompany and stay with Gillian upstairs. He didn't want his boys compromised.

"Please, Annetta," Gillian begged. "Come with me."

"No. They have their business. I have mine."

"You don't like Eddie."

"You hush…"

Judith quickly interceded. "I'll stay with you."

It was hard witnessing the Squad caring for Eddie when she couldn't interfere, but it was their understanding. She learned more about them. Ace didn't need the job, his folks had money, but he didn't like to be idle, and this experience might eventually fit in with his doctoral thesis.

Scranton needed the money and was thinking of going into psychobiology. "Don't know if this will help me. It's worth a try though."

Rex hoped to design equipment for handicapped people someday. He couldn't understand why society didn't help disabled people more. "They can hardly go out of the house. It's so hard for them to get anyplace."

Rex felt that as a pre-med student he should see all there was to see that might have an effect on his career.

Before long, Eddie's room looked like an extension of the U.C.L.A student store with gold and blue U.C.L.A banners, beer mugs on the child's dresser, stuffed Bruin bears scattered around the room, a bear rug, a rocking chair. The fraternity boys had decorated the room to suit themselves for the many long hours they spent there.

They even brought in a bookcase for their most used books that they didn't want to haul back and forth. They requested and received permission to bring in a hot-plate and television.

In late June, at the beginning of summer, Burger suddenly announced his replacement as chairman of the Eddie squad. Judith was heartsick. He'd been so good for everyone, for Eddie, Gillian, herself.

"Why Burger? You said you would be here until the fall."

He was embarrassed. "I know. But I was offered a research assistant job…"

"Burger, please stay on."

"I wish I could. But there's more to it."

"Tell me, Burger."

But he wouldn't. She decided she'd go to his fraternity brothers to learn the truth. Warren told her to stay out of it. "Maybe he's tired of the job."

"I don't think so. He said he wanted to come back on his days off, but he won't be in charge of the squad anymore."

"Then accept his excuse."

"No, Warren. His pride is holding him back."

"Judith, this is a good time to think about a long range plan for Eddie. Gillian is getting to the point where he will interfere with her friendships. She has a right to live in a normal atmosphere. She and Annetta aren't getting along because of the situation. I think we should consider placing him in an institution. There comes a time…"

"I won't have it, Warren."

She defied Warren about Eddie as she always would. She also defied him about Burger and learned the real reason he couldn't stay on. Burger was short of cash and probably wasn't going to be able to attend medical school. His fraternity brothers had spoken about having a benefit for him, but as she knew, Burger had his pride. He wouldn't have it.

Judith decided to handle it her own way and involve Warren. With this, he was in agreement.

* * *

Two weeks later, Burger came flying up the driveway and leaned heavily on the doorbell, yelling for her. "Mrs. Hollis, Mrs. Hollis. I can stay with Eddie. I got a scholarship to medical school. A real good one, for the whole four years."

He was so excited that she couldn't stop him when he went upstairs and woke up Eddie.

She stayed downstairs in the Roy Rogers room and cried.

Even while he was in medical school, Burger remained in charge of the Eddie Squad, taking time from his exhausting schedule to educate the new fraternity boys who took over from the original five. When Roy Rogers horse, Trigger, died and Burger heard it had been stuffed and put in a museum in Victorville, Burger found a small replica and placed it in the Roy Rogers room.

Gillian turned seven and the current Eddie Squad came to her birthday party dressed like the Beatles, bringing guitars and microphones to sing for her.

Then, in no time, she was eight, nine, ten. Eddie was six and looked about half that age.

During those years, Judith tried to get pregnant again and couldn't. Had her body been so traumatized by Eddie's birth that it refused to honor another fetus?

She went to Randall Thorne, but he could find nothing wrong with her.

In despair, she told Warren. "I want so badly to give you another son."

"Don't worry about it." He soothed her. "Having each other is all that matters."

During the many years, Judith kept occupied at the UCLA Guild, with the Girl Scouts, drama groups, and the Junior Philharmonic with Gillian. She took up gourmet cooking and the housekeeper and family cook indulged her whims in the kitchen. The fraternity boys tried each new dish, but always requested their favorite; her chocolate chip cookies.

Gillian developed into a stunning teenager with even more of a mind of her own. She and Warren were at odds on most everything.

Dating: "I want you to go out with several boys. No steadies…"

"Dad, everyone goes steady."

"Everyone, perhaps, except you."

Schooling: "I want you to go to Julliard," he told her as she entered high school."

"That may be what you want, Dad," she answered, "but that's not what you're going to get."

"Would you rather be an actress, or just settle down and get married."

"How about a trip to Europe to really get me out of the way?" She blasted her father with her frustration.

"I'm sorry," he said. "What is it you want to do?"

"You've always known …"

"Medicine is out."

Judith had heard this argument so much that she could have directed the scenario. She couldn't understand Warren's determination that their daughter not become a physician. Very quietly, Judith made sure that Gillian took the subjects that would qualify her for medical school.

In her last year of high-school, Warren was nominated for the Albert Schweitzer Humanitarian Award to be presented in France. He was being honored for his pioneering surgical work with disfigured children. He and Judith decided Gillian should attend the ceremony in France with them as her graduation present.

And perhaps, during this trip, she and her father could make amends with one another for the years when they had not been particularly close.

Warren was contradictory with their children. Judith tried not to think about it, but she wished Warren could care for their son as much as he did for other handicapped children. He never saw the boy unless he needed to be examined for a strep throat or bellyache.

For the second time in his professional life, in order to accept the award, Warren was willing to turn his practice over to another surgeon so that he and his family could make the trek to Europe for the award.

The ceremony was planned for September fourteenth to suit the convenience of the judges. Warren had three months to arrange matters and prepare his acceptance speech.

Judith was kept busy all summer making preparations, insuring that Eddie would have good care. She called Dr. Burgess Selwyn, honorary chairman, long since gone from the duty he'd taken on years ago.

"Just this once, Burger, could you look in on Eddie while we're gone? We've never left him."

"Delighted."

She knew she asked a lot. Burgess Selwyn had become one of the most successful pediatricians in Los Angeles County who regularly endowed a medical scholarship to a student in his fraternity. In fact, through anonymous donations, every boy who was seriously interested in attending graduate school knew his way would be paid if his grades were good…and if he had spent time taking care of Eddie Hollis. Burger eventually had to very carefully screen applicants for the position to be sure their interest in Eddie was sincere.

A week before they were to leave for Europe, Judith received a telegram.

To Judith Stanhope Hollis: Regret to inform you of your mother's death this morning. Please call regarding arrangements.

Greenbridge Hospital for the Insane.

Greenbridge, Vermont.

Chapter Thirty-Three

Judith stood in the foyer of their home, the telegram in her hand, shaking uncontrollably. Her mind was more than twenty years away remembering when she'd angrily turned her back on her mother on the steps of the nurses residence at Memorial Hospital of Los Angeles.

That was when Sarah had said, "Wait, wait…" and now Judith couldn't remember why she'd said it.

Around the same time her mother had let her down. "Why did you betray me?" Judith had asked. And her mother's answer. "I didn't think I had." Judith would never forget her mother's stricken, pleading look.

So many years had passed. Finally the word had come. Her mother was gone.

Judith leaned on the bannister, her head resting in the crook of her arm. She wept, partly from relief, partly from sorrow that she would never know why her mother had cut her off from her life.

After awhile, she heard Eddie screaming upstairs. He would be all right because someone from the Squad was with him. The cook, Esther, had gone down to Westwood Village grocery shopping. Gillian was at the beach. Warren was doing surgery at Cedars of Lebanon.

Suddenly, Judith started to tremble again, an angry horror spreading through her. Her mother in an insane asylum…dead. What had happened that her mother became crazy? Why hadn't anyone ever told her? She cried and cried, wiping her face on her dirndl skirt. She walked in circles, wringing the skirt, trying to contain the agitation exploding inside her.

Then as suddenly as she'd began shaking, she stopped. After all, it wasn't true. Things like this didn't happen. The only people who ever got telegrams were parents of enlisted men killed in war, or people killed in airplane or car crashes.

It was a bad dream, a nightmare that came on her…somebody was playing a practical joke. She thought of the month. Was it an April Fool's joke, a Halloween masquerade? No, it was June and there was nothing funny or frivolous in the month of June.

June was the month of beginnings, weddings, love.

She picked up the telegram, read and reread it. Her mother, dead. Greenbridge Hospital for the Insane. She'd never heard of the place.

She had the ludicrous thought that if she'd never heard of it, it didn't exist. Therefore, the telegram couldn't be true.

Warren…she had to talk to him. She ran to the Roy Rogers room and quickly dialed.

Asking for him was easy. She'd done it for years, knowing she'd have to wait, perhaps not hear from him for hours. Ever since Eddie had been born, an emergency from home seemed to mean something less to Warren.

He was on the line almost immediately. "Hello, darling. Between cases…"

"Warren…" Her voice broke. She couldn't go on.

"What is it, Judith?"

She stared at the wall, her mouth open, trying to tell him, but the words were stuck somewhere behind a trapdoor in her mind.

"Judith…Judith…" Even his alarm didn't shake the words loose.

A sob racked her body.

"Judith, what is it!"

"Warren…" Her voice became a wail. "My mother's dead." It was all she could say and then her body gave up and she collapsed to the sofa, the phone dropping on the couch beside her.

She lost track of time, succumbing to her grief.

Eventually she got up, put the telegram in her pocket and went outside to walk the grounds, to believe that she was alive, that she lived in Bel Air, that she had a husband and two children. But her mind wouldn't give in so easily because it kept taking her back to Santa Monica, seeing her mother ironing her nurses uniforms, polishing her shoes, trying to hide their poverty by covering the cracks in the shoes with layers of white paste, pulling and twisting her fine, long hair into a bun that hid its beauty under a white nurses cap.

She thought about their relationship, how her mother had struggled and struggled, never quite making it, how she had counted on Judith's father's insurance money to get them by and then confessed that there had never been any insurance money…and how she hadn't really appreciated what her mother had gone through.

"You were a snot, Judith," she told herself, bringing fresh tears.

She was laying on a chaise lounge by the pool when Warren came and she fell into his arms, numbly handing him the telegram. He read it.

"I'm sorry, Judith. I'm very sorry."

She cried some more, but the tears were different, tears of relief at his being there to comfort her.

"It may be a mistake," he said. "Cruel things happen and it may be nobody's fault."

"How could anybody make a mistake like that?"

"I don't know. Call, darling. Find out."

She couldn't and he sensed it, picking up the phone on the patio and dialing Greenbridge himself. He told the person who answered that he was seeking information and before long he was talking business. "What were the circumstances of Mrs. Stanhope's hospitalization?"

He listened and then turned to her. "Judith, have you ever heard of a Charles Preston?"

The name was vaguely familiar.

"Your mother's brother-in-law?"

"Yes."

"He took her to Greenbridge years ago."

Warren was talking on the phone again. "About the arrangements…" he began, but Judith stopped him.

"I'm going back, Warren. Just tell them I'll be there tomorrow."

He covered the receiver. "Darling, I can't get away."

"I know. I'm still going. I have to see her to believe it."

"Without me?"

"Yes…"

Warren drove her to the airport for the midnight flight. After a stopover in New York, she flew on to Mt. Pelier and rented a car for the journey to Greenbridge. This time she wasn't going to rely on the temperament of a hired driver.

She drove through lush hillsides, small towns, over bridges, alongside rivers with railroad tracks laid down like flattened fences, past farms, each on its own hill that looked like all the picture postcards she'd seen of New England serenity.

In spite of the sadness of her mission, Vermont had a quiet about it, a peaceful stillness. Perhaps, in happier times, she and Warren could come back here to visit.

She had no trouble locating Greenbridge, a short distance out of Danbury. She parked in front of the immense, brick walled institution and went to the administrative office.

The director introduced herself. "I'm Mrs. Wilton," she said, placing a yellowed folder on her desk. It contained information about Sarah.

She quickly reeled off some facts for Judith. "Your mother has been here for fourteen years and was sixty years of age at the time of her death. She contracted pneumonia and there was nothing we could do for her. She never seemed to have any will to live."

"If only I had known…"

"She never spoke one word the entire time she was here."

That couldn't have been Sarah. It was unlike her. "Let me see her. I think there has been a mistake."

"Of course."

The sensibly dressed matron took her to the basement and led her through a tunnel that showed years and years of wear where millions of feet must have trampled, past walls cracked with long fissures that must have witnessed and held hidden memories, to a stairwell, then down another set of stairs where they passed a steam room with hissing boilers, a man walking between the furnaces. Finally, they stopped at an unmarked door which the director unlocked.

It was a morgue. In one wall were six wooden doors with swing handles like on old ice-chests. The room was cool and Judith felt a rush of dizziness.

Mrs. Wilton offered her a chair.

"No, thank you."

She swung back one of the wooden doors and Judith saw a sheet-covered figure on a metal tray. The director pulled out the tray, hefting it on a set of metal legs that she then rolled to the center of the room.

The figure under the sheet was small, much smaller than Judith remembered her mother as being.

Judith reached for a chair to steady herself, suddenly feeling warm, then cold.

"Sit down," said Mrs. Wilton.

"No," she said, shaking. "I'll be all right."

The director pulled the sheet back from the face.

Judith didn't recognize the woman and was flooded with relief. The woman was emaciated in her thinness with wrinkled, yellow skin, sunken eyes.

Mrs. Wilton explained: "At the last, she refused to eat. We finally found it meaningless to force her anymore."

Judith studied the white hair. She couldn't imagine her mother with white hair. The director drew the sheet down farther and Judith could see the thin hands, the long fingers.

She shook her head, moving away. "This woman is not my mother."

Mrs. Wilton removed the sheet completely.

The woman had a hammertoe, the second toe overlapping the first. Her mother did have that defect.

"I don't think she is my mother," Judith repeated, but now she was less positive and had a crazy thought. Are we remembered for our defects?

Mrs. Wilton did not dispute her as she covered the body and shoved the tray back into the morgue box. She led Judith back to the office.

"Let me tell you more about her," she said. "We know she had a daughter, named Judith, married to a Dr. Warren Hollis. Is that not you?"

"Yes."

"We know that she had a sister who died by her own hand, an aged mother who lived in a Burlington nursing home until she came here."

Although the evidence was specific, Judith rejected the idea that it was the woman she had seen who said she never had a daughter named Sarah.

"Do you know anything more?"

"We believe that she was born in Riverfork, Vermont, and trained as a nurse at the Margaret Ward Training School for Nurses. Beyond that her life is sketchy."

The administrator took a cigar box from a desk drawer and removed the lid. "She brought this with her."

The items inside the box were mostly trinkets and miscellaneous papers: a faded picture of three women, nurses for they wore white uniforms and caps; a bus token from a Santa Monica, California bus company; a few alumni newspapers from the Margaret Ward School; strips of cloth.

Mrs. Wilton picked one up. "When she became extremely agitated, she would take off her clothes, reducing them to torn strips before we could stop her. Then she would lapse into a profound depression that would last for months."

Judith fished in the box. There was the telegram she had sent when she married Warren. It stopped her cold. There was a man's university ring that Judith remembered her mother wearing on a chain around her neck. More evidence that this woman was her mother. The ring showed little wear, the engraved initials in the inner band clearly visible.

"We took that from her when she first came because we felt the chain was dangerous and she might swallow the ring."

Judith carefully put the items back in the box, secured it with a rubber band and placed it in her purse, finally accepting that these had been her mother's attachments to life, symbols, some with meanings clear only to her.

"Why wasn't I ever told that my mother was in this hospital?" With acceptance came anger.

"It was her wish that you never be informed while she was alive. She gave that instruction to us the day she came in, the only message she ever wrote." Mrs. Wilton took the note from the folder and showed it to Judith, adding, "There was some tragedy…"

The note was in her mother's handwriting. "What?"

"I don't know."

Judith was close to breaking down. To avoid it, she quickly made funeral arrangements and settled any expenses that might be incurred with a check drawn against Warren's business bank account.

She thanked Mrs. Wilton who accompanied her from the office. As the two went out, a witch-thin woman with stringy hair and faded eyes stopped in front of them.

"I'm snow…I'm snow…I'm snow…" she implored, touching Judith as if pleading for her to believe it, then when she did not give the wanted response, the woman screamed angrily: "Snow! Snow! Snow!"

Judith was terrified of the wild look in the woman's eyes.

"Abbie!" Mrs. Wilton spoke sharply. "Go back to the dining room!"

"I'm snow," the woman whimpered, hurrying away.

Chapter Thirty-Four

The next day, Judith arrived home in Bel Air. Warren knew as soon as he saw her that the congratulatory cards and telegrams jamming their mailbox and phone lines, the dozens of flowers filling the living room, the celebration and happiness glared against her mood. She was depressed.

He had seen to it while she was gone that preparations were nearly finished for their departure. Everything was ready to go save for a few last minute throw-ins to the luggage. Everything, but he soon found, not everyone. He tried to make Judith feel better and it was impossible. He realized she needed to grieve.

The night before they were to leave, she told him: "Warren, it's no good. I would ruin the trip for both of you. I'm staying home. This is the highpoint of your life and it has to be perfect. When you get back, I'll feel better and you can give me the memories through your eyes."

Reluctantly, he agreed.

She was right. This award did mean a lot to him, representing a culmination of his life's work, a validation of his worth as a human being and surgeon.

First, he was going to Lambarene, West Africa, for a symbolic journey to the hospital complex where Schweitzer had left his own mark for humanity. Then, on to Strasbourg for the award, and finally, Paris.

A dozen times that last day, he passed Judith and hugged her. She slept fitfully that night, waking him, but got up in the morning to drive him and Gillian to Los Angeles International Airport.

He'd hoped to have a private farewell with Judith, but a crowd waited for them. He saw many of their friends and colleagues including Randall Thorne. "Nothing funny, old boy," Warren cautioned him. To which Randall replied with a look of injured innocence. Several well-wishers who were strangers to them, plus newspaper photographers and reporters. They jostled the trio as they congratulated Warren, slapping him on the back, shaking his hand, laughing, joking.

He pulled Judith and Gillian through the crowd and hurried off to an annex for a few last words with his wife. He kissed her, lingering over her warm, moist lips, wishing she were not so sad. For a few moments, they were bound together by the love they'd shared for twenty years, feelings meant and given only to one another, a love that shut everyone else out. He wanted to remember her as she was today, in sandals, a pleated skirt and short-sleeved blouse, the smell of her Guerlain perfume.

He must remember to pick up another bottle in Paris.

Then the three of them went down the ramp to the plane. Just before he and Gillian boarded, Judith called out, "Wait, Warren. I forgot something." He turned back to her. She reached into her purse, pulled out a small, wrapped object and placed it in his hand.

"Darling," she said. "Something for you...a sentimental remembrance of the occasion."

He dropped it into his pocket and headed up the steps. At the top, he turned and waved to her. Newspaper photographers snapped pictures of Judith wiping her eyes and waving to him and Gillian.

In the far reaches of his mind, he thought he had been in a similar situation at another time in his life. But the thought was cut off by the clicking cameras trained on him and his daughter that didn't stop until they escaped into the plane.

During the flight to New York, Warren opened his briefcase, pulling out everything he'd compiled about Dr. Albert Schweitzer. He browsed over the doctor's public speeches, the books written by and about him, pictures of his hospital at Lambarene and its grounds, pictures of the great man playing Bach on the organ at Strasbourg, a copy of Schweitzer's scholarly work on Bach, his proceeds from the book sales financing the Lambarene operation.

Gillian was curled up on the seat beside him, absorbed in a book on genetics, the subject that had always fascinated her and to which she planned to devote her life following medical school.

He was still not happy that she had won her battle to be a physician. She was like him in one respect and that was her fascination with research.

After awhile, he saw she had fallen asleep.

Warren continued to read, write, doze, and during waking time, he found himself musing about Gillian, nearly a physical replica of her mother. Their smiles were the same. Gillian's deep-set eyes were somewhat rounder than Judith's almond-shaped brown eyes, but other than that slight distinction, the only real differences between them were the way they behaved, the flashes of humor and compassion Gillian spread between everyone. The ability to show emotions. But, then, she'd had an easier life than Judith.

Friends remarked at the uncanny likenesses in their behaviors, his, Gillian's, and Judith's. They particularly had the same expressions during serious moments and would laugh at the same things. Judith always seemed to know just what he wanted in terms of gifts or nights out, and could even sense when it was best that they stay home. Why didn't Gillian have the same perceptions? He dismissed the question. After all, she was his daughter and not his wife.

Randall once told him that being with the three of them was like being in a house of mirrors, because they had so many traits in common; identical expressions, likes and dislikes.

Warren couldn't see it, and dismissed the similarities as the result of their living together.

Five hours later, Warren and Gillian arrived in New York, leaving almost immediately for Dakar on the coast of West Africa. Exhausted when they reached the port city, they slept in their hotel until the following morning when they boarded a DC3 for the flight to Doula.

The plane landed in a jungle clearing and natives carried their baggage from the otherwise deserted airstrip to a *pirogue*, a lean canoe used for river travel. The natives' arms and bodies glistened as they pulled the oars, gliding the dugout smoothly up the Ogowe River against the current. The jungle growth around them was isolating, reminding Warren that life was not just people, but here, also, stately cranes soaring above them, kingfishers circling curiously, giant butterflies floating in the air, the green-gold plumage of the *pipilo* shining proudly. After several twists along the river, their craft rounded a bend for their first view of the Schweitzer compound. They couldn't see much, just that there were low buildings, well-worn dirt paths and many people without shoes.

The boat docked next to a huge mango tree and they were met by French speaking missionaries and an interpreter who showed them to their quarters. After a brief period of freshening up, he and Gillian toured the compound and saw hospital wards for mental and dysentery patients, another for the natives, a separate bungalow for the whites.

She leaned close to him so that only he could hear. "Schweitzer was a bigot," she whispered.

"You don't know," he said, sharply. "It may not have been his idea."

They looked into buildings where surgeries were performed, the store rooms, the kitchen, the shed for canoes; and farther away, the leper colony and garden.

When they returned to the central compound for lunch, Warren asked and was given permission to stay in Dr. Schweitzer's private quarters.

Alone, Warren quickly catalogued the room in his mind; the bed, a desk made from packing crates sent to Lambarene with supplies decades ago, a small table, bookcase, shelves for his papers. His white shirts and pants were still neatly folded on a chair. It was as though the doctor, dead for nine years, was expected back momentarily.

Warren had the eerie feeling that he had been here before, a *deja vu* experience. And yet, he knew, this was only gained from the writings and pictures he'd been studying.

He turned once again to his own speech, pouring over every word, checking for accuracy. Glancing up now and again, he saw the doctor's pith helmet that had provided protection from the cruel African sun, a reminder that he had been very human, indeed.

Outside the window, rain began to fall, the humidity becoming even more oppressive. Warren threw his coat over the end of the doctor's bed to work in his shirt sleeves. The coat landed upside down and he heard something drop to the floor. He reached over to pick it up. It was wrapped in tissue paper.

He remembered Judith slipping something to him as they parted. He unwrapped it, smiling when he recognized it as being a University of Vermont ring. He turned the ring over and over, examining it carefully, seeing letters on its inner band, letters he couldn't read in the dimming light of the room. Imagine, he thought to himself, Judith being clever enough to tie up this event with his beginnings in medicine.

He slipped the ring on his finger, a perfect fit, and went back to his studies.

That evening, at supper, the talk somehow seemed subdued in the humid air, the pounding of the rain on the corrugated roof increased with the severity of the storm, making him feel even more isolated. It was easy to see why the jungle and weather were the masters.

As they dined on fruits from the plantation orchard, oranges, mandarins, grapefruit, guavas, avocados and fruit from the Pomme de Cythere tree, corrosol, Warren became acutely aware of the ruby ring accompanying his every hand move. It fit so well that Judith must have used his wedding band as a model. He'd stopped wearing it years ago because he was afraid he'd lose it after he took it off to perform surgery.

Gillian eventually noticed the addition to his hand. "Where did you get that gorgeous ruby, Dad?"

"From your mother. She gave it to me to commemorate this occasion. Very thoughtful." He took it off and handed it to his daughter.

She admired it. "There are initials on the band. W.T.H." She looked at him. "Yours, naturally. And there's a date…1929. What is the significance of that?"

"The year I graduated from medical school," he said, spearing a mango.

He went to bed that night, the ring nagging his finger until he had to take it off. He doubted that he could ever get used to wearing a ring again.

The next morning as they were getting ready to board the *pirogue* for the return boat ride to the airport landing and clearing, Gillian stopped him.

"Where is your ring, Dad?"

He'd forgotten about it. "I must have left it on the table in Dr. Schweitzer's room."

"For shame," she chided, getting out of the boat, running up the hill to retrieve it. When she returned, out of breath, she said, "If it hadn't been for me, you'd have left it. And then you would have had some explaining to do to mother."

He laughed. "You're right about that."

Natives released the dugout canoe from its ropes and they moved away from the shore toward the middle of the river, waving to their hosts. As they glided through the water, Warren's memories went back to another river and another time. The emotions he had felt then were at least as overwhelming as those of the past two days.

It was at the edge of the Winooski River in Vermont. He looked at the ring on his finger. It was exactly like one he'd given away, half a world and lifetime away, more than thirty-eight years before, to a girl who'd fulfilled him as had no other woman until Judith.

Too bad he'd given away the original ring. It would have been nice if he could have given it to Judith. But as soon as the thought occurred to him, he rejected it. The first girl had been worth it.

It took him a moment to remember her name. Sarah. Yes, her name was Sarah. And every day with her had been worth a lifetime of feeling. Then his heart was torn with the old confusion, forgotten for years. Why had she spurned him as soon as he'd left Vermont? How could she have let a love die that had been as pure and deep as theirs, simply because miles had come to separate them? He had only intended that they be apart for a short while. Yet, she had made it permanent.

How could he have been so wrong about a woman?

Chapter Thirty-Five

At least Warren had Judith to make up for it. Now, his mind was brought back to the present for the plane was cruising into Strasbourg, a city foot-balled between France and Germany since 1871, reverting to France in 1918.

He nudged Gillian.

"Don't wake me until we land," she protested, pulling the blanket over her head.

His first impression of the city was of its aged charm, heavily industrialized along the inland port and freight center at the junction of the Rhine-Marne Canal and the River Ill. It was here that iron ore and steel from Lorraine passed into the shipping corridors.

He patted Gillian awake in the seat beside him. "Look, there's St. Nicholas Church where Schweitzer played the organ...where the award will be given."

She took a quick peek and went under the blanket again.

Below them Warren saw the wineries in the Alsatian Valley whose yearly harvests predicted economic happiness or sadness for the city. There were miles of comfortable, gabled houses in the city, seeming as close and friendly as long standing neighbors.

Two hours later, he and Gillian waited in the vestibule of the great church. She was tired from the traveling, he was hot in the cumbersome doctoral robes. The members of the Schweitzer committee shook his hand warmly and solemnly.

Warren heard organ music of Bach coming from inside the church and he knew that it was from recordings made by Schweitzer before his death.

He took Gillian's hand and was surprised at its clammy palm. Was she a case of nerves, his usually self-assured, assertive daughter, reduced by her awe to the young, innocent girl she pretended not to be? He gave her a pat of encouragement and sent her hurrying down the side aisle to her seat of honor in the front row.

As soon as she was seated, the center doors of the church were opened, releasing the soaring sounds of Schweitzer's playing. The seven committee members proceeded singly and slowly down the middle aisle. When the last of them was seated on the stage, Warren moved forward, drawing in his breath, briefly closing his eyes to steady himself, to gain control of this, the most momentous occasion of his life.

He could feel heads turning, respectfully following his progress.

When he reached the stage, he stood next to Henri Beavois, the French scientist and chairman of the Schweitzer committee. He explained to the assembly the significance of the award, of the lengthy committee deliberations in choosing the recipient. Then he presented Warren to the audience.

The applause was polite as Dr. Beauvois stepped away and Warren placed his own notes on the lectern.

His acceptance speech was titled: "Our Past is Our Present." He had hoped to compare his life with Schweitzers' to show how the totality of everyone's experiences follows him always, in known and unknown ways. But, in his heart, he knew he did not measure up to Schweitzer.

To provide the bare necessities for his hospital, Schweitzer always had to struggle in the West African jungle, where the weather and diseases could be cruel. In contrast, Warren only had to do a few more face lifts, breast augmentations or reductions, and he could bankroll anything he wanted.

Once Schweitzer had decided to devote his life to the needy, they and their lifestyles became his. Warren went to the needy, but at night returned to the opulent life, idyllic, except for Eddie.

"We do not learn from the past," he told the audience, "but repeat each mistake as if it were a rough-hewn diamond in need of constant grinding, or a precious metal requiring a fine polish before any vision can be seen. Even then we often fail to see our mistakes. We are blind to them as if blindness were a basic need for survival.

"We continue to have wars as though they involved only power, not killing. Those of us who war with our minds, try to find alternatives with which we can live. Thus, Albert Schweitzer had his mission in life, and I humbly submit that I, too, have a mission.

Both of us recognized our obligation to the less fortunate. The kind of work that Albert Schweitzer did will always be necessary. There will be needy peoples for centuries to come. With the rapid progress of science, my work should become unnecessary. Much of my work is devoted to potentially preventable tragedies and accidents of nature. In time, when we are able to control genetic errors and environmental insults to developing fetuses, there will be no need for my services."

He made reference to Schweitzer's Reverence for Life philosophy, a respect for the lives of all beings.

"Unfortunately, I do not totally share the great doctor's thinking. I believe that, for some, life is without living. It is these that we must protect, or should I say, spare?" He thought of Eddie writhing in his crib in Bel Air, tearing at the bandages on his arms, eating his own skin and lips.

"We do agree on a major point, however, that we who are able, should rid others of the Mark of Pain. Let me tell you in his words. The members of the fellowship who bear the Mark of Pain have *'learnt by experience that physical pain and bodily anguish, belong together all the world over; they are united by a secret bond. One and all they know the horrors of suffering to which man can be exposed, and one and all they know the longing to be free from pain. He who has been delivered from pain must not think he is now free again, and at liberty to take life up just as it was before, entirely forgetful of the past.*

"'Doctors should go forth to carry out among the miserable in far-off lands all that ought to be done in the name of civilization, human and humane.'

"Let me conclude, again with his words: *'Sooner or later the idea which I here put forward will conquer the world, for with inexorable logic it carries with it the intellect as well as the heart.'*"

The audience stood to congratulate Warren as he bowed to the thunderous applause pounding the walls of St. Nicholas' Church. As he did so, he thought that he'd never had to travel to far off lands to find suffering. All his life the tragedies had been close, coming to him; his defective brother in Vermont, his parents moving away from the town from grief and shame. Eddie...

He swiftly came back to the present, smiling and bowing, grasping the Schweitzer medal that had been placed around his neck. He saw Gillian beaming below him, her cheeks pink with excitement. He felt a thrill, a peace flow through him, the peace of one who has achieved and been acknowledged. He felt the ring on his finger brushing against the medal...he could hardly wait to tell Judith...and when the clapping died down, he walked down the steps from the stage to Gillian, who accompanied him up the aisle. He held her hand tightly as Schweitzer's organ music swelled with the sounds of "Jesu, Joy of Man's Desiring," played at Warren's request.

By nightfall, he and Gillian were once again back in Paris and were driven by limousine to the Crillon Hotel, once the palace of the Duke of Crillon, converted to a hotel in the early part of the century. Situated across from the American Embassy, it was convenient, within walking distance of dozens of attractions.

Without waiting to be escorted to his room, Warren sent Gillian on her way with the porter, checked the international clock in the lobby and phoned Judith in Los Angeles. Nothing mattered to him but hearing her voice.

"Darling," she said, excitedly. "I could hardly wait for your call. Congratulations are pouring in over your speech. Randall phoned, even Denise spoke with me, Kate…your picture is in every paper in Los Angeles. I haven't been able to sleep, I've been so excited for you."

He could visualize her pacing, even then, as she spoke. If only it weren't for time and distance, he could be holding her, feeling her warmth. Instead, he had to settle for the damned phone.

"Darling," she chided, "your hand covered the medal in all the pictures. I couldn't read the inscription."

"Now you're teasing. You wouldn't be able to read it, anyway." He went on to describe it to her, feeling the pewter medal. "On one side is a relief of Schweitzer's head, bushy mustache and bulbous nose. His character shines. The years 1875-1965 are engraved at the top. Beneath his likeness are inscribed these words. '*Truth is now* '.

"On the obverse is an engraving of the hospital at Lambarene with my name and the year, 1973.'"

"It sounds beautiful."

"It is. Nearly as fine as the ring you gave me as I left Los Angeles."

"Do you like it?"

"What do you think?" He looked at the ruby in the subdued light of the phone booth. "It's my crystal ball," he said. "I can see you in it."

She laughed.

"It fits exactly as the one I received on graduation from medical school. How original of you to connect that milestone with today's ceremony. I'm curious, how did you know what the ring looked like so that you could reproduce it?"

"I didn't. It's just a coincidence, but I loved the ring. It belonged to my mother. It was one of the few things she'd kept. It's been locked up in the director's office at Greenbridge since mother was first admitted there."

Warren absorbed the information, but it made no sense to him. No sense at all.

"Whatever," he shrugged. "Gillian and I will be home shortly."

"When is 'shortly?'"

"Gillian wants to shop for a few things. That means about two days."

They lingered over their farewell and then Warren went up to his hotel room, sleeping soundly for the first time in days.

The next morning he met Gillian and, following breakfast, they went on a bus tour of the city, and finally on their shopping trek.

They caught a cab to the Right Bank where they shopped alongside students from the Sorbonne and then at the city's largest department store, Au Printemps. Gillian settled for a book and a fine handkerchief. "For mother," she said, dropping it into her bag.

Then it was on to the Galeries Lafayette where Gillian bought several dresses and suits. At Hermes, it was silk scarves, two handbags, one for herself, one for her mother.

They stopped at Freddy of Paris where Warren bought Judith more Guerlain perfume, longing to be with her.

Gillian purchased bracelets for her friends and a dress from Pierre Cardin's couture collection. Warren obligingly carried her packages and whenever he set them down, the glow of the red ruby in his ring reminded him of Judith.

For some reason, the ring seemed warm on his finger as if not wanting to be forgotten. While Gillian turned this way and that before a boutique mirror, studying a hat she debated buying, he studied the ring.

When they stopped at Gucci's for still another handbag, he slipped off the ring and, once again, wondered at the date and initials inscribed on the inner band. *1929 WTH*. Did somebody else have the same initials who had bought an identical class ring that year? He ran through all the names he could remember. None had his initials. Perhaps, it belonged to someone graduating from another department of the university.

If so, what connection did this person have to Judith's mother?

Gillian interrupted his thoughts. "Daddy, if I buy this hat, will they think it's too silly in Beverly Hills?"

"Nothing is ever too silly in Beverly Hills," he said, solemnly. "Nothing, or everything, depending on your point-of-view."

"Good. Then, I'm going to buy it."

It was a broad brimmed hat with streamers running down the back. Her curly hair puffed up to the edges of the brim accenting her face, making her look like a Modigliani cherub.

"Enough," he said. "I can't carry anymore."

"Yes, Daddy." She kissed him. "Just one more dress for tonight…from Pucci's…"

He sighed indulgently. "If you must."

"I must."

That evening, she wore the tight fitting black dress from Pucci's as he escorted her to dinner at *La Tour d'Argent*. They passed by the mural, an outrageously fanciful family tree of the restaurant, supposedly dating back to Adam and Eve, when it couldn't possibly have existed that long.

Once seated, Warren ordered for them: *Potage Claudius Burdel* made with sorrel, cream, butter and chicken broth. Then a main course of *Duck D'la Orange*, and finally *peches flambes* for dinner.

During the meal, Gillian reached across the table for his glass and impudently sipped his wine. As she looked over the edge of the glass at him, she reminded him of someone other than Judith. Someone he'd known years before Judith. Someone from another lifetime. Maybe it was her coloring. Or was it her face, not as long as her mother's? Or was it again the eyes?

The image of the other girl came to him through a haze and almost as quickly disappeared. But he knew who she'd been. Again, Sarah.

Perhaps the myth was true, that men were repeatedly attracted to the same kind of woman. First Sarah, then Judith. And now here was his daughter who looked, if nothing else, like a composite of the two.

Gillian, slightly drunk, spoke: "Daddy, order some escargots."

"Do you know what those are?"

"Certainly. Snails."

"Be reasonable, Gillian. We've already had dessert."

"Daddy. Have fun. This is Paris and who knows if we'll ever return."

"We'll return, if only to get you escargots. Besides, if you want to go to the Folies, we must hurry."

A short while later, as they watched the scantily clad girls doing kicks in their high-topped boots, the skirts with miles of taffeta slips bouncing from side-to-side, he glanced at Gillian, her eyes sparkling.

A thought came to him that had nothing to do with her, a thought remote from the evening and the time. Judith's mother's name was Sarah and she was a nurse. Why, oh why, did this come to his mind? For what purpose?

At intermission, Gillian confessed. "I never want to leave this city. I want to stay forever."

"That's the way it is when you travel. You'll probably feel that way about the next city you visit."

"I didn't feel that way about Lambarene."

"What a pity."

He had given the ring to Sarah in 1930. What was the year of Judith's birth? He chided himself for asking himself such stupid, meaningless questions. What point was there in trying to establish a link between this ring and his family when there couldn't possibly be any? Sarah hadn't been pregnant. Surely, she would have told him. Besides, Judith's father was a physician killed in World War II.

After the Folies, Warren took Gillian for a stroll along the lamp-lighted Seine.

Sarah had been a nursing student at the Margaret Ward School of Nursing near the University of Vermont.

An unaccustomed nervousness overtook him as he steered Gillian back to their hotel.

"Pack tonight," he warned her. "We must be out of here by six in the morning." He kissed her goodbye at her door.

He went to his own room, turned off the lights, opened the drapes, lay on his bed and watched the sights of Paris, the moving cars, the protective dim yellow street lamps, people hurrying along in the night to destinations unknown to him, but seeming very clear in their purpose. He slipped off the ring and set it on the bedside table.

Something was churning in his mind. A question burrowing to the surface.

After awhile, with dread, he went downstairs to check the international clock, went to the same phone he'd used earlier and dialed Judith in Beverly Hills. But before anyone answered, he thought better of it, and hung up.

A name had suddenly come to him. Morgan.

He froze in the phone booth, sweat pouring off him, as if it were the most humid, hot day of the year instead of a cool fifty-eight degrees. He seemed to pass in and out of consciousness. Black spots bombarded his eyes. His body began to shake, his teeth knocked against one another like boats against pilings during a hurricane. He could hardly breathe. He rushed from the phone booth, tore loose his tie, ran out to the street to draw in great, deep breaths, frantically reaching for support on a pole at the hotel's entrance.

"May I help you, sir?" The doorman reached out to him.

"No," Warren said, brusquely, fearfully.

"Perhaps assistance to find your room?"

"No, Goddamit!"

Embarrassed by his overreaction, he apologized, hurrying towards the Seine. He ran beside the low stone-wall trying to escape the truth chasing him. His stomach doubled him over in pain. He wasn't used to running. He retched, hanging over the murky waters. A boatman looked at him dispassionately as he scraped something off a metal plate with a large spoon into the river.

If he hadn't been there, Warren would have leaped into the Seine, sinking to the bottom, holding his breath until he could no longer do so, then taking in giant gulps of dirty water and be through with life.

Instead, he placed his palms against his pounding head and sobbed.

Judith's grandmother's name was Lillian Morgan and she'd had sons like Eddie. "No, no, no," he cried out to Paris, the gutteral tones choking in his throat.

His body, wracked with panic and shaking, felt as if it would fly apart.

He ran back to the hotel, took the elevator up to his room, unable to take his eyes from the ring resting innocently on the bedside table, the ring that had suddenly tied his past to his present with seemingly unrelated thoughts and the horrible truth that finally crashed down.

He could not think what his relationship to Judith was. There wasn't a word in the English language to describe it. She was his wife, but she couldn't be, because he couldn't be married to her.

Albert Schweitzer never knew the Mark of Pain as thoroughly as Warren did at this moment, the horror of the revelation crucifying him.

All that he understood was that his wife was also his daughter.

There was no other conclusion that could be reached. It was the ring that told the truth. And Judith's words: "It belonged to my mother. It was one of the few things she'd kept." Sarah had lied to Judith about her father being killed in the war.

Warren spent the night pouring out his insides in the bathroom, pacing the floor between the door and the window, the scene of Paris a blur, and finally exhausted, flopped on the bed. At six in the morning, Gillian knocked on his door. "Time to leave, Dad," she sang out as he let her in. "Aha! Look who isn't ready."

He tried to get hold of himself. "I've been up all night with something unique to Paris," he said.

"Poor Daddy," she said, with mock pity. She stroked his arm and the feel of her hand on him broke through his reserve, his resolve not to share his burden with her.

He threw his arms around her, sobbing, "Gillian, Gillian, my baby."

"Dad, what's the matter." She tried to extricate herself from his hold.

He could tell he'd frightened her and he hadn't meant that to happen. He let her go, turned away, wiping his eyes. "It's nothing, Gillian."

"It is, Dad. What is it?"

"I don't know. The excitement, the ceremony, getting the medal. The importance hit me all of a sudden…and then, on top of that, the Paris disease. I'll be all right."

"Dad, your clothes aren't packed."

Frantically, she threw his things in the suitcase, slamming the lid.

At the same time, he slammed the lid on his mind, vowing that it would stay closed forever on what he knew.

"If that's what happens to you when you get honored," said Gillian, "I'm never accepting an award in my whole life." She shoved the ring and Schweitzer medal at him. "Dad, put these on and don't take them off. You're going to lose them for sure. Wear them forever."

The last twelve hours had been forever.

Chapter Thirty-Six

When Warren came down the plane's steps in Los Angeles, he hardly noticed the photographers blinding flashbulbs, for he had loaded himself up with pills in an attempt to control his nerves. For the entire flight from Paris, he was either in the airplane bathroom, his bowels cramping and knotting, or thinking about getting there.

When they were about to land, Gillian put him together, washing the puke from his tie, straightening it, combing his hair. All the while admonishing him, "Dad, you're a wreck."

He braced himself against the railing when he saw Judith breaking through the crowd, rushing toward him, her arms out. He caught her, leaning his full weight against her and what began as an embrace ended with her supporting him, dragging him across the field.

"What's the matter, Warren?"

He couldn't get the cotton out of his mouth to answer.

"Mother, he's got the tourist thing."

Judith brushed aside the reporters, apologizing. "Please, my husband is very tired." They hurried into the limousine brought to the field for them. Reporters clamored at the windows, but Curtis proceeded as if they weren't there, dropping them off like ants from a burning log.

When they arrived home, Curtis helped get Warren into the house and Judith had him led to their bedroom. "No, no," he protested. "I don't want you to get this."

"I won't dear…"

He stumbled past their room, up the stairs to the spare bedroom beyond Eddie's and fell to the bed.

He felt Judith lift the medal from around his neck. Even though he was seeing double, he could tell she was admiring it, holding it to the light.

"I'm so proud of you, darling." She leaned over him. "When you feel better, it will have been worth it."

She crushed herself against him, her breasts pressing, as she kissed him. He pushed her away. "Don't touch me! You mustn't get this."

She stood back. At first she was hesitant, then her eyes filled with tears. He knew he'd hurt her. "I'll let you sleep," she said, her voice trembling. "You probably have jet lag, too."

"Yes, yes, I do." He turned away from her.

Mercifully, she left the room.

He got up in the night and drank glasses of water. His head had started to clear and the horror of his situation was renewed. He wanted pills from their bathroom and he tried not to wake her, but she sat up. "Something I can get for you, darling?"

"No. I just need some medicine." He took all the bottles he could find from the bathroom and bedroom drawers that had collected over the years...codeine, phenobarbital, seconal...and stuffed them in his robe pockets.

When he passed Eddie's room on the way back to bed, a big, muscled, sandy-haired man from the Eddie Squad was hunched over the desk, studying. He turned around to speak and all Warren got out of it was that his name was Russell Jordan and he'd been on the job for ten days.

"Appreciate it," Warren mumbled. As soon as he was alone again, he downed a half-dozen pills, guaranteeing that he'd be knocked out for the next day.

Warren lost track of time. Gillian came to his bed. Judith came to his bed. Gillian and Russell Jordan came to his bed.

Once, he was vaguely aware that Gillian was saying goodbye to him. "Dad, I'm leaving for pre-med classes at University of California at San Francisco. I expect you to be well when I come back next month. Or, I will take care of you myself." There was a mischievous glint in her eye.

Russell Jordan had his arm around her. Now Warren was more than aware of this member of the Eddie Squad, taking liberties with his daughter. Mighty soon, too, since they'd just returned from Paris.

As soon as he was alone, he went for the pills, but they were gone. Frantically, he searched the bed, underneath it, and with a brilliant idea, he opened the dresser drawers. Yes, somebody had cleaned and dropped them all in there. Not taking any chances, after popping several, he hid them.

When next he awoke, Randall Thorne was standing over his bed. "I saw the medal, Warren. It's a richly deserved honor."

Warren felt as if his eyes were stuck in their sockets, his head ready to burst like an over-inflated balloon, his body kept from falling by the support from the bed. If only he had siderails..."Thanks."

Randall sat on the side of the bed. "What's the problem, Warren?"

"Too much Paris."

"Warren, you've been home for days. Paris has been gone for a week. And so have you."

"A week..." No, that was unbelievable.

"And that's not all. If you want the truth, you look and smell as if you've been living in a dumpster. I'm taking you into the hospital for a work-up."

"The hell you are," Warren roared. "You're an obstetrician. I'm not going to any goddam maternity ward."

"You're going to general medicine. I've already spoken to Jerome Gardner."

Jerome Gardner was chairman of the medical school faculty at the University and a classmate of Randall's. His reputation for being a crack diagnostician was unparalleled in the country.

"I'll be all right."

Judith stood behind Randall, worried, gaunt. Warren felt guilty when he saw her misery. But what could he do about it?

"Please, Warren," she begged.

"I'll be all right," he repeated loudly, turning away from them. He closed his eyes hoping they'd leave. Eventually, he felt Randall get up from the bed and then the bedroom door closed and then he felt someone on the bed again. Alarm ripped through him. Judith had returned, alone.

But the voice was Randall's and the firm hand on his shoulder was his friend's. "Warren, turn over. Look at me."

Against his better judgment, Warren did as he was told.

"Give up the pills, old buddy."

Warren protected his bathrobe pockets as Randall wrestled his hands loose, taking the bottles away from him. Most of them were empty.

"Anymore?"

"No." None except for the stash under the pillow, between the mattress and box springs.

"What is it, old buddy? What's really going on with you? You've just gotten the highest honor possible and you're a mess. What happened?"

Warren studied his friend and measured Randall's strengths next to the burden he carried within himself. He started to speak, but something prevented his tongue from moving. He interpreted it as a warning to keep silent.

Randall persisted, his voice barely above a whisper, comforting, empathetic. "Warren, what is it?"

The emotions broke loose from Warren, flowing from every pore in his body, great, wracking sobs tearing him apart. He clung to Randall's arm, begging him to understand without knowing. "It's going to be all right," Warren sobbed to his friend.

"Let me help you."

"No one can help me. I'm alone in this."

"Alone?" Randall was patient. "In what?"

But Warren was wary. The truth, once exposed, would destroy more than him. It would ruin his whole family, Gillian, Judith. He kept quiet.

"Why don't you go back to your own bedroom, Warren? Be with Judith. She's worried sick about you."

"No."

With that, Randall took matters into his own hands and pulled Warren out of the bed. He went limp as Randall dragged him into the hall.

"Stand up, you damn fool. You're going with me."

Warren mustered what strength he could, knocked Randall down, and ran back into the bedroom, locking the door. He turned off the light, fell into the bed and clamped his hands over his ears, covering his head with blankets.

Randall picked himself up, more perplexed than ever. He went downstairs and took Judith into the den where he mixed them stiff drinks.

"I don't know what to think," he began.

She was in tears. "It's just been since he came back from receiving the Schweitzer award."

Privately, Randall was sure something traumatic had happened, but it was best not to upset Judith more. At first, he thought Warren needed a good internist and a rest. Now he was positive that he needed a psychiatrist instead.

He couldn't be sure, but as he had pulled Warren down the hall, he had sensed that his friend was terrified of Judith.

He handed her the marguerita. "What did Gillian have to say about the Paris trip?"

"She said everything went well. The last evening, they ate at the *d'la Argent*, overlooking the Cathedral Notre Dame. The next morning he was sick." She looked at him beseechingly. "But that should have passed, don't you think?"

"Yes."

She turned away, wiping her eyes, her nose.

Randall wondered, did it have something to do with religion? Or Eddie? No, Warren wasn't that much of a believer.

After awhile, Judith spoke through her tears. "Do you suppose there's somebody else?"

He was curious. "How can you tell?"

Warren lapsed into a profound depression. Judith tried to feed him, but it was hopeless.

Another week passed, Randall came around again and said that he would hospitalize him against his wishes.

Warren was able to muster up the strength to fight him off again. He heard him talking to Judith outside his bedroom.

"He's got pills someplace."

"His office is calling twice a day wanting to know when he's coming in. Surgeries are backed up..."

As if this presented the solution to his problem, Warren waited until he heard the two go out the front door and he could see them talking in the front drive. He phoned his secretary and told her he'd be there in three days and not to call his house again. Warren willed himself to quit the self-destruction, stopped taking tranquilizers and sedatives and forced himself out of his depression.

When he did go in to his office, he filled his schedule so thoroughly that he never had time for anything else and, often, he slept at the hospitals where he attended new surgical cases.

Before long, Judith was convinced there was another woman. And she was heartsick.

After he'd been back to work for a month, he gifted her with a Rolls Royce and a strand of natural pearls. He took her to dinner, but would not return to their bed.

"Why?" She begged him. "Please..."

They were in the vestibule of their home by the stairs leading to the second floor.

"I love you too much to tell you the truth."

"Not knowing is worse, Warren."

Thinking of her despair and tears of the last several weeks, he decided that, perhaps, she was right. He let her have it. "I am no longer able to function as your husband."

"What kind of textbook excuse is that?"

"You wanted the truth."

At first she didn't understand, but then her confusion lifted and she said, almost in a whisper: "You mean you've become impotent?"

"Yes, my darling."

"But Warren, that isn't uncommon. It often happens following traveling…time zone changes, jet lag, and the rest. It's only temporary."

"I'm not so sure…"

"Warren, I need you. Come to our bed. We can try…" She carefully began slipping her hand into his trousers.

He gently removed it. "No, Judith."

That hurt look was back again, the look he'd seen in her eyes when Randall was sitting on the bed.

Suddenly she was angry. She threw back her head. "Why don't you tell me the truth, Warren? You've got guilt written all over you. It has nothing to do with impotence. It has nothing to do with Paris. Those are just grand excuses. I know the real reason…" She glared at him. "A Rolls, Royce, pearls, expensive dinners…what gift will you give me next to cover up that I am not the only one?"

The outburst was his opportunity to be levelheaded. "I would be happier if you didn't come to that conclusion, Judith. It's not that at all."

"Not at all? Certainly it is. You've been unfaithful for a long time. Just how long, Warren?" She didn't wait for an answer before slamming into her room.

Of course, she would draw that conclusion. Perhaps it was just as well.

Within a month, Warren knew that she'd been to a psychiatrist, for the psychiatrist was his colleague, Rob Cannon, with an international reputation for theories on the mid-life crises. He spoke at several conventions each year and had to beg off just as many more.

He told Warren about Judith's visit and the content of the session.

"Rob, I love my wife, but she must believe what she needs to believe."

"It could be a temporary crisis for her," the psychiatrist said. "After all, she's nearing forty and wonders about her attractiveness. Women do have these periods of doubt."

"Yes," Warren agreed, wanting to punch the bastard. "Incidently, Rob, you'd better pull up your pants on your ethics. If my wife is stupid enough to come to you, the least she deserves is confidentiality."

Warren had always dreaded the middle-of-the-night calls for his expert surgical skills when there was a horrible, disfiguring automobile crash, a boat fire in the marina, a plane gone down. But six months after his estrangement from Judith, he was almost relieved when two disasters required his services. The first was a small plane crash in the Valley, where a young, married couple miraculously escaped with their lives, but leaving the bride needing years of reconstructive surgery to her face, where one side had been torn away.

The second was a Los Angeles hotel fire, an old building that went up like kindling, taking most of the victims to a quick death. A few got away completely. A few lived, but might as well have been dead.

Warren was called in immediately for plastic surgery. The cases kept him busy for weeks. He would take quick meals in the hospital cafeteria where the buzz centered around a second-rate burglary involving the White House. It was front page news for months and Time Magazine showed Nixon's secretary doing contortions to prove that she was, indeed, the culprit who erased eighteen minutes from damaging tapes that Nixon had recorded with unsuspecting associates.

Warren found it hard to believe that this single, incident could take up an entire nation's time and energy. If politicians lived with death every day as he did, they might change their priorities. And then he was back in surgery.

He was kept busy for weeks on end, too bone-tired to think about his own problems. Judith continued to see Rob Cannon, twice, sometimes three times a week and Warren paid the bills, hoping the advice Rob gave her at least kept her pulled together.

She left him alone and he thought she'd accepted his marital conditions. Then, one night, eight-months later, he felt her beside him. He murmured and reached to caress her. The blood was pulsating through his penis and she grasped it hungrily.

An alarm went off in him when he realized what was happening. For just a moment, the old feelings had been there, his happiness at having her near, the glow of contentment...and then, he woke up, as if a bomb had burst outside his bedroom window.

"It's all right, my darling," she was saying. "It's going to be just like it used to be."

His throbbing organ fought to keep from responding. His mind fought with his feelings. Is it incest if she doesn't know, he asked himself, and then the desperate answer came. Yes, because I know it and I cannot do it. He took her hands firmly, holding them away from his body. They tightened in anger and hurt.

"It's no good, Judith. Leave things as they are." His heart tore at what this was doing to her and he didn't know any way of making it easier.

He could smell Rob Cannon at the other end of this scene and he hated him more than ever.

She never came to his bed again or made overtures. And she refused to let him take her out in the evenings. She became a recluse, reading books she ordered from Martindale's, dozens at a time, and had sent. She took over more and more of Eddie's care, giving the Squad more days off. Russell Jordan was about the only regular sitter now, and he spent half the night writing letters to Gillian.

As a married couple, Warren and Judith might as well be two separate continents divided by an ocean. And he feared there was no vessel large enough to sail across it.

Shortly after an empty New Year's celebration with medical colleagues including the Thornes', Warren learned that Judith had seen a lawyer. How? Thurston Wright, their family lawyer and social acquaintance, called and told him so.

"Warren, I thought I'd better let you know your wife was in."

"Why?"

"To discuss divorce."

Warren wasn't shocked, but had a deep sorrow. It didn't have to be this way. It was no resolution. "I'll fight it, Stew. I don't want a divorce."

"Neither does she."

Maybe he could stall Judith. Somehow convince her that everything would be all right. "Look, Stew, I need to come in about a will. I want to set up a trust fund for Judith and Gillian." He neglected to mention Eddie. "We've had problems...not her fault. I want to be sure she'll always be financially secure."

"Why don't you two see a marriage counselor?"

"Not a bad idea. I'll mention it to her."

Inside, he hated Thurston for violating Judith's confidence. Warren fully realized that she was a victim of his success. And he knew that he'd never see a marriage counselor. It would be the ultimate hypocrisy, because he'd have to go into it lying. He would never tell the truth about his relationship to Judith. Not to anyone. And, certainly not to her.

Two weeks later, Thurston duly reported that he'd told Judith he couldn't represent her. Conflict of interest.

"In what way?"

"There isn't, but I would have come up with something if she'd asked. Incidently, she refused a referral to someone else."

Chapter Thirty-Seven

"Unexpected news from afar. Meet with old friend." Judith read her daily horoscope to Warren. It was innocuous enough, and fit well within the framework of their marital relationship.

They were eating breakfast together, keeping their structured schedule, carefully avoiding sensitive subjects. She'd come to realize the impossibility of a divorce. As bad as her situation was, Eddie had better care here than any she could provide for him if she were alone.

She thought about the horoscope, trying to give it substance. "I'm having lunch with Randall's wife, Denise. Is she an old friend?"

He paused in spooning out his grapefruit. "Is she a friend?"

"Probably not." She folded the paper.

"Wait! What's my horoscope?"

"Sorry. I didn't know you believed in them."

"I don't."

She opened the paper and found Capricorn. *"Surprise communication comes from a distance."*

"There you are," he said. "The message is the same as yours except using different words."

"Warren, it's just for fun. Besides, sometimes they come true."

"Yes...most generalizations do."

* * *

After Warren left for the hospital, Judith bathed Eddie, fed him, bound his hands and waited for Ralph from the Squad. Then she left to meet Denise at Bullocks in Westwood Village for lunch and the fashion show.

Denise was nervous and looked haunted with dark circles under her eyes, lines around her mouth. She'd never lost her sleek figure, but her makeup barely hid the baked, dried out look of her skin from too many hours in the sun.

They ordered the standard diet luncheon, fresh peaches and cottage cheese with a small grilled sirloin patty.

Denise chattered about Beverly Hills. "Have you tried shopping on Rodeo Drive? Impossible. Those terrible tourists. And those foreigners moving into Bel Air...middle-easterners..."

"How is Brian?" Judith interrupted, changing the subject to her son.

"Fine." She held up two crossed fingers of one hand. "Maybe the two years in jail helped. We think he's clean and he's talking about going back to school. How is Gillian doing in pre-med?"

"Fine."

"She's so talented with her music," said Denise. "It's a shame her violin and piano have to suffer."

"I hope they won't. They just won't be her career."

"I can't imagine a woman having a career."

Judith became nervous with the conversation flying all over the field like wild baseballs. What was it that Denise wanted?

Midway through the meal, Denise put her fork down. "I don't know how to bring this up, so I'll just say it." She laughed nervously.

"Go right ahead."

"Are you and Warren having trouble with your marriage?"

Judith was careful. It was none of Denise's business. "Why do you ask?"

"Randall says he's been with Warren every evening. Problems between you two. He says that ever since Warren came back from Europe, something has bothered him."

"Yes, but I didn't know he'd told Randall." That was a lie. Of course, he'd told Randall.

Denise's mood brightened as if storm clouds had passed by. Confirming Judith's bad news was obviously good news to her. "Is it something I can help you with?"

"No."

Denise soon excused herself, saying that she was late for a hair appointment.

When Judith got home, there was a large envelope addressed to her from Burlington, Vt. Inside was a letter from her mother's old friend, Jane Barnett.

Judith had written to tell her of Sarah's death, remembering Jane's closeness
to her mother from the picture of three women among her effects. Judith had
taken a chance that Jane still lived in Burlington.

The letter read:

Dear Judith:

*I am so sorry about your mother. She was a fine, admirable person.
What a puzzle that you never knew what had happened to her all of
those years.*

*We missed her at the 40th reunion of the Margaret Ward Training
School.*

*If you ever come to Vermont, I would like to have you as a house guest.
Perhaps I could tell you about the days when Sarah was a student
nurse, although I know little about her after she went to California.*

Included with the letter was an alumni bulletin announcing the class
reunion, the class roster of that year and an old picture of a few girls taken at
Battery Park.

Her mother looked so happy, young and innocent. What ever had
happened, that was so painful that she'd ended up in a mental institution?

When Warren came in that evening, Judith said, "Maybe there's some
truth to horoscopes."

"In what way?"

"I've received unexpected news from afar."

She showed him the letter.

He read it and looked at the picture in the alumni bulletin. His face became
ashen and he quickly handed it back to her, turned away and went into the Roy
Rogers room to fix drinks for them.

She was sure his hand was shaking as he gave her the glass.

"How do you know that woman from Vermont?" he asked.

"She and my mother were close friends."

"But you've never heard from her before."

"Yes, twice before. When my mother first disappeared. And last month, I
wrote to tell her mother had died. She sent condolences while you were in
France."

He changed the subject as they sat down to a late dinner.

"How is Denise?"

"Fine. The lunch was a fishing expedition. She wanted to know if you and I were having trouble with our marriage."

"What business is it of hers?"

"None. She says Randall is with you most every evening. She offered to help me with our problems."

Warren was silent.

"Is he spending a lot of time with you?" she asked.

"No."

"That's the answer I gave her when she asked if she could help me." Judith couldn't keep her mind on Denise for she kept thinking about the letter from Vermont. Before they had finished eating, she'd made a decision. "Warren, I think I'll write and ask Jane Barnett if I might visit her for a few days. I really would like to know more about my mother. I wonder if Jane knew my father…"

Warren got up from the table and fixed another double scotch.

The next morning Judith wrote to her mother's old friend, even though she couldn't find Jane's letter or the alumni bulletin. She hunted and hunted, but never found them. Luckily, she had Jane listed in her address book.

*   *   *

Jane Barnett had been upset when she learned of Sarah's death. She'd often thought of her old friend and how strange it was that she had broken off communication, the memory of their friendship kept alive only through her daughter. Asking Judith to visit was an impulsive afterthought, but Jane was pleased when she accepted the invitation.

It had been years since she'd had anyone into her house for an extended visit. Until retirement, she'd always worked hard. In the beginning, after graduation from nurses training, she'd had private duty cases. Then she did public health work in the rural areas of Vermont, finally returning to Burlington during World War II to work at Fanny Allen Hospital in nearby Winooski.

Most of the women she knew were married and she saw little of them for they were involved in family matters, church socials, later caring for grandchildren. Jane had never married and liked being alone. And now, crippling arthritis kept her from social contacts even more.

She scrubbed every inch of her house, her painful, knarled hands protected by gloves. She washed the antimacassars, curtains, all the sheets and towels, sprayed the rooms with scents of spring flowers, piled homemade oatmeal and raisin cookies into the cookie jar, filled the freezer with steaks and roasts. She brought home a honey baked ham for Judith's first meal with her.

She was sure that Judith had done well by herself since she had a Bel Air address. Had she become a success in the movie industry? Perhaps she was a writer. She could even be a physician for she had never married. Whatever, she was extremely modest about herself, only mentioning her mother, Sarah, in her letters.

When Judith arrived, the spring day was made for a happy occasion…a crisp morning, followed by warming sunshine, the last of the snow melting away with new grass proudly smiling its approval.

Jane hugged her warmly and held her at arm's length.

This was the first time she'd seen Judith and she was struck by the resemblance to her father. Dear Dr. Hollis, killed in the war, so young…

"Judith, my dear, you must be exhausted. I'll show you to your room where you can freshen up and rest."

"I'm too excited to rest. I want to hear all about my mother and the other nurses from your class."

"Not yet. First, you go do your business while I do mine." She sent her protesting guest to the spare room.

Jane turned on the oven to warm the ham and made tea, which she poured in her special china service. She fixed a plate with cookies and cheeses and brought out the few old pictures she had found. When everything was in place to suit her, she called for Judith.

Jane showed her a picture of three nurses: "This is your mother with me and another student, Abbie Kirley." She omitted details of Abbie's losing her mind, struck by the thought that she, herself, was the only one of the three who hadn't. In fact, that's all she knew of Abbie. The day she left the Margaret Ward Training School was the last anyone had ever heard of her.

"There was lots of sadness in our class. Only five of us are still alive, so far as I know." She told her about Elsie Robinson, Eunice Thompson, Carrie Whitney and Mary Drury, all married with different names, two of them widowed.

Judith listened intently.

"Your mother was a fine woman, very compassionate, especially with children. She'd had an unhappy childhood herself, and her heart went out to small, ill children. She didn't think children should ever have to suffer. She'd had brothers and a sister who died from something that runs in the family."

"Yes," said Judith, sadly. "I have a son with the problem."

This shocked Jane. "I didn't know you were married."

"Oh, yes. Very much married." She took out pictures of Gillian and Warren.

Jane studied them. "These must be old pictures of you with your grandfather."

Judith laughed. "No. Guess again."

"Well, it can't be your daughter and your father." She tried to think of a delicate way of expressing it. "Your father is no longer here."

"That's true, but you're half right. This is my daughter and my husband."

Jane, flustered, tried to make light of her error. "You know, there's a Vermont folk saying: 'Fall in love and marry an old man. Any troubles you have will soon die along with him.'"

It was a mistake. She should not have said it for it upset Judith.

"I hope my husband never dies."

"I'm sorry, my dear. We New Englanders are sometimes too blunt. But you surprised me. I thought your maiden name was Hollis."

"No, my maiden name was Stanhope."

Jane fingered the pictures for a long while. Gillian was a darling, a carbon copy of Sarah.

"Did you know my father?"

Jane looked at her friend's daughter for a long time, debating what to tell her. A nagging voice from the past warned her, 'Mind your own business'. "No, I didn't know your father. I believe your mother met him in California."

From the kitchen came the smell of the ham burning.

* * *

Jane sat in the living room that night, reading the Burlington Press and back issues of Vermont Life. Judith had gone to bed right after dinner, pleading exhaustion, leaving Jane to herself.

Something puzzled her. How could Judith's married name possibly be Mrs. Warren Hollis? If her mother had been married to Warren Hollis, then why was Judith's maiden name Stanhope? Had Sarah's second husband adopted Judith?

She thought for hours. She had the eerie feeling that the past had never happened. It had only been a dream that had only recently become a reality. She had somehow confused Sarah's life with her daughter's. It was as bad as the days in nurses training with Miss Bradford when it had been impossible to distinguish the truth from lies even on the basis of first hand knowledge.

It was nearly morning when Jane went to a box in her closet and found more pictures of their student days at West Vermont Hospital. There was one snapped at Battery Park during a July 4th celebration, one that she had never shown to Sarah. It was taken on the sly, a picture of her with Warren.

Jane took it and compared it to the photograph of Warren with Gillian that Judith had left on the coffee table. Jane had to use her imagination to bridge the years, but this man was the same Warren Hollis pictured with Sarah forty years ago.

Had Sarah lied to her daughter about her past? Had the deception finally destroyed Sarah? Is that why she died insane at Greenbridge?

How could Judith marry her own father? What circumstances would ever make it possible? Did she knowingly marry her own father? For what reason? Certainly not for revenge or to spite Sarah. Jane could see no hate there.

Jane rationalized a dozen ways that her conclusions might be false, but there was no escaping the facts. Finally, her head spinning and spinning, the revulsion reaching the pit of her stomach, she hobbled into her bedroom, threw open the window with agonized fingers, and fell into bed, fully dressed. She took in great gulps of the clear, Vermont night air and never slept a minute.

She was too ill the next day to attend to her guest.

"I'm sorry, Judith, but my arthritis has flared up terribly." She rubbed salve on her miserable joints. "I won't be able to go out today."

"Do you mind if I go alone? I'd like to see mother's old hospital and the Winooski River flowing below it that she loved, stop at the home where my grandmother lived out her last years…walk along Lake Champlain at sunset, relive her memories…"

When Judith returned that evening, Jane felt even worse. Judith offered to take her to a doctor, but Jane urged her guest to return to California.

In spite of her promise to Sarah, she never wanted to hear Judith's name again.

300

*   *   *

On the return flight to California, Judith wondered what had disturbed Jane so. And she thought back to Warren. He'd become just as upset when he learned about the letter from Jane.

What did those two know about one another?

Judith was sure they'd never met because Jane hadn't known she was married. And yet, from their reactions, they certainly weren't strangers. Had her mother been the common denominator between them, concealing a secret?

Judith intended to find out.

Chapter Thirty-Eight

Judith arrived in Los Angeles just after five a.m. Curtis was there to meet her...alone.

"Dr. Hollis sends his regrets that he could not be here. He is still in surgery."

In a way, she was glad. She had become nervous as the flight progressed towards California. She had started out with such resolve, but it had slowly weakened.

Admiring heads turned as she walked with Curtis through the LAX terminal, crowded even in the early morning. It was times like this that boosted her confidence. She must have something that attracted people. Although her full hair was graying, she wore it loosely piled at the crown of her head, emphasizing her elegant, clean profile. Her figure was as slim as the day she had married and she could afford to dress well.

Curtis carried her Vuiton luggage, opened the door of the limousine for her where she escaped, settling against the seat away from the prying, curious eyes.

It was a swift ride home before the morning commuter traffic paralyzed the Los Angeles freeway system.

Warren still wasn't there so Judith went to bed and slept all day. She awoke refreshed and he still hadn't come home. She waited for him in the Roy Rogers room, reading, her velvet robe wrapped around her legs. It was nearly midnight when she heard his car drive in, the door slam, then a second car door.

Her heart leaped, adrenalin alerting her body. He hadn't expected her home. Who was he bringing? She dreaded the worst and the confrontation if it was another woman.

The backdoor opened. She heard male voices. Her relief was instantaneous as she hurried to meet them.

Randall Thorne was with Warren. Their friend was unshaven, his black hair unruly, his clothes rumpled.

Warren hugged her and she was aware, again, that he always held her slightly sideways so that he never pressed against her. It was odd, but that's the way it had been since his return from West Africa and France.

She could feel his fatigue. "Has something happened?"

"Denise, got a botched face lift," Randall said, bitterly.

Warren's expression was grim. "She went to one of those boy wonders who does cosmetic surgery in his office. Of course, he isn't board certified. She waited five days before calling me and by that time, infection had set in. I did what I could, but it was almost impossible with the swelling from the earlier surgery."

"Why didn't she consult with you in the first place?" Judith asked.

"Pride," said Randall. "She told me she was going to a spa for three weeks to lose weight, but it was a actually a private home where women go to stay after having plastic surgery."

Judith made them snacks while Warren mixed drinks. The men drank several doubles rapidly, chewing on peanuts, potato chips, pretzels, rye bread sandwiches with cold cuts.

"You're staying the night," she told Randall after his third drink.

He followed her as she went to prepare the spare bedroom for him.

"If Denise could be more like you...a real woman."

She kissed him lightly, her heart breaking for him.

She went back to the den, thinking of what he had said, and her husband's lack of responsiveness to her. "Warren, Randall says I'm a real woman."

"Yes, you are."

"But not a real wife..."

"Judith, please don't...I'm much too tired."

He stood and it was an effort.

She felt an unaccustomed resentment and insisted he stay longer.

"Darling, I just got back from Vermont. Aren't you interested in my trip?"

"Of course." His eyes wavered, his lids drooped.

She plunged into her prepared questions. "Warren, what is there between you and Jane Barnett?"

"Between us? What do you mean?"

"What do you know about her?"

"Nothing." In spite of his being half-asleep and drunk, his defenses were up. "What are you implying?"

"I'm implying that you know one another. She became physically ill after she saw your picture with Gillian."

"Judith, I couldn't possibly know her."

Her frustration was building, the knowing and feeling that there was something to her suspicions, but never able to identify what.

Suddenly, a thought broke through and the words tumbled from her. "Warren, what is there about you and my mother? What do you have in common?"

His reaction was immediate. "You."

She was exasperated. "You just won't tell the truth, will you?"

He looked at her for a long time and she thought that he was going to say something more. Instead he came to her, placed his hands on her shoulders, squeezed them lovingly, and kissed her on the forehead. "It's good to have you home."

* * *

Judith asked Warren about Denise every evening. "The nurses say she won't come out of her private room at Cedars. Refuses phone calls and visitors. Why don't you go and see her?" he suggested.

"I'm the last person she'd want to have visit, especially if she wants to be alone."

"Perhaps not."

So Judith went. Denise was pathetic, her face swollen, black and blue with weeping sores, dark roots betraying her bleached hair.

"Oh God, Judith, I don't want you to see me like this." She pulled the sheet up under her eyes like a veil.

"You're not that bad."

"Yes, I am. I don't dare go out in public. If it wasn't for Warren, I would have killed myself." She was downcast, reached over and picked up nail polish from the bedside table. "I can't even get the energy to use this." She plunked it down, too hard.

"It's not important."

Denise gave her a stricken look, her eyes tearing. "Randall has filed for divorce."

The news stunned Judith. Those two fit like matched thoroughbreds. Class. Money. Worldwide vacations with the beautiful people. Superstars of the jet set. She'd thought the face lift was just to keep the never changing glitter, not as a means of keeping Randall.

Disregarding the gulf that had always been between them, Judith hugged her gently. "Denise, I'm sorry…"

"He's got someone else," she cried. "She's younger, with long, straight hair. Almost no makeup. Wears sandals, loose fitting clothes. She does sports, swimming…very athletic looking. She's not his type at all. Just the opposite from me." She reached for a tissue to dab at her black and blue eyes. "I can't believe he's leaving me. I have no skills. He never wanted me to be useful. Just beautiful. Now he's tired of that."

Judith was lost for the right words. "He'll take care of you."

"He doesn't have to. This is California. It's fifty-fifty, right down the line."

"Randall would never leave you without resources."

"I'm not so sure. Remember when you and I went to lunch? I thought Warren was cheating on you. All the time, it was Randall lying to me."

* * *

Judith went home, shaken. She went up the stairs to be with Eddie. He kept her busy without intruding on her thoughts. And she needed time to think.

Russell Jordan was with him.

"Hello, Mrs. Hollis."

"Hello, Russell."

He went with her to stand by Eddie's crib. Russell really was a thoughtful young man. She couldn't understand why Warren didn't like him. He was conscientious, determined, about to receive his bachelor's degree in engineering. When he stayed nights, he always dimmed the light in Eddie's room when the boy was sleeping. She thought it strange since Eddie was blind, but decided it was Russell's way of adapting Eddie to the outside world. Which, of course, never happened.

"Do you know something, Mrs. Hollis. He's quieter than he used to be. And he looks thinner."

"Maybe he's sick."

Russell looked at her queerly. "He's always been sick."

"Maybe a cold or something." She worried about him and tried not to think about it, but the little knowledge they had was that children like Eddie seldom lived past their teens. Eddie was in his teens.

She had Warren look at him when he came home, but he said the boy looked all right to him. Judith called Selwyn Burger who broke into his jammed schedule to make a house call to see Eddie. He prescribed antibiotics.

* * *

The following Thursday, she was still upset about Warren's attitude towards Eddie, her trip to Vermont, Denise and Randall, when she kept her appointment with Rob Cannon. He was glad to see her.

"Rob, Eddie's not doing well. I'm afraid for him."

He asked her to describe her fears.

It was hard to do and it seemed hollow to say that Eddie was an important part of her life. How could he be when he couldn't share experiences, feelings or love? She finally had to admit that she needed him, but was it fair to him? Wouldn't he be better off dead?

Rob had no comment, letting time pass in silence. Then he lit his pipe and settled back. "Tell me about your trip," he said.

"It was very interesting. Don't think I'm crazy, but my mother's friend became very upset when she saw Warren's picture."

"Why?"

"I had the feeling she knew him."

"Did you ask her?"

"Of course. I haven't been coming to you without learning something."

"And..."

"She said she didn't know him. I came back and asked Warren what my mother had in common with him and he said, 'you'. Naturally. She's my mother and he's my husband."

Rob Cannon sent a couple of quick puffs into the air. Judith hated the smell of his cigar smoke.

"Do you suppose he's trying to tell you that he's tired of your innuendos?" he said.

"What do you mean by that?"

"Ever since your mother's death, you've been trying to construct a past that never existed. Judith, you're not living in the real world. You've stopped sleeping with your husband…"

"No, he stopped sleeping with me."

"Possibly because of these crazy ideas of yours."

She was stunned and hurt. Rob Cannon had suddenly changed. He'd always been so supportive, now he was insinuating that her problems with Warren were entirely her fault.

Rob put down his pipe and came to stand over her. "Judith, you've forgotten how to respond as a woman. You did not die along with your mother."

He sat down beside her, facing her. She wasn't sure whether she should be comforted or move away from him.

"You've been coming to me for months. Your discussion is mostly questions about your husband. You have to make up your mind if you want to solve them or get out of the marriage."

She couldn't keep up with him. What was he trying to tell her?

"Judith, you need a kind of help that you've never considered."

"What kind?"

He was taking off his belt.

"What are you doing?"

He was unbuttoning his trousers and reaching inside. Gradually she realized what he had in mind.

She wanted to ask him how this would solve her problems, but he had stood, dropping his pants. She tried to get up, but lost her balance when he pushed her down on the couch and got on top of her. She could feel his hardness against her as he pulled up her skirt and ripped her underwear.

"Don't! Don't!"

His face was coming down on her. "The trouble, Judith, is that you've forgotten how to love. See how frightened you are? You're not being fair to yourself."

She tried to push him away. "I'm having my period."

"Why should that make a difference? It's perfectly natural. Did that bother your husband?"

"That's none of your business."

He gazed into her eyes, holding her hair. "You're a beautiful woman, Judith."

"I don't want this, Rob."

He was caressing her breasts. She began to fight and he became strong, beast-like. All she could think of were Doberman dogs that killed on command and that Rob Cannon was going to do that to her.

He forced himself on her brutally, jamming himself into her dry insides, searing her with pain. His thrusts were vicious and hard. He had his hands on her legs keeping them apart, his chin pressing into her chest. She yanked at his hair which only seemed to increase his animal passion.

When he was through, he calmly stood up, wiping himself with his handkerchief, drawing up his pants. She pulled her skirt down and stood, reaching for her panties and shoving them in her purse.

"You are low, Rob Cannon. Low. If my husband had ever treated me like that, there's no question what I would have done with the marriage. Wait until I tell him about this."

"He would never believe you. My dear, all women fantasize sleeping with their therapists. You are no different." He went back to his desk and picked up his pipe.

She slammed out of his office, infuriated and humiliated. He'd raped her, pure and simple. If anyone got therapy from it, it was Rob Cannon.

* * *

A few months later, Warren observed, "Rob Cannon isn't sending bills."

"I've stopped seeing him."

"Is everything resolved?"

"With him, yes. He's given me all he has to offer."

"In my opinion, that probably wasn't much."

She shrugged.

Chapter Thirty-Nine

The next four years passed rapidly. For Warren, there was no letup. After he'd patched up Denise, he suffered through Randall's divorce from her. She promptly married a Palm Springs import half her age, half as rich and she was ecstatic.

Randall married his mistress, and the marriage took the same pathway as his first, only faster. He hit the bottle, despairing that there was no place called paradise.

Warren knew there was. He and Judith had visited there often before it was lost to them. Even though she never knew what had happened between them, she finally accepted the compromises in their marriage. For this, he admired her.

She began overseeing their philanthropic finances and volunteering at U.C.L.A again. He bought her a beach house at Malibu where she could dream, where being alone was part of the landscape. But she didn't use it. She wouldn't be that far away from Eddie.

Instead, Gillian and Russell used it, staying there every chance they found.

In Bel Air, when Judith wasn't in Eddie's room, she spent hours in the dayroom, warmed by the sun streaming through the windows. She read, filling up notebook after notebook, writing out her comments to various classics. Camus made sense to her as did Dostoyevsky.

One evening, she and Warren were together in the Roy Rogers room. She sat sideways on the couch, a patchwork quilt over her legs. He read at the other end of the couch. She laid down the Kafka she was reading.

"Warren, do you think these writers would have kept pouring it out if they'd ever had answers that satisfied them?"

"I don't know."

She looked at him, too long for his comfort. He held his breath, sure that this was leading to something.

"Warren, you should take up writing." She smiled and picked up her book again.

That's the way it was with them now. He never had gotten used to it, but she'd stopped asking questions. Thank God, for he could never have been honest with her. Every time he wrestled with his conscience, he ended with the same conclusion. There was nothing he could do to ease her burden.

Eventually, she turned to the women writers: George Sand, Virginia Woolf, Anais Nin. Warren wondered if she knew what she was searching for.

He knew what he wanted, but it, too, was impossible. He was feeling his years and longed to cut back his practice, limit it to consulting, eventually retiring, but he feared the effect it would have at home. Avoiding one another would become impossible.

Gillian was in her third year at the University of Southern California School of Medicine where she'd transferred from San Francisco to be closer to her family. She was bringing Russell Jordan home with her for the weekend. Warren still didn't like him any better than the first time he'd met him.

It was May and the weather was California perfect. Not too hot, too cool, or too smoggy. When they arrived, Russell headed for the swimming pool while Gillian stayed behind, asking to speak to him alone. She was dressed in her tennis outfit and hardly looked more than fifteen years old.

"Dad, I want to ask your permission to do genetic tests on Eddie."

It seemed a casual request, almost as if she were asking for a credit card to use for the afternoon. But it caught him by surprise. Genetic testing was the last thing he would have expected her to be doing.

"Are you studying that in medical school?"

"No. I'm working ten hours a week in the genetics lab. I want to be sure that's what I want as my specialty."

Warren thought back to his own exposure to genetics. Mendel, the monk, and his peas. Drosophilus matings. Endless counting of sex, wings, belly spots. What would she find out? She'd see the different cell divisions, some chromosomes. Nothing more. Nothing threatening to him. Maybe he could even help her, tell her something she'd never find under the microscope. "I don't see why not. But please don't tell your mother."

"Why not?"

310

"You're probably interested in Eddie's disorder. I'm sure you're aware that it's genetic in origin, sex-linked, passed on through the maternal line."

"I suspected it might be. If it is and we can identify the defective gene, then I'm going to find out if I'm a carrier."

"Is that possible?"

"Of course. Dad, when did you last read up on genetics?" She was exasperated.

"I haven't had the time." His excuse was lame and he was surprised at his resentment that his daughter might know more than he. He should have known that surgery wasn't the only field with advances.

She sensed his chagrin. "I'm sorry, Dad," she said, throwing her arms around him. "I should be more tolerant. You've been so busy during the years that genetics knowledge really exploded. Almost all advances in the field have been made since 1959 with improved cell culture techniques."

He was puzzled.

"You mean you can culture DNA cells the same as you can bacteria?"

"Certainly, with special mediums. It's exciting. One cell can tell you everything you might want to know about someone."

Now he was alarmed. Maybe he'd been too quick to give permission. "Even who your parents are?"

"No," she laughed. "For that, you have to test both of the suspected parents, too."

His relief was monumental. When he learned that, he was more than willing to help her obtain the blood specimen from Eddie, holding the boy while she withdrew blood and placed it in a special medium.

As soon as Gillian had taken the specially preserved blood back to medical school, Warren forgot about the incident. He had more important matters on his mind.

Namely Russell Jordan.

At the conclusion of that weekend, Russell had come to him and he, too, asked to speak to him privately.

They went to the Roy Rogers room where Warren offered to mix him a drink.

"No thanks," said Russell. "I want my head clear for this. I'll settle for Perrier water, if you have that. Otherwise, nothing."

"Then, unfortunately, it will be nothing."

Nevertheless, Warren mixed himself a scotch and water. When he was settled, he waited for Russell to state the nature of their meeting.

"Dr. Hollis, I would like your permission to marry Gillian. Yours and Mrs. Hollis…"

Warren's immediate reaction was negative, but he cooled the lava in his head and kept quiet, hardly able to believe that Gillian was old enough to marry. Why, oh why, of all the young men she'd known, was she stuck on this one?

"Does she want to marry you?"

"I haven't asked her. I want your approval, first."

"That's thoughtful of you. But perhaps you should ask her. Asking us may be immaterial."

Russell rose and shook his hand. "If you feel that way…"

"No, no, let's discuss it more. When would you like to marry her?"

"As soon as she finishes medical school."

"I suppose you'll be able to support her."

"She doesn't need that."

Warren bristled. "What do you mean she doesn't need to be supported?"

Russell was obviously ill-at-ease. "She doesn't want to be supported. After all, she'll be a physician…"

"It bothers me the way you young men want your wives to be independent of you."

"It isn't that…"

"Then what is it!" He knew he was intimidating Russell, but he irritated him.

"I'm willing to support her. That's why I want to wait a year before we marry. These last two years have been a bitch for me. Getting my Ph.D. has been like walking through a minefield. My thesis chairman can always find a reason to blow it apart. Getting the tuition money is killing me. I even have to go to a sperm bank in order to get the money to take Gillian out."

"You what!"

It was as though he'd put a clamp on Russell's mouth because he shut up, refusing to expand on his statement.

The two men glared at one another, the one hating, the other confused.

"Look, Dr. Hollis, forget I said anything. Just forget it."

"No, out of fairness to you, I'll ask her mother and let you know."

He and Judith discussed it.

"As far as I'm concerned, it's up to Gillian," she said.

"I think she can do better than Russell Jordan."

"That's not really our business. He's a decent, conscientious man. Determined, too. Warren, he's brilliant. He was originally an engineering major, but he switched to physics which he finds more exciting. He's been offered a research position with the Pentagon.

"How do you know all this?"

"Because I know Russell. He's been loyal in caring for Eddie for almost nine years. I can always count on him, the same as I could Burger."

"He's no Selwyn Burger."

"How do you know? You've never given him a chance."

He didn't care to, either. The more he thought about Russell, the more he found to dislike. The wide, stubborn jaw, his lack of confidence. "We don't know enough about him. What about his background? What about his parents, his grandparents?"

"You didn't ask me all of those things before we married. Why are you so particular with Gillian?"

He backed off. "Let's just say that Russell Jordan is going to have to prove himself to me."

"How?"

"I'll think of something."

"Why not try to like him? Then maybe the rest won't be necessary. If Gillian wants to marry him, she'll do it with or without our permission. It's the wrong way to start, Warren. After all, he will be the father of your grandchildren."

And of how many others, he wondered, thinking of the sperm bank.

Two weeks later, Gillian came to Warren and took him into the Roy Rogers room, locking the door. He could feel her excitement. Her words rushed out. "Dad, I've got good news…"

Had she decided to give up Russell Jordan? That would be the best news of all.

She took some photographs and a diagram from her brief case. "Dad, remember when you told me Eddie's disorder was sex-inked? Well, it isn't. Isn't that great?"

"You mean, it's not genetic?" After all these years, would he learn he'd suspected wrongly?

"It's genetic, but not sex-linked."

"Are you sure?"

"Yes, more than sure. Positive. In fact, my instructor, Professor Burroughs, identified the affected chromosome." She placed the photograph on the desk before him. As she talked, she pointed to numbered black lines and curves which looked like pairs of thin-waisted dancing girls without heads or feet.

"Genetics has certainly progressed farther than I imagined," he said, awed and worried.

"At first, we thought Eddie had a disease known as Lesch-Nyhan. His behavior certainly suggests it and that is a sex-linked disorder. But his sex chromosomes are normal." She circumscribed one chromosome. "Do you see this one? Do you see this band?"

"Yes."

"Here is the abnormality. This is a body chromosome, or autosome. The problem is a translocated gene, very unusual. Even more unusual is that it is a recessive gene."

She didn't continue for a moment, but studied him, examining every facet of his expression as if to gauge his understanding. Before he could figure it out, she told him.

"That means Eddie had to inherit the defective gene from both of you."

His whole being crashed in, his self-image shattered with this discovery. Never had he considered that he, too, might be responsible for Eddie's condition.

"Professor Burroughs is so interested that he wants blood samples from you and mother. He'll come and get them so he can see Eddie."

Never. He felt his facial muscles tighten. "Gillian, I don't want your mother to know about this. I told you that in the beginning."

"Why? She should be happy to know it isn't her fault. And so should you."

He had to stop her delving. "I suppose my real reason is that I feel this is an invasion of my privacy. I don't want any more genetic testing done on me."

"Why not?"

"I just don't. Personal identities are gone. My God, the IRS knows everything about your finances. The insurance companies have a central registry with the inside track on your health history for your entire life. And now, you want to add fuel to this assault on individual autonomy and have genetic maps of your family."

"I certainly do. You owe it to your family so there won't be any more Eddies." Her flashing eyes filled with tears.

Did she have to be so determined? Couldn't she be a little more like Judith and a little less like him? "I'll have to think about it," he said, already knowing what his decision would be, terrified that Gillian might learn of his true relationship to Judith.

As it was, he didn't have to decide right away. The next week, Gillian came down with chicken pox, and came home to recover, losing valuable time from medical school.

For the first few days, she felt too miserable to care whether she lived or died. After that, her body covered with pustules, she lay in bed studying, scared that she wouldn't have finished enough clinical hours to graduate with her class.

When she finally felt better and the pustules had dried, she went back to the university health office. They refused to release her for classes until every last scab had dropped off, for even they were contagious.

Discouraged, she went back home. Russell called and wanted to see her, but she refused.

"It's too much of a risk. Your committee chairman would love the chance to delay accepting your thesis and your getting chicken pox would sure do it."

Reluctantly, he agreed and stayed away.

The problem was that no one from the Eddie Squad could come to the house and care for him while Gillian was considered contagious. Judith had the job all to herself and she finally became exhausted.

Feeling sorry for her, Gillian stepped in. "I'll dress from head to foot with long sleeves and pants and put rubber bands around my wrists and ankles and take care of him, Mother. You have to rest."

"If I weren't so tired…" Judith hesitated. "All right, I'll lie down for an hour."

Gillian took care of Eddie for an hour, two hours, three hours and still her mother never came out of her room. Knowing she needed sleep, Gillian bathed, dressed, and fed Eddie. Surely, this one little exposure couldn't affect him.

But it did.

Two weeks later, she'd gone back to medical school and Judith was alone with Eddie. Warren was involved in a long surgery case when the fever struck their son. Within hours, he was convulsing, his body twisting and contorting.

Frantic, Judith called Selwyn Burger who came right to the house.

He examined Eddie, his temperature raging to 106. "I think it's more than simple chicken pox, Judith. I suspect the worst possible complication. Encelphalitis."

She looked down at Eddie, too sick to chew at himself, his face red, but calm, his eyes glazed.

"I think we'd better take him into the hospital," Selwyn said.

She started to get a blanket to wrap Eddie in, a bag for his clothes and items, found herself stalling, folding and refolding his special pajamas.

"He won't need anything, Judith." Selwyn was quietly patient with her. "The hospital will provide everything."

Everything but care, she thought, bitterly. No different than most others, the nurses would be afraid of Eddie. Still, she knew that wasn't her only motivation for delaying taking him.

"Selwyn," she said, near to breaking. "Maybe it would be better to keep him here."

"Judith, you can't possibly manage his intravenous fluids. He needs an extensive workup."

"I was thinking that we should just leave him alone."

She fell against him, crying.

"No, Judith. I can't neglect him."

"I don't see it as neglect. I see it as the real test of caring."

Selwyn didn't press.

Eddie was having a convulsion.

They discussed sponging him off to get the fever down, but neither moved to get the necessary equipment. As sick as Eddie was, he seemed better than when he was well. He wasn't a frantic bundle of nerves, searching for something to bite, something to ease the impulses that tortured his brain.

It happened faster than she expected. After a long convulsion, he stopped breathing. She waited for the next breath. Selwyn was counting the seconds on his watch. After a time, he reached into the crib, but she stopped him.

Eddie's body had completely relaxed for the first time ever. His hands lay limp in the bed, his face peaceful, his eyes closed.

She wept and so did Selwyn. And, for her, it was the perfect way for Eddie to go, helped to the angels by two of the people who most cared for him.

She covered her son and turned out the light in his room.

Chapter Forty

The next month passed in a fog for Judith. She knew that in it someplace was life, structures, some kind of order, but first she had to fight her way through it, arrive at a sense of resolution.

She shared the first days of grief with Gillian, never telling her the true cause of Eddie's death, and with Warren, who seemed relieved. Would this make a difference in her relationship with him? Would it improve?

It didn't because Warren was annoyed with Russell Jordan.

"He has no reason to come here anymore," Warren told her. "Is he homeless or doesn't anyone else want him either?"

"It's quieter here. Besides, he has to come to terms with Eddie's death, too. After all, he took care of him and studied in his room for years."

"It's a habit he'll have to break, and the sooner the better."

"Then you tell him."

She didn't know when the two spoke, but before long, Russell stopped coming to the house.

Now the only people she saw were the cook, housekeeper, gardeners, and Gillian, who would dash in on weekends to collect a refill on clothes. Then she and Russell would go to the beach house. It got so that he waited in the car for her and Judith would go out to see how he was doing.

Warren was being unfair, she decided. As it was, she didn't see any more of him than before. He, too, had formed habits which it didn't look as though he'd ever break. Too busy, over-booked, both in surgeries and speaking engagements. Judith felt sorry for his secretaries, placating patients and others who had to put up with his crammed schedule.

In a way, she envied him. He didn't have time to waste thinking about himself. Thinking about herself had become her primary occupation. It wasn't long before she wondered what she was doing on this earth. She felt useless, no longer needed. All meaning for her had vanished.

Very briefly, she came out of her depression to assert herself with Gillian. She and Russell were planning to marry with or without Warren's consent.

"No, Gillian. You won't have a good marriage without your father's permission. He's had too much of an influence on your life. Wait. Eventually, he has to change his mind. Besides, I want to plan a lovely wedding for you with your father giving you away in an exquisite white gown."

"Forget that, Mother. Russell and I want to go off to Hawaii and be married on the beach. There's a rock over there that we want to stand on...I've seen pictures of it in the National Geographic..."

"You wouldn't dare."

* * *

Judith took to driving to the Malibu house when no one else was there, walking on the beach, sitting, watching the ocean for hours, idly sifting sand through her fingers and toes. How easily it slipped away.

Warren called every night to see how she was.

At first, she thought nothing of it. But as the weeks went on, she realized that he was happier with this situation. His voice lost the tenseness he had when they were near each other and she knew it was because he was afraid she would display intimacy, perhaps touch him.

Strange. She just couldn't reconcile his attitude.

It had been nine years since they'd had intimate relations. Nine years since he'd received the Schweitzer award which she came to hate, seeing that it had castrated him.

The summer came and went. An extremely hot fall broke through in southern California, capricious fires traveling through Porter Ranch in the Valley, Topanga Canyon above Malibu, jumping across the coast highway, racing towards the beach houses.

Judith watched dispassionately as the flames tore down the hill and she evacuated the house only when the firefighters forced her to.

It would be a heaven sent conclusion for her to go with the house. But the house was spared while two others nearby were caught and taken.

October came.

She checked the calendar and realized she'd been at the beach for four months. And not once had Warren suggested she come home. He sent her gifts of fruits, nuts, had steaks flown in from the east, sent her fine chocolates. But he never came to visit.

She left the fruit to rot in the winter sun, the chocolates running like mud between the wooden patio slats.

She sent for more books from the bookstore, read and read, eventually throwing the finished novels and biographies in the trash. She kept her life tidy, for she never knew…

One day she knew. She'd read all she cared to read. She'd grieved all she cared to grieve. The weather was overcast, windy, cold. She started a fire in the living room fireplace. Through the massive glass window that gave her a view and protection from the elements, she could see the surf crashing down, the fingers of the waves crooked in her direction, the waves becoming giant hands, the white caps beckoning to her. "Come, Judith," they said.

She heaped more logs on the fire.

But her restlessness and the relentless sounds of the surf compelled her. She slipped on warm knee-high socks, shoes, long, woolen pants, turtle neck sweater, a scarf. Finally her woolen coat, taking huge safety pins and pinning one beside each large button through all the layers to be sure that the coat would stay closed.

She looked at the fire one last time, stoked the hot coals, and set the poker aside.

She pulled open the sliding glass door, the blast of cold air briefly breaking the spell of her being turned in on herself. She went down to the water's edge, knelt down, the water licking at the hem of her coat, at her shoes. She gazed out at the ocean, where the horizon met the water. There was no difference between them. It was impossible to see where one ended and the other started. A continuity.

Was that the way it was with living and dying?

She sifted sand idly through her fingers, and gradually found herself placing handfuls of the cold grains in her pockets.

When they were filled, she stood, and it was difficult because the pockets were so heavy, pulling her shoulders down. She lost her balance, but righted herself.

Then the surf called and she walked into it.

As the first wave rolled over her, she heard voices, muffled, through the water.

"Mother! Mother!"

"Mrs. Hollis! Mrs. Hollis!"

She wasn't sure whether the voices were real or not. She had expected to be panicked when she finally couldn't get her breath and the sea would claim her, but she didn't and it seemed almost a pleasure to give herself up to the swirling, jealous salt water.

She felt something hit her and grab her legs. Of course there were sharks here, but, she wouldn't feel their grasp for long...

She was buffeted about, her head thrown back, her hair pulled...cold hit her face, but it wasn't water, it was air.

She was being dragged.

"For Christ's sake, Gillian, she was drowning."

Somebody was talking about her.

"Mother! Mother!" Gillian was sobbing as Judith was dragged up the beach, choking, gasping.

They stopped and Judith could hear someone else gasping for breath. She recognized Russell. Gillian bent down beside her.

It was hard for Judith to get the words out. "Why didn't you leave me alone?"

Gillian dropped on her, sobbing.

Russell lifted her off. "Gillian, we've got to get her to some warmth."

Together, the pair carried her along the beach, up the steps, unpinned the dripping coat, dropping it on the patio, and lay her on the floor in front of the fire.

Gradually, her head cleared, and instead of gratitude that they had saved her, she was angry. It would have taken just a few more seconds. Did they have any idea how tired she was of being depressed, of having no purpose to living, of having a husband who disregarded her as a wife? Did they have to save her to become a shriveled, even more bitter shell of a woman?

Russell and Gillian sat on the couch watching her. She closed her eyes to shut them out.

She had no idea how much time passed, but she heard the front door open and Warren was talking to them, and then they went away and she was alone with Warren.

He knelt beside her on the floor.

"Judith, I'm sorry. I've neglected you too long."

It had been years since she'd heard that kind of pain in his voice, but his words were stone to her.

"Judith, Judith..." He stroked her hair.

She wouldn't open her eyes.

"I've not been fair to you..."

She wished he would just go away.

"My darling, I am going to tell you something, something that I probably should have told you years ago."

She waited, not caring.

"It's something I learned and it has destroyed me. I wanted to save you from it, but I've seen what you've been through..."

Why didn't he just get on with it?

"...you've made me realize that not knowing can also destroy."

So...

"Judith, open your eyes. Look at me."

"No..."

"Please...I'm begging you."

Wearily, she did so.

"Judith, sit up. I want you to be looking at me. I want you to know that you have not dreamed this."

She didn't budge. He forced her to a sitting position.

"Look at this." He held his hand before her. He was holding something. A ring. She remembered that it was the one she'd given him to commemorate his receiving the Schweitzer award.

"Judith, did you know that this ring belonged to your father?"

"I thought it might."

"But you never saw any connection between your father and me..." He paused a long time before continuing. "...because the idea is inconceivable. Is it not?"

"What do you mean, Warren?"

"Judith, could you ever believe that I gave this ring to your mother the year before you were born?" He fell silent and she saw a sorrow in his eyes and behind them a broken heart.

"What are you trying to tell me?"

"Judith...I'm trying to tell you that I am your father...and that it's been too horrible for me to handle." He lay her down and sobbed beside her.

The waves crashed down on her again. Finally, after all of those years, maybe she could understand. She reached for his ring hand, looked at it for a long time and all her energy flowed away. She let his hand drop and she closed her eyes, wishing that the waves had taken her. They lay there, seemingly for hours before his sobs subsided and she was through thinking and their relationship emerged from her confusion, only it had changed. It was moons away from the one she thought had been theirs.

He quietly stood, left the room and brought back Gillian and Russell. His arm was around Russell, who smiled.

"Judith," Warren took her hand. "They came here today to tell you that Russell's thesis was finally accepted. I would like you to meet Dr. Jordan."

Gillian and Russell were beaming.

"And the future Mrs. Jordan."

Too much was happening. There was a total breakdown between what was real and what was not real. Nothing seemed real and yet she was still here, alive. That was real.

It took months before Judith came back to being able to separate fact from fantasy. Even then, she was never sure. There was so much she wanted to forget and still keep just one dream; the dream that had to be true where she watched Gillian coming down the aisle on her father's arm, dressed in white satin with a lace train that trailed along behind her farther than the eye could see.

No, that wasn't a dream. It did happen, didn't it?

Epilogue

*"...there can be no hereditary disease.
since matter is not intelligent and cannot
transmit good or evil."*

Mary Baker Eddy

Printed in the United States
64051LVS00002B/229-249